DAMNATION ON HALFADAY CREEK

James B Hendryx

DAMNATION ON HALFADAY CREEK

JAMES B. HENDRYX

ILLUSTRATIONS BY
PETE KUHLHOFF
BILL HANLEY
NICK EGGENHOFER

POPULAR PUBLICATIONS • 2021

SERIES EXECUTIVE CONSULTANT

Richard Hall

PUBLISHING HISTORY

"Yukon Twins" originally appeared in the August 1933 issue of *West* magazine (vol. 36, no. 6). Reprinted by arrangement with the Estate of James B. Hendryx.

"Black John and the Sky Pilot" originally appeared in the May 1952 issue of *New Western* magazine (vol. 24, no. 3). Copyright 1952 by Popular Publications, Inc., and assigned to Steeger Properties, LLC. All rights reserved.

"Black John—Bushwhacker" originally appeared in the November 1952 issue of *Dime Western* magazine (vol. 62, no. 4). Copyright 1952 by Popular Publications, Inc., assigned to Steeger Properties, LLC. All rights reserved.

"Black John's Bear Trap Trouble" originally appeared in the February 1951 issue of *Dime Western* magazine (vol. 60, no. 2). Copyright 1951 by Popular Publications, Inc., and assigned to Steeger Properties, LLC. All rights reserved.

"Cheechako Trouble" originally appeared in the September 1952 issue of *New Western* magazine (vol. 25, no. 1). Copyright 1952 by Popular Publications, Inc., and assigned to Steeger Properties, LLC. All rights reserved.

"The Damnation of Black John" originally appeared in the December 1950 issue of *Dime Western* magazine (vol. 59, no. 4). Copyright 1950 by Popular Publications, Inc., and assigned to Steeger Properties, LLC. All rights reserved.

"Death Stakes this Claim!" originally appeared in the January 1953 issue of *New Western* magazine (vol. 25, no. 3). Copyright 1953 by Popular Publications, Inc., and assigned to Steeger Properties, LLC. All rights reserved.

"Justice—Yukon Style!" originally appeared in the September 1951 issue of *Big Book Western* magazine (vol. 29, no. 4). Copyright 1951 by Popular Publications, Inc., and assigned to Steeger Properties, LLC. All rights reserved.

"Superstition" originally appeared in the January 5 & 12, 1958, issues of *The Boston Sunday Globe*. Reprinted by arrangement with the Estate of James B. Hendryx.

"White Hell" originally appeared in the September 1953 issue of *Big Book Western* magazine (vol. 32, no. 4). Copyright 1953 by Popular Publications, Inc., and assigned to Steeger Properties, LLC. All rights reserved.

THANKS TO

Robert Loomis, Cynthia Whyte, & the Leelanau Historical Society

TABLE OF CONTENTS

YUKON TWINS

THE YUKON HAD been running ice-free for a week. The break-up had come with a rush, rendering the trails to far diggings impassable successions of slush, mud, surface water ponds, and bare ground. Creeks became raging torrents freighted with ice cakes and debris which jammed at the bends and tore loose to jam again. Many prospectors, caught in the hills, faced a season of short rations until such time as these creeks should subside to permit canoe travel. Men scowled at the sodden snow of high hillsides, and puttered about the flumes and sluices of their soggy claims.

Then, one night, the wind veered, the ground and the sodden snow banks and the little rills froze, the creeks subsided like magic, and for twenty-four hours it snowed. And on the snow the prospectors swarmed into Dawson with their sleds and their dogs for supplies.

It was a big night in the Tivoli where these men foregathered to drink, and to dance, and to gamble, and listen to the news of the diggings.

At a table near the side wall opposite the crowded bar, five sourdoughs were playing poker, apparently oblivious to the hubbub of conversation and the tinny jangle of the piano in the adjoining dance hall, through whose wide doorway a continuous procession of men and girls passed to and from the bar.

"There's them Condons," observed Camillo Bill, tossing his hand into the discard. "I never can tell which is which. Damn if I believe their own mother knows 'em apart."

1

"What would she want to fer?" asked Moosehide Charlie. "One's jest like the other; so what difference would it make?"

"Well, she might," grinned Swiftwater Bill. "Women's kind of whimmish."

"They're good men on the trail," said Burr MacShane. "An' they sure can handle a canoe."

"Good men any place you put 'em," agreed Camillo. "Always mindin' their own business." The glances of the sourdoughs rested approvingly on the two young men who stood near the end of the bar taking in the scene with evident enjoyment. As like as the well-known two peas in a pod, they were—well set up, tall and broad shouldered, with long flat hips, no bulge at the waistline, and blue eyes that looked out from clean-shaven, clean-cut faces in good humored enjoyment of life as they found it.

"If their ma can tell 'em apart; er can't," said Swiftwater Bill, "I'll bet it was their pa that done the namin'—Tom an' Jerry, their names is."

"Them's prob'ly jest nicknames," opined Moosehide. "They tell me they've be'n twins from birth."

"The hell!" chuckled Old Bettles. "I figgered, mebbe, they'd jest twinned up fer the stampede."

"I mean," scowled Moosehide, "they say they've looked alike ever since they was borned. They put a good one over on Dad Thrush, the barber today."

"How's that?"

"**WELL, THEY** hadn't be'n in since Chris'mas, an' they'd both grow'd 'em quite a beard. Tom, he hits fer the barber shop, 'long about noon, an' sets down in Dad Thrush's chair. 'Give me a good clost shave,' he says, 'I ain't shaved since early this mornin'.' Dad, he looks him over an' grins an' they git to joshin' back an' forth, an' when Dad's through with him Tom looks in the glass an' runs his fingers along his jaw. 'Guess that'll do till suppertime,' he says. 'I'll be in then fer another. Beats hell how fast my whiskers

grows. It's a damn nuisance. Bet you the drinks they'll be as long as they was when I come in here.'

"Well, 'course Dad bet him the drinks, thinkin' he was kiddin' him. Tom he hunts Jerry up an' puts him wise, an' long about suppertime Jerry he strolls in an' set down in Dad's chair. 'Well, I come back fer that other shave,' he says 'I sure wisht I could git holt of somethin' that would slow whiskers down a little.'

"Dad's eyes bunged out till you could hang yer cap on 'em, an' the other barbers crowded around, them havin' heard Tom an' Dad kiddin' one another at noon. But, the folks in their chairs was hollerin' at 'em to finish 'em up, an' they went back to work while Dad lathered Jerry up an' went at him. They claim each one of them other barbers cut their man, them not bein' able to keep their eyes off 'n Dad's chair. When Dad finished, Jerry he looks in the glass an' run his fingers along his jaw. 'Guess that'll do till mornin',' he says. 'How about that drink?'

"Dad, he turns to the other barbers. 'Come on, boys—yer all in on it,' he says. 'I thought first off, there was some shenanigan somewheres—but, there ain't. This here's the same feller I shaved this noon—same clothes, same eyes, same whiskers. You might fool a man on all them—but, boys, it's the same smell—an' you all know damn well you can't never fool a barber on the smell!'

"The barber business declares a mor'torium on work, right there, an' they all files into The Antlers, next door, an' Dad sets 'em up to the house. When they'd drunk up, the other barbers buys, an' then Jerry buys a round, an' Dad's jest about to buy another, when Jerry touches him on the shoulder: 'Hey,' he says, 'I'd like fer you to meet my brother.' Dad, he looks around an' there they stood—both of 'em lookin' jest alike standin' side by side, grinnin' at him. Dad, he turns kind of white around the gills, an' he blinks an' he gawps, an' he gawps an' he blinks fer mebbe it's half a minute. Then he steps up clost, an' he sniffs each one of 'em—like a dog sniffin' a dead moose. Then he busts out in a grin; 'S'all right, boys!' he says, lookin' mighty relieved. 'The drinks is on me! I thought fer minute I was fooled—thought I was seein' double, an' was gittin' a touch of my old trouble, the deelirium tremens, an' would have to lay off drinkin' fer a spell—but I won't! A man can see double, but I'll be damned if he can smell double! There's two of 'em, all right! An', we can go ahead with our drinkin'!' Which," concluded Moosehide, "I guess they're doin' yet—er was, white coats an' all, when I come by there a few minutes ago. Tom an' Jerry kind of eased theirself away an' left 'em alone in their glory, as the feller says."

WHEN THE laughter had subsided, Old Bettles ran his fingers down his cheek. "I was figgerin' on steppin' over fer a shave after a bit," he said. "But some other day'll do. Them barbers is prob'ly too damn full of glory to do a heedful job."

As Bettles finished speaking a bellowing voice shouting *"There'll be a hot time in the old town tonight!"* drowned out the blare of the tinny piano. The next moment a hulking figure barged through the broad doorway, a dance hall girl astride his shoulders, followed by a rabble of men and girls, all roaring out the chorus of the popular song of the day. The crowd parted as the huge man surged into it and sat the girl on the bar.

"Fill 'em up!" he roared. "Bull McClosky's buyin' a drink!" And again the huge voice roared forth the words: "*There'll be a hot time in the old town tonight!*"

The sourdoughs remained seated at their table as the crowd swarmed to the bar.

"Bull McClosky's on the loose ag'in," observed Camillo Bill.

"Yeah," agreed Burr McShane, "An' there's three of his Sunk Crick gang along with him."

"Someone ought to knock his damn head off," opined Moosehide Charley.

Swiftwater Bill grinned. "Go to it, Moosehide. He'll be hurlin' his *defy* pretty quick, an' you'll git yer chanct."

"Hell—I don't want none of his meat! He could lick four like me. Onct down to Forty Mile, I seen him clean out a hull barroom."

"I wouldn't drink with the son of a gun," said Old Bettles, dean of the sourdoughs. "Not till some of the doin's out in the hills has be'n cleaned up. The last one was that young Englishman, Farnsworth, his name was. Couple of the boys found his body weighted down an' sunk in a rapids. That's six that's disappeared—all while they was comin' in from their claims to deposit their dust. Farnsworth is the only one they've found, so far."

"Looks like the police had ought to do somethin' about it," said Moosehide.

"There ain't much they can do when they don't find the body," said Buck Hammond. "Corporal Downey's workin' on the Farnsworth case. The fellows that found the body brought it down to detachment."

"How was he killed?" asked Burr MacShane.

"Knocked on the head from behind. Some kind of a heavy club. Caved in his skull."

"Not much to go on," grunted Swiftwater Bill. "A man can't hardly blame the police fer not ketching the murderers right away. Tellin' you about me, I believe young Downey'll git to the bottom of it if anyone will."

"You an' me both," agreed Old Bettles. "An' when he does, it wouldn't surprise me none if we-all will be lookin' at plenty of daylight between the soles of the Sunk Crick gang's feet an' the ground."

"They'll have to hang McClosky with a log chain," grinned Camillo. "He must run two-sixty er -seventy of good hard meat. There wouldn't no rope hold him."

"He's jest about drunk enough to start in an' raise hell with us fellers fer' not drinkin' with him," opined Moosehide.

"Not much hell—he won't," said Buck Hammond, grimly, as he loosened a couple of buttons at the front of his shirt, and slipped his hand to the butt of his six-gun. "If he starts anything with me I'll pattern a button hole around his belly button an' save the police huntin' up a log chain. We know he's a damn murderer—an' so does Downey—but, he can't prove it—yet."

OLD BETTLES grinned: "He won't bother us none. McClosky's no damn fool. He don't want none of our meat. He has better luck with *chechakos*."

From the bar came the bellowing voice of McClosky: "I kin lay any two men in the house on their back fer the drinks!" The announcement was followed by comparative silence, broken after a moment by further challenge: "I can lick any damn man in Dawson! Come on, you gravel hogs! Where's yer guts? Step up an' lock horns with the rarin', rantin', ravin' Bull o' the Woods!"

Once again silence greeted the words, and seizing the girl whom he had set on the bar in his huge hands, he tossed her, screaming to the ceiling, caught her, and returned her to the bar, amid the loud-voiced laughter of the crowd. "Come on!" roared McClosky, glaring about him. "I'm the best damn man in the Yukon! I kin fight harder, run faster, jump higher, lift more, yell louder, an' spit further than any other damn man north of sixty—er, by damn—south of it!"

"That's quite a bit of territory, when you come to think about it," grinned Old Bettles. "Why don't you clip his wings fer him, Buck—like you done Black John?"

"Hell, Black John's a gentleman!" retorted Buck Hammond. "I wouldn't dirty my hands on this scum! I notice he didn't say nothin' about shootin', an' look at the two big white-handled guns stickin' out of his holsters! If he says anything to me I'll tell him to draw 'em both, an' then blow his guts out before he can pull a trigger."

"He knows that," grinned Bettles, "an' he ain't goin' to give you no chanct to. He knows all about you shootin' the eyes out of that picture on the wall, yonder. I seen him glance over here a minute ago. He seen we wasn't drinkin' with him—an' he never let out a yip. Look at him! I b'lieve he's goin' to start in on them twins!"

II

THE ROVING GLANCE of McClosky had come to rest on the two Condons standing side by side near the end of the bar. Elbowing his way through the crowd, the huge man, closely followed by his three satelites, brought up directly in front of them where, for a long moment he stood glaring from one face to the other.

"Is there two of ye, or only one?" he roared. "An', if so, which one?"

The two grinned good-humoredly without answering, and McClosky scowled: "By gosh, if ye can't talk I'll find out fer meself!" he bellowed, and reaching out a pair of hamlike hands, he jammed the caps of the two roughly down over their eyes.

"By gosh, he touched off dynamite that time!" cried Old Bettles, delightedly, as he shoved back from the table and stood up in his chair to see over the heads of the crowd that had surged back as the two Condons sprang suddenly into action.

The wicked thud of hard-driven fists on flesh, was followed by a grunt as McClosky recoiled from the two blows that had landed simultaneously on his protruding jaw. A one-two to the belly sent his great arms flailing just as his three Sunk Creek followers projected themselves into the row.

"Fair play, there!" shouted Camillo Bill, who had also climbed upon his chair. "Someone stop them three damn coyotes!"

Someone did! It was one of the Condon twins—and he stopped them effectively and conclusively in less time than it takes to tell it. As his brother crowded in on McClosky, he met the onrush of the three with three lightning blows that landed with the precision of bullets squarely upon the points of three chins, and the three Sunk Creekers crashed to the floor amid wild whoops and yells of surprise and delight from the men who shoved and elbowed for points of vantage, crowding onto chairs, tables, and even the bar in frenzied effort to miss no single detail of the epic battle.

Meanwhile the other Condon was facing McClosky who had recovered from the jolting surprise of the first swift onslaught and was flailing and lashing out with his huge fists in blows which, had they landed, would have crushed the bones of any man. But they didn't land. In and out, weaving this way and that, jabbing, feinting, hooking, Condon was stinging the giant to blind fury that found vent in the lashing blows and in bull-throated bellowing curses.

AND HIS brother was not idle. Slipping behind the hulking McClosky his two hands shot out, and the next moment two white-handled six-guns flew over the heads of the crowd and thudded against the opposite wall well out of reach of the rage-crazed giant

"By golly, he got what he was huntin' fer—an' he ain't none happy!" cried Moosehide Charley, from the vantage point on top of the table that he shared with Buck Hammond, and Swift-water Bill.

"Look at that bird fight!" yelled Bettles. "Them fists of McClosky's don't miss him by more'n a inch! Look at him duck! Man oh man! If that one would of hit him it woulda knocked him through the wall!"

"An' he's landin' on McClosky damn near every time he hits!" echoed Swiftwater Bill, thumping Bettles on the back in an ecstasy of delight.

"He's workin' on his belly an' gettin' his wind," opined Buck Hammond. "McClosky's puffin' like a walrus—"

"Yeah," seconded Camillo, "he's workin' from his belly clean to his eyes! Look at the blood in his whiskers! What a fight!"

"Look at that foot-work!" cried Buck Hammond, himself no mean fighter.

"Foot work—hell!" cried Bettles, "It's the fist work I'm watchin'! By hell, movin' as fast as he is, I can't figger why he ain't winded! McClosky's damn near all in! Look at his eyes bung out! Why in hell don't the other Condon sail in?"

"My gosh!" yelled Camillo, excitedly, "that *is* the other Condon! They're two-timin' him—an' he don't know the differ-ence!"

Wild whoops of appreciation welled from the throats of the sourdoughs as realization dawned upon them that the brothers were, every few minutes, changing places—shifting so swiftly and so cleverly that neither McClosky, nor the majority of the spectators realized the fact.

"Spellin' each other off," laughed Swiftwater Bill, "an', fair enough! McClosky attacked 'em both simultaneous. He's damn lucky they don't gang up on him both to onct!"

"He's damn near all in," chuckled Bettles. "Listen at him puff. He ain't got no wind left fer cussin'."

"It won't last much longer," opined Buck Hammond. "He's groggy right now."

SCARCELY WERE the words out of his mouth before, with a lightning shift, the two brothers once more changed places, and a barrage of flying fists landed on McClosky's face. The two huge arms ceased their labored flailing and rose sluggishly to guard against that rain of stinging blows. With a swift shift of footing, Condon stepped back, measured his distance, and sent a long, powerfully driven right straight to the hulking midriff.

With a whistling, grunting sigh the huge form collapsed and pitched forward on hands and knees, while the man who had delivered the blows stood grinning down on him with fist cocked for action should he attempt to rise.

A hullabaloo of yells and cries filled the room:

"Finish him off!"

"Kick his damn liver out!"

"He asked fer it—give it to him!"

"Kick his teeth down his throat!"

"Kill the big slob!"

"He's got it comin'!"

Camillo grinned into the faces of the sourdoughs. "He don't seem to have many friends."

"His friends is asleep there on the floor," chuckled Bettles. "All three of 'em."

"That's what a man gits fer takin' in too much territory," opined Swiftwater Bill. "If he'd of stuck to north of sixty, he might of got away with it—but, south of it! He bit off more'n he could chaw."

On hands and knees the big man rested, air surging in and out of his lungs in great panting sobs, as blood dripped from his battered nose and swollen lips to form a widening red pool on the floor.

One of his henchman stirred, wriggled a bit, and sat up blinking groggily, and uncomprehendingly at his inert companions, and at McClosky on all fours panting like a wounded bear, bleeding at the nose. He reached out a hand and shook the form nearest him, and that one, too, sat up groping with fumbling fingers for his jaw.

With a roar of fury McClosky leaped erect, grabbed a half filled whisky bottle from the bar, and hurled it with all the force of his mighty arm. With a sickening crash it struck Condon squarely, in the forehead, broke in half, the neck portion flying through the air to crash through the front window and fall at the feet of young Corporal Downey of the Royal Northwest Mounted Police, who was intently examining the wire wrapping that had been wound around a broken sled runner.

Inside the Tivoli, a sudden and ominous silence followed the sound of smashing glass. Leaping to the side of his brother, who had dropped like a polled ox at the impact of the bottle, the other Condon dropped to his knees and raised the bleeding head on his arm. He looked up, straight into the blazing eyes of McClosky.

"Damn you!" he exploded, in a tone that cut the silence like the voice of doom, "if my brother dies, I'll kill you if it's the last thing I do on earth!"

AT THE words the pent-up emotions of the crowd burst forth in a torrent of curses and threats as men surged toward McClosky like a pack of avenging wolves.

Then, sudden silence once more reigned, as the street door opened, and a voice rang loud and clear above the pandemonium of noise: "Stand back, there! What the hell!" Revolver in hand, Corporal Downey of the Mounted advanced as the crowd gave way before him. "What's comin' off here?" he demanded, his eyes sweeping the faces of the crowd.

When all started talking at once, he held up his hand for silence. "I'll tend to this case later," he said. "First off, I want to know who owns that sled out in front—the one with the busted runner?"

One of the Sunk Creek men rose dazedly from the floor, and eyed the youthful officer stupidly. "That's my sled," he mumbled, thickly. "What about it?"

"Just this much about it," answered Downey, evenly. "You come along with me. I've be'n huntin' for a piece of wire like you mended your sled with for quite a while—ever sence young Farnsworth was murdered, to be exact. An' there ain't another piece like it in Dawson!"

The man's face went a shade paler. His eyes lost their dazed look and stared wildly about the room. "I never done it!" he cried. "I got that wire—" He stopped abruptly as his eyes met the glaring eyes of McClosky, who stood with his back to the bar.

"You can tell me about it later," said Downey, curtly. "Come along to headquarters." Seizing the man's arm, he shoved him on ahead, and made his way rapidly across the floor. At the doorway he turned. "I'll be back in a few minutes to straighten out this ruckus," he said. "But, first, I want to see this bird safe behind the bars."

Mention of the Farnsworth murder had thrown the room into a new buzz of conversation, and when, a few moments later, the sourdoughs followed Old Bettles to the bar for a round of refreshment, McClosky and the two remaining Sunk Creekers were nowhere to be seen.

III

THE FULL MOON rendered the street as light as day as Corporal Downey halted before one of four loaded sleds while his prisoner stooped to untoggle the dogs.

"Since when is it agin the law fer to mend a sled runner with wire?" growled the man, surlily.

Downey grinned. "It ain't the mendin' that's got you in bad," he answered, "It's lack of judgment in choosin' yer wire. String them dogs out an' head 'em for the police detachment. What was all the rookus in the Tivoli about?"

"You can't prove it by me," answered the man, sulkily. "Seems like McClosky started in to have some fun with a couple of ginks, an' the next thing I know'd I woke up with my jaw hurtin'—an' it's hurtin' like hell yet."

Downey fell in a couple of paces behind, as the man struck off down the street at the head of his dogs, "You started to tell me where you got that wire," he reminded.

"How the hell do I know where I got it? Where someone throw'd it, I s'pose. Where does anyone git a piece of wire?"

"That's what I've be'n wonderin'—where anyone would get a piece of gilt picture wire in Dawson. I've be'n tryin' to locate a piece ever since they brought in young Farnsworth. There was a rock wired to his neck with that same kind of wire."

They were passing a space cluttered with lumber piles and the frames of buildings in course of construction. "I'll see you in hell before I—" The man whirled half around and crashed forward onto his face, his legs and arms thrashing convulsively, as a rifle roared from among the lumber piles.

For a single instant Corporal Downey stood staring down in horror upon the twitching form as blood gushed from the mouth to redden the hard-trodden snow. Then, drawing his pistol he dashed among the lumber piles and for ten minutes he prodded into every nook or angle that could have afforded shelter to the killer. He concluded the futile search and paused to scowl down at the snow, hopelessly tracked up by the feet of the carpenters and workmen. "Knocked him off so he couldn't squeal," he muttered between clenched teeth. "An' right in under my nose. It's that damn McClosky, all right—but, suspectin' an' provin' is two different things. No tracks—not a damn clue—not even the bullet. It was a rifle, an' a hundred to one, the bullet went on through him. But—I've got the wire—an'… I'll get McClosky! It's me for Sunk Crick!"

RETURNING HASTILY to the street he found Constable Peters, who had been attracted by the sound of the shot, bending over the body of the man. "Take him an' that sled down to detachment! An' take the sled inside. Make me up a four-day trail outfit, an' load it onto one of them light stampedin' sleds, an' hook a good string of dogs to it, an' have it back at the Tivoli as quick as the Lord'll let you! Here, I'll help you h'ist him up on the load. Grab holt of them feet. Get a-goin', now! Mush!"

Back at the Tivoli Corporal Downey found a bartender pasting a square of paper over the shattered window pane, and a rabble of men drinking and talking excitely at the bar, while in the dance hall the "professor" was banging out a catchy waltz on the tinny piano.

Hunting up Curley, the proprietor, he called him aside: "What the hell was comin' off here when I come in?" he asked.

Curley, regarded the young officer seriously: "To start off with, it wasn't nothin' but Bull McClosky on one of his sprees. You know his stuff—blusterin' an' brass-lungin' his merits fer everyone to hear—challengin' everyone to anything from a fight to a spittin' match.

"He picks on them two Condon boys, an' when they don't pay no heed to him he shoves their caps down over their face an' they light into him—an' not only him, but three more of the Sunk Crickers that was trailin' along with him. Jeez that was a fight! The Sunk Crickers went to sleep, one, two, three—jest like that—an' then while one Condon was makin' a monkey out of McClosky in front, the other slips up behind an' throws his guns away—jest in case. Then come the slickest trick I ever seen pulled—an', believe me, I thought I'd seen 'em all! They begun two-timin' him—switchin' off, one keepin' after him while the other got his wind—an' they done it so slick, an' lookin' jest alike, McClosky never know'd the difference, an' it wasn't long before they had him plumb winded. Boy, kin them fellers fight! McClosky never landed on neither one of 'em, an' they both played tunes on him from his belly to his hair roots!

"Everyone was damn good an' tired of McClosky's bluffin' an' blusterin', an' what with the talk that's be'n goin' around about them men that's disappeared in the hills the Condons had the crowd with 'em from the start. Man, you'd ought to heard 'em yell when McClosky went down!"

"Went down!" exclaimed Corporal Downey. "I didn't think there was anyone in camp that could put him down."

"I'll say he went down! Not plumb out—like them others. But down—good an' proper. Down an' helpless on his hands an' knees with the blood drippin' off'n his whiskers. An' the Condons too damn square to finish him off. One of 'em stood by the bar laughin', an' the one that downed McClosky standin' ready to down him ag'in if he got up. An' the crowd whoopin' an' yellin' at him to kick the daylights out of the big stiff!

"Boy, she was great doin's—up to there! Then, them Sunk Crickers begun to come to, an' the Condon that was waitin' on McClosky to git up swung his eyes onto 'em, an' while he wasn't lookin', McClosky jumps up an' grabs a whisky bottle off'n the bar an' throws it fer all he's worth, bouncin' it off'n Condon's head, which the bottle busts an' the half of it goes out through the window. Condon, he drops like he was shot, an' his brother drops down beside him an' raises his head off'n the floor—an' then he looks up at McClosky, an' he tells him that if his brother dies he'll kill him if it's the last thing he ever done—an' I don't blame him! It was a damn low down dirty play McClosky pulled, an' it showed the rotten yellow guts of him! It's too damn bad they didn't polish him off when they had him down."

"Is Condon hurt bad?"

"**I DON'T** know, but it stands to reason he is—what with a half-full bottle of whisky bustin' over his head. Moosehide Charley went to fetch old Doc Pettus, an' Bettles an' the rest of the sourdoughs helped the other Condon carry him down to their shack."

"Where's McClosky? I notice those other three sleds were gone when I got back."

"Don't no one seem to know. Him an' the other Sunk Crickers jest naturally faded away whilst the boys was millin' around the Condons. There's strong talk of a lynchin', if young Condon dies."

"There won't be no lynchin'," said Corporal Downey, his lips tightening.

"Yer damn right there won't," echoed Curley, "Nor, no legal hangin' neither. Man—you'd ought to looked, like I done, into the other Condon's eyes when he told McClosky he'd kill him! They glittered hard an' cold as green ice!"

"I'll step over to Condon's," said Downey, "an' then I'll hit out after McClosky. I'll have somethin' to hold him on, now, even if Condon don't die."

"Well—you've got one of the gang, anyway. I hope—"

"The devil's got him by now," interrupted Downey. "He's dead."

"Dead!"

"Yeah—someone shot him right in under my nose when I was takin' him in. Got away with it, too."

"Well, I'll be damned!" exclaimed Curley. "He prob'ly know'd too much."

"What he know'd he took with him," replied Downey. "If Peters comes in before I get back, tell him to wait for me."

At the board shack occupied by the Condon brothers, Corporal Downey found the sourdoughs anxiously awaiting the verdict of old Doc Pettus who was bending over the still form stretched out on the bunk. An oil lamp shed a sickly yellow light upon the interior where the men stood in awkward silence. Finally the doctor turned from the bunk, fumbling at his beard with his fingers. "There ain't nothin' I can do, boys. The frontal bone's fractured pretty bad. He'll either git well, which ain't likely; er he'll die, which is. I'd say he's got about one chanct in ten thousan'—maybe not quite so much."

"If Jerry dies," said Tom Condom in a hard, low voice, "I'll leave you boys to bury him—while I go after McClosky."

"I'm goin' to hit out for Sunk Creek after him, now," Corporal Downey said. "If I bring him back, I'm promisin' you that the law will take its course."

"Let it," replied Condon, "—if you bring him back. But, if you don't bring him back, Downey—I'll take my own course with McClosky."

"I wouldn't shoot him if I was you," advised the young officer. "Much as you'd like to. Much as I think you've got a right to. But—it ain't accordin' to—"

"I won't shoot him!" interrupted the other. "Shooting's too damn good for him—after the play he made! Low down as he is, I'll give him a break. I'll kill him, damn him! I'll choke him to death with my two hands!"

Corporal Downey shook his head. "He wouldn't give you no breaks," he said. "He's yellow. You couldn't never get him to fight you, again!" and turning, he abruptly quitted the room and hurried back to the Tivoli which he reached just in time to meet Constable Peters coming up with the trail outfit. Swiftly he threaded the streets of the big camp, and a few minutes later, headed the dogs onto the Sunk Creek trail.

IN THE Condon shack Old Bettles grinned a bit sheepishly at Burr MacShane. "I kind of hate to double-cross young Downey, at that," he opined. "He's one hell of a good policeman."

"He sure is," agreed MacShane, "but, just the same, Tom's entitled to the first chance at McClosky. Jerry's his own brother."

"That's right," seconded Moosehide. "A trip up to Sunk Crick won't hurt Downey none—an' he might pick up some evidence about them other murders out in the hills."

"Hell," exclaimed Bettles, in a husky whisper. "They can't hang him but once! If Downey had McClosky he'd sure have evidence enough to hang him high as a mountain. If Jerry dies there's plenty of us seen him kill him—an' then, Camillo follerin' McClosky an' watchin' him shoot his pal right out from in under Downey, as you might say! An' then follerin' him on to the river an' watchin' him head upstream in a canoe! He's hittin' fer Half-aday Crick, all right. By gosh, follerin' McClosky thataway, is smarter'n what I thought Camillo was!"

"I expect we might's well go over an' have a drink," suggested Swiftwater Bill.

Old Bettles nodded emphatical assent: "An' that's the smart-est opinion I've heard you voice in quite a while, too." He turned to Condon who was seated upon the edge of the bed, his eyes on his brother's face. "We're goin' to step over to the Tivoli, boy," he whispered. "We can't do no good here. If—if—er—anythin' happens—you'll find us there. Buck Hammond, here, he'll tell you all about how to get to Halfaday."

Young Condon nodded without looking up: "Thanks, boys. I appreciate what you've done."

"Hell—that ain't nothin'!" assured Bettles. "Would you admire fer one of us to fetch you over a quart er two?"

The man shook his head, and the sourdoughs tip-toed from the room, and made their way to the Tivoli, while out in the hills Corporal Downey urged his dogs on, and on, and on, as the moonlight waned.

Just on the edge of daylight, Jerry Condon died. For a long time young Torn stood looking down into that still face that was the exact duplicate of his own. Then he turned away, blew out the lamp, and walked slowly toward the Tivoli.

IV

THE FIGHT IN the Tivoli had been more or less of a blur to Bull McClosky. One moment he had been smashing the caps of a couple of *chechakos* down over their faces, and the next, he was staggering backward under the impact of a terrific blow on the jaw—two blows delivered simultaneously, had he but known it—and from that moment on it had been just one long succession of blows, with a man dancing in and out in front of him, punching, jabbing, weaving about—and always just out of his reach.

Red fury blinded McClosky even more than his rapidly closing left eye. In vain he bellowed and charged and swung his ponderous fists. In vain he spread his huge arms to gather and crush his antagonist. A man can't fight a man he can't hit—a man he can't crush, or choke, or hurl crashing to the floor.

McClosky had been in fights before—hundreds of fights—but, never in one that held that furious pace without pause nor let up. His, wind was going. He sucked the air in great sobbing gulps—but apparently the man who danced in and out before him and delivered that never ceasing rain of stinging blows was as fresh as when he started. No man could stand that furious pace—no man had lungs enough. But, this man was doing it! And McClosky couldn't hit him!

With his ears ringing, his head whirling dizzily, and with a thick red fog blurring his vision, he felt himself falling. Bull McClosky knocked off his feet for the first time in his bullying, blustering life! Down—but, not out—not quite out.

On hands and knees he waited for the inevitable rain of kicks and blows that would flatten him. Waited, with the warm blood trickling from his nose and lips, soaking his beard, dripping onto the floor. Waited, and yet strove with every nerve and fiber of his hulking body to summon strength to regain his feet and smash his elusive antagonist with one shattering blow—one blow would do it—if he could only land. But his hands were like hands of lead—his body a vast weight, solidly fixed to the floor, as his laboring chest surged like a bellows pumping the oxygen into his lungs.

But, the kicks and the blows for which he waited did not come. His whirling brain cleared, and above the ringing in his ears he could hear the roars and the shouts of the crowd. What was it they were saying? Jumbled, meaningless, at first, the loudly shouted words shaped themselves into ideas: "kick his liver out!" "kill the big slob!" Whose liver? Who was the big slob? Suddenly

it dawned on the man that it was his liver they were demand-
ing be kicked out—he was the big slob—he, Bull McClosky, he,
himself, who could make mince meat out of any one of them,
any two—or three—or four! Drinking with him one minute—
laughing when he swung the dancing girl to the ceiling and sat
her on the bar—and the next minute howling for his liver—for
his very life like the pack of damn coyotes they were. Damn 'em!
He'd show 'em! He'd show 'em all!

BUT FIRST, he'd show the man that had brought him to this—
the dancing, punching, jabbing *chechako* that didn't play the game
according to rule—that didn't back away and circle around stall-
ing for wind—that didn't finish a man when he had him on his
hands and knees! What the hell was he waiting for?

An abysmal, all-encompassing rage surged through the brain
of McClosky. He leaped to his, feet, his undamaged eye sweeping the room in a red glare of hate. There, before him stood the
man who had floored him—fists doubled—ready to spring
in—ready to begin that battering hell of blows all over again—
grinning!

McClosky's fingers closed, about the neck of a bottle of
whisky that stood forgotten on the bar, his arm drew back and
he let it fly straight at that grinning face, not ten feet from him!
There was the sound of smashing glass, and the man collapsed
at his feet! He'd show him! He'd learn him not to stall for wind
in a fight—not to finish a man off when he had him down!

Then, there was silence in the room—silence, and a sea of
faces—all staring down at the man on the floor. Someone
knelt beside the man—raised his head. The head was bloody—
served the damn *chechako* right—he'd learn him! Then, a face
was looking up into his own. Good gosh—it was the same face!
No—another—not bloody! But—the same face—he ought to
know—wasn't it the face he'd been swinging at and missing for
the last half hour? The man was speaking—that voice—hard
and clean-cut—like the blows that had floored him—"Damn

you—if my brother dies, I'll kill you if it's the last thing I do on earth!" And the eyes—harder—colder even than the voice that cut from between those hard, firm lips.

Then—there was a policeman in the room—Corporal Downey—they all claimed he was the smartest of the bunch—and he was talking—he had his service revolver in his hand—and he was talking about a sled—a sled with a busted runner. What the hell had busted sleds got to do with this rookus, anyhow?

Then, Piggy Dixon was getting up off the floor, fumbling at his jaw. What was Piggy doing on the floor? Well—that's where he would be—in a fight. No guts—wallering on the floor to keep out of the way—that was Piggy, every time. What was he saying—it was his sled with the busted runner? Well—what if it was—what had Piggy be'n up to, now?

The policeman was talking again—talking about some wire and young Farnsworth—good gosh—Farnsworth—wire! McClosky's brain cleared instantly—Farnsworth—wire! And Downey was saying that the wire on Piggy's sled was like—! He remembered his piece of baggage that had burst on the dock at Seattle, and that he had ducked into the nearest store, and bought wire to wind it with—gold picture wire—it was all the man had—and he remembered that it was a piece of that wire he had used! And he remembered that just as they were starting out on this trip from Sunk Creek, Piggy Dixon had found a cracked runner, and he had stepped into his shack and grabbed up the first piece of wire he had come to to fix Piggy's sled—gold picture wire—his gold picture wire—McClosky's!

And, now Downey—the smartest policeman of the bunch—was asking about it—and Piggy—Piggy was saying—McClosky met Piggy's wildly roving glance—and Piggy swallowed his words.

Then, Corporal Downey was taking Piggy along—arresting him, for the Farnsworth murder—and Piggy scairt, and with no guts at all! When the police got to working on him, he'd spill everything he knew—and he knew plenty!

SILENTLY UNOBTRUSIVELY, while the crowd was talking and watching the officer shoving his prisoner along toward the door, Bull McClosky, eased himself out the back door where he was joined a moment later by the other two Sunk Creekers. It was then that he noticed that his two white-handled six-guns were missing from their holsters, and he cursed vehemently under his breath.

"Bull," whispered one of the two, from between chattering teeth, "Piggy'll squeal, sure as hell. He ain't got the guts of a louse!"

McClosky whirled on the man with a snarl. "I'll tend to Piggy!" he rasped in a hoarse whisper. "My side guns is gone. I'll git my rifle off'n my sled—it's on top in under the ropes. You an' Billings hit fer the crick as fast as you kin leg it. There's more of that damn wire in my shack! Destroy it—hide it—"

"Where'll we hide it?" sniveled the man referred to as Billings.

McClosky cursed under his breath like a mad man: "Where? Anywhere, you damn idiot! Where Downey can't find it! The hull Yukon spread out around you—an' you can't hide a piece of wire! Git goin', now—take my outfit along with you. I'll git my rifle an' 'tend to Piggy 'fore the police has a chanct to work on him. Then, I'm hittin' downriver fer a while—Alasky—see!"

"You leavin' us!" cried Billings. "Leavin' us to take the fall—an' you hittin' fer Alasky!"

"Listen, you damn fool! There ain't a thing on you—on any of us—if you hide that wire! The wire Downey found was on Piggy's sled—not your'n!"

"Nor your'n, neither—but, you're beatin' it!"

"Not on account of Farnsworth, nor them others! Piggy's the goat—an' he'll be dead in three minutes! It's from that, in there, I'm runnin'. I killed that guy with a bottle! An' if the law don't git me that other guy will! I seen it in his eyes! A man with an eye like that don't bluff. Git on up the crick, now! Here—give me what dust you've got on you! You'll have all the dust in the cache—but, don't fergit that a quarter of it's mine—I'll be comin' back some day—an' if my quarter ain't still in the cache—you'll answer to McClosky! Shell out! There goes Downey an' Piggy, they got the dogs ontoggled!"

Two small pouches of dust changed hands and went into McClosky's pocket. Swiftly, the big man ran along the side of the saloon, and stepping to a dog sled, slipped his rifle from under its lashings, and darted back into the shadows.

Again McClosky ran in a course parallel with that taken by Downey, and his prisoner—keeping in the rear of the stores and the saloons that fronted on the street. With the grimness of desperation he clutched his rifle, nor did he glance to the right, nor to the left, nor behind him—else he might have caught a glimpse of the figure that followed—a figure that held well to the shadows.

AMID A clutter of lumber piles McClosky took a stand that gave a clear view of the street in the bright moonlight. One minute passed—two—then a man appeared walking at the head of a string of dogs. A few feet behind him walked another man—a man in the uniform of the Mounted Police. Deliberately, McClosky raised his rifle and fired. The man spun half way around and fell. McClosky turned and ran. Not back toward the Tivoli, this time, but at a right angle—toward the river. He gained a cross street, and slowed to a walk, and at a walk he continued until he came to the little group of shacks occupied by the Siwashes that worked in the saw mill. At the third shack he paused and knocked on the door. When it opened, he stepped inside and spoke in hurried tones to a young Indian. A pouch of dust changed hands, and the Indian stepped out into the night, leaving McClosky in the shack. A half-hour later he returned, carrying a well-filled pack sack. McClosky accompanied him to the river bank where they overturned and launched a canoe.

With the pack sack amidship, McClosky took his place in the stern, and with a parting injunction of silence, shoved off, and headed up the Yukon.

The moon sank behind the mountains and a period of comparative darkness was followed by a gray dawn. McClosky landed, boiled a pot of tea, and fried some bacon. Breakfast over, he filled and lighted his pipe, and stretched out for a short rest. "Downey'll hit out fer Sunk Crick," he mused, "an' if Billings an' Blinky beats him an' gits red of that wire, he won't have a damn thing on me, as fer as Farnsworth goes—it's that rookus last night that puts me in Dutch.

"Wisht, now, I hadn't beaned that guy—but, I was too damn mad to think. He'll die, all right—an' if Downey does find that wire, it don't make much difference, now—they can't only hang a man onct. Blinky an' Billings are goin' to be wild when they find out I moved the cache! The damn crooks, I mistrusted somethin' might happen down to Dawson, er that one of 'em might slip back an' swipe the dust on me—so I cached it where they'll never find it. They'll be sore as hell—but, they can't blab nothin' on me about them other jobs without gittin' theirself hung too. They'll prob'ly squawk that I hit downriver fer Alasky—an' that'll sound reasonable—that's where the police'll figger I went.

"When they don't stop me at Forty Mile er Eagle, they'll think I made her. An', me—I'll be up on Halfaday—an' mebbe lock horns with Black John Smith, hisself. Looks to me like it's time Halfaday had a new king. Then, when the excitement's died down, I'll slip back on Sunk Crick, an' gather in that cache. Billings an' Blinky'll be gone by then—there ain't even wages on the crick—an' them two ain't got neither the guts nor the brains to pull off no more robberies."

WELL PLEASED with himself, McClosky knocked the dottle from his pipe, and kneeling at the water's edge, washed the dried blood from his beard, and bathed his battered lips and swollen eye in icy water. Stepping into the canoe, he pushed on upstream, keeping close in shore to take advantage of the eddies, and also to escape observation from the boatloads of *chechakos* that were pouring into the Yukon on the heels of the big stampede. He paddled steadily, but not hurriedly, landing at frequent intervals to hide among the rocks as a boat passed, Dawson bound.

In the early evening he beached the canoe on a narrow strip of shingle, swung the pack to the gravel, and concealed the light craft between two rocks. He was tired, and hungry, and what the hell was the hurry? Downey wouldn't be back from Sunk Creek for a couple of days, and when he did get back, he'd go kihootin' off downriver—so, what the hell!

He collected firewood, and unrolled his blankets. Picking up his tea-pot he stepped to the water's edge, and the next instant leaped back, scattered the little pile of firewood with a kick, tossed his pack among the rocks, drew his canoe into further concealment, and with his rifle clutched in his hand, crept behind a rock and gazed downriver toward a canoe with a single occupant that was forging steadily upstream. The craft was only twenty or thirty yards out from shore, and not more than a hundred and fifty yards away. The man's face was not distinguishable in the waning light, being partly concealed by the visor of his cap. Some prospector heading upriver, thought McClosky. But, what if he, too, should decide that this narrow strip of beach was a good place to camp for the night? McClosky had no desire for company. He had no wish for any man to know that he had not gone downriver. He cocked his rifle. If the fool headed in, it would just be too damn bad for him—that's all. What's one more killing? They'd never find the body, anyhow.

THE MAN was nearer, now—a hundred yards. He looked up—and McClosky stifled a cry. It was the other *chechako*! The one who looked up with his eyes like ice and promised to kill him if his brother died! His brother must have died, then. But—how in hell did this one know that he had headed upriver? Had that damn Siwash talked? Sure—it was the only way he could have known. Well—he'd kill the Siwash, for that! He'd learn him to talk! But, first, he must kill this *chechako*.

A man couldn't take any chances with a man with eyes like that! Look at him! He worked his paddle like he worked his fists—never tiring. Seventy-five yards, McClosky judged, as he sighted along the barrel of the rifle that rested over a rock. He couldn't miss at seventy-five yards—not a mark like that—the whole width of the man's chest! Carefully he lined his sights squarely in the middle of the chest, then a hair to the left—sixty yards now! With steady finger, McClosky pressed the trigger. The rifle roared. The result was just what he had expected. The man in the canoe, whirled halfway around—why did they always whirl half way around? wondered McClosky, as he watched the man plunge forward on his face over the side of the canoe. The next instant, the light craft was bottom up, floating sidewise with the current. And, near it was a thrashing and splashing of water. Then, two hands shot upward, for a single instant a white face seemed staring straight into his—as it stared once before from the barroom floor—then the face disappeared, and the hands followed, making scarcely a ripple on the surface.

Farther on, the canoe spun slowly and lazily as the current carried it into the gathering darkness.

McClosky heaved a sigh of vast relief. And the next instant flattened himself low among the rocks, as with a wicked whining "ping" a bullet ricocheted from the rock not a foot from his head, showering his face with a spray of stinging particles. From the river came the roar of the rifle, and another and another, as bullets whined and flattened themselves close about him.

Peering around a rock, McClosky cursed the occupants of a boat that, a hundred yards out in the river, was sweeping downstream. It was a clumsy craft made of unpainted whipsawed lumber. In it were four men, two who worked furiously at the crude oars, and two others who, clutching their rifles, were staring toward the shore. Even as he looked, the boat was swallowed up in the gloaming.

"Damn *chechakos*!" growled McClosky, aloud. "Always buttin' in where they ain't wanted! They seen me drill that guy—but, what in hell was it any of their business! They'll shoot off their head in Dawson about seein' a man killed upriver, an' the police'll come up to investigate. They won't know it's me—but, it means I got to keep movin' damn lively till I hit Halfaday! Onct I git there I'll organize the boys, an' if Downey or any other damn police comes snoopin' around there we'll blast 'em to hell!"

McClosky gathered his scattered firewood, cooked and ate a hurried supper, rolled his blankets, loaded his outfit into his canoe and pushed on. Crossing the river, he hugged the opposite shore, and despite his fatigue, paddled on and on through the night.

At daylight he camped, carrying pack and canoe well back into a spruce thicket. "I'll camp days an' travel nights," he muttered, "as long as I'm on the big river. That way I won't be meetin' all them damn *chechakos* an' leavin' a trail fer the police. Chances is they'll think them *chechakos* is lyin' about what they seen, anyhow."

ON THE White River, of which Halfaday Creek is a tributary, McClosky resumed daylight travel. The danger from *chechakos* had passed, and the ascent of the White with its shallows and its rapids is no night work for any man.

One evening, fifteen days later, at a point some hundred and fifty miles from the Yukon, McClosky camped on a sandbar close against the edge of a thicket of spruce on Halfaday Creek. He kindled his little fire and stretched out on his blankets waiting for the water to boil. "Tomorrow," he mused aloud, "I'd ought to fetch the Halfaday diggin's—an', then to hell with the police! I'll hit this here Cushing's Fort with a whoop an' a holler—let 'em know right off the reel who's boss. There'll be some of 'em there that's heard tell of McClosky."

V

IN THE EARLY gray of dawn, Tom Condon opened the door of the Tivoli and walked slowly to the bar where the little group of sourdoughs stood regarding him in silence. "Jerry's gone," he announced, in a hard, flat voice. "The best damn brother a man ever had."

"That's a hell of a note," opined Moosehide, in awkward sympathy.

"Have a drink," invited Old Bettles. "Another glass, Curley!" he called, shoving the bottle toward Condon.

The young man poured his drink with a steady hand, and downed it at a swallow.

"We're—er—plumb sorry," blurted Bettles shifting uncomfortably from one foot to the other. "He could fight like hell. Er—have another drink."

Condon shook his head: "You boys see that he gets a decent burial. I'll be goin' after McClosky, now."

"I'll say we will!" boomed Camillo Bill, heartily. "How's 'Condon' spelt?"

Buck Hammond called for a pencil and paper, and drew Condon aside. "You get to Halfaday like this," he said. "I'll draw you a map. You prob'ly won't need it. You'd ought to overtake him in a day or so on the Yukon."

"We got my canoe all ready," said Burr MacShane. "Stampedin' pack an' grub fer a month."

"Black John Smith and old Cush are damn good friends of mine", added Buck, as Condon stowed the folded paper in his pocket. "Tell 'em all about it—an' mention my name."

Old Bettles downed three stiff ones in a row, and stuck out a gnarled leathery hand: "Good luck boy. Take a fool's advice an' don't give him no breaks—like you told Downey you would. He won't give you none. Shoot the son first, an' choke him afterwards!"

"The canoe's down' by the wharf," said Swiftwater Bill. "We'll go 'long an' see you off. Then we'll get to work thawin' out a spot fer Jerry."

Fifteen minutes later Tom Condon stepped into the canoe provisioned and ready for the trip, with packs neatly lashed to the thwarts, a spare paddle on top. A six-gun bulged the front of his shirt, and beneath the lashing of the packs, he carefully wedged his rifle. Then, with a wave of his hand he was gone.

All day, with grim, set face, and untiring muscles, young Condon forged steadily upriver keeping, as McClosky had done, close to the bank to take advantage of the eddies. He stopped for no meals. In the bitterness of his soul, the thought of food never occurred to him. Boatloads of *chechakos*, Dawson bound, called greeting to which, scarcely hearing, be paid no heed.

The sun sank, and the valley of the mighty Yukon purpled in the dusk. Toiling mechanically, dipping his paddle and leaning on it with a full, sweeping stroke, his eyes rested on a narrow strip of shingle some distance ahead. Dully, he realized that he was tired—hungry, too. A square meal and a boiling of tea would go mighty good. He leaned heavily on the paddle—only a few more yards.

THE NEXT instant he was diving head foremost into the river. The black water gripped him with a numbing chill. Before he went under the sound of a rifle shot roared in his ears. He was up in an instant, struggling against the grip of the river. Shaking the water from his eyes, he stared shoreward to see a thin puff of smoke, and below it, showing just over the rim of a rock, a face— the bearded face of McClosky! And McClosky still had the rifle!

Discarding the impulse to strike out for shore, he turned toward the canoe floating bottom upward, his brain working with lightning rapidity. If McClosky should think he had killed him—so much the better! He turned to face the man, took a long, deep breath, threw his arms up over his head—and sank.

A few swift underwater strokes brought him to the canoe. Reaching upward, he grasped it by the gunwales, and thrust his head up inside. It was dark as a pocket in there, and the icy water chilled him to the marrow. He shifted his grip from the gunwales to the ropes of the packs, and relaxed. He couldn't stand the numbing cold long, but at least, he was safe from a bullet. McClosky had seen him sink. McClosky would think he was dead—and in a few minutes the canoe would be carried out of sight in the rapidly gathering darkness, and he could work it ashore. He was only a few yards from the bank.

Suddenly something bumped against the canoe, and through the thin shell came the sound of voices. What the hell! He had expected McClosky to be alone! But—what was he doing at the canoe? Surely he thought he had killed his man. Oh, yes—he didn't want the empty canoe drifting down past Dawson where it might be found by the police. He couldn't distinguish the words—evidently there were several men—all talking excitedly. Loosening his grip on the ropes, Condon's right hand tore at the buttons of his shirt, and his fingers closed about the butt of his six-gun. He wondered whether the gun would explode—with the barrel full of water? What difference if it did—he was a goner, anyhow. But—if it didn't, he'd get McClosky, before the others got him! The canoe seemed to be moving across the current. The men had made fast, and were towing it ashore. Now was his chance. Old Bettles was right—he wouldn't give McClosky a break—not now—not after he had shot from ambush! Better, here in the river than ashore. McClosky wouldn't be looking for it. Drawing a deep breath, Condon sank, and came up beside the canoe. He shook the water from his eyes—and raised the gun above the surface, holding to the gunwale with his left hand. Blurred forms were in a boat, close beside him.

"Good gosh!" A voice, shrill and strained with surprise and terror, sounded almost in his ear. And then—"Don't shoot, feller! We're savin' you!"

ONE SWIFT glance showed four tense, white faces. None of the faces was bearded. McClosky was not among them!

A moment later the boat touched the bank and a man leaped ashore and drew the canoe onto the rocks, while fingers twined into Condon's shirt collar and drew him from the water.

"We seen him shoot!" cried one. "We thought he'd killed you!"

"Never touched me, I guess," said the bewildered Condon. "But—what in hell made the canoe turn over?"

"Right here!" cried a man, holding up the blade of a broken paddle. "She busted plumb in the middle when you had yer weight on it! Look!" he paused and pointed to the broken end. "A bullet done it! Yes sir—cut the paddle in two right in yer hands!"

"We was jest comin' past, when we seen it," said one. "We sure thought he'd killed you, an' we cut loose on him with our rifles! But it was gettin' dark, an' we couldn't see him good. I got one look at his whiskers an' begun shootin' at the place we seen him duck down. An', besides Pete, here, an' Joe—they wouldn't quit rowin'."

"Not by a damn sight!" agreed another of the men. "Hell— we'd jest seen him knock off one man! We was gittin' to hell out of there!"

"I hope you didn't hit him," said Condon.

"Hope we didn't—Well, I'll be damned. If anyone ever cuts down on me with a rifle, I hope every son of a gun on the river takes a crack at him—don't none of 'em miss!"

Condon smiled: "This is a private matter, boys," he said. "Just between me and him. I hope you won't say anything about it in Dawson. I'd rather the police didn't horn in."

"Jest as you say," grinned one. "It ain't none of our funeral— but, it come damn near bein' your'n. If it was me, all the police in the country wouldn't be none too many—an I'd wish there was more."

"I'll camp here," said Condon, pointing to a level spot back from the shore. "I've got to dry out my outfit. After a while I'll slip up and see if the man that shot at me has pulled out."

"We'll camp, too. I don't like this damn river at night. Gosh—you northern fellas are hard! Tellin' you about me, that guy could pull out fer hell an' gone—the further the better. I'd never go huntin' him!"

Later, the four watched with undisguised admiration, as Condon slipped silently into the dark, armed only with his six-gun. Two hours later, he was back.

"He's gone," he announced. "Probably figured you fellows would report what you saw to the police."

"If I was in your shoes, that would suit me fine," said one of the men. "Will you be goin' on back with us to Dawson?"

"No, I'll keep on his trail. I'll overtake him, sometime."

"Suit yerself, pardner," said one of the men. "An', good luck to you. You've sure as hell got more guts than I have—an' that ain't no lie, neither."

TOM CONDON found no further trace of McClosky on the Yukon. When he hit the White, however, he ran onto a series of recent campfires at likely camping places, and in the mud and the sand about these, he saw the tracks of a large man. He knew by the tracks and the ashes that the man could not be more than a day ahead, and he traveled with his eyes well to the forefront, having no desire to run into another ambush.

Then, late one afternoon, on Halfaday Creek, far back from the Yukon, he rounded a bend just in time to see his man disappearing around another bend a short distance ahead of him.

Landing, Condon drew his canoe from the water. The sun sank behind the high hills as he secured the craft and hastened forward on foot, keeping well within the shelter of the bush. "He'll be camping pretty quick," he breathed. "A man can't run this crick in the dark."

A quarter of a mile farther on he paused, and peered through the scrub. The man had beached his canoe on a broad sandbar that terminated in a thicket of dense spruce.

Condon watched as he removed his packs, drew the canoe from the water, overturned it, and carried the packs to the edge of the scrub. The man cut firewood, filled his teapot at the river, kindled his fire, and spreading his blankets, threw himself down to wait for the water to boil.

Tom Condon loosened two buttons in the front of his shirt, drew his six-gun and inspected it. He returned the gun but left the buttons unfastened. His chance had come. The moment for which he had waited and toiled was at hand. He would cover McClosky, back him away from his rifle, and throw it in the river. Then, his own six-gun would follow it, and there on the sandbar the two would battle barehanded to the death. He would kill the great hulking brute—kill him with his two hands—just as he had told Downey he would kill him. Then, he would go back to Dawson and take a look at Jerry's grave. Good old Jerry—a fight or a frolic—it had always been the same to Jerry. And now Jerry was dead—lying there in the frozen ground where the sourdoughs had laid him with rough tenderness. Tom was glad he had not been there to see it. He might have broken down.

His lips tightened into a grim, hard line, and he crept forward, swiftly—silent as a snake, into the thicket of spruce. Twilight deepened. Only the nearest of the small tree trunks were visible as Condon silently approached the little fire that flickered on the sandbar.

WHEN HE was within a few feet of the sprawling figure, a twig snapped sharply beneath his knee. Instantly he was on his feet, gun in hand. Instantly, also the huge figure on the sandbar leaped erect—staring into the bush—staring straight into Tom Condon's face! Condon saw the huge jaw drop open, as the man's eyes seemed fairly to pop from their sockets. Then the voice—loud and shrill with terror—not the bellowing bull-throated voice with which he had roared his challenge that night in the Tivoli. "You!… You!… Which one!"

"The one you killed on the river!" answered Condon, in a queer, toneless voice. "My brother—that you brained with the bottle, is there behind you."

With a choking shriek of horror the man lunged forward, and came up with his rifle in his hand. Condon's own gun spat fire—both reports rang simultaneously, and McClosky pitched forward onto the sand, red blood welling in spurts from a hole between the eyes.

Condon felt as though someone had struck him on the shoulder with a club. He stepped out onto the open sandbar, and stared down at the fallen man. Something warm and wet trickled down his side, and he threw back his shirt to gaze stupidly at a hole in his shoulder from which blood was flowing freely. "I—I thought he'd whirl around, and I could step between him and his gun," he muttered, "when I told him Jerry was there. But—oh—well—he's dead. But, I'm damn sorry I couldn't have killed him the way he deserved to be killed."

With his handkerchief he bound up his wound as best he could, and struck out for his own canoe. Before he had covered half the distance he realized that his wound was more serious than he had supposed. He was weak—and momentarily growing weaker. The bullet had gone on through, and his shoulder was bleeding profusely from behind where he couldn't reach to bandage it.

The last few yards he made haltingly, pausing frequently to lean against the trunks of trees. He reached the canoe at last. He would unroll his blankets and take a rest. He reached for the blanket roll, and then darkness overwhelmed him. Queer it should get black dark so quick—a soft, heavy darkness. He could feel it pressing in on him—pleasantly pressing.

ALMOST AT this same moment back in Dawson young Corporal Downey smiled across his flat top desk into the faces of the five sourdoughs who had filed into the little office at detachment headquarters. "Well, boys," he asked, "what can I do for you?"

The sourdoughs shifted uneasily upon their feet and glanced one toward another. "Hell," grinned Corporal Downey, "you look like you'd be'n stealin' sheep."

"It might even be worst than that," admitted Swiftwater Bill. "You tell him, Bettles. You're the oldest."

"Burr's got the best eggucation," said Bettles.

"Buck can run fastest," grinned Mac-Shane.

"Camillo done it," cut in Moosehide Charley. "He'd ought to tell."

"What the devil are you fellows driving at?" asked Downey, a puzzled frown supplanting the grin,

"Like this," began Camillo Bill. "We overheard some *chechakos* talkin' in the Tivoli."

Downey's grin widened: "They can't be arrested for that!"

"They'd ought to be," grumbled Old Bettles, in deep disgust, "—some of the questions they ask! Gosh! Is kerosine good fer chilblains? An'—which snowshoe goes on the left foot!"

"But, these here *chechakos*," persisted Camillo Bill, "they come downriver a couple of weeks ago, an' they claim that, one evenin', jest about a day's paddlin' above here, they seen a feller with whiskers shoot from the bank at a feller in a canoe, an' the canoe tipped over."

"Why didn't they report the matter to the police as soon as they got here?"

"The feller asked 'em not to."

"Well, I'll be damned!" snorted young Downey. "A man shoots another, an' these damn fool *chechakos* don't report it because he asks 'em not to!"

"It was the other fellow asked 'em," explained Old Bettles. "They took some shots at the one with the whiskers."

"The man wasn't killed, then?"

"Wasn't even nicked. The bullet busted his paddle when he was leanin' on it, an' over he went. He dove down an' come up under his canoe, an' the *chechakos* pulled him ashore."

"No harm done, eh? Well, we're too busy to bother with busted paddles, an' canoes tippin' over."

"But," ventured Moosehide, "This here's a kind of a particular case. We kind of figger the feller with the whiskers was McClosky."

"McClosky!"

"Yeah," supplemented Bettles, "an' the other was prob'ly Tom Condon."

CORPORAL DOWNEY eyed the clearly perturbed sourdoughs through narrowed lids. What had got into these old-timers—these sourdoughs whose word, for years had been the law of the North? Why were these self-sufficient men who had battled the North, and won, standing there in front of his desk, shame-faced, and uneasy as a bunch of small boys who had been caught drowning an old maid's cat?

"What the hell would McClosky an' Tom Condon be doin' upriver?" he snapped. "When I got back from Sunk Creek you fellows told me McClosky had hit downriver for Alaska—an' that Condon was on his tail!"

"We lied," announced Old Bettles.

"Lied!"

"Yeah," admitted Bettles, who had assumed spokesman-ship for the sourdoughs, "we lied like hell. It's like this—when McClosky skipped out, Camillo, here, was the only one of us that had the brains to foller him. He seen him shoot yer pris-oner, an' then hit out upriver in a canoe. He come back an' told us, an' believin' that Tom Condon was entitled to the first crack at him, we shut up an' let you go on to Sunk Crick. When you come back an' figgered that McClosky had prob'ly hit fer Halfa-day, we give you the tip that he'd pulled out downriver an' Tom had took after him. We thought we was doin' the square thing by Tom—it was his brother that was killed. But, now, we ain't so sure. You see, Tom lit out after McClosky right soon after he pulled out, an' from what them *chechakos* told, he ketched up to him that same evenin'. McClosky bushwhacked him, but he didn't git him—that time. Tom kep' on after him, an' should of overtook him ag'in, in a day or so, an' done his job, an' come back. But—that's two weeks ago—an' he ain't back. We're figgerin' that, mebbe McClosky had better luck next time."

Corporal Downey turned to Camillo Bill: "You saw McClosky shoot my prisoner that night?"

"I sure did."

"Well, it looks like you fellows had raised hell. I told Condon that McClosky would never give him a break. It's too damn bad. I ain't blamin' you. From your standpoint, Condon did have the right to get McClosky. I'm glad you had the sense and the guts to come an' tell me about it. I'll be pullin' out for Halfaday in the mornin'."

VI

BLACK JOHN SMITH stepped into the barroom of Cushing's Fort, the outland trading post that was the rendezvous of the little community of outlawed men on Halfaday Creek, close against the Alaska-Yukon boundary line.

"There's a dead man," stated Old Cush, setting out bottle and glasses, "on a sandbar."

Black John digested the information as he filled his glass. "What," he asked, "is he doin' on a sandbar?"

"Jest like any dead man. He's layin' there."

"Who did he used to be?"

"I couldn't say. Accordin' to Joe Brown, he's an important lookin' corpse, fer size."

"What's Joe Brown got to do with it?"

"He fetched in the news. It was him found him."

"A dead man," opined Black John, judicially, "*per se*, in an' of hisself, ain't nothin' to get excited about. Some folks dies natural."

"Not," replied Old Cush, "with a forty-five bullet in their head they don't."

"Such bullet," admitted Black John, "might have a bearin' on the case. Where-at is this sandbar which contains the corpse, if any? Joe Brown might of lied.

"A man," argued Old Cush, "could think up a better one than that in case he aspired to lie."

"There's times," opined Black John, refilling his glass, "when any lie at all is better than the truth."

"The sandbar is down to Olsen's bend," informed Cush, tugging at his drooping moustache. "An' jest in case you might fergit, that there second drink is on you. What good would it do Joe to claim he seen a dead man on a bar, if he didn't?"

"No good, in the long run," admitted Black John. "In fact, it would prove a detriment to Joe. But it might be his sense of humor yearns him fer to see someone paddle them sixteen miles fer nothin'."

"That wouldn't be my idee of a joke."

"Mine, neither," agreed Black John. "An', henceforth, as the feller says, it won't be Joe's."

"He might of be'n tellin' the truth."

"Yeah, that's got to be considered. But, ag'in, he might jest be'n braggin'. A man that seen a dead man on a sandbar would be more important than one that didn't. Joe, he might have one of these here inferiority complexions, an' picked out that way of bein' took notice of."

"He looked like a man that was tellin' the truth."

"Hell!" retorted Black John, "that's the way to look if yer lyin'! If a man's really tellin' the truth he don't give a damn how he looks."

"We'd better be gittin' along if we're goin' down there an' investigate that corpse," reminded Old Cush. "S'pose Corporal Downey, er some policeman should happen along!"

"I expect yer right," agreed Black John, pouring a third drink. "Fetch a spade. If he's dead as what Joe claimed, he'd ought to be buried. Prob'ly some *chechako* killed him, er he'd had sense enough to do his own buryin'. *Chechakos* is a damn nuisance—like havin' a dog around, er a cat, that ain't house broke. Some folks' ain't never had no proper fetchin' up. But it looks like even a *chechako'd* ought to know that leavin' dead men around on bars ain't so good! Believe me, if we go clean down there an' don't find no corpse layin' on that bar; there'll be one layin' on your'n when we git back—an' the joke'll be on Joe!"

A COUPLE of hours later these two beached their canoe on the bar at Olson's Bend, and stepped ashore to stare down at the body, sprawled on the sand.

"He's sure a big man," said Old Cush.

"Yeah, he'll take a hell of a lot of buryin'—an' us with only one spade. You better start in diggin' whilst I kind of look things over."

"You're a better hand at diggin' than I be."

"I know," grinned Black John, "but, it's your spade. Look," he added, disengaging the rifle from the man's grasp and working the lever, "he went out a-shootin'. His finger was on the trigger, an' an empty shell in the chamber."

"It might be," opined Old Cush, glancing toward the thicket, "that there's two dead men."

"We'll take 'em one to a time," said Black John, after a hasty survey of the man's pockets and his pack. "Barrin' a couple of kind of lean sacks of dust, an' his rifle, an' blankets, which we'll divide amongst us fer our trouble, the rest of his effects is plumb trivial. Let's git his grave dug. Maybe we'll have better luck with the next one."

Search of the thicket, revealed no other body, but the damp ground showed tracks that led down the creek. They followed, and a few minutes later, came upon a canoe drawn up on the shore. Across the canoe was sprawled a body.

"This 'un's alive," announced Old Cush. "But, he's lost a hell of a lot of blood."

Carefully, the two lifted the wounded man from the canoe, and laid him upon the ground where Black John proceeded swiftly and effectively to bandage the wounds. He drew the revolver from beneath the man's shirt, and throwing open the cylinder, pointed to the single exploded cartridge. "Got his man the first shot," he said, approvingly, "an' right between the eyes. He's ondoubtless a likely lad, an' worth savin'."

Stooping, Old Cush held a flask to the man's lips and forced a splash of liquor between the teeth. The man choked as the fiery liquor trickled into his throat—swallowed, and opened his eyes. Raising his head, Cush again held the bottle to his lips, and nodded approval as he swallowed several gulps of the whiskey.

"Do you know Old Cush, and Black John Smith?" asked the wounded man, feebly.

"We're them," stated Black John.

"Buck Hammond—he said you were friends of his—told me to tell you all about it—I—killed—"

"Listen, fella," interrupted Black John, heartily. "You've told enough. Quit worryin'. If yer a friend of Buck's you could kill half the men in the Yukon, an' it would be all right with us. We stand fer law an' order on Halfaday, an' we've buried yer *corpus delicti* fer you. We'll be loadin' you in the canoe now, an' takin' you up to Cush's where the *klooch* can look after you till you git well. You ain't in no shape to talk, now nohow."

One day, two weeks later, young Corporal Downey pushed open the door of Cushing's saloon and entered, to be greeted vociferously by Black John Smith, who stood at the bar shaking dice with the somber faced proprietor.

"Well, damn if it ain't Downey! Come on up an' name yer licker, Corp'ral! I jest hung one on Cush!"

"That was only the first horse," reminded Old Cush.

"What the hell's a horse er two amongst friends? Go ahead an' set 'em up! What you goin' to have, Downey?" asked Black John with a grandiloquent wave of the hand toward the four bottles on the back bar. "We've got Conyac, Sour Mash, Rye, an' Bourbon—an' you can't go wrong. Cush draws 'em all out of the same bar'l."

"It keeps the boys from mixin' their drinks," explained Old Cush, somberly, "which is, bad fer their stummicks."

WHEN THE drinks were poured, Black John slanted the young officer a glance. "Be you huntin' someone," he inquired, "er jest takin' the census?"

"I'm lookin' for a man," answered Downey.

"One that's mebbe, committed some-thin?"

"A matter of a few murders—three, at least—prob'ly a half a dozen more."

"H-u-m-m," uttered Black John, "kind of done himself proud didn't he?"

"They're damn slimy murders—every one of 'em."

"What fer lookin' was he? Me an' Cush might be able to help you out. We aim to keep Halfaday moral."

"He was a big man with a bushy reddish beard."

"A big man did you say" asked Black John with sudden interest. "An,' he had reddish whiskers?"

"Yes. He'd weigh around two-seventy. Big, an' yellow to his guts. Loud mouthed an' blusterin', an' noisy as hell."

"H-u-m-m, seems like we seen a big man, 'long about two weeks ago. But, he was an awful quiet fella. Wasn't he Cush?"

"He didn't make no noise whilst I seen him," admitted Cush.

"Prob'ly learnt his lesson," grunted the officer.

"He kind of looked like a man that had, at that," admitted Black John.

"Where is he?" asked Downey, eyeing the two sharply.

"I couldn't say," answered the noncommittal proprietor.

"It kind of seems like he passed on," said Black John. "We only seen him the onct."

"Did he cross the divide?"

Black John nodded emphatically. "He shore did."

Corporal Downey swore softly. "I'm damn sorry that bird got across to Alaska," he said. "He's one hombre, I wanted to see hang! I don't suppose you saw anything of a good lookin', clean-cut, upstandin' sort of a lad about that same time, did you?"

Black John shook his head: "Nope. There ain't no upstandin' young feller showed up on Halfaday, er we'd of seen him. Wouldn't we, Cush?"

"I couldn't say," answered Old Cush, fumbling among the glasses on the back bar.

"What's he got to do with it—the upstandin' one?" asked Black John.

"The big one, McClosky, murdered his brother, an' he took out after him. I don't blame him—I'd have done the same thing. I suppose McClosky ambushed him somewhere along the White. He tried it on the Yukon."

"Suppose," queried Black John, "that the upstandin' one had come up with this here McClosky, an' shot it out with him, fair an' square?' Would there be anythin' on him?"

"Hell—no!" Downey exclaimed. "Young Tom Condon was a fine lad! So was his brother. It's too damn bad McClosky got 'em. The Condons were worth a thousand of him! I only wish it had happened the way you said!"

A slow grin overspread the bearded face of Black John Smith. "Per onct, Downey, you git yer wish," he said. Then, raising his voice so that it carried to the room above: "Hey, Tom! Kin you make it down here without help? Corporal Downey's here—an' I'm buyin' a drink!"

BLACK JOHN AND THE
SKY PILOT

OLD CUSH, PROPRIETOR of Cushing's Fort, the combined trading post and saloon that served the little community of outlawed men that had sprung up on Halfaday Creek, close against the Yukon-Alaska border, set out a bottle, two glasses and the inevitable leather dice box as Black John Smith crossed the floor and elevated a foot to the battered brass rail. Picking up the box, the big man rattled the dice noisily, and rolled them out onto the bar. "I'm leavin' them three fives in one," he said.

Cush failed to beat the three fives, and took three shakes to collect three sixes which Black John promptly beat with four treys. As both filled their glasses, Cush pushed the square-framed, steel-rimmed spectacles from nose to forehead. "I seen a piece in that there newspaper Red John fetched up from Dawson where it tells how some perfesser name of Langley in Worshin'ton, er somewheres, went to work an' built him a flyin' machine."

"Flyin' machine, eh? Where did he fly to?"

"He didn't. They loaded this here machine, which it had a engine in it to make it go, on top of some kind of a boat an' anchored it out in some river. Then this fella gits in it, an' they starts the engine an' shoves the damn thing off'n the boat."

"Yeah—an' what happened?"

"Jest what anyone with any sense would know would happen—it fell in the river an' sunk. Looks like even a perfesser would have more sense than to figger he could fly."

"Oh, I don't know," the big man replied. "It ain't so damn long ago there wasn't any railroads, an' here only a month or so back there was a picture in the Police Gazette of some fella steerin' a horseless carriage down Fifth Avenue in New York. A man can't never tell about these inventions."

"Yeah, but railroads is built on the ground where they can't fall nowheres, an' them horseless carriages, too. But a flyin' machine—what the hell's goin' to hold it up in the air? Cripes, it's bound to fall down!"

"The sun an' the moon an' the stars stays up there, don't they? An' there's nothin' holdin' them up."

Black John stared wide-eyed at the two forms sprawled on the ground...

"Yeah, but they're a hell of a ways off—an' besides, how do you know they ain't nothin' holdin' 'em up? No one's ever seen the other side of 'em. They might be hangin' from somethin' solid that's so damn fur away you can't see it."

The big man grinned. "What would hold this theoretical solid thing up in the air?"

"How the hell would I know? But, at that, John, if anyone could fly it would save a hell of a lot of work. Look at the room he'd have to git around in. An' look at the time an' hard work he'd save. Cripes, he wouldn't have to foller no trail, or road, or paddle up some damn river, or climb up over no mountains. He could jest take off an' go straight to where he's goin'. You know, sometimes I git mad as hell watchin' the geese go by, way up there—slidin' along fast an' easy like."

The big man downed his drink and grinned. "I'm afraid it won't do you any good watching 'em, Cush. The life you've led—by no stretch of the imagination will you ever sprout wings."

"Yeah? Well, I don't see no pinfeathers stickin' out through your shirt, neither." He glanced toward the open door. "Here comes a Siwash. Wonder what he wants?"

The Indian stepped into the room, crossed the floor and paused beside Black John. "Dat tam you tak' de hooch man off Ladue Crick an' hang him, an' give us back de fur we trade for de hooch."

"Yeah. I remember. What about it? Didn't you get all your fur back? Or do you want him onhung so you can get some more hooch?"

"We git all de fur back. Dat damn good t'ing you hang um. You good mans—*kloshe talicum*. I'm like you good. Me, I'm fin' leetle crick. Ron into nudder crick. Ron into Pelly. I'm fin' gol'—*pil chickimin*." The man paused, produced a small moosehide sack and poured its contents onto the bar. Both Black John and Cush were impressed with the little pile of dust and nuggets.

"What's your name? An' how long did it take to pan this stuff out?" John asked.

"Nem Tom Big Axe. I'm work two day. Pick up de nuggets by de rocks in de rapids. Pan de dus' in my frypan."

Cush slid the gold onto the scale: "Eleven ounces," he announced. "That's a hundred an' seventy-six dollars—without no shaft, jest snipin'."

"If you made this strike up the Pelly what are you doin' on Halfaday? Why didn't you hit for Dawson an' record your location?"

"Me, I'm like I'm pay you back for git all de fur back, dat tam. I'm show you de crick so mebbeso you stake claim by me. Crick only so beeg for two claim. W'en day fin' out I'm tak' out mooch gol', mebbeso som' damn *chechako* com' 'long an' tak' de odder claim. Mebbeso steal my gol'. Mebbeso shoot me, tak' my claim. I'm lak you got dat claim. You hones' mans, Black John."

"Come on," Black John said, as the Indian pocketed his dust. "What are we waitin' for? Let's get goin'."

ONE EVENING ten days later, after a day spent in test panning and clawing about in the gravel in the bed of the tiny creek, Black John eyed the Indian. "We've got somethin' here, Tom," he said. "She's good—might even be damn good. We'll go pardners on this proposition. We can stake fifteen hundred feet in two Discovery claims—an' short as the crick is, that'll damn near take it in from one end to the other. In the mornin' we'll sock in our stakes. You stay here an' work the claims an' I'll hit out for Dawson an' record 'em. I'll leave you my rifle an' a box of shells, an' you can make out with what grub we fetched along till I get back with more. I might be gone a couple of weeks, er even a couple of months. But I'll be back. Cache the stuff you take out, an' if anyone comes nosin' around tell 'em you ain't doin' no better'n wages."

At noon, several days later, paddling down the mighty Yukon, Black John landed on a gravelly point a few miles below the mouth of the White River, for lunch. As he stepped into the bush to gather wood for a boiling of tea, a gleam of white caught his eye, and peering through the underbrush, he saw a tent pitched in a tiny clearing at the foot of a huge rock. He called loudly and receiving no answer, pushed his way through the bush. A few moments later he stood at the edge of the clearing and stared wide-eyed at the two forms sprawled on the ground between the doorway of the tent and the remains of a tiny fire with an empty tea pail lying on its side in the ashes. One of the men lay on his back, his face covered with blood that had gushed from a wound in his forehead, his hands still grasping a cocked rifle. The other lay on his belly, his face buried in a crooked forearm.

Dropping to his knees, Black John grasped the man's shoulder and turned him over. He rolled limply, and the next instant, tearing the man's shirt open, Black John detected a feeble heartbeat, and exposed a bullet wound high up on the right side of the chest from which a few drops of blood oozed. Leaping to his feet, the big man crashed through the underbrush to his canoe, and lifting out his pack sack, rummaged in it for a clean suit of underwear from which to rip a bandage. A smudge of smoke caught his eye, and a moment later a steamboat, paddle wheel churning, appeared around a bend, headed downriver. Stepping into the canoe, Black John paddled out and flagged her down. A few minutes later, the *Racket* nosed into the bank, and willing hands carried the wounded man aboard and placed him in a bunk. The dead man was also taken aboard, as was Black John and his canoe, and the steamer headed full speed for Dawson. There was no physician aboard, but between them, Black John and the captain did a creditable job of bandaging the wound after liberally smearing it with antiseptic salve.

Black John was the first to speak as the two stood staring down at the man in the bunk. "Downey's got a murder on his hands now—an' a damn dirty one. These men were shot with a revolver. If it had been a rifle the bullets would have gone on through."

The captain nodded. "Yeah—two murders. This man will be dead before we hit Dawson. Cripes, you can't even see him breathe!"

"But his heart's still goin'. Maybe if we could get a little whiskey down him it might help."

"Hell, weak as he is he couldn't swaller! If we tried to get whiskey down him we might choke him to death."

"A shot of whiskey might keep his heart goin'," Black John persisted. "If he don't get it he'll die, anyway. For myself, I'd rather choke to death on whiskey than lay in a bunk an' fade out like he's doin'. Hell, man—goin' that way, a man would never know he was dead! Go fetch a bottle an' we'll try to get some down him. If we can get him to the hospital Doc Sutherland'll fetch him around. He's cured fellas a damn sight deader'n this man is."

"We better thin it out with water," the captain said, as he handed Black John the bottle a few minutes later.

THE BIG man shook his head. "Nope. Weak as he is, he ain't goin' to swallow much anyhow—an' what he does get, the stronger the better." Holding the bottle close, he allowed a few drops to trickle into the open mouth. The man's throat moved slightly and for several minutes he continued to swallow feebly as the liquor trickled from the bottle.

"By God," the captain exclaimed, "if he ain't dead when we get to Dawson he'll be drunker'n hell!"

Black John held up the bottle and eyed its contents. "We got a damn good drink down him, anyhow." Placing his hand on the man's chest, he nodded. "His heart's picked up already. I believe that whiskey done the trick. Anyways, I'd ruther be drunk than dead any day—who the hell wouldn't?"

"Wonder who these fellas is?" the captain speculated. "Couple of *chechakos*, prob'ly."

Black John shook his head. "They ain't *chechakos*. The clothes they're wearin' are Yukon bought. My guess is that they're a couple of men who maybe made their stake an' were headin' outside. An' that some snake knew about it, an' followed 'em up here an' knocked 'em off an' robbed 'em. Anyhow, that's Downey's headache, not ours."

The captain nodded, "The Mounted does a damn good job. I shore hope Downey ketches up with whoever done it."

"Or, if he don't, I hope the damn cuss hits for Halfaday."

The captain grinned. "I hear how you boys up there don't do so bad with your miners' meetin's."

"We do the best we know how. If a man's guilty we hang him—an' if he ain't we turn him loose. There ain't no quibblin' like a judge turnin' him loose because his name was spelt wrong in an indictment, or the crown prosecutor makin' a grammatical error in summin' up his case, or an appeal court turnin' him loose because some juror was held to he prejudiced. All we want to know—did he do it or didn't he? I shore hope this bird pulls through. He might be able to identify the cuss that shot him." Black John paused and glanced at the two pack sacks he had carried aboard. "If they were packin' out any dust they've been robbed, all right. There's their packs, an' neither one of 'em's heavy enough to have much gold in it."

"They might have traded in their gold for bills at the bank," the captain suggested. "Maybe we better run through their stuff—jest in case one of the crew might slip in here an' do a little sneak-thievin'."

Nothing of value was found in the packs, and the big man frowned. "They've been robbed all right. Either that, or they didn't have anything when they started out—an' if that was the case, no one would have shot 'em. Whoever done it knew they were well heeled, or he'd never risked his neck to rob 'em."

AS THE *Racket* docked at Dawson, the wounded man was rushed to the hospital, and Black John proceeded to detachment headquarters of the Mounted Police, where he turned over the two pack sacks belonging to the victims to Corporal Downey. "It's murder, all right, an' a damn dirty one," he said. "Bettles an' Swiftwater Bill was at the landin' when the *Racket* pulled in an' they identified the two as the Bronson brothers who sold out on Squaw Crick an' headed upriver a few days back with twelve hundred an' sixty ounces of dust, claimin' they was goin' back to North Dakota an' open a store. Accordin' to Bettles, they sort of spread around a couple of days before hittin' out, so the chances are some damn cuss followed 'em upriver, an' knocked 'em off an' robbed 'em. Cap Blakely an' I went through their packs there, an' there wasn't a damn ounce in either one of 'em."

Downey nodded. "Yeah, I remember seein' the Bronsons in the Klondike Palace a few nights back. They was feelin' pretty good, swingin' the girls high, wide an' han'some. Prob'ly done too much talkin' for their own good. When you headin' back upriver?"

"As soon as I get through at the recorder's. I was comin' down to record a couple of locations when I run onto their camp. I flagged down the *Racket* an' me an' Cap bandaged Sam up an' got some whiskey down him. We fetched Joe's body down, too."

Corporal Downey reached for the phone and called the hospital. After a few moments of conversation he hung up the receiver. "Doc Sutherland says he dug a .38 bullet out from under Sam's shoulder blade. Gives him a fifty-fifty chance of pullin' through. He dug another .38 out of Joe's head—revolver bullets, soft lead, no jackets. Get along to the recorder's, an' I'll be ready. I'm goin' up an' have a look-see. Prob'ly won't do no good. But you never can tell. I'll have Peters an' Blake keep an eye open around here—see if any of them damn cusses that hangs out around the Palace is throwin' around too much dust. Or it might be that one of 'em's missin'. Meanwhile, if any suspicious-lookin' stranger shows up on Halfaday, you slip me the word, an' I'll come up an' get him."

The big man grinned. "So you can take him down to Dawson an' give some jury a chance to turn him loose because his hair was parted on the wrong side, eh? I'll promise to let you know all right if the murderin' skunk shows up on Halfaday—an' if you want him when we get through with him, you're welcome. Miners' meetin's have kept Halfaday Crick a damn sight moraler than the law court has kept Dawson."

"If we bring 'em in, it ain't our fault if the court turn 'em loose."

"Shore it ain't," Black John agreed. "But the fact is the guy is apt to be turned loose to commit another murder. Up on Halfaday the evidence is heard, an' if he's guilty he's hung right then an' there. If he ain't, he's turned loose. Them boys in our graveyard layin' there with an H carved on their slab don't never repeat."

NOTHING OF importance was found at the camp, and Black John took leave of Downey and headed up the White. On the evening of the second day he rounded a bend several miles above the mouth of Ladue Creek to find a canoe drawn up on the gravel, and a man seated beside a tiny fire above which a tea pail was suspended. Beaching his canoe beside the other, he stepped ashore to be greeted by a long faced, sad-eyed bewhiskered individual. "Ah, brother, welcome to my little camp. I was about to prepare my evening meal. I trust you will join me."

"Might's well. We can go halves on the grub. I was about to camp, myself. Where you headin'?"

"I am heading for Halfaday Crick where, I am told, a band of outlaws hold forth at a place called Cushing's Fort. I left the Yukon several days ago. I was told that Halfaday Crick runs into the White River from the north. So, upon reaching the White I headed up the first crick I came to, and two days later I met an Indian who told me that I was on Ladue Crick—that Halfaday is many miles farther on."

Black John nodded. "Yeah. You an outlaw?"

"No! No! I am a minister of the gospel, the Reverend Ishmael Saunders. And like my namesake, the Ishmael of old, I wander through the wilderness seeking to do what good I can, and to carry the Word to such benighted souls as are in danger of hell-fire."

"Figure on convertin' some of the boys, eh?"

"If I can snatch one brand from the burning I will have done a worthy deed. And who knows—I may be the means of turning many from the error of their ways—even the notorious Black John Smith, himself, who I understand is king of these outlaws."

The big man nodded. "Yeah, you might, at that. You're welcome to try. But I'll give you fair warnin'—us brands snatch hard. A man might get his fingers burnt in the snatchin'. You see, I'm Black John Smith."

"Then you have no objection to my sojourning among you?"

"None whatever. Fact is there's undoubtless a few characters along the crick that a little religion wouldn't hurt none. You don't look like no priest. Methodist? Or maybe a Baptist, eh?"

"I belong to no sect. No pope, nor bishop, nor moderator can tell me what to do, or where to go, or what to say. I simply preach the Word as it stands in the Book."

"Like to be your own boss, eh? That's a good way. So do I."

As he spoke the big man removed a light pack from his canoe as the other lifted a heavy pack sack aside and indicated a spot beside the fire.

"Sit down there, Brother Smith, and we'll soon have supper ready," he invited as he removed a chunk of bacon from his pack.

"Never mind the bacon, Parson," Black John said. "I just come up from Dawson an' I fetched along a couple of big thick beef-steaks. We'll throw one of them in the pan. Man gets kind of tired of bacon an' moosemeat, so when I hit Dawson I generally fill up on beef. I like mine fried damn near raw. How about you?"

"That suits me fine. While you fry the steak I'll boil the tea and warm up a can of beans."

The meal over, Black John filled his pipe, and tendered his tobacco pouch to the other, who accepted it and produced his own pipe, with the remark that he saw no harm in smoking inasmuch as there was nothing against it in the Book.

The big man grinned. "Sir Walter Raleigh hadn't discovered tobacco yet when the Book was wrote, or it would be in there, all right."

"Ain't it the truth?"

Black John glanced at the other, who was lighting a twig in the fire. "How's that?"

The man held the burning twig to his pipe and puffed vigorously. "I say the truth is set down in the Book, and if it doesn't prohibit using tobacco there can't be any harm in it. Likewise I don't see any harm in taking a drink, now and then. St. Paul himself says to take a little wine for thy stomach's sake, so if a man can't get hold of any wine, he'd have to make hard liquor do. A man shouldn't get drunk, though. The Book holds that drunkenness is a sin."

The big man nodded. "Guess you'll get along on Halfaday all right, Parson. The boys'll appreciate your liberal-mindedness regardin' smokin' an' takin' an occasional drink."

"How about accommodations on Halfaday Crick? Could I find a cabin to live in? And maybe a building large enough to hold meetings in?"

"Oh, shore. You can move into One Eyed John's cabin. An' you won't need to worry none about a place to hold meetings. I'll speak to Cush an' he'll let you use the saloon. There's no other buildin' on the crick that would do. It's what you might call our community center. We do our drinkin' an' stud playin' there, an' likewise hold an occasional miners' meetin'."

"Miners' meeting! Then you already have a preacher on the crick?"

"No. A miners' meetin' ain't a religious gatherin' It's more like a court of law. If someone commits murder, robbery or any other form of skullduggery, we call a miners' meetin' an' try him. If he's guilty we hang him. If he ain't, we turn him loose."

After a moment of silence the other asked, "These crimes you try a man for are all committed on the crick, I suppose."

"Oh, shore—on the crick an' the adjacent an' subtendin' territory."

"You spoke of my moving into One Eyed John's cabin. Does this One Eyed John still live there?"

"Not since we hung him, he don't."

"Why did you hang him?"

"Oh, damn if I remember. It was a while back. I think it was for murder an' robbery. But I ain't shore."

"Are you sure that this Cush, as you call him, won't object to my holding religious meetings in his saloon?"

"No, he won't object. He won't sell no drinks while you're preachin', neither. Go right ahead, long as you get the meetin's over with in time for the stud game to get goin'. If I was you I'd go kind of light on preachin' agin stud. The boys sort of favor it on Halfaday. It's about the only recreation we've got."

"Many regular preachers hold forth against gambling, but I have never found anything in the Book that says gambling is a sin. I enjoy a good game of stud myself."

Black John nodded. "Like I said, Parson, I believe you'll get along all right on Halfaday—as long as you remain amongst us."

ONE MORNING, some two weeks after his arrival on Halfaday accompanied by the Reverend Ishmael Saunders, Black John stepped into Cushing's saloon as Cush set out bottle, glasses and dice box.

After winning a round of drinks, he eyed the big man across the bar. "This here reverend you fetched in—Cripes, we didn't need no preacher here on Halfaday! You know damn well even Downey claims we're the moralest crick in the Yukon, a'ready. It's miners' meetin's keeps us' moral—not no preacher. What I claim is, one good hangin', where the boys kin see some damn skulldug, kickin' around on the end of a rope, will keep a crick moraler'n a dozen preachers."

The big man filled his glass from the bottle Cush shoved toward him. "You got me wrong, Cush," he said. "I didn't fetch him in. He was headed for Halfaday of his own accord. I overtook him on the White an' we came on in together. He claimed he'd heard about the gang of outlaws that hung out here, an' he figured on comin' up an' snatchin' some of us sin-blistered souls from the grip of hell. What with my pa bein' a preacher back home, I figured a little religion wouldn't hurt the boys none, so I didn't try to keep him away."

"Well, jest between you an' me, I don't believe he's no more of a preacher'n what *I* be. He plays a damn good game of stud. An' he takes a drink whenever he feels like it. Claims the Bible says a little wine is good fer the stomach ache, an' bein' as he can't git no wine here he drinks licker. His stomach must ail him somethin' fierce the way he pours it down. He shore takes plenty o' medicine."

"But you've got to admit that he holds his liquor well. An' as for stud—did you ever see anything in the Book against stud playin'?"

"No, but I ain't got only as fer as the Axe of the 'Postles in that there Bible my fourth wife had. I got quite a bit more to read yet. Prob'ly stud playin' comes in there."

"He's held two meetin's since he's been here, an' the boys seemed to enjoy 'em."

"Yeah, but I take notice he was damn careful not to step on no one's toes. The first time he preached agin strumpets an' the like of that, an' he know'd damn well there ain't no strumpets on the crick—nor no other woman. An' the next time he preached agin makin' gravy images an' fallin' down an' worshipin' 'em. An' I'm bettin' two to one, they ain't a man on the crick, outside of you, would know what a gravy image is, let alone how to make one, or fall down an' worship it." Cush frowned. "I figure this here reverend is a damn fake, an' all the big words you kin think up ain't a-goin' to change him."

After another round of drinks, Black John eyed the safe. "Better make up a pack of dust an' I'll take it down to the bank," he said. "The clean-up's about over, an' I see the safe's kind of bulgin' at the seams."

"That's a good idee, John. Quite a few of the boys ain't fetched in their dust yet an' the safe's damn near full. Better take down about three thousan' ounces. I'll do it up whilst you throw yer stuff in yer pack."

Half an hour later, with nearly two hundred pounds of gold in his pack sack, Black John turned from the bar and headed for the door. "Good luck, John," Cush called after him. "If you can't find no more preachers to fetch back, mebbe you could git holt of a good horse doctor. We shore need one here on the crick—bein' as there ain't a horse within a thousan' miles of us."

ARRIVING IN Dawson, Black John proceeded directly to the bank where he exchanged the gold for bills of large denomination, and after a drink or two at the Tivoli, sauntered over to detachment headquarters to be greeted by Corporal Downey.

"Back again, eh?" Downey said. "How's everything on Halfaday? Any newcomers on the crick?"

"Everything's okay. Business as usual, as the fella says. The boys have just about finished their clean-up. Most of 'em done pretty good. Speakin' of newcomers—did you have anyone in particular in mind?"

"Well. I was hopin' that the bird who shot up the Bronson boys an' made off with their dust might have hit for Halfaday."

"Our hopes runs similar on that score. You ain't had any luck on that case, eh?"

Downey shook his head. "Not much of any. We've got one suspect in mind. But that's about all it amounts to."

"How about Sam Bronson? When I left here about six weeks ago Doc Sutherland give him an even chance to pull through."

"Sam pulled through, all right. He's good as ever. Figures on workin' a lay for Bettles over on Shorty Crick."

"You've talked with him, I s'pose. Does he think he could identify the cuss that shot him, if he saw him again?"

"He knows damn well he could. Sam got a good look at him when he shot Joe. That's howcome we've got this suspect in mind. Sam described him as near as he can remember. Of course, a man's got to take that kind of a description with a dose of salts—he only saw him once, an' then only for a few seconds, an' under the excitement of seen' his brother shot an' gettin' shot himself. Sam says he was a tall, sort of sad-faced-lookin' character, wearin' a beard."

Black John grinned. "Cripes, that description might fit me! I wear a beard, an' I'm tall—an' I'll bet I'd look sad as hell if I was to sneak up an' shoot a couple of fellas in cold blood."

Downey returned the grin. "I guess we can give you a clean bill of health on a job of that kind, John. Leastwise, you ain't the character I've got in mind."

"Thanks for the vote of confidence. Who do you figure done it?"

Downey cleared his throat. "You remember a while back when they called a halt on Soapy Smith's outfit, back in Skagway. After Frank Reid shot Soapy the vigilance committee took over an' scattered Soapy's gang all over hell. There was Old Man Tripp, George Wilder, Slim Jim Foster, Yeah Mow Hopkins, an' others, includin' the Reverend Bowers. We got descriptions of all of 'em, so after Sam Bronson described the man that shot him an' Joe, I put in a day or so, checkin' over the files of men wanted, an' men to watch. This Reverend Bowers come nearest to fittin' Sam's description, so I checked up on him." Downey paused and reaching into a drawer, drew out a sheet of paper. "This Bowers was one of Soapy's steerers who claimed to be a preacher—an' looked like one. Here's what we've got on him since he was chased out of Skagway. A year ago he showed up in Rampart, an' George Bribrilters, the U.S. marshal, told him to move on. Jack McQuesten an' Bob Steele claim he hung around Circle City for a while, an' later Bergman says he hung around Fortymile, snipin' the bars along the crick. Then, a couple of months ago, Bill Tanner, one of Cuter Malone's bartenders, slipped me word that Bowers was hangin' around the Klondike Palace. Tanner used to tend bar in Skagway, an' he knew Bowers. So the other day I got in touch with him an' he says Bowers hung around the Palace for a couple of weeks an' then disappeared. That would he just about the time the Bronson job was pulled off.

"I told Tanner about seein' the Bronson's spreein' around in the Palace just before they pulled out upriver, hopin' to get a line on the exact time of Bowers' disappearance, but he says he didn't know the Bronsons, an' there's so many guys whoopin' it up in there nights that he don't remember 'em."

"Preacher, eh?" Black John said, as Downey returned the sheet to the drawer. "Prob'ly resorted to murder an' robbery just as a sideline to sort of eke out his salary."

Downey grinned. "Anyway, you know as much about it as I do. So if anyone shows up on Halfaday that would fit that description, especially if he claims to be a preacher, you slip me the word, an' I'll be up there pronto."

"If he shows up. I'll slip you the word. An' like I told you before, if you want him after we get through with him, you can have him. Guess I'll hunt up Sam Bronson an' have a word with him. Might be he can remember somethin' he overlooked when he was talkin' to you. You say he's over on Shorty Crick workin' a lay for Bettles?"

"Bettles offered him a proposition. I don't know if he took him up or not. You might ask Belinda Mulrooney. He was puttin' up at the Fair View Hotel."

STOPPING IN at the Tivoli, Black John was greeted by Gordon Bettles, who stood at the bar with a younger man. "Hey, come over here an' meet a friend of yourn. You'll remember him, but he won't know you—never havin' had no formal introduction." He paused and turned to the other. "Sam, this is Black John Smith, the man that fetched you downriver."

Bronson thrust out his hand. "I'm mighty glad to meet you, John. I've heard a lot about you from Downey and Doc Sutherland and the sourdoughs. And on top of that, I owe you my life."

The big man grinned. "Oh, I guess you can thank Doc Sutherland for that. I wouldn't have given a hell of a lot for your life the last time I saw you."

"He did his part, all right. But if it hadn't been for you, he'd never got to work on me. I'd have died up there on the river."

"All right—me an' Doc'll divide you up, fifty-fifty, then." The big man paused and filled the glass the bartender slid toward him. "I just been over talkin' to Downey. He claims you got a good look at the bird that shot you."

"You bet I did! I'll never forget that face! I'd know him if I saw him in hell!"

"You ondoubtless will—if you're headed that way. But how'd you like to get a look at him before that?"

"What do you mean?" the other asked eagerly.

"Meanin' that maybe you an' me had better take a little trip."

"A trip? Where to?"

"Oh, back off the river a ways—Halfaday Crick, to be exact."

After a moment's hesitation Bronson replied. "Bettles and I were about to hit out for Shorty Crick. The fact is, I'm flat broke. That twelve hundred and sixty ounces the robber made off with was every cent Joe and I had in the world. So when Bettles offered me a proposition on Shorty Crick, I took him up on it. And the sooner I get to work, the better."

Bettles grinned. "This here little side trip John mentioned might not be a bad idea. I'd take him up on it, if I was you. About that Shorty Crick lay—I'll hold it open for you. But I've got a hunch that when you get back from Halfaday you won't be wantin' it."

Bronson smiled and shrugged. "I don't know what it's all about. But if that's the way you fellows feel about it, I'll play along with you. When do we start?"

"About three drinks from now," Black John replied. "The *Delta's* due to pull out upriver in an hour. Cap Freely'll nose her in at the mouth of the White an' save us eighty miles of upriver paddlin'."

ARRIVING AT Halfaday some ten days later, Black John slipped Bronson into his own cabin and sauntered over to the saloon. Cush counted the roll of bills the big man tossed onto the bar, placed them in the safe, and made the proper entry in his book. "Looks like you got back in a hell of a hurry," he said, as he set out bottle and glasses. "What's the matter? Weren't there no stud players in town?"

"Oh, shore, there was plenty of stud players," Black John replied as he filled his glass. "But I remembered you wanted me to fetch back a horse doctor, so when I couldn't find none I got so damn disgusted I just turned around an' headed right back here."

Cush filled his own glass and glanced at the big man over the rims of his spectacles. "Speakin' of horse doctors, you know that there reverend you fetched in—by God, I got him all wrong! You re'lect I figgered him fer a fake. Well, he ain't. He's all right. I ketched him a time or two sort of eyein' the safe there, like—well like a man might if he figgered on bustin' into it. So, knowin' we didn't want no sech a damn cuss on the crick, I got holt of Red John an' Pot Gutted John, an' told 'em to git the reverend off to one side an' cook up a scheme fer robbin' the safe. I figgered to wait till you come back, then have the three of 'em go ahead an' start in on the safe some night, an' we'd be layin' fer 'em an' ketch 'em at it. Then we'd hold a miners' meetin' an' vote a hangin' onto 'em. We'd hang the reverend first, so he wouldn't never know we turned Red John an' Pot Gut loose."

Black John nodded. "Not a bad idea, at that. A trifle onethical, maybe—but not bad. When's the play comin' off?"

"It ain't. Like I told you, I got the reverend wrong. Not only he wouldn't have nothin' to do with the deal, but he up an' give Pot Gut an' Red John hell fer figgerin' it out. Then, on top of that, come Sunday, when we was havin' church in here, he r'ared up an' preached the damndest sermon you ever heard agin' robbery an' murder an' such like. An', believe me, he kin preach to beat hell, onct he gits started—specially when he gits a few drinks in under his belt. I'm a-tellin' you he had some of the boys sort of shiftin' around in their chairs when he told about hell."

"So you figure he's okay, eh?"

"Shore I do! Look at it sensible. If we got to have a preacher on the crick, it's a damn sight better to have one that's lib'ral minded enough to smoke an' drink an' play stud—but which wouldn't rob no safe—than it would be to git one which he'd raise hell with the boys fer drinkin' an' gamblin', an' then turn around an' rob the safe."

The big man grinned. "I believe you've got somethin' there, Cush."

"Yer damn right! But you ain't got to take my word fer it. This here's a Wednesday. An' Wednesday nights the reverend has what he calls prayer meetin's. They start early an' don't last no hell of a while, on account the boys like to git the stud game goin'. Some of 'em ain't finished their clean-up, an' they don't like to stay up too late when they got to work next day. He don't do no reg'lar preachin' tonight, like Sunday—but he kin pray damn near as good as he kin preach. Come on over tonight, an' I'll bet you the drinks you'll claim you never heard no better prayin'."

Black John downed his drink and turned from the bar. "I'll take you up on that, Cush. I'll be over right after supper."

Early in the evening he paused in the doorway of the saloon and peered in to see a dozen or more men seated in chairs listening to the impassioned words of the Reverend Ishmael Saunders who knelt before the bar in an attitude of rapt devotion.

SEVERAL MINUTES later he closed with a fervent "Amen," and rising to his feet, reached for the bottle and glass Cush had placed conveniently at hand. He filled the glass and turned as the men rose from their chairs and crowded to the bar. Catching sight of Black John standing in the doorway, his lips parted in a welcoming smile. The next instant the smile died on his lips and his eyes widened, then suddenly narrowed at sight of the man who had stepped into the room and stood beside the big man. The next instant the newcomer pointed a finger. "That's him! That's the skunk who—"

Like a flash the glass dropped to the floor. The hand that had held it plunged into the front of his shirt and came out with a six-gun. A shot rang out—and the Reverend Ishmael Saunders reeled backward against the bar, then suddenly collapsed and slithered to the floor, as the men of Halfaday stared wide-eyed at the big black revolver in Black John's hand.

Cush was the first to find his voice. "What—what the hell?" he cried, as he stared at Black John.

The big man shrugged. "Nothin' much, except you've got to readjust your estimate of the Reverend Ishmael Saunders. The fact is, he shot this man an' murdered his brother an' made off with twelve hundred an' sixty ounces of their dust down on the river a few weeks back. I run onto their camp when I was comin' back from that trip with the Siwash, an' when I saw that Bronson here wasn't dead, I flagged down the *Racket* an' we got him to Dawson where Doc Sutherland give him a fifty-fifty chance to pull through."

"But," Cush asked, "did you know the Reverend there was the one that done it when you fetched him up here?"

"Oh shore. That is, I had a damn good notion he was when I noticed that his pack was small—but damned heavy—about twelve hundred an' sixty ounces heavy, to be exact. I knew onct he got to Halfaday he'd stay here to keep away from the police. So, when I took that batch of dust back, an' found out that Bronson had recovered, I hunted him up, figurin' that if he could identify Saunders as the man who murdered his brother an' robbed him, we'd hold a miners' meetin' an' hang him." The big man paused and glanced into the faces of the men. "You all saw him identify Saunders. An' under the circumstances, you all understand why I figured a miners' meetin' was impractical. We'll adjourn to One Eyed John's cabin now, remove them twelve hundred an' sixty ounces, turn 'em over to Bronson—an' the case will be closed."

BLACK JOHN—
BUSHWHACKER

BLACK JOHN SMITH, reputed leader of a band of outlawed men that hung out at Cushing's Fort on Halfaday Creek, a tributary of the White River, was heading for Dawson. The sun hung low over the western mountains as his canoe shot out of the mouth of the White River onto the broad surface of the mighty Yukon. The big man paddled steadily for an hour or more, heading the light craft downriver in the slowly fading twilight. Casting about for a camping spot, his glance was attracted by a thin column of smoke that rose beside the river.

"Might be Bob Henderson or Art Harper," he muttered, as he swung the canoe shoreward, "but chances is it's a *chechako* camp." The lips beneath the heavy black beard twisted into a grin. "If it is, I can get in some psychological research, as Doc Sutherland would say. I ain't never yet been able to figure out what most of the damn *chechakos* uses for what they call brains."

As he drew nearer shore a young man appeared on the gravely beach, and catching sight of the canoe, waved his hat frantically.

Beaching the canoe, Black John eyed the clean-cut youngster, who appeared to be not a day over eighteen. Beyond him, a fire crackled brightly in a small cleared space in front of a small A tent.

"You heading for Dawson?" the youth asked.

The big man nodded. "Yeah, but I've put in a long day. It's about time to camp."

"I'm glad. It sure is lonesome camping alone."

"Alone? How come you're alone? Where's your canoe, or boat, or whatever fetched you here?"

"I haven't any partner. That is," he amended, "I have one, but he's on Hunker Crick. And night before last my canoe disappeared."

"What do you mean—disappeared?"

"I landed here about this time two days ago and pitched my tent, intending to camp for the night. In the morning, when I stepped to the river to get water for my coffee, the canoe was gone. All day yesterday and today I've been trying to signal to the passing boats that I needed help. Lots of boats have gone down the river, but none of them stopped. The men in some of them waved back, but most of 'em didn't pay any attention. At that, though, I guess they wouldn't have had room for me. They all seemed to be loaded to the gunwales with men and dogs and outfit."

"Didn't hear nothin' durin' the night?"

"I'd put in a long day on the river, and I was pretty tired. I went right to sleep after supper and I guess I slept pretty soundly. I did wake up once when a steamboat went by heading upriver, but went right to sleep again. Whoever took the canoe probably didn't make much noise."

"Where was the canoe? Did you pull it clear of the gravel?"

"No. I pulled it about half out of water and left it there on the beach."

Black John smiled. "You heard the culprit, all right. The upriver boats hold in pretty close to shore along this stretch of river an' buckin' the current they kick up a wash that would float any canoe that was only half out of the water."

THE LAD looked crestfallen. "I guess I've got a lot to learn," he said.

"All *chechakos* have. An' it's the things they learn the hard way they remember longest."

"My Dad told me a lot of things about this country, but he didn't say anything about drawing my canoe clear of the water. Guess he thought any fool ought to know enough to do that."

"Your dad here in the Yukon?"

"No. He was here. My name's Bob Wilson, my dad, Sam Wilson, sold his farm near Sauk Centre, Minnesota, and bought a house in town. When news of the Klondike gold rush got around he tried to get someone to hit for the Klondike with him. Most of 'em had been reading about what a tough country the Klondike is and didn't want any part of it, but dad finally persuaded Lem Brink to sell his livery stable and throw in with him.

"Lem didn't have a very good reputation around town. He drank quite a bit, and folks said he was a pretty slick article when

The lad's eyes widened.
"What's this—a holdup?"

it came to horse trading. He killed a man with a neck yoke over a horse trade a few years ago, but his lawyer got him off on the grounds of self defense. The only witness was a stable boy that worked for Lem and he swore that the man came at Lem with a pitchfork and Lem had to hit him. But lots of people think that Lem told the kid what to say, and he was afraid not to.

"Mother didn't like the idea of dad hitting out with him, and tried to talk him out of it. But dad was determined to get in on the gold rush, and he wouldn't listen to her. He claimed that any partner was better than no partner, and as long as no one else would go, he was going with Lem.

"That was two years ago this spring. They made a strike on Hunker Crick, and got a lawyer to draw up a partnership agreement—a fifty-fifty proposition, with a clause that if either party died during the life of the contract, his entire interest reverted to the other."

"Was this clause Lem's idea, or your dad's?"

"When we went over the contract, just before I started out, dad said that Lem suggested it, claiming that if one should die, the other one's heirs wouldn't get anything anyway. The lawyers would see to that. They worked the claim that winter, and the test panning showed that they were taking out a thousand ounces a month.

"Late in the winter mother got sick, and the doctor was afraid she couldn't live, so we got word to dad, and he hit out for home before the spring clean-up. Lem promised to hire men to help him clean up the dump, and send dad his share.

"Along in the summer dad got a letter from Lem telling him that the gravel wasn't as rich as they figured it was, that he had hired four men to help with the clean-up. He said they sluiced out forty-two hundred ounces, that came to sixty-seven thousand, two hundred dollars. That figures thirty-three thousand, six hundred dollars apiece. The labor and expenses amounted to thirty-one hundred and twenty dollars, or fifteen hundred and sixty dollars apiece. He sent dad a bank draft for thirty-two thousand and forty dollars, together with a statement from the bank that he had deposited a like amount to his own credit.

"Then in June, this year, he got another letter from Lem, enclosing a draft for twenty-four thousand and ninety dollars. He said the gravel was running leaner, and he had hired four men all winter sinking new shafts, and kept them on till after the clean-up, so the expenses were high.

"Dad don't believe the claim is running out—and he thinks that last year's clean-up should have amounted to right around seven thousand ounces, instead of forty-two hundred, as Lem claimed. He wanted to come up this summer and find out for himself what was going on, but mother is still sick—it's her heart, and the doctor says she never will be any better. I got through high school this year, and talked 'em into letting me come up and look things over—sort of take dad's place in working the claim. So I hit out—and here I am."

Black John swung his pack from the canoe, pulled it clear of the water, and after supper, filled his pipe and eyed the lad. "You've done all right, so far, barrin' losin' your canoe. From Minnesota to here is quite a trip for a youngster to make alone—an' it ain't an easy one. It shows you've got guts. The way I see it, the job you've come up to tackle ain't an easy one, neither. Looks like your ma prob'ly had this Lem pretty well sized up when she tried to keep your dad from throwin' in with him."

"I'm not afraid of Lem Brink. Gosh, he's about half drunk most of the time," the lad said, a note of contempt in his voice. "Used to keep a jug of whiskey under his bed in the office of the livery stable."

"You might not be afraid of him—but watch your step. Plenty of drunk men have knocked off sober ones before this."

"I'll keep an eye on him. But I'm going to find out whether or not he's cheated on those two clean-ups—and I won't quit till I do."

"How do you aim to work it?"

"Why, I'm going up to Hunker Crick and take my dad's place. He assigned his share in the partnership over to me."

"So you're this here Lem's pardner now, eh?"

"That's right. And believe me, if I find out that he has been cheating dad, he'll come across—or else."

"Or else—what?"

"They've got police and law courts in this country, haven't they?"

The big man nodded. "Yeah, we've got police, an' we've got courts. We've also got a hell of a lot of country where even a half-drunk man might knock off a sober one—an' no one know the difference. A lot of right good men have been buried along the cricks. Some of 'em died natural. Some by accident. An' some died otherwise."

"It's a job I came here to do—and I'm going to do it—no matter what happens."

"That's right, son. But, from what you've told me, I judge this Lem to be a character that will stand plenty of watchin'. We'll be hittin' for Dawson in the mornin'. My name's John Smith. I've sort of knocked around a little, here an' there. Just happened to think—I know a fellow name of Burr MacShane that's got a claim on Hunker..."

"Burr MacShane! Why, he's got the next claim to ours. Dad told me about him—said he's a fine man—a sourdough, and a man I could depend on if I ever needed help of any kind."

"That's right—a man can depend on Burr. As I was goin' on to say, he'll prob'ly be in Dawson. There ain't much doin' on the cricks this time of year. I'll get hold of Burr, an' sort of find out how he's got this Lem doped out. You say Lem hires quite a bit of help there on the claim. Fact is, I'm sort of at loose ends, right now. I'm plumb out of a job, an' it might be that this here Lem might be able to give me one."

"I'll say he will!" the lad exclaimed. "Remember, I'm a partner in that claim. You'll get your job, whether Lem wants you, or not."

"That's right kind of you, son. Maybe I'll take you up, on that. It's accordin' to what Burr's got to say. I sure need the job, all right. But maybe it would be better to have Lem hire me. You stick around town till after I've talked with Burr."

THE TRIP down the Yukon was uneventful, and leaving young Wilson at the hotel, Black John dropped in at the Tivoli Saloon, to be greeted by Burr MacShane and Gordon Bettles who stood near the end of the bar. "What in hell you doin' in town?" Bettles asked. "Cush's safe get to bulgin' again?"

Black John filled his glass from a bottle the bartender set before him. "No. Fact is, I happened to glance in the lookin' glass when I got up the other mornin', an' it looked like I needed a shave."

MacShane grinned as he eyed the heavy black beard. "What's the matter—couldn't you find the barbershop?"

"Oh, sure, I found it, all right. But there was another fella settin' in the chair, so I says to hell with it. I'll get my shave some other year."

"Swiftwater Bill an' Moosehide Charlie's in town, an' Camillo Bill an' Doc Hamilton ought to be back upriver today. Looks like we might have a stud game tonight."

"Sounds reasonable," the big man replied, and turned to MacShane. "How's things on Hunker?"

"Oh, about so-so. Most of the boys done all right last winter. But, if you're figgerin' on buyin' in up there, you better look the proposition over pretty careful. She's spotted. One claim might be payin' out big, an' the next one to it not worth a damn."

"I ain't buyin' in on the crick. By the way, ever run acrost a feller name of Lem Brink, up there?"

"Lem Brink! Shore I know him. I've got Number Ten above Discovery, an' he's on Number Nine."

"Pretty good feller, is he?"

MacShane slanted the big man a glance. "If he is, then so's the devil. I wouldn't trust him far as I can spit. Him an' his pardner, Sam Wilson, located the claim a couple of years ago. Sam was a good man anyways you look at him. They was both from the same town somewheres in Minnesota. But why Sam ever throw'd in with a dirty son like Lem Brink is more'n I can figger. Along in the spring, a year ago, Sam hits outside, leavin' Brink on the claim, him promisin' to hire help fer the clean-up, an' sendin' Sam his share. They've got a hell of a good proposition there. Lem hired a hand an' sluiced out the dump, all right, an' it run between eight an' nine thousan' ounces. I don't know how much of it he sent Sam—but I'm bettin' it wasn't nowheres near what he had comin'."

"What makes you think Lem is crooked?"

"I don't think he is—I know damn well he is. When I said he hired a hand to sluice out his dump last spring, I mean he hired two hands, one to a time. He worked hell out of the first one, then accused him of stealin' dust on him an' kicked him off the place without payin' him. An' the other one had to knock hell out of Lem to collect his pay. Then, durin' the summer he kep' three, four men workin' sinkin' shafts all over the claim. They'd go down to where the seepage made 'em quit, then sluice the stuff out, shovel the gravel back in the shaft, level it off an' sink another shaft. Looks to me like he's workin' that claim fer all it's worth—milkin' it dry, so when Sam Wilson comes back there won't be a hell of a lot left in the gravel. Last winter he worked four men an' they done even better than the winter before. Come Christmas time, three of the men knocked off fer a week an' come down here fer a jamboree. One of 'em stayed on the claim with Lem. When the others come back, the one that stayed on the claim was missin'. Lem claimed he'd changed his mind a couple of days after the others left, an' hit out fer Dawson, too. But no one's seen him since. I'm bettin' Lem knocked him off to keep from payin' his wages."

"Where does Lem hang out when he hits town?"

"He don't hit town. He don't never leave the claim. When he needs supplies, he sends one of his men for 'em."

"Don't he never loosen up—come down for a time with the boys—play a little stud—do a little drinkin'?"

"Not him. He don't play stud. He drinks plenty—but he drinks alone, there in his shack. Keeps a jug in under his bunk, an' stays about half soused all the time. They've got two shacks on the claim, one at each end. Sam claimed Lem snored all night an' kept him awake, an' wore his clothes till they stunk, an' wouldn't wash no dishes. So he put up another shack an' lived there. Since Sam's been gone the hired hands uses his shack.

"The way things is goin', if Sam don't show up pretty quick, Brink's goin' to have that proposition milked dry as a bone. Then again, if he does show up, an' finds out what's be'n goin' on, chances is he might disappear—like the hand did. If Lem would knock a hand off to keep from payin' him wages, he'd shore as hell knock Sam off to keep what he'd stole off 'n him. Like I say, I don't know what he's been sendin' Sam—but I'm bettin' it ain't a patch on what it ought to be."

BLACK JOHN nodded. "Sam ain't comin' back. His wife's got a bad heart, an' he can't leave her. But his boy's here. He's a damn fine kid. I run acrost him on the river where a steamboat had washed his canoe loose durin' the night, an' I fetched him on down with me. Bob, his name is, an' he's over to the hotel right now. His dad transferred the pardnership contract over to him, an' he's goin' out to the claim to see what's wrong. Lem Brink sent Sam a bank draft for thirty-two thousand an' forty dollars for the first year's clean-up, an' twenty-four thousan' an' ninety dollars for this spring's. He wrote Sam that the stuff in the dump wasn't as rich as the test pans showed, an' that it's runnin' leaner all the time."

"My God!" MacShane exclaimed, "I knew Lem Brink's a crook—but I didn't know he was that crooked!" Drawing a pencil from his pocket, he figured on the back of an envelope.

"Lem panned out eight or nine thousan' ounces a year ago— call it eighty-five hundred. He skinned off right around four thousan' ounces that summer, an' this spring's clean-up was a good twelve thousan' ounces—that makes twenty-four thousan', five hundred ounces—three hundred an' ninety-two thousan' dollars. He sent Sam fifty-six thousan', all told, an' claimed that's all he kep' for himself. After takin' out Sam's cut, that would leave three hundred an' thirty-six thousan', of which Lem's honest cut would he the same as Sam's, fifty-six thousan'. Takin' that out, it would leave two hundred an' eighty thousan' dollars that Lem has got salted down somewheres."

"Yeah," Black John agreed, his eyes on the penciled figures. "I wonder where?"

"He could have banked it—but I doubt it. He never goes to town."

"I'd sure like to know whether that dust was deposited in the bank. I know the boys in the bank, all right—havin' deposited plenty of dust from time to time. But—well—owin' to circumstances, and all—maybe it would be better if you was to step over an' find out how much Lem's got on deposit. You can tell 'em Lem's sort of figurin' on buyin' you out—you holdin' the adjoinin' claim, an' you'd like to know if he's got enough on deposit to cover the price."

"I'll do it!" MacShane exclaimed. "By God, I'd hate to see a damn skunk like him put anything over on a feller like Sam, or his kid."

He stepped out and returned shortly.

"He hasn't got a damned cent in the bank. He did make a couple of deposits—one last year for thirty-two thousan' an' forty dollars, an' another one this spring for twenty-four thousan' an' ninety—an' asked for statements of these deposits—then he withdrew the money within a week."

"Okay," Black John said. "Then he's got it cached somewhere—right around three hundred an' thirty-six thousan' dollars—twenty one thousan' ounces of dust—an' that's damn near three quarters of a ton! The amount is worth contemplatin'. This here Lem—he must figger he's done pretty well fer himself."

MacShane nodded. "Yeah. An' it looks from here like he has. He's a pretty slick article, Lem is… too damn slick fer any eighteen-year-old kid to tackle. Chances is the kid could never locate the cache. Even if he did, he'd never get the chance to get into it. Lem's right there on the claim all the time. If he even suspected the kid had located it, it would be jest too damn bad for the kid—you can bet yer life on that. I sure hate to think of that kid goin' up there, when Lem's got everything to gain an' nothin' to lose by knockin' him off."

Black John nodded, slowly, as he toyed with his glass on the bar. "Yeah, it is a kind of a doleful thought, at that. You say Lem hires him a hand, now an' then?"

"That's right—an' he could use a couple, right now. The two he had workin' fer him quit a couple of days ago. Jim Sutton's located on the claim below Lem's—Number Eight. I seen him in the A.C. store, this mornin', an' he says Lem told him to try an' locate a couple of new hands. Jim stopped in to the Klondike Palace where there was a lot a *chechakos* hangin' around broke, an' he tells 'em that a feller up on Hunker wants to hire a couple of hands. Some of 'em spoke up, wantin' the job, till one guy asks who it was wanted 'em. An' when Jim tells him it's Lem Brink, on Number Nine Above, the guy starts in an' spills 'em an earful. He's the one Lem kicked off the claim without payin' him—an' when he got through onloadin' what he thought of Lem, there wouldn't none of 'em take the job."

"The kid goin' up there would give him one more hand. An' then, if some feller should happen along, someone that was broke an' needed a job, Lem would prob'ly hire him."

MacShane's eyes widened. "You mean…"

"I don't mean nothin', except jest what I said," the big man interrupted. "An' then, after this feller was hired, if someone should happen to slip Lem the word that his new hand was a crook—one the police would give their right hand to locate—bein' as he's wanted for a couple of robberies an' a murder or so, somewheres downriver… it might be that Lem might figure he could make use of his new hand, over an' above the routine chores of minin'. Even if he didn't, this new hand might take a likin' to the kid an' sort of keep an eye on him."

MacShane and Bettles exchanged glances, both grinned, broadly, and Bettles ordered a round of drinks. When the liquor was poured MacShane raised his glass. "Well here's to Lem Brink. I wish him all the luck in the world—of the kind he's got comin!"

Returning to the hotel, Black John found Bob Wilson seated in the lobby reading a magazine. "If I was you I'd go on out to Hunker an' get to work on your claim. I'll hang around here for a couple of days, an' then go out an' hit Lem Brink for a job."

"Why not both go out together? As I told you, I'm a partner in that claim, and I'll give you a job whether Let wants to, or not. It's the least I can do—after what you did for me."

"Listen, son—I know you told me that. An' I remember you told me that you an' your dad suspect that this Let ain't been givin' him a square deal on this partnership proposition. An' after talkin' to Burr MacShane, I know damn well he ain't. Lem knows it, too. If you show up there alone he'll prob'ly figure that bein' jest a kid, an' a *chechako* to boot, he can outguess you without much trouble. But if two of us was to show up together, he'd prob'ly figure the odds was agin him. From what Burr told me you're goin' to need all the help you can get. So when I go up an' hit Lem for a job, don't you let on you ever saw me before. Two heads is better'n one—'specially when you're dealin' with a damn crook like this Lem Brink."

"I guess you're right, at that. I'll do as you say, and believe me—if things work out for dad and myself you'll never regret it."

"No, son, I don't expect I will. Fact is, I don't never remember of regrettin' seein' some damn skulldug get what's comin' to him."

II
BAD BILL REDDICK

ONE DAY, A week later, as Lem Brink and Bob Wilson were repairing a sluice box on the lower boundary of their claim, Burr MacShane strolled over from his adjoining claim, passing close to Black John, who was busy at the upper boundary.

"Well," said Burr, "I see you got the two hands you wanted. I was talkin' to Jim Sutten the other day in the Tivoli an' he told me you wanted him to find you a couple."

"Yeah, but Jim never located me none. He went down to the Klondike Palace an' told them loafers about this job, an' when a couple of 'em says they'll take it, an' asks what claim they was to go to, another guy butts in an' tells 'em a lot of lies about me, claimin' I'd worked hell out of him an' then kicked him off the job without payin' him. I'd kicked him off the job, all right—but it was because I ketched him pocketin' a bunch of nuggets, he'd picked outa the dump. This here kid is my new pardner—an' the other one drifted along couple of days ago an' I hired him."

"Your new pardner? Did Sam Wilson sell out?"

"No. This here's Bob Wilson—Sam's kid."

MacShane's glance shifted to Black John. "This hombre you hired—did he tell you his name?"

"Said it was Smith."

MacShane grinned. "About as handy as any name, I guess. I'd sort of keep an eye on him if I was you. He's Bad Bill Reddick. Used to be smooth-faced. Prob'ly figures no one would recognize him with that beard—an' I guess he's right, at that. I sure wouldn't of spotted him, except when I passed close to him I happened to see that scar on the back of his left hand where a breed knifed him one night in the saloon in Rampart."

Brink's eyes rested for a few moments on the big man, and shifted to MacShane. "You claim his name is Bad Bill—what's so bad about him?"

MacShane shrugged. "Plenty, I guess—to hear the police tell it. I know Corporal Downey would sure as hell like to pick him up. There's a couple of robberies an' a murder he'd like to ask him about, down around Fortymile. The police figure he hit downriver. They've notified the marshals to be on the lookout for him over on the American side. There's a thousan' dollar reward out for him—dead or alive."

"How long ago did he pull off that there murder an' them robberies?"

"It was a couple of years ago, right after the spring clean-up."

Brink shrugged. "What he done before he come here ain't none of my business. He's a good worker, an' as long as he keeps on workin' good I sure ain't goin' to turn him in fer no thousan' dollars."

MacShane nodded. "Me neither. But if I'd spill what I know about them crimes Bill Reddick would stretch rope damn quick. What I claim, if a man's goin' straight, now—he'd ought to be given a chance."

"That's right," Brink agreed. "Thanks for the tip, though. I'll sort of keep an eye on him."

Black John and Bob occupied the cabin Sam Wilson had built for himself, leaving Brink to his own cabin, and the big man noted with amusement that since MacShane's visit, there seemed to be a slight aloofness in the lad's attitude toward him. The youngster was neither hostile nor openly suspicious, but several times Black John surprised a puzzled, questioning look in his eyes.

A FEW mornings later the two finished breakfast and were met at the sluice by Brink, who greeted the younger man jovially. "Hi, Bob! Fine mornin'! Say, I was jest thinkin' some fresh moose meat would go good—save on the grub bill, too. Couple hours ago when I went to the crick fer a pail of water I seen a bull an' two cows headin' up that draw, yonder. My eyesight ain't no good fer shootin', no more, so why don't you take that there new rifle of yourn an' go after 'em. If you don't ketch up with 'em in the draw, cross the rim, an' you'll find 'em in the next valley. There's a slow-runnin' crick that widens out into a kinda pasture like where there's plenty of feed. If you git one, come back to the top of the rim and send up a smoke, an' me an' Smith'll fetch the packsacks."

"Sure I'll go!" the lad exclaimed. "I've been wondering when I'd get a chance to try out that rifle."

Returning to the cabin, he came out a few moments later, rifle in hand. "So long," he said. "Keep an eye on the ridge and watch my smoke!"

When he disappeared into the mouth of the draw, Brink eyed the big man. "Ever take a little drink, Smith?" he asked.

Black John grinned. "Not when I can get a big one."

Brink returned the grin. "Come on over to the shack an' we'll see what's left in the jug."

Inside the shack, Brink indicated a bench beside a table littered with dirty dishes. Reaching under the bunk, he drew forth a jug, and shoving the dishes aside, slopped liquor into two murky water glasses and shoving one toward the big man, seated himself opposite. "Drink up, *Smith*," he said, with a wink, "there's plenty more in the jug." When the glasses were emptied and returned to the table, the man reached for the jug on the floor beside him and refilled them. "How do you like it, here, *Smith?*" he asked, again obviously emphasizing the name.

"Oh, I like it all right—far's I've got. One job's about like another. Shovel gravel fer a spell. Draw yer pay. Go to town an' blow it in. Then go back to the gravel."

"How do you like my pardner?"

"The kid? He's all right, I guess. Them *chechakos* is all alike—don't know nothin'."

"Like it here better'n Fortymile, Bill?" Brink asked, abruptly.

The big man's eyes narrowed. "Bill? Fortymile? What the hell you talkin' about?"

"About you. You ain't foolin' me none, with this Smith name. Yer Bill Reddick—Bad Bill they call you down Fortymile way."

Black John found himself staring into the muzzle of a nickel-plated revolver. He leaped to his feet, his glance shifting to Brink's narrowed eyes as the other spoke.

"Jest keep yer pants on, Bill. Set down. Me an' you's got things to talk about."

The big man settled slowly back onto the bench, a look of fear in his eyes. He moistened his lips with his tongue. "I guess you got me," he said slowly. "But—how'd you know me—with these whiskers?"

Brink grinned. "Far as the whiskers goes yer safe enough, but you'd ought to wear a glove on that there left hand of yourn to cover up that scar—where the breed knifed you that time down in the saloon at Rampart."

Black John glanced at the scar left by a wound he'd received smashing a window to rescue a man from a burning cabin several years before, and nodded, slowly. "I guess you're right," he said. "But how come you know about that scar... an' about—Rampart—an' Fortymile?"

Again the man winked knowingly. "Oh, I been around some. An' I'm a-tellin' you, I ain't the only one that knows—the police does, too—about that scar, an' about a couple of robberies an' a murder that was pulled off a couple of years ago on Fortymile. This Corporal Downey—he'd give a pretty penny to pick up Bad Bill Reddick."

After several moments of silence the big man met the other's glance. "But—you wouldn't turn a guy in, would you, Brink?" he asked in a voice that trembled slightly.

"Well—mebbe I would, an' then again, mebbe I wouldn't. It's accordin'."

A ray of hope flashed into Black John's eyes. "Accordin' to what?" he asked, eagerly.

"Accordin' whether you throw in with me on a proposition, or not. If you do, you kin stay right here an' what with them whiskers an' a pair of gloves, the police wouldn't never spot you in a thousan' years. An' on top of that, there'll be quite a bunch of dust comin' yer way, beside yer wages. If you don't, we'll be hittin' fer Dawson in a few minutes—you walkin' in front an' me behind, with this here gun on yer back. An' I wouldn't be makin' no bad play, at that, bein' as there's a thousan' dollar reward out fer you, dead or alive."

"I guess you got me, Brink," Black John said, after a few moments of silence. "What's your proposition?"

"It's like this—I an' Sam Wilson located this claim a couple years ago. We worked all winter an' the test pannin's showed the gravel was rich. Along in the spring, jest before the break-up, Sam got word that his woman was ailin' bad, an' he hits out fer home. I hired help an' cleaned up the dump. She was rich, all right, but I short-changed Sam on his cut which I sent him a bank draft an' writ him a letter claimin' the gravel kep' gittin' leaner an' leaner. Sam's woman didn't git no better, an' he didn't come back, so this spring I done the same thing.

"Then this here Bob shows up. He's Sam's kid—an' he claims his ma ain't no better an' never will be, an' his pa won't leave her, so he transferred his share of the location to him. The kid, he's a *chechako*, an' like you said, *chechakos* don't know nothin'. But I figger this here Bob is smart, an' it ain't goin' to be long before he'll know the gravel's runnin', an' then he'll know damn well that I double-crossed his old man on them two years' clean-up. Not only that, he could prove it, too. 'Cause this here Burr MacShane on the next claim—he knows damn clost to what I took out them two springs—an' he liked Sam Wilson a damn sight better'n what he likes me. He'd swear to what he knows in court—an' I'd be in a hell of a fix."

BLACK JOHN nodded. "Yeah, it kinda looks that way, don't it? An' even if they couldn't make no criminal action stick, the kid could bring a civil suit, an' tie up every damn cent you've got in the bank."

Brink grinned, and winked. "I ain't afraid of no civil suit. Let him sue an' be damned. I ain't got a nickel in no bank. I've got plenty—but the dust's cached where no court order would ever touch it. But what with provin' I beat Sam out of plenty of dust—which jest between you an' me I done—they could throw me in jail fer God knows how long. An' I don't aim to do no time in no jail!"

Black John grinned. "Can't no one blame you for that. Cripes, look where I'd be—if the police could pin them Fortymile jobs on me."

The other nodded. "That's right. But like I says—if you throw in with me, you ain't in no danger. Here's how we'll work it. Tonight I'll make up a hundred-pound pack of dust, an' tomorrow I'll send the kid to Dawson with it, tellin' him to open an account in the bank in Brink an' Wilson's name an' deposit it. He'll hit out around noon. You take my rifle, there, an' lay fer him at that bend in the trail, where it swings in between them high rocks, an' that deep gulch. You let him have it an' shove him into the gulch an' cover up his body—an' fetch the dust back here. Then I'll split it with you... fifty pound of dust is what you git— that's eight hundred ounces—twelve thousan' eight hundred dollars—an' that ain't chickenfeed in no man's language."

Black John frowned. "It's a sight of money, all right. But— God, I kinda hate to shoot the kid, at that."

Brink's eyes hardened. "Listen, Reddick—they can't hang a man no higher fer two murders than one. If you don't do like I say, you'll swing fer that Fortymile murder as quick as I can git you to the police! You can't never make twelve thousan' no easier. An' besides, chances is, no one'll ever know anyone was knocked off. The kid ain't got no friends in the country—no one, outside of MacShane even knows he was here. It'll be a long time before his folks will be askin' about him, an' if the police comes inquirin' around we kin say he went off on a moose hunt, or a prospectin' trip a while back an' never showed up yet. Then with the kid outa the way, the hull claim is mine."

"Okay," Black John replied. "If I've got to, I've got to. You make up the pack of dust an' start the kid off with it—an' I'll do my part."

"That's the talk. Here, have another drink, an' we'll get to work on that sluice. I shore hope the kid knocks off one of them mooses. A nice thick steak would go good."

DARKNESS WAS settling when Bob Wilson returned without having seen a moose. Dog-tired, he rolled into his blankets immediately after supper and was soon sound asleep. Shortly thereafter Black John slipped from the cabin, and took up a position in a thicket of scrub willows on the bank of the creek.

An hour passed—two hours—then the door of Brink's cabin opened, and the man stepped out, paused and peered about him in the dim light of the stars, and carrying an empty pack-sack, walked rapidly to a pile of firewood a short distance from the cabin. Throwing aside a few sticks of wood, he dropped to his knees, and clawed away some six inches of gravel from the mouth of one of the filled-in shallow shafts. He lifted out numerous moosehide sacks of dust which he placed in the pack-sack. Returning the loose gravel, he leveled it off, repiled the firewood on it, shouldered the pack and returned to the cabin, pausing once more to scrutinize the landscape, before stepping into the cabin.

When the door closed behind him, Black John slipped from his place of concealment, and sought his bunk without disturb-ing young Wilson, who slept soundly between his blankets.

Toward noon of the following day Brink called the young-ster aside, and with a glance toward Black John, who was busy about the mouth of a new shaft, spoke in a low tone. "Y'know, Bob, ever sence MacShane give us the low-down on Smith—er, Bad Bill Reddick, there, I been kinda wonderin' like. He's a good worker, all right, an' if a man's goin' straight, I sort of hate to turn him over to the police fer somethin' he done couple of year ago. At the same time, what a man done onct an' got away with he's apt to do agin."

Bob nodded. "I've been thinking about that, too. Smith seems to be a nice fellow—the last man in the world I'd figure for an outlaw. But Burr MacShane seemed to know what he was talk-ing about, and he isn't the kind of a man who would deliberately lie about a thing like that."

"Yer damn right he wouldn't! He ain't a guy that would lie a murder an' robbery onto no man,"

The younger man nodded. "As you say, Smith, or Reddick, or whatever his name is, is a good worker, and as far as I can see, we might as well keep him on the job for a while, at least. We haven't begun taking out any gold yet, so there wouldn't be any point in his murdering us."

"I ain't so shore about that," Brink replied. Fact is, I've got sixteen hundred ounces in my shack, there, that I tuk out before you come. Half of that, of course, is yourn, bein' as you've took over yer pa's half of the claim. I never said nothin' about it, figgerin' it wouldn't be no hell of a while till you got a yen to hit fer town fer a couple of days or so—most young fellers does—an' then I'd let you pack the dust down an' start us a j'int bank account with it. But here yesterday, whilst you was moose huntin', I told Smith I was goin' up to MacShane's to borry a file. Instid of which, I slipped into the bresh an' snuck down through them willers an' watched Smith. Figgered to find out if he'd soldier on the job when he thought we was both gone.

"Pretty quick he throw'd down his shovel an' looked all around. Then he slips into my shack an' stays in there mebbe' it's three, four minutes. Then he came out agin. 'Course, he didn't fetch that dust out with him—nor no part of it, 'cause I checked up on it when I got back. But he damn well could of located it, figgerin' to watch his chance an' git holt of it later."

"Why—he could even slip out some night without waking me, and murder you there in your shack! I'd never know it till morning and he could be miles away."

"That's right," Brink agreed, "It don't look so good from my angle, does it? But, like you said, if there ain't no dust here fer him to git away with, he ain't goin' to do no murderin'. So instead of firin' him, we'll keep him on the job fer a while anyhow, an' you take that dust to the bank this afternoon. Sixteen hundred ounces—that's a hundred pound, worth twenty-five thousan' six hundred at the bank. It's in twenty eighty-ounce sacks. I'll make sure Smith knows what's in yer pack when you start out, so he'll know the dust ain't in my shack no more. An' I'll damn well keep him workin' right close to me clean up till dark, an' by that time you'll have the dust in the bank."

Shortly thereafter Bob Wilson shouldered the pack, stepped from Brink's shack, and headed down the creek. "Don't let them damn bank clerks claim no short weight on you!" Brink called, loudly, as the lad passed the shaft where Black John was work-ing. "There's a full eighty ounces in all twenty of them sacks—an' be sure an' fetch the empty sacks back!"

A half hour later, Brink beckoned to Black John from the doorway of his shack. He poured half a tumbler of liquor and handed it to the big man. "Throw that into you an' git goin'. Here's the rifle. You kin easy overtake him. Like I said, wait till you git to where the trail runs between them high rocks an' that gulch, then let him have it. Cover up his body, an' wait till dark so no one could see you, then fetch the dust back here an' we'll divide it up. An' don't git no fool notion of makin' off with that dust, 'cause if you do you'll have every damn policeman in the Yukon on your tail before midnight."

Black John downed the drink and picked up the rifle. "Like I said, I hate to do it—but you've got me. I sure as hell ain't goin' to swing fer that Fortymile job." He turned, left the cabin, and headed swiftly down the creek. Rounding the first bend, he doubled back and keeping well into the bush, swung around to MacShane's claim.

"This is it, Burr. Here's where we get that dirty double-crossin' son dead to rights. He started the kid fer Dawson with sixteen hundred ounces of dust to deposit in the bank. I'm s'posed to lay fer him there on the trail, knock him off, bury him, an' fetch the dust back to Brink's cabin, where he'll split it with me—fifty-fifty. You wait here till the kid joins you. Then both of you lay in the willows till you see me come back. It'll be an hour or so after dark. Then, when you see me step into Brink's cabin, you slip over an' glue yer ears to a crack between the fifth an' sixth log, clost to the window. I punched out the chinkin' behind his calendar an' you can hear every word that's said. I've got a hunch that you two'll catch you an earful, an' when the play's over, Brink'll be hittin' the high spots. He sure runs off at the head when he gits too many drinks down him—an' I'm bettin' he'll drink plenty between now an' dark to steady his nerves till I get back with that dust."

III
RECRUIT FOR HALFADAY

BOB WILSON MUSHED steadily down the trail, stopping to rest now and then and ease the burden of the unaccustomed pack. And as he walked his brow drew into a frown. "Maybe Lem isn't as crooked as dad and I figured he is," he muttered. "Take this gold—sixteen hundred ounces—I didn't even know he had it on hand. Half of it, more than twelve thousand dollars worth, is mine. He could have kept it all, and I'd never known the difference."

His thoughts reverted to the big man who had befriended him on the river and was now working on the claim. "It's hard to believe he'd be guilty of murder and robbery. In spite of what MacShane said, I can't help liking him."

As he was about to pass between the rim of a deep ravine and a mass of jumbled rock a man stepped suddenly into the trail barring the way. The lad's eyes widened as his glance shifted from the rifle resting in the crook of the man's left arm to his face. "You?" he cried.

The big man nodded. "Yeah. It's me."

"What's this—a holdup?"

"Yeah—you might call it that. Just slip out of them straps an' let the pack drop to the ground!"

The youth flushed angrily as he complied. "Then you are an outlaw, just as MacShane said!"

"Not knowin' exactly what Burr said, I couldn't say. Plenty of folks claims I'm an outlaw, at that."

"I see you've got Lem Brink's rifle. I suppose when you found out that I was packing this gold to the bank, you murdered Lem and took out after me."

The lips beneath the heavy black beard smiled. "I've noticed conclusions that's jumped to is damn near always wrong. The fact is, I didn't knock Lem off—much as I'd ought to. Bein' as I'm workin' for him, I'm just carryin' out his orders—that's all."

Something in the smile, the tone of voice, the twinkle in the gray-blue eyes dispelled the younger man's anger. "His orders? I—I don't understand."

"You will understand, by midnight, son—if you do like I tell you. Your dad knew Burr MacShane, an' liked him. An' he was right. There ain't a better man in the north than Burr, anyways you look at him. I'm savin' my breath. The way this play come up, you might, or might not believe me. If you do as I say, by midnight tonight you'll know all about what kind of a pardner you've got—an' you'll hear it from his own lips, too.

"Leave the pack where it is. I'll take care of it. You hit back up the crick an' slip into Burr's cabin without Brink knowin' it. Burr'll tell you what to do. He'll take over from there. Believin' I'm an outlaw, an' all, I know it's askin' quite a bit of you to hit back an' leave this dust with me. But it's for your own good, son. You've got to believe me."

Only for a moment the younger man hesitated, his eyes on the big man's face. "I do believe you," he said, suddenly. "I—I may be wrong. But I believe you. I'll do as you say." And turning abruptly away, he headed back up the trail.

AN HOUR after dark Black John stepped from the trail and headed for the dim square of light that marked Lem Brink's cabin window. As he neared the door he smiled slightly as he saw two figures step from the scrub willows and rapidly approach the cabin from the rear.

Stepping into the cabin, he found Brink seated at the table, a tumbler half filled with liquor before him. He swung the pack to the floor, and stood the rifle in the corner behind the door. Reaching for the jug on the floor beside him, Brink slopped it half full of liquor and shoved it toward him. "You got back, eh?" he said, thickly. "Set down an' throw that into you. Fetched the dust, too, I see."

The big man removed his hat, wiped his brow with his sleeve and loosened a couple of buttons in the front of his shirt. "Oh, shore. I got back with the dust, all right. Kinda hot, what with the pack, an' all. I been pickin' 'em up an' layin' 'em down pretty fast."

The drinks were downed, and Brink replenished the glasses. "Everything work out all right?" he asked.

"There's the dust. I jumped him right where you said."

"Git him the first shot?"

"I wouldn't see no sense in wastin' ammunition."

"Did you bury him, like I told you to?"

"I didn't leave him layin' there on the trail."

"Where'd you bury him?"

The big man grinned. "Listen, Brink—I ain't tellin' where I buried him—just in case you might try to double-cross me—like reportin' your pardner robbed an' murdered on the trail."

"Hell, man—I wouldn't report you to the police! If I wanted to turn you in, I could do it on them Fortymile jobs you pulled—an' collect the reward, besides. Why, I knocked a guy off last year—right here on the claim. Ketched him knockin' down dust on me, an' I whammed him over the head with a club, an' rolled him in one of them shallow prospect holes, throw'd the club in on top of him, an' filled the shaft with gravel."

"Kinda hard-boiled yourself, eh?"

"I'll say I'm hard-boiled! You an' me'll git along, all right. But don't never try to double-cross me."

"Guess we might's well divide up them ounces," Black John said. "You claimed there's twenty eighty ounce sacks in the pack. You promised me half of 'em for knockin' the kid off. I'll take my ten now."

Brink's voice rasped suddenly harsh. "I promised you half of that dust fer knockin' the kid off. With him outa the way, this hull claim is mine. Don't never think I didn't know what I was doin' when I hired you to knock him off. You think you're a hell of an outlaw fer gittin' away with them Fortymile jobs, don't you? Well, you ain't—you ain't nothin' but a damn boob!"

"What do you mean—boob?" Black John cried, slipping his hand beneath his shirt and scratching lustily at his belly.

"I'll tell you what I mean. I kin tell it to you here. I got it all figgered out. The kid's dead. You never drug his body no hell of a ways. It won't take the police long to locate it. When they do, the claim's mine—it's wrote right in the papers. All I got to do is tell the police he hit out fer Dawson with a pack of dust, an' never showed up no more. You done the job fer me—but it's the last job you'll ever do. You don't never leave this shack alive!"

As he spoke, the man drew the nickel-plated gun from his pocket—and the next instant, his eyes widened in terror as he stared into the muzzle of the .45 Colt that the big man slipped from beneath his shirt. The gun dropped from his nerveless fingers and thudded onto the table top.

"What—what the hell!" he gasped, as his eyes raised to the steel gray eyes above the black beard.

Reaching across the table, Black John picked up the nickel-plated gun and slipped it into his pocket. "Hard guys like you hadn't ought to carry pocket guns—you might hurt somebody."

The man moistened his trembling lips with his tongue. "You got me," he wined, "but for God's sake, don't shoot! Take your cut of that dust—take the hull twenty sacks! Take 'em an' git to hell outa here! I'll keep my month shet—about them Fortymile jobs, an' you knockin' the kid off. Hell, I wouldn't dast to squawk, nohow—I told you about knockin' that guy off an' buryin' him here on the claim."

The big man grinned. "You ondoubtless lied, Lem. I've somehow got the impression that you ain't trustworthy."

"I ain't lyin'! I tell you I done it! I kin show him to you in the mornin'—what would be left of him. He ain't only three, four foot down. I shoveled the gravel on him, an' then throw'd them extry sluice planks on top of it, so's a wolf or nothin' couldn't dig him up. Hell, man—if I was to squawk, so could you! We'd both git hung—an' there ain't no percentage in that! You can't git away with shootin' me, no-how. What with the kid disappearin', an' me, too—the police would git on the job, an' MacShane would damn quick tell 'em that you was workin' here, an' they'd be on yer tail before you could git nowheres. It looks like a horse apiece, Bill. Like I says—take that dust—sixteen hundred ounces, that's better'n twenty-five thousan' dollars—an' git goin'. With the kid dead, I'll have the claim."

"You like to shoot off your mouth, don't you, Lem?" the big man said, eyeing the other. "You know, if I ever knocked a man off I sure as hell wouldn't sit around an' brag about it—an' tell where I buried him, to boot."

There was a note of truculence in the other's voice as he replied. "I don't never shoot off my mouth onless I know damn well who I'm talkin' to. You ain't in no shape to squawk—what with them Fortymile jobs hangin' over you, an' the murder of the kid, to boot."

Black John smiled, broadly. "You'd be safe enough, Lem, if you hadn't made three, four mistakes. In the first place, my name ain't Bad Bill Reddick. I never pulled off any jobs on Fortymile—robberies or murders, either. No breed ever knifed me in a Rampart saloon. I got this scar smashin' a window in a burnin' shack to drag a man out. An' I might add that the kid ain't no more dead than you an' I are. You claim you never shoot off your mouth onless you know who you're talkin' to. That's your biggest mistake of all."

Brink's eyes widened, and his mouth dropped open, as Black John raised his voice and called. "Come on in, boys! Lem's spoke his piece!"

THE DOOR opened a moment later, as Burr MacShane and Bob Wilson stepped into the room. MacShane grinned. "Yeah, it was quite a piece, at that. Mighty interestin'."

The blood rushed to Brink's face that had turned paper-white in the lamplight. "It's a damn lie! You couldn't hear nothin' through them log walls—an' the window shet!"

For answer MacShane stepped over, tore the calendar from the wall and pointed to the inch-wide gap where the chinking had been punched out.

There were several moments of dead silence, during which Brink's glance flitted furtively from one to the other of the three.

"What—what you goin' to do?" he asked, at length.

"It ain't what we're goin' to do that'll interest you. It's what you're goin' to do," Black John replied.

"How do you mean?"

"Meanin' that there's some slight adjustments to be made in your personal economy."

"I don't git you."

"You will before the evenin's over. It's like this. You admitted to me, yesterday, that you'd stole plenty off your pardner, Sam Wilson."

"I lied. Them twenty sacks in the pack there is every damn cent I've got in the world—an' half of them belongs to the kid."

The big man nodded. "That's right, Brink. An' half the claim belongs to you, now. But it won't in a few minutes."

"What do you mean—won't in a few minutes?" the man cried, his glance flashing to the butt of the six-gun that protruded slightly from the big man's shirt front.

"Oh, I ain't goin' to shoot you—much as you deserve it. I mean that it hadn't ought to take more than a few minutes for me to write out the assignment of your half of the claim to the kid. He's got the assignment his dad made out to him. It's all wrote out legal, an' I'll copy it, substitutin' your name for Sam Wilson's as the assignor. Then you can sign it, an' the kid can get it recorded. That will leave him as sole owner of this claim."

The man's fact flushed angrily. "By God, I won't do it! Half of this claim's mine, an' I'll hang onto it."

Black John shrugged. "Suit yourself. You'll hang, all right, but it'll be on a gallows—not onto this claim. An' when you do hang, it'll be for the man you clubbed to death an' buried under them planks. Then your half of the claim will revert to the kid automatically. It was your idea—puttin' that clause in the papers, Brink—an' there was murder in your heart when you done it—Sam Wilson's murder—the same as you had Bob Wilson's murder in your heart, yesterday. You better sign over the claim, Brink. Remember there was three of us heard you admit murderin' that man—an' it won't take the police long to dig him up."

"I—I never murdered him. I had to kill him. He come at me with the rifle—an' I had to git him!"

"You'd ought to have thought that one up when you was braggin' about catchin' him swipin' dust. The real reason was to keep from payin' him wages. It won't take a jury long to convict you, Brink—when they see the *corpus delicti* an' hear what we've got to say. It's up to you—sign the transfer an' get to hell out of here by daylight—or refuse to sign it, an' let the court make the transfer after you're hung."

The man turned to MacShane. "If he's Bad Bill Reddick, how's he goin' to testify in court—with robbery an' murder agin him on Fortymile?"

MacShane eyed Black John and shook his head, slowly. "First off I thought he was Bad Bill, but come to look at him closer, I see he's someone else."

"God damn you! Damn you all! You're in cahoots to git me off'n this claim! I'll sign the transfer. I gotta. Damn if I'm goin' to git hung! But, first off, the kid's gotta dicker!"

"How do you mean—dicker?" Black John asked.

"It's like this—half the dust in that pack's mine. An' I've got more dust cached here on the claim—my share of the dust that's been took out of it, an' the dust I beat Sam Wilson out of. I'll give the kid what Sam's got comin'—but, by God, the rest's mine! I earned it, fair an' square!"

Black John's eyes widened. "Why, you dirty, double-crossin', murderin' son—you never done nothin' fair an' square in your life! Now I'm tellin' you one—you'll sign that transfer, an' then you'll get to hell off the crick—an' you ain't takin' no dust with you—not one damn ounce! An' what's more, you've got just thirty days to get out of the Yukon. Thirty day from now, Corporal Downey'll come up here an' dig up the guy you murdered—an' he'll have your description, right down to a gnat's hind leg—an' by God, you'll swing for murder! Tomorrow we three'll dig up your cache there under the woodpile an' apportion the dust equitably. The kid'll get his dad's share. An' your share, amountin' to two hundred an' eighty thousan' dollars, will just about cover my attorney fee for drawin' up the transfer paper. Deprivin' you of the emoluments of crime is the best way I know to teach you damn crooks that crime don't pay."

Just on the edge of daylight, with the transfer duly signed, the three watched from the doorway as Brink, his personal belongings in his packsack, headed down the creek.

Then, at the edge of the claim, he turned and shook his fist. "By God, you'll wish you never done me like this! I'm hittin' fer Halfaday Crick. They're all outlaws, up there, an' the police don't dast to show up! Black John Smith—he'll show you guys where to head in at!"

"Do you know Black John?" the big man asked.

"No, but I know a couple of his men! They'll make me acquainted with him—an' don't you fergit it!"

"I won't," grinned the big man, with a wink at MacShane as the other turned and headed down the creek. "An' when he does meet him, I'm bettin' he'll be plumb surprised."

BLACK JOHN'S BEAR
TRAP TROUBLE

I
SOLOMON OF HALFADAY CREEK

OLD CUSH, PROPRIETOR of Cushing's Fort, combined trading post and saloon that served the little community on Halfaday Creek, close against the Yukon-Alaska border, folded his newspaper and placed it on the back bar. Then, without haste, he took up a bottle, two glasses and the leather dice box as Black John Smith stepped into the room and up to the bar. Old Cush won the drinks, made the proper entry in his day book and faced the big man who was filling his glass from the bottle.

"It looks to me," he began, as he filled his own glass, "like the world's goin' to be in a hell of a fix if the damn' doctors don't quit inventin' new kinds of medicine to cure folks of what they've got, an' then turnin' around an' inventin' new ways of keepin' 'em from ketchin' somethin' else."

Black John grinned. "I don't quite follow your line of thought, if any. It looks to me like the world is better off every time the doctors find out how to cure a disease or to prevent folks from catching one."

"Maybe you're right," said Cush, "but I ain't sold on medicine."

"I wouldn't lose no sleep over it, if I was you, Cush." The big man grinned and turned toward the door which had opened on a parka-clad figure. As the newcomer advanced he threw back the parka hood to reveal a cascade of silver hair. "Well, Father Cassatt, in person!" Black John said. "Welcome to Halfaday! Step right over by the stove an' peel off your parka while I fetch

A glance at the unwavering rifle muzzle decided him against trying anything…

you a drink." He called to One Armed John who was puttering about in the storeroom, "Go out an' look after Father Cassatt's dogs an' I'll buy you a drink, too."

The priest smiled. "A dram of liquor works wonders in driving the chill from an old man's bones. It is growing colder. I am thankful to have reached this haven."

"Where you headin', Father?" the big man asked.

"I am on my way to Dawson to consult with Corporal Downey."

"Someone be'n botherin' yer Siwashes?"

"Yes, a bad man. A very bad man. He is a half-breed—Louis Harp—the bastard son of Pierre Harp, a French free trader

who, years ago, built a cabin and lived on a creek not far from my mission. Despite all I could do to prevent it, a young woman of my people went to live with him there, and in due course a son was born to her. Shortly thereafter Pierre Harp disappeared, and the young woman returned with the infant to her people. She did not live long and the child was raised by her parents. He attended my school at the mission, and was by far the smartest of all my pupils.

"But he was ever a wayward lad—a scoffer and a blasphemer. While still in his teens he forsook the abode of his grandparents, repaired to the deserted cabin of his father and shortly became the best trapper among all the Indians. Then, while still a young man, he disappeared.

"For a number of years thereafter I would hear rumors of him. He worked as a whaler... he became a notorious gambler... he traded liquor to the Indians along the Koyukuk... he killed a man over a card game at Nulato. Then he hit for the outside but got no farther than Skagway, where he became an habitué of the saloons, the gaming houses and the brothels.

"Then, early in the autumn, Louis Harp reappeared in the Feather Creek country as suddenly as he had disappeared, and has again taken up his abode in the cabin of his father. Ostensibly he is trapping, but I have noticed of late that my people have been obtaining liquor. I have, as yet, no direct evidence that he is supplying this liquor. But I am morally certain of it, because until his return my people have had no liquor since the time you so effectively rid the country of those two malefactors who were cheating them out of their treaty money."

"I WENT to him and remonstrated, but he laughed at me, and assured me he was merely trapping. He has added a log addition to his cabin and this room is already half filled with fur. When I accused him of obtaining this fur from the Indians in exchange for liquor, he assured me that I was wrong—that he himself had trapped it all. But this is manifestly untrue, for no man could trap that much fur in the time that has elapsed since his return."

"Where do you figure he's gettin' the hooch from," Black John asked.

"I suspect that he obtains it from Cutter Malone. I know he is a friend of Malone, and it has been my experience that any friend of Malone is open to suspicion."

"There's no question about that," Black John Smith agreed. "Cutter's as ornery as they make 'em."

"Day before yesterday," the little priest continued, "I saw Louis Harp swing his dog outfit onto the river and head downstream, so I decided to go myself to Dawson and lay the matter before Corporal Downey."

"You say the breed has traded your Siwashes out of half a roomful of fur. He's prob'ly takin' a big sledload of it down to Dawson to buy more hooch with."

"No. His sled was empty. He was running light."

"This room where he keeps the fur, is it stout built?"

"Yes. It is strongly constructed of logs and the door is secured by means of a huge padlock."

Black John smiled. "Considerin' your problem from the viewp'int of an innocent bystander, it don't look so tough. If I was you I'd forget this trip to Dawson. You can stop overnight with me, an' in the mornin' you can hit back to Feather Crick an' pick out half a dozen husky Siwashes an' have 'em fetch along an ax, an' either knock off that padlock or chop out part of a wall, an' reclaim the fur. Then when the breed gets back with another load of hooch he'll find out that his tradin' venture ain't showin' a profit. What with you havin' a bunch of Siwashes, an' only one of him, the odds wouldn't look right for him to stage a reprisal."

The priest shook his head. "No, John, while your suggestion might well be a practical solution of the problem, I cannot consider it. I have labored for years among my people in an endeavor to instill the virtues of honesty, sobriety and truth into their hearts. The fact that Louis Harp has caused many of them to stray from the path of sobriety cannot justify my advising them to also stray from the path of honesty. Despite the methods he used in obtaining the fur, it is his property now, and the plan you propose is nothing short of burglary. And I could not for a moment condone it."

Black John Smith's smile widened. "Well, of course, Father, when it comes right down to splittin' theological hairs, I'll admit that you'd use a razor where I'd use an ax. But I maintain that the good old practice of fightin' fire with fire still works."

BEHIND THE bar Cush nodded emphatically. "John's right, Father. It would serve the damn cuss right. I ain't no priest. But if I was one I wouldn't give a damn what my Siwashes done to a hooch-trader, jest so they done it damned thorough."

"Two wrongs cannot make a right. I appreciate the sympathy of you men, but I must turn a deaf ear to your advice. I cannot condone a violation of ethics as a means to an end, no matter how propitious that end might be."

Cush shrugged. "Huh—John, he's allus talkin' about these here ethics, an' claimin' how he's got 'em. An' now you claim that what he told you to do would be agin ethics. If he's got ethics, an' you've got 'em, an' he claims it's all right to rob a hooch-runner, an' you claim it ain't, how do you figger that out? It looks to me like them ethics ain't worth a damn no ways you look at 'em."

Black John regarded the speaker loftily. "The apparent discrepancy in viewp'int is easily explained. As you say, both Father Cassatt and I adhere to a code of ethics. The explanation is that the good father's code is not as flexible as mine." He turned to the priest. "Ain't that so, Father?"

The little priest smiled. "Ethical flexibility is a remarkable concept, to say the least, John. I must adhere to my determination to go to Dawson and invoke the aid of the law in righting this grievous wrong."

"I'm doubtin'," the big man said, "that Downey can do you any good. If he should go up there an' the breed has the hooch cached where he couldn't find it, an' the Siwashes would clam up on him, he couldn't get no evidence to go to court with, even if he arrested the breed."

The good father's brow drew into a frown. "Clam up? I do not understand."

"I mean, if they'd shut up—refuse to squeal on the breed. An' that's just what they'd do, for fear they wouldn't get any more hooch if they squawked."

The priest nodded. "I am afraid you are right. But there must be something the police can do. Surely the Lord will point the way to right this wrong."

Black John nodded. "Ye-e-a-h, He might, at that. But just in case the police might get balled up on the way He was p'intin', I'll go along down to Dawson with you. It's a long trail down there, Father, an' you ain't as young as you used to be. Anything could happen."

"But, John, I—I cannot permit you to make the trip merely to insure my safety. I have lived in this country for many years, and have traveled many trails, both in winter and summer. I'm not exactly a novice. I'm not afraid."

"Shore you ain't, Father. But you know as well as I do that on a long winter trail two men are better than one, every time. An' as for permittin' me," he added, with a grin, "when I feel a lucky streak comin' on I ain't in the habit of askin' permission of the clergy to ride it. I feel it my bounden duty to journey to Dawson an' instill some of the basic principles of the game of stud into the minds of them damn benighted sourdoughs. We'll take my dogs. You can leave yours here an' pick 'em up on the way back."

The priest smiled broadly. "Very well, John. Far be it from me to interfere with any man's bounden duty. I shall be very glad of your company on the trail."

ON THE afternoon of the twelfth day thereafter the two stepped into Corporal Downey's office at detachment headquarters of the Northwest Mounted Police. The officer smiled as his eyes shifted from the frail little priest to Black John's hulking figure. "Which one of you is bringin' the other one in—an' what's the charge?" he asked.

The big man returned the smile. "I'm fetchin' him in, an' he's charged with harborin' a suspicious character up there in the Feather Crick country."

When the two were seated, with their pipes going, the officer listened while Father Cassatt explained the situation. When he had finished Downey nodded. "Louis Harp, eh? I know him. In fact, he's in town now. I saw him on the street this mornin'. He's a bad actor. An' his father, old Pierre, was a bad actor before him. This Louis is the worst of the two because he's smart. He's be'n in trouble both sides of the line, but so far he's managed to keep in the clear. There's half a dozen jobs I know damn well he's pulled but so far I've never be'n able to get the evidence to go to court with."

Black John grinned. "You know, Downey, I've often wondered why they don't pick out honest folks to make the laws."

"What do you mean?"

"You'd ort to know—it's your job to enforce 'em—or try to. An' you know that the way the law is, every cheap crook that breaks it knows his lawyer can find loopholes for him to slip through.

"Take it on Halfaday, now: if we know a man is guilty we go ahead an' hang him after callin' a miners' meetin' an' givin' him a chanct to try an' lie out of it."

"You boys do a good job, up there," Downey admitted. "I wish every crick was as free of crime as Halfaday is. But just the same, John, the law recognizes the fact that every one is entitled to a fair trial."

"Oh, shore. We give 'em a fair trial, too—'cause we know damn well they're guilty before we try 'em." Black John knocked the dottle from his pipe and rose to his feet. "Bein' steeped in rectitude myself, I can't see no p'int in settin' around discussin' the fallibility of the law. Guess I'll just drift around a bit an' see if I can't stir up some of the boys. Might be we could rig up a stud game."

II
MAN-BAIT FOR A BEAR TRAP

IN THE NOTORIOUS Klondike Palace Cutter Malone, the paunchy proprietor, mouthed his big black cigar and eyed the half-breed who faced him across the bar. "If you've got two thou-san' dollars worth of fur in yer cache, like you claim, why didn't you fetch it down when you come?"

"I couldn't fetch it down. I've only got five dogs. It's loose fur. My fur press is broke. It's an old press—my father's old press. He left it in the cabin when he went away, years ago. The cabin laid empty many years and the Siwashes stole most of the iron off the press. I'm takin' new iron back when I go, an' then I fix the press an' bale all the fur an' bring it down in a York boat on the high water when the break-up comes in the Spring."

Malone frowned. "Looks like you could have fetched part of it down. How the hell do I know you ain't lyin'? How do I know you've got any fur in yer cache? Here I stake you to twenty gallon of hooch, an' you pull out with it, an' in six weeks yer back fer more hooch, an' not a damn fur to show fer it, an' claimin' you want forty gallon more hooch. We went in on this deal, fifty-fifty. I furnished the hooch an' you was to do the tradin'. If you've got two thousan' dollars worth of fur, the half of it belongs to me, an' by the good God, I want it!"

"You'll get it, an' plenty more with it," the breed insisted. "Listen, you know damn well I wouldn't dare to double-cross you—even if I wanted to. I know you've got plenty of men that would kill me in a minute if you give 'em the nod. But I don't want to double-cross you 'cause we've got too good a thing the way it is. Any time we can get two thousan' dollars worth of fur for twenty gallon of hooch, we got a good thing. I cut it plenty—make four gallon of trade licker out of a gallon, an' get six dollars a quart for it. We've got a good thing. There's a couple hundred Siwashes up in the Feather Crick country and they're doin' all right with their trappin'."

"How about that priest, up there, Father Cassatt? Won't he raise hell about his Siwashes gittin' hooch?"

The breed shrugged. "What can he do? The Siwashes won't tell him where they get the hooch. If he gets the police up there they won't find anything. An' the Siwashes won't talk. I keep the hooch cached where no one can find it. An' me, if they come to my place, I'm only a trapper. I keep a line of traps set—just in case."

Malone seemed mollified. "Guess you wouldn't dast to double-cross me, at that," he admitted. "It wouldn't be exactly healthy to. Okay, I'll shove in forty gallon more. But, I'm warnin' you, I'll have some boys of my own up there jest before the break-up. They'll help you bale the fur an' run it down. You couldn't git out of the country with the fur anyhow, an' even if you did you'd never dast to show up in the Yukon agin."

THE DOOR opened and a large man with a heavy black beard stepped into the room, paused for a moment as his eyes swept the interior, then turned on his heel and went on. The breed, noting the frown with which Malone had eyed the man, smiled. "That man, you don't like him, eh?"

"Like him! I hate his guts! That's Black John Smith, the damndest outlaw in the country. He don't hang around here none. Prob'ly stepped in lookin' fer someone."

The breed nodded. "Ah, yes—Black John. I've heard of him and his outlaws on Halfaday Crick."

"Heard of him! Ain't you never saw him? Hell, Halfaday Crick can't be so damn fer from the Feather Crick country where you hang out."

"About two days travel. I have passed the mouth of Halfaday many times on the White, but I have never gone up to Cushing's Fort. The Siwashes stay away from there. Cushing will not sell them any hooch. He would not sell me any either for I am half Indian."

Malone shrugged. "Yeah, Cush nor Black John won't stand fer sellin' hooch to Siwashes. He's smart as hell, Black John is. I know of four or five fellers he's knocked off fer peddlin' it."

The breed shrugged. "I am smart, too. I am not afraid of Black John."

"You might not be afraid of him now, but you better watch yer step. He's a friend of Father Cassatt's an', by God, one of these days he'll be hangin' yer hide on a tree limb—an' you in it! I ain't no damn fool—an' he's took me fer plenty. An' he's took plenty of big crooks fer their pile, too—the more they had, the more he took 'em fer. Take it, first an' last, I'll bet he's made more'n a million. They claim he keeps better'n hundred thousan' in cash in Cush's safe all the time."

"I have read much in books. There have been many smart men. But always there comes someone who is smarter. And this Black John—because he has knocked off many men, that is not saying that he cannot be knocked off when a smarter man comes along."

Cutter eyed the breed sharply. "Listen," he said. "The day you prose to me you've knocked Black John off, I'll hand you a thousan' dollars in cash. An' that ain't all. You could have a hell of a good thing up there, 'cause with Black John out of the way I could put one of my men up there to run Halfaday, an' you could peddle hooch the hull length of the White, an' no one to bother you."

The breed smiled. "You can keep your thousand dollars, Cutter—an' your hooch trade on the White. Because when I knock Black John off, I'm going to take him first, as he has taken many others. And when I take him I will take him for plenty.

For so much that your thousand dollars and your hooch trade on the White will look like chicken feed."

AFTER TWO nights stud-playing in the Tivoli Black John met Father Cassatt in the hotel lobby. "Well, how'd you an' Downey make out?" he asked.

"Corporal Downey has promised to start for Feather Creek the week after next. That should give Louis Harp time to get back there with his liquor, and Downey may be able to secure his evidence."

The big man nodded, "Yeah, he might. I'm takin' my sled to the blacksmith shop to get that runner fixed, so you be ready to start back about daylight tomorrow."

"If it's just the same to you, John, I believe I shall remain here and go back with Corporal Downey. Father Judge has asked me to accompany him on a visit to his mission on Fortymile."

"Okay, Father. You'll be stoppin' in to Cush's for your dogs. I'll see you then. So long."

As he approached the blacksmith shop, Black John saw the breed he had noticed talking with Malone in the Klondike Palace, just leaving the place. He noted that the man eyed him narrowly as he passed. In the shop the blacksmith was putting the finishing touches on a huge trap. "What the hell is that you're makin'?" he asked, eyeing the object.

"Bear trap."

"A bear trap! Who the hell would want to trap a bear? An' look at the chain he's got on it. Cripes, that damn thing would hold an elephant."

The blacksmith nodded. "Yup. I told him it was bigger'n it needed to be, but he claimed that's the way he wanted it. He's a breed name of Louis Harp. Wanted the jaws twenty inches long an' ten inches high—double springs, an' fifteen foot of heavy log chain on it."

"Cripes," Black John grinned, "the work it'll take to haul that thing out an' set it would be more than the bear was worth."

"Yup. Chain an' all she'll weigh right around seventy pound. He claims a big bear has been robbin' his meat cache, an' he aims to ketch him!"

"I see he's got a big padlock on the end of the chain."

"Yup. Jest come in a few minutes ago to see how the trap was comin' along, an' he pulls the padlock outa his pocket an' snapped it on the chain. Hell, fer's I kin see, he could of run the chain around the tree, er log, er whatever he was anchorin' the trap to, an' then wired it together, an' saved the price of a padlock. But, long's he's payin' fer it, I'm makin' it like he says."

The sled runner was soon repaired, and the following morning Black John hit the trail for Halfaday. Ten days later, as he swung from the White River, he shot a young moose that leaped from a thicket at the bend of the creek. As he stooped, knife in hand, to bleed the animal, he paused and a grim smile twisted the lips beneath the black beard. Removing a pint flask from his pocket, he pulled the cork, swallowed the remaining liquor, stuck the moose, and filled the flask with blood. Corking it, he slipped it into his pack sack.

"Puttin' two an' two together makes four," he muttered. "I seen Cutter an' the breed eyein' me that day in the Palace. Cutter ondoubtless warned him about how I treat guys that peddles hooch to Siwashes. Prob'ly told him I ain't exactly no pauper, too. Then the breed gets a big bear trap made, an' he sticks a padlock on the end of the chain. A bear couldn't onwire the chain if he got caught—but a man might. Also, a man with his leg in a bear trap might dicker to get out. I've got a hunch that the tranquility of Halfaday is due to be enlived by an incident." Whereupon he butchered the moose, loaded the meat on his sled and pushed on to Cushing's Fort.

"WHERE'S FATHER Cassatt? An' how did he make out with Downey about that there hooch-runner he was tellin' about?" Cush asked as Black John stepped into the saloon the following morning.

"He made out all right. Father Judge wanted Father Cassatt to make a trip down to Fortymile with him, an' when he gets back Downey's promised to go on up to Feather Crick with him an' investigate the matter."

"Huh," Cush grunted. "Them hooch-peddlers is smart. Chances is Downey won't git no evidence again' him if the Siwashes keeps their mouths shet. What we'd ort to do is go over there an' grab the damn cuss an' fetch him over here an' hang him fore Downey gits there. By God, onct you hang a man, he don't peddle no more hooch to no Siwashes!"

"The suggestion has merit," Black John admitted. "But the fact is, Cush, what I'm more interested in at the moment is a strike a couple of fellas made in them mountains over south of the White. I run acrost one of 'em in the Tivoli an' he had plenty of dust in his poke, an' if what he says is true, they've hit one of them rich pockets.

"They're *chechakos*, an' don't like the country an' he wants to sell out an' go back to the States. I told him I wasn't investin' in no property till I'd looked it over first. He pulled out of Dawson to go back to his location the other mornin' an' wanted I should go back with him. I'd set in a stud game all night an' was too tired to hit out. I wanted him to wait a couple of days, but he said he had to git right back with a load of grub. He claims they've got a couple of Siwashes an' breeds workin' fer 'em an' the grub was runnin' low. So I told him to go hack with the grub an' send one of them Siwashes or breeds over after me an' I'd go back with him an' look the property over. So if anyone shows up lookin' for me, an' I ain't here, send him over to my cabin. Sometimes them *chechakos* makes a damn rich strike an' I ain't overlookin' no bets."

"Yeah, sometimes they do but mostly they don't," Cush replied. "This gent prob'ly had a few drinks in him an' was runnin' off at the head, Damn if I'd go kihootin' all over hell in the winter on the word of no *chechako*. I'm bettin' no Siwash don't show up."

"The weather's good for travel, an' from what the fella said this crick can't be more'n two, three days from here. Anyway I'm goin' to take a shot at it if someone does come for me. An' I've got a hunch someone will."

True to Black John's prediction, several days later an Indian stepped into the saloon, glanced furtively around, and motioned to the big man who stood at the bar with several of the men of Halfaday. When Black John joined him near the door the Indian peered into his face. "You Black John Smit'?" he asked.

"Yup. If you've got anything to tell me, come on over to my cabin. Cush don't allow no Siwashes here in the saloon."

Inside the cabin the Indian shifted uneasily from one foot to the other. "You Black John, you frien's wit' Fadder Cassatt?" he asked.

The big man nodded. "Shore I am. Was there somethin' he wanted?"

The man nodded. "Fadder Cassatt, she say 'you go Halfaday Crick, fin' Black John Smit', tell heem com' queek to Fadder Crick. Ees a breed, nem Louis Harp—ver' bad mans—sell hooch to de Siwash an' git hall de fur. De Siwash, dey hall git dronk.' She say you mak' heem git to hell out of dere."

"H-u-u-m—sellin' hooch to the Siwashes, eh? That's bad."

The Indian nodded. "Ver' bad. Dem dronk all tam."

"Why didn't Father Cassatt come down after me himself?" Black John asked.

"Fadder Cassatt, she seek. She no feel good. She stay een de bed."

"Did you just come from there—come straight over here?"

"Yes. Me, I'm com' fas'—two day. Fadder Cassatt she say you no com' to mission. Louis Harp, she got cabin on leetle crick 'bout seven, eight mile 'fore you git to mission. She say you go to mission, de Siwash see you an' dey know he sen' for you an' dey git mad on heem. She say you go to Louis Harp cabin an' mebbeso you tak' heem to Halfaday an' hang heem."

"Not a bad idea," Black John agreed. "An' how about you—will you show me where this Louis Harp lives?"

"I show you. I tak' you to de mout' of Louis Harp crick. Hees cabin 'bout two miles up de crick. I no go up de crick. Me, I'm 'fraid from Louis Harp. She mad on me 'cause I ain' buy no hooch."

Black John nodded. "Okay, I'll go along. I'll just throw my blankets an' some grub in my pack sack. We won't bother with a dog outfit."

TWO DAYS later the Indian paused and pointed to a trail that led to a small creek some distance below the mouth of Feather Creek. "Dat Louis Harp crick," he said. "De trail she go to Louis Harp cabin. Me, I'm no go dere. I'm 'fraid."

Shifting his rifle to the crook of his elbow, Black John took leave of the Indian and struck off up the creek. He preceded slowly, his eyes on the snow of the trail. He had gone a mile and a half to a point where the trail passed between two enormous rocks with only room for the passage of a sled between. A grim smile twisted his lips as his eyes searched the apparently undisturbed surface of the snow. Stepping to the foot of a tree that grew at the base of one of the rocks, some ten feet off the trail, with his mittened hand he scraped the snow away from its base and encountered a chain.

It was a heavy chain, secured to the tree trunk by means of a padlock—the chain and the padlock he had seen in the blacksmith shop in Dawson. Seizing the chain, he jerked the huge trap from beneath the snow in the trail between the rocks—at a point where anyone following the trail must certainly have stepped squarely into it. Reaching beneath the jaws he sprung the trap, then dragged it about for several minutes, roughing up the snow to the full length of the chain. Then, removing the bottle of moose blood from his pack sack, he sprinkled the snow with blood and poured some on a blanket which he unrolled.

With the trap pulled well to one side of the trail, he laid down, wallowed about in the snow, then with his leg lying across the jaws of the trap, he spread the blood-stained blanket to conceal both leg and trap. A few minutes later, he opened his mouth and gave voice to a shriek of anguish. Again and again he shrieked and screamed, but his only answer was the weird sound of his own voice screaming back at him from the far rock rim. With his rifle ready he lay, his eyes on a bend of the trail only fifty yards beyond the opening between the rocks.

Surely, if the breed's cabin was only half a mile away he could hear those agonized shrieks for help, and the moment he rounded that bend he would get a rifle bullet square through the middle. Again he shrieked at the top of his lungs, and turned his head sharply at the sound of a low derisive laugh, to stare into the dark saturnine face that showed above the muzzle of a rifle at the edge of a spruce thicket scarce a dozen yards away.

"Get me out of here!" he cried. "I stepped in a trap—a bear trap—there on the trail between the rocks! I've be'n yellin' fer half an hour. For God's sake—get me out!"

"I heard your cries, and I came to release you. But first you must toss your rifle beyond reach into the snow."

"Why would I shoot you? Hell, man, if I shot you I'd die here in this damned trap!"

"I take no chances. Throw away the gun".

Black John tossed the rifle into the snow. The breed still kept him covered. "And now the big revolver you carry beneath your shirt. I can see where it is bulging your parka."

As Black John's hand slipped beneath his parka and grasped the six-gun he considered for an instant his chance of a quick shot as he drew it out, but a glance at the unwavering rifle muzzle decided him against trying anything, and he tossed the revolver out of reach in the snow.

III
GHOST ON TWO LEGS

THEN THE BREED stepped from the thicket, an evil smile widening his lips. "S-o-o—Black John Smith—the big outlaw—the man Cutter Malone says outsmarted other outlaws and has taken a million dollars from them and kept out of the clutches of the law. This Black John is so dumb he has stepped right in the middle of a trap."

"Get me out of here!" Black John cried. "Get me out before my leg freezes stiff!"

"I will release you in due time. I am Louis Harp, the man you came here to hang, as you have hanged others, for selling hooch to the Siwashes. But those others were not smart, or they would not have been hanged. I tell you now—it was I who sent for you, not Father Cassatt. I sent for you for a reason—but the reason is not to rid the country of a hooch trader. I laid my plan well. I set my trap and the big outlaw, Black John, walked right into it. It is to laugh. No matter how smart a man is, there is always someone who is smarter."

"You've got me. But for God's sake get me out of this trap! I tell you my leg is freezin'!"

"I will release you—but for a price."

"A price! What do you mean—a price?"

"Well, let us say one hundred thousand dollars. Surely, if you have a million, one hundred thousand dollars is not too big a price to pay for your life."

Black John scowled. "How can I pay you a hundred thousan'? I ain't got that much change on me."

"I did not expect you to have it with you. But you have it in the safe at Cushing's Fort, on Halfaday. Cutter Malone told me so."

"Cutter's a damn liar. I've got sixty thousan' in the safe—an' not a damn cent more."

"Very well—sixty thousand, then. I will settle for sixty thousand."

"Okay. You've got me. I'll pay it. Let me out of here an' haul me down to Cush's, an' I'll pay you."

The breed laughed. "Sure you would pay me—with a rope! Do you think I am a fool! I have here a pencil and paper. You will write out an order for Cushing to pay the bearer sixty thousand dollars and I will collect it myself."

"But, good God, man—it will take you two days to get to Cush's an' two days to get back. An' by that time I'd be froze stiff!"

"That is true. But you will not freeze. My man—the same who guided you up here, will release you and take you to my cabin where it is warm and comfortable. Then he will summon Father Cassatt, who will look after you. I am not coming back. When I obtain the money from Cushing, I shall leave this country for good."

He called loudly, and the Indian appeared from the thicket, carrying two heavy clamps.

The breed continued. "Write out the order, and I will start at once for Halfaday. One half hour after I leave, Kumtux, here, will clamp down the springs of the trap and release you." Retrieving Black John's revolver from the snow, the man cocked it, and handed the pencil and paper to the Indian. "Give it to him, so he can write out the order." He glanced into the big man's face. "Do not resort to any trickery. That order better be good—for if I do not receive the money, I shall return and kill you."

"Oh, Cush'll turn it over to you, all right. I'll say here that I need the cash to pay a couple of *chechakos* for a location I aim to buy. I was tellin' him about that proposition not so long ago, an' he'll think that's where I'm at, now. You can tell him you was workin' for these boys, an' I sent you over for the cash."

WHEN THE breed received the paper he read it carefully, folded it and placed it in his wallet. Then his thin lips twisted into a sneer of contempt as the black eyes rested on the prostrate man's face. "Black John Smith—king of the outlaws! Pouff! You have hanged many men—and now it is your turn to die. But you will not die quickly, on the end of a rope. You will die slowly—miserably, right here where you lie. You thought you would hang me. You did not know that I am smart enough to turn the tables on you. You can lie here and think of that as you die. You can think also of your million dollars and wonder what will become of it. And you can think of me spending your sixty thousand amid women and wine and song in places far, far from here."

He turned to the Indian, and reaching in his pocket, tossed him a key. "Here you are, Kumtux, that is the key to the fur room. The fur is yours, now—the fur and the forty gallons of liquor that I just brought up from Dawson. I told you that if you would stick with me you would never regret it. Go back to the cabin now, and in the morning come back down here and release Black John. He will be frozen stiff by then. Drag his body back off the trail and leave it for the wolves." Retrieving a pack sack from the spruce thicket, he adjusted it and struck off down the trail to the White.

When he had disappeared around a bend Black John appealed to the Indian. "Come on, get me out of here. You wouldn't leave a man to freeze to death with his leg in a bear trap."

The Indian scowled. "I'm no let you go. You hang me sure—for it you com' oop here—for trade de hooch to de Siwash. Dat better you die—den I ain''fraid no mor'!" And, turning his back, he stepped between the two rocks and headed up the trail.

Leaping to his feet Black John kicked his rifle out from under the snow, and leveled it at the Indian's back. "Hold on!" he cried. "You forgot somethin'!"

The Indian whirled at the sound of the voice, then his eyes widened and his mouth sagged open as he stared incredulously at the man who approached in swift strides. "You! You een de trap!" the man faltered. "How you git hout?"

"Chawed my way out. Hell, that trap ain't nothin' but steel! Turn around an' head fer the cabin."

When they arrived Black John continued, "Fish out that key an' roll them kegs out of the fur room." When the man had complied, Black John picked up a piece of rope. "Now, lay down on your belly an' put your hands behind your back an' hold 'em there till I get 'em tied." When the man's hands were secured, the big man picked up an ax and smashed the kegs, allowing liquor to gush out over the snow. Then he locked the fur room, pocketed the key and turned to the Indian. "Get up, now, an' head down the crick. You an' me are headin' for Halfaday."

LOUIS HARP had struck out for Halfaday following the back trail Black John and the Indian had left. Also following this trail, the two made good time. Darkness fell as they topped a ridge and the flicker of a fire showed at the edge of a spruce copse a quarter of a mile away where the breed had camped for the night.

Glancing at the Indian, Black John warned. "Listen. You open your mouth to yell an' I'll kill you. We're campin' here—an' we ain't makin' a fire. I've got a blanket apiece, an' we'll roll up in the snow. We won't sleep—but we won't freeze." He fed the Indian without releasing his hands. Later, when the breed's fire had died to a mere flicker, Black John filled his lungs and a weird shriek rent the still air. "Help! Help! Get me out of here! My leg's in a bear trap! Help!" His lips twisted into a grin as he saw a shower of sparks shoot upward from the breed's fire, then the flames leaped upward as the man tossed on dry wood.

From his vantage point on the ridge Black John's grin widened as he watched the breed, standing erect beside the leaping flames, peering this way and that into the surrounding blackness. He rolled up in his blanket, but slept fitfully in the cold. Each time he awoke he could see the breed's fire blazing high, could see, also, the form that sat bolt upright close beside the flames. At midnight, he again gave voice to a series of agonized shrieks. And again watched the breed leap to his feet and peer fearfully into the darkness.

SHORTLY AFTER dawn the two ate all that remained of the moose meat in the pack sack and hit the trail. Black John grinned as they passed the breed's camp of the night before. The fire had died to ashes. Evidently the breed had been gone at least an hour. "He won't lose no time gettin' to Cush's," he opined. "He ort to make it by suppertime."

The prediction proved correct. Darkness was falling as Black John handcuffed the Indian to a bunk stanchion in his cabin, and hurried to Cush's, where he slipped into the storeroom and glued his eye to the 'peek hole', a slit placed close beneath a shelf, that gave a view of the interior of the barroom.

Cush and the breed were alone in the room and the breed was recounting bills as Cush counted them out onto the bar. Finally, he finished, pocketed them, and turned from the bar. "You better stop here tonight," Cush said. "You kin git an early start in the mornin'."

The breed shook his head. "No, I promised I would return as quickly as possible. There will be starlight. I can reach the White before I camp."

Slipping swiftly around to the door, Black John confronted the breed as he opened it. As the man leaped back into the room with a muffled cry on his lips, Black John held out his hand. "I'll take the sixty thousan' here, Louis," he said.

The breed's eyes widened in horror as they shifted from the bearded face to Black John's legs. Spittle drooled from his mouth as words faltered from his lips. "*Tahamanawas!*" he cried, reverting to the lore of his Indian forbears. "*Kultus tahamanawas!* I heard it in the night! Shrieking at me from the dark! But you—in the trap—your leg was in the trap—I saw blood on the snow!"

Black John grinned. "Oh, shore—that was moose blood you saw. Trouble with you birds that think you're smart—you jump to conclusions. If you'd been really smart, Louis, you'd have jerked that blanket off me, an' then you'd seen that when I sprung your trap I left my leg out of it."

The man went suddenly limp and leaned against a card table for support. "Cutter Malone... I should have listened to him.

He said you were smart, smarter than all the others. He warned me to watch my step—or—or you would hang me."

"He did, did he? Well for onct in his life, Cutter was right." He turned to Cush, "Send One Arm out to fetch in a quorum. We got to call the miners' meetin', an' get this damn cuss an' his Siwash hung before Downey gets here, or he'll defeat the ends of Justice."

CHEECHAKO TROUBLE

IT WAS LATE in the afternoon of the day after Christmas when Black John Smith and Lyme Cushing stepped into the Tivoli Saloon in Dawson to be greeted heartily by the little group of sourdoughs that had foregathered near the end of the bar. Swiftwater Bill eyed the big man with a grin. "Speak of the devil an' up he pops! We was wonderin' if you'd show up this Christmas, John, but we sure never expected you'd fetch Cush along."

Black John returned the grin. "Hell, it was him that fetched me! Personally, I prefer the peace an' quiet of Halfaday, but Cush got his mind set on the bright lights an' was ra'rin' to go so I give in."

Old Cush, the lugubrious proprietor of Cushing's Fort, the combined trading post and saloon that ministered to the wants of the little community of outlawed men that had sprung up on Halfaday Creek, close against the Yukon-Alaska border, scowled. "Huh, it was him that was ra'rin' to go. One mornin' when he come in the saloon an' we was pourin' our drink I says how the squaw that does my cookin' an' cleanin' around the place was aimin' to go way off in the hills somewheres where her folks is goin' to have a big potlatch.

"I know them damn potlatches is apt to last for two, three weeks, an' I tried to talk her out of it. But I might of know'd better. A man can't talk no woman outa nothin' once she gits a notion in her head."

118

"Then John, he starts in about what a hell of a good time we could have down here to Dawson, what with everyone in off'n the cricks an' all, an' how I hadn't been nowheres in a hell of a while, an' what a hell of a lot of work it would be if I had to take care of things without that gal to help—an' he went at it till I kinda seen it that way myself. So, bein' as how no one but me an' John knows the combination of the safe, I give in, an' hired Pot-Gutted John an' One-Armed John to run the place till I got back. John warned 'em if they stole any more'n we figgered they ought to, we'd call a miner's meetin' an' hang 'em higher'n hell."

"Looks like you got here a day late, at that," Burr MacShane said.

"We never got here no day late," Cush replied. "By God, the way John put them seven big dogs of his'n over the trail, you'd thought the devil was after us! We got in yesterday mornin' an' put up at the Fairview Hotel an' rolled into bed. We never woke up till ten, last night. So we got supper over to the Northern Restaurant, an' then we went over to the Pavilion an' danced all night. I'm gittin' old for sech doin's. My feet hurt, an' I couldn't of got no tireder if I'd of stayed to home an' done my work an' the squaw's chores on top of it."

Old Bettles, dean of the sourdoughs, grinned. "I'm buyin' a drink. Cheer up, Cush, we'll be startin' a stud game pretty quick, an' you can rest up."

AS THE drinks were poured, Moosehide Charlie joined the group. "I was jest talkin' to Constable Peters. Accordin' to him, young Bill Amberdahl's wife found him layin' dead on the portage trail around Elbow Rapids up there on Johnson Crick with a bullet hole in the back of his head. The day before Christmas, Bill went down to Clem Orkey's roadhouse at the mouth of the crick for some supplies, an' when he didn't come home that night she hit down the crick, figgerin' they was probably a bunch in Clem's place an' Bill had got soused. It had snowed

durin' the night an' damn if she didn't trip over Bill's corpse layin'
there under the snow."

Art Harper, a sourdough who had been in the country longer
than any of them, spoke up. "Young Bill ain't the man his dad
was, by a damn sight. Old Ben Amberdahl was some man,
anyway you look at him. God, I'll never forget the day he cleaned
up on them Roosians down at the mouth of Seventymile, on
the American side! Ben, he was a cowpuncher that got shang-
haied in 'Frisco an' woke up aboard a whaler. He deserted at St.
Michael an' come on upriver. I come into the country in 'seventy-
three, overland from the Mackenzie, an' Ben was snipin' the bars
on Fortymile when I got there.

"I rec'lect it was the day before Christmas of 'seventy-four I was mushin' upriver with a sled load of trade goods when I met Ben comin' down hell-bent ridin' an empty sled draw'd by six big Siberian dogs. He'd got soft on a Siwash gal an' they aimed to hit down to Fort Yukon an' get married, come spring, an' he told me the Roosians had kidnapped her.

"A big Roosian name of Ivan had built that log tradin' post at the mouth of Seventymile. There was always three, four Roosians hangin' out there an' they was a damn tough outfit. The Siwashes would fetch in their fur an' Ivan would get 'em drunk, take the fur an' claim he'd paid 'em for it an' then kick them out. An' they'd steal Siwash girls an' run 'em downriver an' sell 'em to the whalers.

"There wasn't no law in the country them days, an' Ben was alone. I told him he better not tackle them Roosians single-handed, but he claimed he wasn't afraid of 'em, an' hit on down-river. I hated to think what would happen to him, so I turned around an' follered him down. It wasn't only a little ways back, an' when I got there an' was slippin' my rifle out from under the lashin' of my load, I seen Ben shove the door of the tradin' room open. Before I got up the bank there was the damndest volley of shots I ever heard, an' a couple of minutes later when I busted into the room with my rifle cocked, Ben stood there shovin' shells into the cylinder of his .44 Colt, an' four Roosians laid dead on the floor—three of 'em with guns in their hands! Ivan an' another one was layin' behind the counter an' two was in front of it. Ben, he'd fired five shots. Each one of them four Roosians had a bullet hole in his forehead, an' one bullet had missed an' hit the picture of the Roosian King right between the eyes."

"Did he get the girl?" Camillo Bill asked.

"Sure he did. They had her locked in a back room. He got her out an' loaded her onto his sled an' shoved on down to Fort Yukon an' they got married without waitin' for spring."

"I've heard about that fight in that Roosian tradin' post," Bettles said. "It's the post that Joe Turner runs now."

Several others had heard of it, and Burr MacShane asked, "What became of Ben Amberdahl?"

Art Harper shook his head. "Don't no one seem to know. He ain't been around for years. Made him a stake on Fortymile, I guess, an' went outside."

"I've seen his gun—that Colt .44. Joe Turner had it hangin' on his wall. It had Amberdahl's initials carved in the wooden grip."

"That's right," Harper said. "Joe bought the layout from Ivan's Siwash wife, an' later he bought Ben's gun an' hung it on the wall right in under that picture with the bullet hole between the eyes. But it ain't there now—it nor the picture neither. I come through there not long ago an' Joe told me someone had stole the gun a year or so back."

"Ain't they got no idea who shot Bill Amberdahl?" Old Bettles wanted to know.

"Accordin' to Peters," Moosehide replied, "along in the fore-noon of Christmas he got to Clem Orkey's roadhouse on a reg'lar patrol. They was a bunch in there from up the Klondike an' some of them cricks that runs into it above Bonanza. Clem didn't have no complaints an' neither did the others, an' Peters was about to pull out when Amberdahl's wife come bustin' in claimin' she'd tripped over his corpse, there at the Elbow Rapids, an' he'd been shot in the back of the head. She stayed there with Clem's woman while Peters an' Clem an' a couple of others went up an' fetched Amberdahl down an' histed him up on the meat cache.

"Clem give Peters a list of everyone that was to the roadhouse the day before. There ain't only three claims on Johnson Crick. Amberdahl an' his wife was the first ones to locate on the crick. They filed a claim a year ago last spring a couple of mile above the Elbow Rapids. Couple months later Duff Regan an' his breed wife located a mile further up, an' in the fall a young feller name of Jack Manners located above Regans'."

HARPER OBSERVED, "Duff Regan must of abandoned his claim on the Kandik. He married Ivan's breed daughter, Sonia, after Ivan got killed, an' they located on the Kandik. Had a pretty good layout there, it looked like."

"Accordin' to what Clem told Peters," Moosehide went on, "Some of the boys was already there when Amberdahl come in about the middle of the forenoon. Duff Regan's wife come in a little later, an' along about noon this here Jack Manners drifted in. Drinks was had an' after a while Amberdahl got kinda ugly an' accused Manners of seein' too much of his wife. Manners told him he was a damn fool. Told him that he never was down to Amberdahl's when Amberdahl wasn't there hisself. Claimed it was lonesome up there on his claim alone an' he'd come down now an' then to play cribbage. Claimed Amberdahl hisself had invited him down, an' so had his wife, an' they'd play cribbage, an' then he'd hit out for home. He told Amberdahl that if he wasn't soused he'd never accused him of seein' his wife.

"Clem says that Amberdahl told Manners to stay away from his place from then on—or he'd shoot him. An' Manners got mad, an' told him that two could play that game. Then he turned around an' walked out. Clem said that Amberdahl got his supplies an' pulled out later, an' then some of the others pulled out.

"The way things looked, Peters hit out fer Manners' place to question him, but Manners wasn't there, an' hadn't been since the snow. So he went back to Clem's an' they loaded Amberdahl's corpse on Peters' sled, an' he fetched it here to Dawson, Amberdahl's wife comin' along. An' damn if they didn't meet Manners right here on Front Street! So Peters took him an' Amberdahl's corpse over to headquarters, an' Amberdahl's wife went to the hotel. Peters says Corporal Downey took over there, an' when they searched Manners they found a .45 revolver on him with an empty shell in the cylinder. Manners claimed he'd shot at a wolf. But they locked him up."

Swiftwater Bill frowned. "Damned if I'll believe Jack Manners shot Amberdahl—leastwise not in the back of the head. I know Manners. He's a *chechako*, but he's a damn good kid. Worked for me for a while. Hell, I was talkin' to him last evenin' over to the Fairview Hotel, an' he didn't look like a man that had jest pulled off a murder, by a damn sight. Accordin' to what you said there was plenty of others in Orkey's place that could have had it in for Amberdahl. I know him. He don't get soused very often, but when he does he's apt to get mean. An' as for Manners runnin' after his wife—that's all bunk. I know Maybelle Amberdahl— know'd her when she was a kid, down there on the Porcupine. She's a damn fine young woman. Manners told me about stoppin' in at Orkey's place for a couple of drinks, an' then he come on here for the Christmas jamboree."

"A hell of a jamboree he'll have locked in a cell over to head-quarters," Moosehide said. "Accordin' to Peters, it looks damn bad for him. An' besides which, that wife of Amberdahl's is a damn good looker. A man couldn't hardly blame this here Manners for makin' a play for her if he got the chance."

Black John grinned. "I fear your ethics are open to question, Moosehide," he said.

"Ethics—hell! I ain't got no ethics—wouldn't know one if I seen it. All I says—it looks damn bad for Manners."

Cush glanced at the clock. "It's goin' on six," he said, "an' I'm goin' to the hotel. I ain't goin' to play stud on no empty stummick. An' neither I ain't goin' to be late for supper an' have to take no leavin's, neither."

"Me an' you both," Black John said, and turned to the others. "We'll be back in an hour or so, an' it ain't no more'n right I should warn you damn gravel hounds, that on Chris'mas nights us Halfaday Crickers plays 'em high, wide, an' handsome."

II
LADY IN DISTRESS

AS THEY WAITED for their order in the dining room of the Fairview Hotel Cush noticed that a good-looking young woman seated at a table across the room kept glancing at Black John. Finishing her meal, she rose and headed for the door, pausing beside the table at which the two were seated. "Pardon me," she said, glancing into the big man's face, "but aren't you Black John Smith?"

"That's right, ma'am. But you have the best of me. I don't rec'lect ever seein' you before."

The woman's lips smiled, accentuating the look of tragedy in the dark eyes. "You probably haven't seen me since I was a little girl. I have changed—but you haven't. I'm Maybelle Bolton. My father, Sam Bolton has a location on the Porcupine. You and Corporal Downey stopped overnight with us the time you went up to Taylor's Post and arrested that horrible Cronin who murdered Mr. Taylor and robbed the safe, and tried to lay the blame on Tom Keith. Mamie Taylor knew Tom was innocent even though Cronin had used Tom's knife to stab Mr. Taylor to death with, and then left it where the police could find it. Mamie's my best friend. She and Tom are married now, running the post, and they both say that if it hadn't been for you, even Corporal Downey would have believed Tom was guilty."

"Oh, sure." Black John replied. "I rec'lect Sam Bolton an' you, too. This Mamie Taylor an' Tom Keith are a mighty fine pair of young folks. But Corporal Downey's the one that deserves the credit for solvin' that murder. I ain't connected with the police. I was jest an unofficial observer—jest went along for the ride."

"You could never make Mamie or Tom believe that," the woman told him. "I know most people think you're an outlaw. But they can't make me believe it, because I know Corporal Downey would never have anything to do with an outlaw, except to arrest him."

White teeth flashed behind the black beard. "Thanks for the vote of confidence."

"My father says you are smart—smarter even than Corporal Downey. And he, too, believes that if it hadn't been for you Tom Keith would have been hanged for Mr. Taylor's murder, and Cronin would have gone scot free. I recognized you the minute you stepped into the room, and I've been trying to get up courage to—to ask you if—if you couldn't help me out."

"Why, sure, m'am, I'll do what I can. What's your trouble?"

"I married Bill Amberdahl and we have a location on Johnson Crick a few miles above Clem Orkey's roadhouse. On the day before Christmas Bill went down to Orkey's for some supplies, and when he didn't return that night I went down to find out why, and I—I tripped over Bill's body lying there under the snow on the portage trail around the Elbow Rapids. I hurried on to the post and found Constable Peters there. Clem Orkey told me that Bill had been drinking and had accused young

Jack Manners of seeing too much of me. The accusation was perfectly absurd, and Bill would never have made it if he hadn't been drinking.

"They brought Bill's body down to the trading post. He had been shot in the back of the head. Orkey said that when Bill accused Jack, Jack denied it, and called Bill a fool for saying such a thing, and they had words bath and forth and finally Bill told him that if he ever showed up at our place again he would shoot him.

"Of course Bill would never have done it, and Jack knew he wouldn't. Bill was drunk, and Jack was mad. But they locked Jack up, and Corporal Downey intends to remove the bullet from Bill's head—and if it's a .45 I'm afraid Jack will be in a terrible position."

Black John nodded. "Yeah—it would kinda look like that, wouldn't it?"

"It certainly would! And I know he never shot Bill. He is a fine young man, and Orkey said he was perfectly sober. Bill would have been sorry when he sobered up—and Jack Manners knew that. He certainly would never have laid for Bill and shot him. There were others in Orkey's that day he had quarreled with at times—maybe one of them shot him, knowing that Jack would be blamed for it.

"I swear to you that there was absolutely nothing in Bill's accusation! I never even saw Jack when Bill wasn't present! You do believe me, don't you? Oh—you must!"

"Why—sure I believe you," the big man said gently, and drawing a well-filled pouch from his pocket, tossed it onto the table. "So you're broke here in Dawson an' need some dust to tide you over till this thing is straightened out, eh? Well, there you are. Take it an' welcome."

"No! No! I don't need any dust! Bill and I did well there on our claim. We have money in the bank here—plenty of money. What I want you to do—if you only will—is to help Corporal Downey—as you did there on the Porcupine. If he removes that bullet, and it should be a .45 they might even hang Jack Manners. And I know he never killed Bill!"

"How about robbery?" Black John asked. "Did Bill flash a heavy poke there in Orkey's place?"

"Yes, Bill had a well-filled poke with him, and I suppose he did flash it. But he wasn't murdered for his dust. His poke with the dust in it was in his pocket when they brought him down to Orkey's. Whoever shot Bill hated him. The quarrels Bill had from time to time with the prospectors and trappers that frequent Orkey's place were never very serious ones, so I'm wondering if whoever shot Bill did it to avenge some thing that happened years ago. If so, the murderer might kill me, too. I'll never feel safe there on the claim alone until the murderer is caught.

"You see, I hadn't known Bill very long before I married him. I've heard that he was pretty wild, in those days. But since we were married he settled down. He drank now and then—maybe once or twice a year. But he soon sobered up and was always sorry. He was a hard worker and really a perfectly wonderful man."

"H-m-m-m. Well," Black John replied, pocketing the poke, "I'll do what I can. I ain't promisin' anything, though. Policin' is Downey's business—not mine. But in a case like this—if it will make you feel any easier, I'll drop into detachment tomorrow an' see what's goin' on."

"Oh, thank you!" the woman cried, in a voice that was half a sob. "I have every confidence in you!" And, abruptly, she turned and left the room.

CUSH SLANTED the big man a scowling glance. "I'll be damned if I kin figger out how every good-lookin' woman that comes along picks you out to have confidence in, an' tell their troubles to—when everyone knows you're the damndest outlaw in the country!"

Black John grinned. "The reason is ondoubtless owin' to the benign an' confidence-inspirin' contour of my features, coupled with the subtle aura of virtue that eminates—"

"If them damn words means anything you better talk 'em to someone that knows what it is!" Cush interrupted. "By God, any woman kin git anything she wants outa you! Hell—tossin' out your poke—a good eighty ounces—jest 'cause she stands there an' claims she's got troubles! If she'd of grabbed up the poke it would served you right. An' damn if I don't wish she had! Like I say, it would served you right—an' mebbe learnt you somethin'. Her claimin' there weren't nothin' goin' on betwixt her an' this here Jack Manners… when anyone would know that any young feller would of fell for her—husband, or no husband! An' when some woman likes some young guy which ain't her husband, an' claims he's a fine young man, it's jest too damn bad for the husband. I've had four wives—an', by God, I know what women are like!"

Black John shook his head slowly. "Your viewpoint on women is incontrovertibly pessimistic an'—"

"An' if you say jest one more big word you'll git this here cup right between the eyes!" Cush exclaimed, waving the item mentioned under Big John's nose. "An' what's more—I'm bettin' that if this here Manners gits turned loose, like she wants him to, she'll be makin' a play to marry one of you two—or mebbe both, before the snow melts on Bill Amberdahl's grave."

Black John's grin broadened. "A man might do worse, at that. Good lookin' young woman—good location—money in the bank…"

"Yeah—an' hell a-poppin' on Halfaday all the rest of your life! Come on, lets git over to the Tivoli. What with all the folks they is in town we mightn't get no seat in the stud game."

ALONG TOWARD the middle of the following morning, Black John stepped into the office at detachment headquarters and greeted Corporal Downey seated behind his flattop desk. "Well, how's things goin' in the ranks of the sinful?"

"Oh, not too bad for the number of people that's in for the Christmas hell-raisin'. Draw up a chair an' sit down. Town detail keeps busy with drunks, an' fights, an' whatnot. We've got one murder on our hands, though, that don't look so good."

The big man grinned. "Well, takin' 'em by an' large, as the Good Book says, damn few murders do look good to the casual observer."

"What I mean—a fellow by the name of Bill Amberdahl was—"

"Yeah," Black John interrupted, "I've heard the particulars—everything up to how you found a .45 gun on Manners with one empty shell in the cylinder, an' Manners claimed he'd shot at a wolf."

Downey nodded. "An' on the face of it, it looked bad for Manners. But here's somethin' else—I got the bullet out of Amberdahl's head. He was wearin' a twill parka, an' whoever shot him slipped up behind him on the trail and fired the bullet into his skull, low down. He slipped up damn close, too. There's flecks of burnt powder around the bullet hole in Amberdahl's parka—black powder. The cartridges in Manner's gun were smokeless. I got the bullet where it had plowed through his brain an' stopped against his skull, high up in front, about where the hair starts. It was a soft lead bullet—mushroomed a little, but in pretty good shape.

"I fired a bullet out of the gun we took off Manners into a tub of mud an' took the two bullets over to the hospital where they've got a good microscope, an' it didn't take but a few minutes to see that it couldn't have been fired from Manner's gun. The butt end of the bullet that killed Amberdahl measured a mite smaller than the other—prob'ly a .44. The two bullets were a different shape an' weight. The lands an' grooves were different, too. But the thing that mattered most is that the bullet I took from Amberdahl's head was fired from a left hand twist gun, and Manner's gun is a right hand twist. The Colt is the only left hand twist I ever heard of—all the rest are right hand. The lands an' grooves show the twist of the barrel the bullet was fired from. One other thing—the course of the bullet slanted upward, showin' that whoever fired it was shorter than Amberdahl, who measures five foot ten. Manners stands six foot one in his socks."

"So you turned Manners loose, eh?" Black John asked.

"I'm goin' to in a few minutes. I jest got back from the hospital a half hour ago an' ain't finished my report yet. Manners seems like a nice young fellow—not one that would sneak up an' shoot a man from behind. I'm glad he's in the clear."

Black John filled and lighted his pipe. "So, the case is closed, I guess."

"Closed—hell!" Downey exclaimed. "It won't be closed till the one that murdered Bill Amberdahl is hung!"

"Might be quite a chore to locate the party. Accordin' to what Peters told Mooseliide Charlie, there was quite a few in Orkey's place, that day that didn't like Amberdahl none too well. Any one of them might have shot him."

"That's right," Downey agreed. "An' the chances are, one of 'em did. My job is to find that one. I'm hittin' out for the Johnson Crick country as soon as I turn Manners loose."

"Yup—quite a chore," Black John repeated. "What with them trappers an' prospectors scattered all over hell, an' the new snow like it is, an' the strong cold due anytime. Some of 'em might still be hangin' around Orkey's, but the chances are most of 'em have pulled out."

"Sure, it's goin' to be quite a chore—an' most likely nothin' will come of it. He was shot with a revolver, all right. A rifle would have drove the bullet clean through his head."

BLACK JOHN nodded. "Yeah, an' when whoever done it finds out you're on the job, it won't be long before that revolver is damn well hid, or throw'd away."

"If Orkey or one of the others don't know who owns a Colt revolver the chances are I never will locate the gun. It's prob'ly a hopeless case. But I've got to make a stab at it. It was a grudge killin'—no robbery. Amberdahl's poke with around seventy ounces in it was in his pocket when his wife found him there on the trail." The officer paused and shrugged. "One of them prospectors or trappers done it, all right—but, which one?"

"Damn few trappers or prospectors pack revolvers."

"Manners packed one. An' so do you."

"Yeah, but Manners is a *chechako*. Time he's been here a while he'll sell it, or throw it away, or leave it home. Me—how the hell could I keep Halfaday moral without it—what with the disreputable characters that keeps driftin' in on us?"

"Some one besides Manners was packin' one," Downey persisted.

"That's right." Black John shrugged. "An' that one held a grudge that called for murder. Your job is to locate the one that had both the grudge, an' the gun, an' the opportunity to use it."

"Yeah—some job!" Downey exclaimed.

"Oh, I don't know," the big man drawled, smiling.

"What do you mean—you don't know?"

"Meanin' I've got a sort of hunch, that's all."

Downey eyed the other narrowly. "An' you'll help me out on this case?"

"You know damn well, Downey, that I never neither help nor hinder the police in their work."

"Yeah, I know. An' I know, too, that there's been plenty of times when, if it hadn't been for you, I'd never have solved a case. How about it—will you? Or, won't you?"

"You rec'lect the time you went down on the Porcupine on that Taylor murder, an' I sort of trailed along, an' how we stopped over night with Sam Bolton? Well, Sam's little girl, Maybelle her name is, is Bill Amberdahl's wife. I was talkin' to her over to the hotel, an' she claims she's afraid that maybe the one that

murdered Bill might take it out on her, too. An' she wondered
if I wouldn't help find the one that done it, rememberin' that I
was along with you that time on the Porcupine. I told her I'd
do what I could—but not bein' in the police, it prob'ly wouldn't
be much. So, if you don't mind, we'll foller this hunch I've got.
But I'm warnin' you, we ain't workin' together. Just what you
might say—parallel. You from the police angle, an' me just sort
of keepin' my promise to Amberdahl's wife."

Downey grinned. "Okay, John. What's your hunch?"

"This here land an' groove stuff you was tellin' about, s'pose
you got holt of a bullet that was fired quite a while back—say
twenty years, or so—from the same gun that killed Amberdahl,
would that microscope up to the hospital show it was the same
gun?"

"It would show whether or not the lands an' grooves were
the same. An' it would show whether the gun that fired it was a
right, or left hand twist. An', yes—I believe in this case it would
show it was the same gun, because all but one of the lands show
clean-cut edges. That one sort of slants down into the groove.
You see, a bullet is slightly larger than the diameter of the barrel
and the hot lead, forced through the barrel carries the marks not
only of the twist, but of any irregularity in the last inch or so of
the barrel. The gun that fired the bullet that killed Amberdahl
had one land that had been damaged near the muzzle."

"Okay—let's go."

"Go! Go where?"

"Down to Joe Turner's tradin' post an' roadhouse there at the
mouth of Seventymile."

"Joe Turner's! Seventymile! This murder was committed on
Johnson Crick, not Seventymile!"

"That's so, ain't it?" the big man grinned. "An' the rookus
started in Clem Orkey's place—not Turner's."

"Sure it did! I'll throw an outfit together, an' we'll hit out for
Orkey's."

"If that's where you're headin' we ain't runnin' parallel no more. 'Cause here's where I split off. I'm headin' for Joe Turner's."

"But, hell, man—that's way over in Alaska!"

"Sure it is. An' there's a good trail on the river. Not like wallerin' through the deep snow huntin' up them prospecters an' trappers that was in Orkey's that day."

"But, I've got no authority on the American side!"

"You won't need none. All you need is a dog outfit, a hand saw, a pick an' shovel, an' enough grub for the trip."

"What the hell do you mean?"

"Meanin' that we're goin' down to Turner's an' saw a bullet out of a log, an' maybe a couple of more out of the skulls of a couple of dead Roosians. Hell, Downey—ain't that clear enough?"

"Clear as mud," grinned the officer. "I'll have the stuff ready in an hour."

III
TIME TO KILL

THE FOLLOWING DAY the two stepped into the trading room at Turner's post to be greeted heartily by the proprietor, who grinned at the officer as he cast a sidewise glance at Black John. "Congratulations, Downey! I see you've run the old reprobate down, at last!"

The big man nodded. "Yeah, he run me down, all right. But I outsmarted him. I hit hell-bent for the line, an' when he caught up with me he was in Alaska, without no authority whatever."

All three joined in the laughter, and Turner set out a bottle and three glasses. "Where you two headin'?" he asked as the drinks were poured. "What's on your minds?"

Ignoring the questions, Black John fixed his gaze on the wall behind the counter. "What become of that picture that used to hang there? Used to be one of them .44 single-action Colt revolvers hangin' under it from a peg drove into the wall."

"Oh, that! Someone stole the gun, a year or so back. An' the picture—it was some old Roosian—it got all blacked up, what with the flies an' smoke, an' all, an' I throw'd it in the stove."

"Accordin' to Art Harper, this used to be a Roosian outfit."

"That's right. A big Roosian name of Ivan owned it. There was always three, four other Roosians hangin' around here, them days—as ornery a bunch of sidewinders as ever got together. There wasn't no law in the country then. But Ben Amberdahl, he didn't need no law. When they stole his gal an' locked her up in the back room there, Ben come b'ilin' down the river. He—"

"Amberdahl!" Corporal Downey exclaimed. "I knew I'd heard that name before! That fight happened long before I came into the country. Before any police hit the Yukon. But I heard about it years ago. This Ben Amberdahl must have been some man."

"I'll say he was!" Turner agreed. "They didn't make 'em no better. It was Ben's gun that I had hangin' there on the wall under the picture. I was snipin' the bars on the Kandik, an' when I heard about the fight, I come down an' bought the outfit off'n Ivan's Siwash wife. An' later I bought that Colt .44 off'n Ben. Claimed he was hittin' outside, an' didn't have no use for it, so I hung it there on the wall."

"So Ben got his gal an' married her, eh?" Black John asked.

"That's right. They had one kid, Bill, his name is. He was a kind of a hell-raiser when he was a youngster. But couple of year ago he married old Sam Bolton's girl over on the Porcupine, an' I heard they'd gone over on the Yukon side, an' was doin' all right."

"He was doin' all right till the day before Christmas," Downey said. "Then someone murdered him—shot him in the back of the head on the trail."

"Well, I'll be damned!" Turner exclaimed. "That's sure too bad. I know Maybelle Amberdahl. She's a fine young woman. Know'd Bill, too."

"That gun of Ben's—when was it stole off'n the wall there?" Black John asked.

"Oh, about a year or so ago. That's when I noticed it was gone. I remember I was gone about a week, down to Nulato, an' when I come back the gun was gone."

"Maybe whoever you left in charge, here, stole it?"

"No, my wife run the place while I was away. There was quite a few in an' out, an' she never noticed the gun was gone, till I come back an' missed it."

Black John nodded, slowly. "Quite a lot of coincidences, eh, Downey? Bill Amberdahl an' his wife locate there on Johnson Crick. A little later, Duff Regan an' his Roosian breed wife, pull stakes an' locate there, too. Just about the same time, Ben Amberdahl's gun disappeared from its peg there on the wall. Ivan was shot by Ben Amberdahl with that gun the day before Chris'mas. Bill Amberdahl is shot the day before Chris'mas. Bill Amberdahl was Ben Amberdahl's son. Sonia Regan is Ivan's daughter."

"By God, I believe you've got it, John!" Corporal Downey cried. "I believe you've hit the nail square on the head! But if she did it, she sure bided her time—avengin' a murder twenty-three years old!"

"Them breeds are patient, Downey. They're canny, too—damn canny. She was in Orkey's roadhouse that mornin', an' heard the row between Amberdahl an' Manners—heard Amberdahl threaten to shoot Manners, an' heard Manners tell him that two could play that game. It looked to her like a perfect setup."

Downey nodded. "An' if we can get hold of some of the bullets Ben Amberdahl fired that day, an' compare it with the one that killed Bill, we've got an open' an' shut case—if we can find the gun in Sonia Regan's possession." He paused and glanced at Turner. "Do you know where those Roosians were buried?"

"Hell, yes! I helped bury 'em. They're out back—an' not more'n two, three foot down. The ground was froze an' we didn't go in very deep."

"An' would you mind if we got that bullet out of the wall—
the one that went through the picture. We'll saw out around it,
an' put the plug back."

"Go to it," Turner said. "To hell with the plug. I can fit one
in place."

"We'll dig up them graves, too," Downey said. "I sure hope
them bullets didn't all go plumb through every one of them
Roosian's skulls."

"None of'em did," Turner said. "Every one of'em had jest one
hole in his head—in his forehead, jest above the eyes. An' I sure
hope you git the goods on that gal. No one likes her. Hell, even
Duff Regan's afraid of her!"

WITH THE bullet taken from the wall, and the three from the
skulls of the dead Russians in their possession, the two thanked
Turner, and headed upriver. In Dawson, the following afternoon,
the bullets were taken to the hospital where the microscope
showed beyond doubt that they had been fired from the same
gun as the bullet that killed Amberdahl.

"Okay," Downey said, as they returned to headquarters.
"Tomorrow we'll hit for Johnson Crick. But tell me, John, how
in the devil did you figure it was Sonia Regan that knocked
Amberdahl off that night at Orkey's?"

"I didn't really figure it. Like I said, it was just a hunch. I was
in the Tivoli when Art Harper was tellin' about Ben Amberdahl cleanin' up on them Roosians. He told about Ben Amberdahl's gun bein' stole off'n Joe Turner's wall. Then Moosehide
Charlie come in an' spilled what Peters had told him, about Bill
Amberdahl gettin' murdered, an' all. An' he mentioned that this
Sonia Regan was there in Orkey's when he had the run-in with
Manners. Art said that her an' Regan had left a good thing on
the Kandik an' settled on Johnson Crick soon after Amberdahl
did—so, puttin' two an' two together, I got a hunch, that's all. I
sure hope the hunch works out."

Downey grinned. "The hunch has worked out already. It's the gun we want, now. Come on over to the Tivoli. I'll buy a drink."

They joined Burr MacShane and Gordon Bettles at the bar. As the glasses were filled, Duff Regan stepped into the room, and Black John motioned him to join them at the bar.

"Come on up, Duff. Wet your whistle. Downey's buyin' one. I just been askin' the boys here where in hell I can get holt of a .38 revolver. We hung a feller up on Halfaday a while back, an' amongst his estate was eight, ten boxes of .38 ammunition an' I'd sure like to get holt of a gun that would fit 'em. It's a damn shame to waste 'em. But I don't know what else to do."

As Regan filled his glass he shook his head.

"I ain't got no .38 gun. Ain't got no revolver. The woman's got a Colt .44. Had it couple of years or so. What the hell she wants with it's more'n I know. She never shoots it. It's one of them old fashioned ones that you've got to cock with your thumb. Got some initials carved on the butt. I'd ought to throw the damn thing in the river—the way she looks at me sometimes."

Corporal Downey tossed off his drink. "Well, so long, you birds. Have a good time. I've got to get back to detachment and take care of things."

Shortly thereafter Black John sauntered from the room, and a few minutes later, joined Downey in his office.

The officer greeted him with a grin. "Well, what are we waitin' for? Let's go! But tell me one thing—why the devil did you ask Regan about a .38? You knew damn well that Amberdahl was shot with a .44."

"Sure I did. An' if I'd asked him about a .44, he might of got suspicious an' shut up like a clam. Askin' about a .38, that way, he just never give it a thought."

"If it wasn't for some—er—eccentricities in your makeup, John, you'd make a wonderful policeman."

"Oh, hell, Downey, I'd never make a policeman. A policeman's got to be smart. It takes everything I've got to keep Halfaday moral—while you've got to handle the whole Yukon!"

THEY ARRIVED at the Regan location just on the edge of dark. The door opened to their knock, and Regan's breed wife eyed them sullenly.

"The jig's up, Sonia," Downey said. "You're under arrest for the murder of Bill Amberdahl. We've got evidence enough to hang you, and it's my duty to warn you that anything you say may be used against you. Get your things together and let's go."

The woman gasped, and stepped aside as they entered the room. "Yes, I'm keel Amberdahl. Amberdahl papa keel mine papa, long tam ago. W'en I'm lettle girl, I'm say I'm git even—I'm gon' keel Ben Amberdahl. But Ben Amberdahl gone 'way before I kin keel heem. So I'm gon' keel he's boy—git even. I'm keel heem wit his papa gon—de gon dat keel mine papa. So I'm steal hees papa gon off Joe Turner wall. I'm always car' dat gon in mine pack, so's wait for chance to keel Bill Amberdahl. W'en Bill Amberdahl git marry an' com' Johnson Crick, I mak' Duff Regan quit Kandik an' com' here, too. He no want to com'—but I'm mak' heem. He 'fraid of me—'fraid som'tam I'm keel heem."

"What made you pick that day?" Corporal Downey asked.

"I wait for chance. Day befor' Chris'mas, I'm go to Orkey for supply. Bill Amberdahl dere. Git dronk. Git in row wit Manners. Den Manners go out. I'm go pret' queek. I'm wait by de rapids, an' w'en Bill Amberdahl com" long, I'm sneak up behine an' shoot heem in de head—lak hee's papa shoot mine papa—day before Chris'mas. I'm got even wit Ben Amberdahl after long tam. Somtam I'm mebbe-so keel Bill Amberdahl woman, too. Git mor' even. How you p'liss know it me keel Amberdahl? Me, I'm t'ink you arres' Manners, 'cause he say he keel heem!"

"We figured it out, all right," Downey said. "We'll pick up the gun, now, an' you get dressed for the trail. We're hittin' for Dawson."

"I git de gon," the woman said and swiftly slipped into the bedroom. Black John loosened the buttons of his shirt, and grasped the butt of his .45, and Corporal Downey drew his service revolver, both with their eyes on the bedroom door. The next moment the sound of a shot roared out, and both men rushed to the door, to see the woman collapse on the bed. She had placed the muzzle of the gun in her mouth and pulled the trigger.

"Well," Downey said, eyeing the big man. "It looks like the case is closed. I'm glad it happened this way. Somehow, I'd hate to have to hang a woman—even one like her."

THE DAMNATION OF
BLACK JOHN

I

THE MUTES OF LITTLE SANDY

OLD CUSH, PROPRIETOR of Cushing's Fort, the combination post and saloon serving the community that had risen on Halfaday Creek, close against the Yukon-Alaska border, folded the well-thumbed copy of the *Police Gazette* he'd been reading and placed it on the back bar. Almost in the same motion he took up a bottle, two glasses and the leather dice box, as Black John Smith stepped into the room and crossed to the bar.

The big man's glance rested momentarily on the folded paper. "I perceive that you've been perusin' the anatomical architecture of the queens of burlesque," he said.

"I ain't no sech a damn thing!" said Cush. "Them wimmin ain't no queens.

They're a bunch of actresses. Fer as I kin see, they run mostly to legs, like them there cigarette pitchers we use' to trade around amongst us when we was kids!"

"It's just as well, at your age, that you can't see no further," Black John grinned as he picked up the box and cast the dice. "Beat them four treys in one."

"Is that so! Well I take notice that I don't fall fer every good-looking woman that shows up on the crick, like you do. An' some time one of 'em is going to take you good. I'm a four-time loser, myself, an' I know." He gathered the dice into the box and rolled two sixes. He followed with three shakes that netted only three deuces which Black John beat in one throw. They filled their glasses as two young men entered and ranged themselves

"Drop it before you get hurt!"

at the bar, one on either side of Black John who greeted them cordially, "Hello, Joe! Howdy, Jack! Fill up! Cush is buyin' one. How you making it over on Little Sandy?"

"I'm doing all right," Joe replied.

"I'm doing fine," Jack said, as he filled the glass Cush set before him, and shoved the bottle along.

"Fellow staked a location on the crick about a mile above us a couple of days ago," Joe observed.

"Claims his name is Baker," Jack added. "Said he sold his location on Squaw Crick."

*The nickel-plated revolver
dropped to the gravel.*

"H-u-u-m, Baker, eh? Squaw Creek." Black John's brow drew into a frown. "Has he got a pair of close-set shifty eyes, an' a high, thin nose curved down like an eagle's beak?"

"That's him. You know him?"

"Only by sight an' reputation," the big man replied, "an' neither one's anything to brag of."

"Nosey Baker!" Cush exclaimed. "He's about as orney a skunk as they is loose. I rec'lect the time the boys run him off'n Fortymile fer tryin' to beat Sally Britton outa half her pa's location the time Sam got squorshed in that rock slide. He claimed Sam had sold him a half interest, an' then got killed before he could record it. Sally, she'd of fell fer it, too, if the boys hadn't stepped in an' run Nosey off'n the crick. You boys better keep an eye on him. He ain't no one I'd want on no crick with me."

"He'll be too busy to bother anyone for a while, at least," Joe replied. "He's getting out poles for his shack."

"He told me," Jack added, "that after he got his shack up, he's going to start cutting wood to burn in with." The drinks were downed, and he ordered another round, tossing a sack well filled with dust onto the bar. "I want ten pounds of sugar, a pound of tea, a pound of tobacco, ten pounds of salt pork and a fifty pound sack of flour. You might as well weigh out the dust for the whole works while you're at it."

WHEN THE glasses were filled, Joe glanced at a slip of paper he drew from his pocket, as he, too, tossed a sack of dust onto the bar. "I want two boxes of .30-40 cartridges, ten pounds of salt pork, a pound of tobacco, five pounds of beans and a sack of flour. An' take out for another round of drinks. Tell Jack I've got twenty pounds of sugar on hand. I can let him have ten pounds. I'll leave it outside my door when I get home and he can pick it up."

Gravely Cush eyed the other, "Joe says he kin let you have ten pound of sugar. It'll save you packin' it from here."

Jack shrugged. "Tell him I've got an extra box of .30-40s he can have. I'll leave it at his door when I pick up the sugar."

Cush turned to Joe. "He says he's got an extry box of ca'tridges you kin have. He'll leave 'em at yer door."

Following Cush into the storeroom, the two slipped the purchases into their pack sacks, and returned to the barroom where Black John ordered another round. When the glasses were empty, the two shouldered their packs and departed.

"Don't it beat hell," Cush observed, "them two young fellas with adjoinin' claims, an' no one elst on the crick, till that damn Nosey Baker showed up—an' them not speakin' to each other!"

Black John nodded. "Yeah, they used to be pardners. Come in together a year or so ago, an' staked adjoining locations on Shorty Crick. They did all right there till both of 'em got to sparkin' Jeff Carter's girl."

"Seems like every kind of trouble they is starts on account of some damn woman," Cush said. "Take them first three wives of mine—I never know'd what trouble was till I married 'em. After that it was jest one damn thing after another till I got shet of 'em."

The big man grinned. "Well, of course, a man's got to know how to handle 'em."

"Handle 'em hell! You talk like a damn fool! Jest wait till some woman gits her hooks into you—an' you'll damn soon find out who does the handlin'!"

"Be that as it may, as I was going to say, accordin' to the sour-doughs up there on Shorty Crick, Mabel Carter sort of played one against the other—"

"Shore she would," Cush interrupted. "That's the way they work it. I tell you, when it comes to wimmin a man ain't got no show. An' two men's got twict as little as one man's got."

The big man grinned. "I'll figure that one out when I git time. Anyway, this Joe Smally an' Jack Bemis busted up pardnership, sold out on Shorty Crick, an' quit speakin' to each other. A short time later the Carter girl married Bill Mahoney."

Cush nodded somberly. "She would. After raisin' all the hell she could, she married someone elst. But Mahoney ain't no prize package, as she's prob'ly found out by now—an' serves her damn good an' right. I like them two young fellers. They mind their own business, an' work their locations, an' don't hang around here blowin' in their dust, an' shootin' off their mouth, an' raising hell like most of the damn *cheechakos* does. Funny, though, they'd hit out an' locate on a new crick right next to each other—an' them not speakin'. It don't look reasonable. If they hate each other, why didn't they locate on different cricks?"

"They don't hate each other," Black John said. "Bemis told me that, last winter, after they'd busted up, Jack broke his leg an' Joe made the run with a dog outfit clean to Dawson an' fetched Doc Sutherland out to 'tend him. An' Camillo Bill was tellin' me that this spring, when Joe got pneumonia, Jack hung around the hospital there in Dawson till Joe was plumb out of danger. An' you just saw how each one favored the other in the matter of supplies. They don't hate each other. Deep down, they're just as much pals as they ever were. They fell out over that girl, an' quit speakin'—an' now each one is too stubborn, or too proud to be the first to speak."

"Hur. Proudness an' stubbornness! Peacocks is proud an' mules is stubborn, but who the hell would want to be a peacock or a mule, neither one! But, at that, I can't figger out why Nosey Baker would quit Squaw Crick an' come up here an' locate on Little Sandy. Accordin' to what I heard, Nosey was doin' all right there on Squaw Crick."

"Yeah, about a month ago, down in the Tivoli, Burr MacShane told me that Nosey had a good thing there. He also told me that he had sold out."

"Why would he let go of a good proposition an' hit out fer a crick like Little Sandy, which no one knows if it's good er ain't good? Them two lads is the only ones on the crick, an' they don't go around shootin' off their mouth about striking it lucky there."

Black John reached for the bottle and filled his glass. Cush did likewise, and made an entry in his day book. "Hey!" the big man exclaimed. "How the hell do you know this round is on me? We haven't shaken for it yet!"

"If you'd retched fer the box before you retched fer the bottle, we'd of shook," Cush replied. "But the way it is, the drinks is on you."

"No wonder we've got the reputation of bein' a bunch of outlaws here on Halfaday, with you pullin' stunts like that!"

"Uh-huh. You take every damn crook that shows up on the crick fer all he's got, an' then claim I'm an outlaw if you've got to buy a drink. You better quit squorkin' about buyin' a drink, an' start figgerin' out why Nosey Baker hit fer Little Sandy."

"I strongly suspect an ulterior motive."

"You do, eh? Well, what good is it, now you've got it suspected? Does that mean we kin go ahead an' hang Nosey 'fore he gits the chanct to rob them boys?"

"**THE CONCEPT** has merit, but savors rather of crudity. You know, Cush, a man never knows when some seemingly trivial bit of information he picks up may prove to be of prime importance. I told you that Burr MacShane happened to mention that Nosey Baker was doin' well on Squaw Crick, an' that he'd sold out. This casual bit of gossip made no impression on me at the time. But in the light of present developments, an added bit of information looms large on the horizon.

"He mentioned that Nosey sold out to Bill Mahoney. Now, putting two and two together, it adds up something like this: Bill's wife tells him that Jack an' Joe had a fallin' out over her. She tells him they sold out on Shorty Crick, an' got a damn good price. Bein' a crook himself, Mahoney hunts up Nosey Baker an' tells him that these boys hate each other, an' that each has got plenty of dust they took out of their claim, besides the price they sold for. He also tells him they located on Little Sandy with no one else on the crick. That fact is common knowledge in Dawson! Nosey figures that if he watches his chance, he can rob one of 'em—maybe even knock him off, an' bein' as they are known enemies, the other will get blamed for it.

"It's my guess that Nosey, in some devious an' onderhanded way known to crooks, ascertained that the boys made no deposit at the bank. If not, he would hardly trail 'em up to Little Sandy on the chance they'd make a strike on an unknown crick. Assumin' that they packed their wealth in with 'em, and that they would cache it up there, Nosey sells out to Mahoney an' locates on the same crick. The way Nosey's got it figured, all he's got to do is locate one of those caches, rob it, knock off the owner— and the other lad will get blamed for it."

"Why, the son of a gun!" Cush exclaimed. "So now all we got to do is hang Nosey 'fore he locates that cache!"

The big man shook his head. "Not so fast, Cush. We've hung men on Halfaday, an' so far we've never hung the wrong man. We've got to wait till Nosey commits an overt criminal act. What I've told you is merely an assumption, an' we can't hang a man on an assumption."

"Assumption hell! Hang him there on the rafter, like we've hung them others! What the hell do you figger on doin', wait till Nosey knocks one of them boys off 'fore we hang him?"

Black John shrugged. "He may not go that far. After all, there's two of them on the crick, an' only one of him."

"What good's that? Cripes—take it here on Halfaday, men has be'n murdered on the crick, an' they's fifty of us here, an' only one of the murderer!"

"Nevertheless, we can't hang a man suspicion."

"The way I figger, Nosey's got a hangin' comin' anyways you look at him! Didn't he try to beat pore Sally Britton outa her claim there on Fortymile? An' didn't everyone figger it was Nosey robbed that gent down on the Flats, that time?"

The big man grinned. "I'm not arguin' that. Takin' it by an' large, as the Good Book says, Nosey ondoubtless deserves a good thorough-goin' hangin'. But of the two things you mentions, as a matter of fact, he didn't beat Sally Britton out of her claim— and as for him pullin' off that robbery on the Flats, that's mere conjecture. Besides, neither of these suspected offences is within our jurisdiction, an' both are ondoubtless outlawed by the statute of limitations—not to mention *habeas corpus*, an' *pro bono publico*."

Cush shrugged. "Jewishdictions, statues of limitations, habus corpses, an' bony publicos! By God, John, you'd ort to steal you another law book sometime, an' mebbe you could read up how to let some other damn cuss loose to pull off a murder! But I'm tellin' you one thing—it won't do that damn Nosey no good to come over here! I won't sell him a damn thing! If you won't hang him, mebbe I kin starve him off 'n Little Sandy 'fore he locates one of them caches!"

Black John frowned. "Listen, Cush. You know damn well that I'd hate to have anything happen to those boys. I've got a hunch that Nosey will overplay his hand, somehow or other. All we've got to do is give him rope an' he'll hang himself. Let him come over here all he wants to. Sell him anything he wants to buy. The more we can find out about him, the better it is for us, an' the worse for him. You've relied on my judgment before—do it again."

Cush shot the other a shrewd glance. "You mean you figger how mebbe Nosey fetched what dust he had, an' what he got fer his claim up on Little Sandy with him—an' you figger on gittin' holt of it, eh?"

The big man shook his head. "Much as I deplore your avaricious and suspicious nature, Cush, there may be a—"

"You don't need to go ahead an' preach no sermon," Cush interrupted. "All I got to say, I'd hate to be them two boys livin' there on the same crick with Nosey Baker. But even worster'n that, I'd hate to be Nosey Baker, if I had any dust in my cache an' you was lyin' to git it!"

WINTER, WITH its long nights and short, cold days settled upon Halfaday. Nosey Baker made occasional visits to Cushing's Fort for supplies, a few drinks and a session of stud. One, day, shortly after Christmas, Black John accosted him at the bar. "Have a drink, Nosey," he invited. "How you doin' over there on Little Sandy?"

"I'm doin' all right. Got a good location. My pannin' shows I'm takin' out anywheres from eight to ten ounces a day—an' accordin' to that, I'd ort to sluice right around seventeen hundred to two thousan' ounces, come clean-up time."

"That's a good winter's work on a new crick," the big man agreed. "How those two young fellows makin' it, Joe Smally an' Jack Bemis?"

"They're doin' all right, too. 'Bout like me, mebbe a little better. Too bad they don't git along together. Won't even speak to one another, an' them workin' locations right side by side. Accordin' to how I heerd it down to Dawson, they use' to be pardners over on Shorty Crick, till they had a fallin' out over Jeff Carter's gal, her that married Bill Mahoney."

"Yeah, that's the way I heard it. Kind of funny they'd hit out for the same crick, an' stake adjoinin' locations."

Nosey downed his drink and slanted the big man a glance. "Might not be so funny as it looks. I've kinda got acquainted with them boys. Play cribbage with 'em now an' then. Sometimes down to one shack, an' sometimes to t'other one. They don't do no talkin', but I got it doped out that each one's sort of layin' fer the other one. Come clean-up time an' I wouldn't be none s'prised if one of 'em'd knock t'other one off an' light out with all the dust."

Black John nodded. "Kind of looks that way, don't it."

"Shore it does. Too bad, too, 'cause they're sort of nice gents, barrin' them hatin' one another like they do."

Occasionally each of the lads visited the fort for supplies. But Black John noticed that since Baker's first appearance on Little Sandy, only one of them came at a time. "Hello, Joe," he greeted as the younger man stepped to the bar one day and slipped his empty pack from his shoulder. "How's everything on Little Sandy?"

"I'm doing fine. I guess Jack is, too. The test panning shows the gravel's getting richer as it goes down."

"How do you like your neighbor?"

"Baker? Oh, he's all right. Works his claim and minds his own business. Seems friendly enough. Comes down and plays cribbage now and then—sometimes with me, and sometimes with Jack."

When Joe had left with his pack of supplies, Cush eyed Black John across the bar. "That Nosey Baker, he's a damn crook, an' allus was. But the way he's stickin' out there an' workin' his claim, mebbe he's got it figgered out that good stidy work pays better'n what crookedness does."

"Yeah, maybe," the big man replied.

WINTER WORE into spring and one morning as Black John stepped into the saloon, Cush greeted him from behind the bar. "The boys here on the crick is gittin' on with the clean-up, an' if they bank much more dust here the safe won't hold it. The sides is damn near bulgin' out a'ready. Looks like you got to take a batch of it down to Dawson an' stick it in the bank." He paused, set out the bottle, glasses and dice box. "So, when we git the drinks shook fer an' drunk, you better throw yer stuff in yer pack sack whilst I make up the package of dust."

When the glasses were filled Black John glanced at the safe. "Yeah, I noticed last evenin' when you put away those six sacks Long-Nosed John fetched in, that the safe wouldn't hold much more. It ain't that I'm averse to slippin' down to Dawson. Them old sourdoughs down there are in need of further instruction in the rudiments of stud. But this time, Cush, I reckon we better send one of the other boys down with the dust."

"Other boys, hell! You know damn well the boys wouldn't trust no one but you to take their dust down to Dawson!"

"It ain't that I'm seekin' to shirk a duty in declinin' this messenger job, Cush. But the fact is I deem that my absence from Halfaday would be inimical to the welfare of the crick till the returns from the outlayin' precincts are in."

"Meanin' what?" asked Cush.

"Meanin' that so far, no one from Little Sandy has banked any dust here, have they?"

"No."

"An' all three of 'em have be'n workin' their claims all winter, an' accordin' to what they say, they're all doin' well. So, with the clean-up about over, there must be quite a bit of dust cached there on Little Sandy."

"By God, that's right, John! An' you figger if that damn Nosey Baker aims to make a play fer them boys' dust you'd ort to be here when he done it?"

"That's the idea, exactly."

"'Course," Cush hazarded, "it might be, like I says a while back, Nosey might be doin' so good on his own claim that he's turned honest,"

"The concept is absolutely untenable."

Cush scowled. "I know what 'the' means, an' 'is'. But you might better kep' them other three words bottled up. I s'pose yer tryin' to say that Nosey—" He paused suddenly and glanced through the open doorway. "Well, speakin' of the devil, an' damn if there he don't come!"

The man barged into the room and approached the bar, an empty pack sack dangling from his shoulder. "I want a canoe an' enough grub to take me to Dawson!" he demanded.

Black John grinned. "What's yer hurry, Nosey? Cripes, you've got all spring to get to Dawson."

"Like hell I got all spring! I gotta git holt of Corporal Downey!"

"What's Downey be'n up to that you've got to get holt of him?"

"It ain't what Downey's be'n up to, it's that damn Jack Bemis over on Little Sandy. It's happened jest like I figgered it would."

"That," said Black John dryly, "I don't doubt."

"What I mean, it's jest like I told you in the winter—that, come clean-up time, hatin' one another like they do, one of them two lads would knock the other one off an' git away with all the dust! Well, it's two nights, now, Joe Smalley's be'n missin'."

"An' Jack Bemis has made off with all the dust, eh."

"He ain't yet. That's why I gotta find Downey, so he kin lay fer Jack 'fore he hits the Yukon. If Downey can nail him on the White he'll find out he's got his own dust an' Joe Smalley's along with it, onlest Jack's smart enough to cache Joe's dust till the stink dies down. Once he gits on the big river, he's liable to git clean outside. What I claim, any son of a gun that would pull a job like that ort to git hung!"

The big man nodded. "You're dead right, Nosey. He shore ort. But there's no use hittin' clean down to Dawson after Downey. In the first place, the chances are that he couldn't get to the White in time to head Bemis off, anyhow. And in the second place we're in the habit of investigatin' our own atrocities here on Halfaday an' vicinity. You an' I will hit for Little Sandy an' investigate this alleged murder an' robbery. Then we'll fetch the culprit back here an' call a miner's meetin' an' hang him."

He paused and glanced toward the ceiling. "There's be'n a sight of men hung from that rafter right over your head, Nosey, a sight of men. An' every damn one of'em had it comin'. They get a fair trial, an' if the boys vote to acquit him, he goes free. I, myself, present the evidence against him. Then he's given a chance to try an' lie out of it. If he's guilty he's never successful, but often amusin'. The boys vote to hang him, an' as quick as Pot-Gutted John gets the noose tied, he's hung. There's no such quibblin' as the law allows for the obstruction of justice. No stay of execution, no habeas corpus, no demurrer, no *nolle prosse*, no monkey work whatever. He's hung, cut down, an' planted in the graveyard, out back, with his name an' check letter burnt into his slab."

"Check letter? What the hell's a check letter?"

"We use three of'em—H for hung. M for murdered. An' occasionally we use D, for died natural—but not often."

II
BADMAN'S CACHE

AS THEY DESCENDED into the valley of Little Sandy, Black John glanced at the other. "We'll slip down to Jack's cabin first, an' hear what he's got to say about Joe's disappearance."

They arrived at the cabin just as Bemis was about to step into his loaded canoe. "Where you headin'?" Black John asked.

153

"I'm hitting for Dawson. Joe has disappeared, and I'm going down to notify the police. He's not only disappeared, but his, cache has be'n robbed!"

"Oh," Nosey sneered, "so you know'd where his cache was, eh?"

"Sure I do. I know where his cache is, and he knows where mine is."

"So it was a cinch fer you to knock him off an' rob his cache, eh?"

"What! Do you mean to say that I did away with Joe and robbed his cache?" His face white with anger, Bemis lunged at Nosey, with clenched fists.

Black John stepped between them. "Hold on, Jack. What Nosey meant is that, knowin' where Joe's cache is, you had the chance to pull the job."

"But—why—Joe was the best friend I ever had!"

"That's a laugh," Nosey sneered. "Hell, everyone in the Yukon knows you hate one another's guts. You ain't spoke to one another sence you busted up pardnership on Shorty Crick. Best friend—hell! Don't try to hand us none of that guff!"

"It's true we never speak to each other. We fell out over a girl. We vowed never to speak to each other again—and we've stuck to it. Sounds foolish—and I guess it is. Just stubbornness, I suppose. But we're not enemies. We're friends."

"Nosey an' I want to look around a little," Black John said. "Will you show us Joe's cache—an' yours?"

"Sure I will." He led the way to a crevice between two upstanding rocks on Joe's claim and pointed to the empty aperture. Returning, he showed them his own cache beneath an overhanging ledge of rock.

"I see you're cache is empty, too," Nosey said. "Did this here robber git your dust, too?"

"No. I've got my dust there in the canoe."

"Oh," Nosey sneered, "yer hittin' hell bent to Dawson to tell the police about this job, eh? An' you figger you could make better time with a lot of dust in yer canoe, than you could runnin' light, eh?"

The younger man restrained his anger with an effort. "I was taking my dust with me because I was afraid that the same thief that robbed poor Joe's cache, would rob mine, while I was gone. If he knew where Joe's cache is he probably knows where mine is, too. Neither of us suspected that anyone else knew where the caches were till this happened."

"This here dust of yours, what did you keep it in?" Black John asked.

"It's in eighty-ounce moosehide sacks. So was Joe's."

"Were the sacks just alike, yours an' Joe's?"

"Yes, just alike. An Indian woman made them for us over on Shorty Crick. We sewed little private marks on 'em so we could tell 'em apart. They're stitched on the inside near the top with black thread. Mine is an *X*, and Joe's is a *V*."

Black John nodded. "Well, I reckon that's about all we can find out here." He eyed the younger man. "Nosey an' I are goin' to poke around a bit an' see if we can locate Joe's body. You wait here till I come back."

As the two headed up the creek, Nosey frowned. "Hell, John, what with all the places they is to hide a corpse, chances is we could hunt fer a week er a month, mebbe, an' never find him."

"Oh, shore. That is, if we just went at it blind. But if we use our heads it ortn't to take so long." As they reached Nosey's claim, Black John glanced around. "Let's stop here an' try to figure things out," he said, seating himself on the sluice box.

NOSEY FROWNED. "How the hell could anyone figger where Joe is hid at, when they's a thousan' places?"

"Well, for instance—if you were doin' the job—where would you hide him?"

"Who, me! I don't know!"

155

Black John filled his pipe, his glance sweeping the valley. "Yeah, there's a hell of a lot of places, ain't there?" His glance rested on the mouth of the open shaft. "Down in the bottom of a shaft wouldn't be a bad place, would it?" He wondered whether Nosey's eyes didn't twitch just a trifle as he continued. "Speakin' of shafts, looks like you done pretty well for yourself here, Nosey."

"I done all right. Best location I ever had, an' I've had a lot of 'em."

"Took out a lot of dust, eh?"

"Yer damn right I did!" the man replied boastfully. "It'll figger right around thirty thousan' dollars fer my winter's work—an' that ain't bad money!"

"That's right," Black John agreed. "Got her all weighed up an' cached, eh? I s'pose you use eighty-ounce sacks, too—most every one does—handy to pack one of 'em in yer pocket, barrin' the weight."

"Shore. I filled twenty-three of 'em, an' about half of another one."

"Let's take a look at your cache, Nosey."

"My cache!"

"Shore. We looked at Joe's an' Jack's. You've got the only other location on the crick—so let's have a look at yours."

"But, hell, John, you don't figger I robbed Joe, do you? Cripes, if I done it I wouldn't of be'n hittin' fer Dawson to tell Downey, would I? An' I wouldn't of told you about what come off over here, would I? Not by a damn sight I wouldn't! I'd of stuck the dust in my pack sack an' hit fer the outside, that's what I'd of did!"

Black John grinned. "You might, at that. But, such preceedure would have been pretty dumb, Nosey. Dumber, even, than I think you are. You'd know that Jack would report Joe's disappearance and yours, too—an' that he'd report the matter to the police, an' you'd be picked up before you could hit the pass. But if you knocked Joe off an' robbed his cache, believin' as you do that those two lads are mortal enemies, it would look like a smart play to be the first to report the fact that Joe was missin'."

"Yeah, an' that's jest what come off! Any damn fool would know that!"

The big man nodded. "Yeah, any damn fool might, but the trouble with your argument, Nosey, I ain't a damn fool. That's why I want your cache."

"I ain't got no cache. Never had none. So I kep' my dust right there in the shack."

"Okay. Let's step inside. I'd like to look them twenty-three an' a half sacks of dust over. You don't happen to have no identifyin' marks on your sacks?"

"No, I don't. An' they ain't no dust in the shack, neither. I packed it down to Dawson quick as I clent up my dump. I was scairt someone might rob me."

"Deposited it in the bank, eh?"

"No. I ain't got no fish in banks."

"Where is it?"

"It's gone outside, that's where. You see, when I hit Dawson I run acrost an old pal of mine, which he was hittin' fer the outside. So I sent my dust out with him."

"Rather trust this pal than the bank, eh?"

"Yer damn right I would! This guy wouldn't dast to double-cross me! I've got enough on him to hang him higher'n hell in three states!"

"Never heard of a guy gettin' hung in three states," Black John grinned. "But, bein' a pal of yours, he ondoubtless would have it comin'."

"How do you mean by that?" Nosey demanded.

THE BIG man knocked the dottle from his pipe on the edge of the sluice box, and rose to his feet. "Meanin', Nosey, that I've listened to about all the damn lies I can stumick at one settin'. Come on, let's have a look at your cache."

"I tell you I ain't got no cache!"

"Okay, Nosey. In that case we'll just step over there to the rimwall an' follow it along a piece, an' then we'll stoop down an' pull a chunk of rock out of a crack in the wall, an' see what we find. I ain't sayin' it's a cache. Maybe it's just a spring where you get your drinkin' water. I happened to be strollin' along the rim, one evenin', not so long ago, an' I saw you step out of your shack here, look all around, an' then head for this spot in the wall. You knelt down, pulled out a chunk of rock, put the rock back, an' came back to the shack. An' you weren't carryin' no pail of water neither."

Nosey's eyes suddenly narrowed. His hand flew to the front of his shirt and came out with a revolver.

"Drop it before you get hurt!" The man's narrowed eyes widened as they stared into the muzzle of Black John's .45, and the nickel-plated revolver dropped to the gravel. "Turn around an' get goin', Nosey. Head for the rimwall just above that dead tree—in case you've forgot." A few moments later Black John spoke again. "This is the place, Nosey. Stoop down an' jerk out that slab of rock an' we'll see what's behind it." One glance at the unwavering muzzle of the six-gun and Nosey, his face chalk-white, dropped to his knees and removed the slab. Stooping, Black John peered over the man's shoulder into the aperture. "Pull 'em out, Nosey—an' keep on pullin' 'em out till the hole is empty." When the man had finished forty-three and a half little sacks lay on the ground. "The last twenty of 'em I assume belonged to Joe Smally," the big man continued. "But just to make shore, open one of 'em an' see if there ain't a little V stitched on the inside, near the top." When the V was uncovered Black John nodded. "Well, I reckon that clears up the case. Tie it up again, Nosey, an' we'll shove on over to Halfaday an' get on with the hangin'."

Rising to his feet, Nosey stood shaking like a leaf as his quavering voice rose to a scream. "Hangin'! By God, you can't hang me!"

"Maybe not. But we can try damn hard. I recollect that you said that a son of a gun that would pull a job like this ort to get hung."

"But you can't hang me! Joe Smally ain't dead!"

"Ain't, eh?"

"No, he ain't! But, by God, if you hang me he will be! He's in the bottom of an old abandoned shaft way to hell an' gone back in the hills, where no one couldn't never find him before he'd starve to death. An' if he ain't dead, there ain't no murder—an' you can't hang me!"

"You're in error. Accordin' to the code of ethics in effect on Halfaday an' vicinity, cache-robbin', an' every other form of skull-duggery is a hangable offence."

"By God, if you hang me, Joe Smally will die, too!"

"I doubt it. There's fifty-odd men on Halfaday, an' every damn one of 'em knows the country. If they'd scatter out in the hills they'd be sure to find Joe before he starved. However, if Joe's alive, I'll admit you have a bargainin' p'int. Tell you what I'll do. You take me to where you've got Joe hid, an' if he's alive, like you say, I'll promise to turn you loose instead of takin' you to Halfaday to stand trial by miner's meetin'. That's my proposition. Take it, or leave it."

"How about my dust, them twenty-three an' a half sacks? Do I take them along? By God, no dust—no Joe! I ain't goin' to work like hell all winter fer nothin'."

Black John grinned. "Okay, Nosey. If that's the way you feel we'll just call the deal off, an' hit over to Halfaday. I'll get the boys out into the hills. Chances are they'd find Joe before night, anyhow."

NOSEY'S BROW drew into a frown, and he shifted about uneasily. "They might find him, at that," he admitted. "I guess you've got me. I'd hate to git hung."

"Yeah, most of the boys did."

"How much of my dust will you let me keep?"

"Not a damned ounce! There's grub in your shack. Fill your pack sack an' get goin' the minute we get back here with Joe Smally. An' once you leave, don't never come back. This ain't a pardon. It's a twenty-four hour reprieve. If you're here tomorrow you get hung. An', speakin' of grub reminds me—when did you stick Joe down that shaft?"

"It was day before yesterday. I aimed to pull out yesterday but it was rainin' like hell, so I waited till today!"

"Did you leave him anything to eat?"

"No. I hung around till I located this shaft, then I went down to his place like I was goin' there to play cribbage, an' pulled my gun on him, an' made him come along. When we got to the shaft, I tied him up with a lenth of rope an' lowered him down. Here's the rope, we'll fetch it along to haul him up with. It ain't only about twenty foot deep. I told him I was takin' his dust, but I'd leave a note where Jack could find it so he could haul him out after I'd got away."

"Did you leave that note?"

The other scowled. "No. I'd be'n a damn fool to."

"Left him there to starve to death, eh?"

Nosey shrugged. "He might of got out."

"Damn you!" Black John cried. "If I was dead sure the boys would find Joe before he starved, I'd go back on that bargain an' hang you anyhow! If anyone ever deserved a hangin', you do. Throw some grub in your pack an' fetch it along. He's goin' to need a big feed when we git him out of that shaft, or he'll be too weak to walk."

Nosey led the way across a ridge, and for an hour they moved up the valley of a small creek, then turned into a deep gulch, and a few minutes later arrived at the shaft. They found Joe alive and, save for a ravenous appetite, little the worse for his imprisonment. Returning to Nosey's shack, Joe thanked Black John profusely, retrieved his dust, and headed for home.

Nosey shouldered his well-filled pack and reached for his rifle. Black John picked it up. "No firearms, Nosey," he said.

Nosey scowled. "An' who gits that thirty thousan' I worked fer?"

"W-e-e-l-l, off hand, I'd say I do. For years I've considered it my duty to instill the rudiments of honesty into the minds an' hearts of damn scoundrels like you. An' I've found that by far the most convincin' method of demonstratin' to 'em that crime don't pay, is to deprive them of the emoluments of crime—an' I make it a p'int never to shirk a duty. So long, Nosey, you better begin pickin' 'em up an' layin' 'em down."

On his return to Halfaday with the twenty-three and a half little sacks of dust, Black John saw Jack and Joe standing side by side at the junction of their claims. He grinned to himself. "I guess they've made up," he muttered. "It took a jolt like that to put some sense in their heads."

Both greeted him heartily as he paused beside them. "So long, boys, an' good luck," he said. "Be seein' you at Cush's one of these days!"

"That's right!" Jack replied. "And, say, John. Tell Joe I'm sure glad he's back." The big man stopped in his tracks and glanced at Joe. "Jack says he's glad you're back," he announced gravely.

"Tell him thanks," Joe said. "Tell him I'm glad I'm back, too. Tell him I wish him luck."

Black John turned to Jack. "Joe says thanks. He's glad he's back, too. He says he wishes you luck."

Then he turned and headed down the creek. "Well, I'll be damned!" he muttered, as he paused on the rim and glanced back into the little valley.

DEATH STAKES THIS CLAIM!

BOB BAXTER STEPPED into the cabin where his wife was busy at the stove, lifted the scale from the shelf, and weighed and pouched the dust he had brought in from the sluice. Then he returned the scale and pouch to the shelf, and stepping outside, busied himself at the wash bench, while Elsie placed supper on the table. The meal was eaten in silence, and in silence the two washed and dried the dishes.

Seating himself Bob filled and lighted his pipe as Elsie removed four moosehide pokes and a small account book from the shelf and seated herself opposite him. "This is it," she said, eyeing the four well-filled pokes. "This is the clean-up. We'll see how we stand."

The young man nodded somberly. "Yeah, this is it. And I can tell you to an ounce how much dust we've taken out—how much we've got to show for a winter's hard work. Just three hundred and twenty-one ounces—five thousand one hundred and thirty-six dollars."

Elsie raised her eyes from the book and nodded. "That's right, Bob. And we put in two hundred and twelve days to get it. Anyway, that's better than wages."

"Better than wages! I don't see how you figure it's better than wages. It figures only about an ounce and a half a day."

"Yes, and wages are figured at an ounce a day."

"So we would have had two ounces a day if we'd made wages. You've worked just as hard as I have—harder, in fact—because you've chopped wood, tended the fires, shovelled gravel, and cranked the windlass right along with me. And you've done all the housework, besides."

"I didn't mind it, Bob. I loved it—working along with you. Why, ever since I can remember, I've helped Dad do all those things."

"Your dad was a wonderful man, dear. You could go the whole length of the river and you wouldn't find a man that was better liked or more respected than Sunset McCarthy. I've heard the sourdoughs talk, and I know. And that's what hurts—to think that his daughter married a failure. Worse than a failure," he added, bitterly. "She not only married a failure but also a man who sank every cent he left her in a business that won't even pay wages."

The girl's face flushed and her eyes flashed. "Bob Baxter, you shut up! You're not a failure! You've worked hard—harder than any *chechako* I've ever heard of! It isn't your fault the claim's no good. And as for sinking that money in it—it was my money— and you couldn't have invested one cent of it if I hadn't been just as much interested in buying this location as you were. I'm the one that's to blame. I was born and raised in this country. I've heard of salted claims all my life, while you couldn't be expected to know." Tears glistened in her flashing eyes, and her voice faltered slightly. "Calling yourself a failure! I could smack you one for talking like that! Bob Baxter, where are your guts?"

A smile twisted the corners of the young man's lips as he glanced into the glistening eyes. "Gee, Elsie, you're beautiful when you get mad. You're... you're wonderful!"

"You won't think I'm beautiful, or so wonderful either, if I ever hear you call yourself a failure again," the girl replied as she dabbed at her eyes with her handkerchief.

"If I had any guts, I'd hunt up that damned Homer Griffin and shoot him!"

"Oh, sure! Then Corporal Downey would arrest you, and they'd hang you, and everything would be lovely for me, wouldn't it?"

"At least, he'd never cheat another orphan out of everything she had in the world."

"No, but the hangman would cheat one orphan out of everything she's got or ever expects to get in the world. Get hold of yourself, and let's get down to business. We've got a situation to face. It's all right here in the book. We've got five thousand one hundred and thirty-six dollars to our name. We owe Al Scougale twenty-nine hundred and forty-seven dollars for supplies. We owe Dr. Southerland a hundred and twenty-five dollars, and the hospital two hundred and ten, for the time I got that infection. We owe the A.C. Company two hundred and ninety-six dollars, and Campbell's drug store twenty-seven, and the N.A. T. & T. Company three hundred and four dollars. That makes thirty-nine hundred and nine dollars we owe. We'll have to pay seven hundred and seventy dollars and forty cents royalty

"Damn if one of 'em ain't a woman!" he exclaimed.

on this dust—so that leaves us just four hundred and fifty-six dollars and sixty cents."

"Not even enough for a grubstake," Bob muttered. "And you had twenty thousand in cash last fall. So our winter's work netted a cash loss of nineteen thousand five hundred and forty-three dollars and forty cents. And you say I'm not a failure!"

"Listen. Dad went broke three different times—once on Mastodon, once on the Kandik, and again on O'Brian Crick. Yet he never called himself a failure, and neither did anyone else, because he never was one! You're going to make good. We're going to make good. You and I together. Do you hear? We've got to make good! We've got our whole lives before us. Why, Dad was past sixty the last time he went broke, but he came back because he never gave up. He had guts!"

Bob Baxter leaned suddenly forward and banged the table with his fist. "And we'll make good, too, dear! You've got guts, and I'll have to keep up with you. We'll make good together! We'll borrow enough for a grubstake and start all over."

The girl nodded. "We could borrow it, dear. Any one of the sourdoughs would stake us. But if we do it that way, we'll have to split with whoever staked us. We'll go back to Dawson, and I'll go back to work at that Fairview Hotel. Waiting table isn't hard work. The pay is good, and the tips count up mighty fast. You can get a job, either in town, or on some claim at an ounce a day. We'll save every cent we can, and by fall we'll have enough to hit out on our own. There are hundreds of cricks that have never been prospected—maybe thousands of them. We'll just have to shove on farther back than the *chechakos* go. We'll hit up the Sixtymile and work back toward the Alaska border. I've heard Dad and the sourdoughs talk, and they figured there ought to be some good cricks in there, near the border."

OLD CUSH, proprietor of Cushing's Fort, the combined trading post and saloon that served the little community of outlawed men that had sprung up on Halfaday Creek, hard against the Yukon-Alaska border, scowled. He glared at the dice that Black John Smith had rolled out onto the bar. "After this you roll them dice out clean, an' don't foller 'em along with the box! When I first looked there was only three sixes, but now there's four to beat."

"Well, why don't you beat 'em?"

"Four sixes is hard to beat in one. Three ain't so bad. An' that's all I'd had to beat if you hadn't flipped one over with the corner of the box!"

"Your premise is manifestly untenable," the big man grinned, eyeing the leather receptacle into which Cush was returning the dice. "The box, being circular in form, has no corners. If, in castin' the dice, I inadvertently..."

"One more big word outa you, an' by God, I'll set the box on the back bar an' charge you up with a round of drinks! I'd trust you with all the dust I've got in the safe an' never lose an ounce. But when it comes to shakin' dice for the drinks, there ain't no low-down ornery trick you wouldn't pull. Then you try to hide behind a string of big words which anyone would know is a damn lie to start with!" He cast three fours and, gathering the dice, set out a bottle and glasses. "The drinks is on me," he said. "But after this you hoist up the box clean after you roll them dice out, an' don't follow 'em along like you done."

As Black John filled his glass, Cush's eyes widened as he glanced past him toward the open door. "Here comes someone, an' damn if one of 'em ain't, a woman!" he exclaimed. "By Cripes, just as if we don't have trouble enough on Halfaday—what with the damn riff-raff that drifts in on us—one of 'em's got to be a woman! One woman can raise more hell on a crick than forty men, an' the devil of it is, you can't hang 'em!"

"Oh, I don't know, Cush," the big man grinned. "We've never tried it."

"Well, who the hell would want to? Somehow it don't seem right."

"Considerin' your postulate in its broader aspect, I'm inclined to admit that promiscuous woman hangin', takin' it bye an large..."

"Yeah, an' you kin chop it off right there!" Cush interrupted. "Cause here they come. This here woman done me one good turn, if she never done another. She saved me from havin' to listen to a damn lecture."

As the two newcomers stepped into the room, the eyes of the young woman widened. "Oh, aren't you Black John Smith?" she asked. "Isn't this Cushing's Fort, on Halfaday Crick?"

White teeth flashed beneath the black beard. "You hit the bull's eye twice. An' I might add that the party behind the bar is Lyme Cushing, better, an' more or less favorably, known as Old Cush."

Cush bobbed his head in acknowledgement of the introduction, and set out two more glasses. "Step up," he invited. "The house is buyin' one."

As they approached the bar, the young woman smiled. "I'm Elsie Baxter, and this is my husband, Bob. We're on a prospecting trip."

"Shoved up the White, an' then up Halfaday, eh?"

"No. We shoved up the Sixtymile, and then struck out overland. We've put in a month prospecting in the mountains."

"You mean you come through from the Sixtymile afoot?"

"That's right," Baxter replied. "We've panned gravel on a lot of cricks. But we haven't struck anything worth-while."

Black John shoved the bottle toward them. "Drink up," he said. "There's a lot of rough country between here an' the Sixtymile."

The young man poured his liquor, and his wife smiled as she picked up the bottle. "I've lived in this country all my life," she said, "and this is the first time I've ever had a drink over a bar."

The big man returned the smile. "Well, live an' learn, as, the Good Book says. You mean you were born in this country?"

"Yes. I was born on Mastodon Crick, over on the Alaska side. You knew my father, Sunset McCarthy."

"Sunset McCarthy! You bet your life I knew him! I was sure sorry to hear he died, about a year or so back. He did me a good turn once—a damn good turn. But he died before I got a chance to even up the score."

"Yes, Dad died last year. We had a location on Steele Crick, on the Fortymile. When Dad died, I sold the location and went to Dawson where I worked for Belinda Mulrooney, waiting table at the Fairview Hotel. Then I met Bob, and we got married. I've seen you a good many times in Dawson."

Black John nodded and raised his glass. "We'll drink this one," he said, "to the memory of Sunset McCarthy, one of the best men that ever hit the country." When the glasses were returned to the bar, he indicated the bottle. "Fill 'em up again. Sunset would never have quit on one drink."

The young woman smiled. "No, but his daughter would. The fact is neither Bob nor I drink much. You'll excuse us, won't you?"

"Why sure! Non-drinkin' isn't a bad fault, if done in moderation. You say you got here overland. Where's your packs?"

"We slipped them off at the edge of the clearing. You see, we didn't know where we were, nor what kind of a place this was. When we saw those graves, with the rows of slabs, we thought maybe it was a mission of some kind. But this didn't look like a church."

Black John chuckled. "No, this isn't exactly a church. An' there's damn few saints buried in the graveyard. Mostly they're characters we hung for one thing or another. Some of 'em was murdered. An' a few died natural deaths."

"You hung them!" Baxter exclaimed. "You mean there's a police post here?"

"No. These miscreants were hung without benefit of the clergy or the police. They were tried an' convicted by miner's meetin'."

"Bob's a *chechako*," the young woman said. "So he doesn't know about miner's meetings. But he's the pick of all the *chechakos* I ever saw. So I married him."

The big man smiled. "He won't be a *chechako* long—married to you. I'm bettin' that if any woman could make a sourdough out of a *chechako*, it would be the daughter of Sunset McCarthy. There was a real sourdough!"

"He'll make a sourdough, all right. He isn't afraid of hard work. By the way, I've heard a lot about Cushing's Fort, here, your miner's meetings, and how you're all supposed to be outlaws. I've heard Dad and the sourdoughs tell about how a lot of crooks hit for here because it lies close to the line. And they all say that you do a better job than the police could in keeping the crick free of crime. Even Corporal Downey admits it. I've heard that this is a trading post as well as a saloon. I sure hope so because we're mighty short of supplies."

"Oh sure. You can get anything you want. Where you headin' from here?"

The young woman shrugged. "We aren't heading for any place in particular. We're prospecting every crick we come to. And some place we're going to make a strike."

"I suppose the country around here has been pretty well looked over," Baxter said.

"Well, there's been some prospectin' done. Some of the boys struck it pretty lucky. It isn't so bad. A man can take out wages on Halfaday or any of the feeders."

"We're not hunting a wages proposition," Elsie said. "We want a real strike. And we're going to keep on shoving back into the hills till we make one."

A PUFF of cold air fanned the room, and Black John's glance sought the open doorway, where a thin scattering of snowflakes swirled past. Then he looked again at the girl. "It's gettin' pretty late in the fall to go shovin' back into the hills from here," he said. "The freeze-up isn't far off now. If you made a strike, you wouldn't have time to put up a decent shack before winter hits. You're a sourdough so I'm not tellin' you anything—just remindin' you of it."

Elsie Baxter nodded. "Yes, I know. But both Bob and I worked for wages all summer in Dawson. Then we hit out on our own. We're going to make a strike. And we won't turn back now. We don't want to work for wages again. Dad wintered through once with nothing but a shelter tarp on the Kandik. And if he could do that, Bob and I can winter in a tent."

The big man nodded. "Yeah, you prob'ly could. But it's a mighty rough country you're tacklin'. Plenty of snow. Plenty of cold. Even if you struck a good proposition, it would have to lay close to a brulee or you couldn't get the wood to burn in with. You know as well as I do that it's a hell of a job to burn in with green wood."

"We're not afraid of hard work," Baxter said.

"No one that's come through the country you've just tackled is afraid of hard work."

"You're suggesting that we go back to Dawson and start out in the spring? Go back and work all winter for wages?"

Black John shook his head. "No. But I've got a suggestion to make. There's a feeder a few miles above here—Whiskey Crick, we call it, on account of a fellow name of Whiskey Bill located there a while back. There's a good cabin on it. Bill did all right there. A lot better than wages.

Then he quit an' hit back for Indiana, or Kentucky, or wherever he came from, with dust enough to buy a farm. He got so homesick for a whiff of a barn that he couldn't stand it any longer. You two could relocate that claim an' winter there. There's plenty of dry wood handy, an' Bill's sluice an' rocker could be fixed up without much work. That location might be damn good. Whiskey Bill pulled out just as quick as he took out dust enough to buy a farm. Two, three others has moved into the shack temporarily, but none of 'em leaned very heavy on a shovel. If you don't strike it lucky there, if your clean-up don't suit you in the spring, you can hit out an' have all summer to prospect in the hills."

The young woman's eyes lighted. "I believe you're right!" she exclaimed. "I knew it was going to be tough wintering through in a tent. But it would be better than working for wages. We'd be on our own. But this way we can winter comfortably and still make better than wages. But, won't Bob have to go to Dawson to record the location?"

"No. The law says that five people or more, providin' they're a hundred miles from a recorder's office, can appoint a temporary recorder. When the boys drop in this evenin', I'll have myself app'inted. I'll be makin' a trip to Dawson before long an' record the location for you."

"Oh, that's just wonderful! How can we ever thank you?"

"Listen, Sunset McCarthy has already thanked me for anything I can do for his daughter. Don't you forget it!"

"When can we hit for Whiskey Crick?"

"You better throw your stuff in One-Eyed John's cabin for the night. It's only a little way from here. Then I'll take you up to Whiskey Crick in the mornin'."

"But," Baxter asked, "won't this One-Eyed John object?"

"You might slip out to the graveyard and ask him," the big man grinned. "We hung him a while back."

II
THE SOURDOUGHS' BET

A WEEK AFTER the Baxters moved into Whiskey Bill's cabin, Black John made a trip to Dawson. After recording the Whiskey Creek location for the Baxters, he strolled into the Tivoli Saloon to be welcomed by the little group of sourdoughs who had gathered at the end of the bar.

Old Bettles greeted him with a grin. "By Cripes, John, it's about time you was showin' up! We ain't seen hide nor hair of you since the Fourth of July. We was worried for fear you'd broke some law an' skipped the country before Downey caught up with you."

"Yeah? Well, if all the laws I haven't broke was piled one on top of the other, a tall man couldn't see over the top of 'em."

Burr MacShane chuckled. "An' if all the laws you have broke was piled up similar, two tall men, one standing on the other's shoulders, couldn't see over the top of 'em."

Camillo Bill turned to the bartender. "Set out the bottle, Curley. Maybe about three drinks from now, I'll have them propositions figgered out."

As the glasses were filled, two men stepped into the room and took places well down the bar. "There's that damn Homer P. Griffin," Bettles said in an undertone. "Dresses up like a dude an' hires two rooms at the hotel, instead of one, an' an office down the street."

"Yeah," Moosehide Charlie added, "real estate office he calls it, but it ain't nothin' but a damn gyp joint."

"Keeps a good dog team an' a Siwash to handle 'em," Camillo Bill said. "An' when he hits the trail, he rigs out in one of them fancy Eskimo parkas with tails down the back, an' a fur-trimmed hood, an' his mukluks is edged around the top with white fox fur."

"An' in the summer he hires two Siwashes to do his paddlin' for him," Burr MacShane sneered. "You should see him!"

"Who's that with him?" Moosehide asked.

"I dunno," Swiftwater Bill replied. "Some poor sucker he aims to trim, I guess. Look at him slappin' a hundred dollar bill on the bar to pay for them two drinks. The damn four flusher!"

"He's got plenty of ready cash, all right," Bettles said. "He bought Sid Mercer's location for sixty thousan' in cash, an' sold it next day to the Consolidated for a hundred an' ten thousan'."

"He's welcome to what money he's got—the way he gets it," Swiftwater Bill growled. "Some of his deals might be on the up-and-up, but most of 'em ain't, by a damn sight. He beat poor old Joe Casper out of his location on Hunker, an' took Fred Simms for all he had on Fortymile."

"Yeah," Bettles agreed, "an' he's beat plenty of others out of all they had, too. Nothin' rough. Trick clauses in contracts, salted claims. Any damn racket he can think up that keeps inside the law. Someone ought to shoot the son of a gun."

"What," Black John grinned, "an' let the public administrator handle all that ready cash! Shame on you, Bettles! Don't you know that shootin' a man is illegal?"

The sourdoughs chuckled, and Burr MacShane slanted the big man a glance. "God be with you, John, if you've got any ideas in your head. I'd sure like to see someone take him for what he done to young Bob Baxter an' his wife. He sold 'em a salted location there on Ophir. This Bob Baxter's a damn good kid. He worked for me all summer on Bonanza. He's a *chechako*, but he's got most of the *chechakos* beat a mile. He ain't afraid of hard work, an' he don't claim to know it all. He married Elsie McCarthy last fall. You rec'lect Sunset McCarthy, don't you, John? He died a while back on Steele Crick."

Black John nodded. "Yeah. I knew Sunset McCarthy. He did me a good turn once. It was one of them things a man don't ever forget. You say this Griffin sold them young folks a salted claim?"

"Sure, he did. They know'd they was gypped, but they never done no whinin'. They saved money, an' this fall damn if they didn't hit out on a prospectin' trip. I tried to talk 'em out of it—told 'em to wait till spring to start out. But they wouldn't, and Elsie said they was goin' to hit further back from the river than the *chechakos* ever go. I sure hated to see 'em pull out. I'd say they ain't got more'n an even chance to winter through—let alone make a strike. What do you think, John?"

"Well, takin' it by an' large—what with her bein' Sunset McCarthy's daughter, an' all—I'd say, off hand, that they might do all right."

"You wouldn't like to make a bet on it, would you?" Swiftwater Bill asked. "I mean an even money bet that they'll winter through an' come out with better'n wages to show for it?"

"Why, yeah, I might take a bet on them terms."

"For how much?" Swiftwater asked.

"Well, let's see," the big man grinned, "there's five of you here—the same five, I rec'lect that set in on that stud we had on the night of the Fourth of July, the last night I was in town. An' I rec'lect that you boys took me for fifteen thousan'. This here Elsie Baxter, bein' Sunset McCarthy's daughter, born an' raised in the country, an' a sourdough right down to her boot heels—an' this Bob Baxter, bein', as Burr says, a good hard workin' young fellow, it looks to me like they've got a fair chance of comin' out in the spring with better than wages.

"Now, I wouldn't want to gouge you boys none, bein' all friends together, but I'd kinda like to get that fifteen thousan' back, along with a fair profit—say fifteen thousan' more on top of it. Such bein' the case I'll bet thirty thousan', even money, that them two young folks will winter through an' come out in the spring with better'n wages to show for the venture. You can split the bet anyway you want to. Just let me know so I'll know who to collect from in the spring."

"Who to pay, you mean!" Swiftwater jibed. "I'd sure like to take it all. But I'm no hog. Suppose we all go after that thirty thousan', takin' six thousan' apiece for the five of us?"

EACH OF the sourdoughs claimed his share of the bet, and Moosehide Charlie glanced at his watch. "Seven o'clock," he announced. "How about startin' a game of stud? If we git goin' now, we kin have a good long session."

Black John shook his head. "I ain't had supper yet. Just hit town an' stopped in here for a drink or two before I eat. You boys go ahead. I'll slip over to the restaurant an' be back pretty quick."

As he headed for the door, Griffin stopped him. "Aren't you Black John Smith, of Halfaday Creek?" he asked.

The big man nodded. "That's right."

"You were pointed out to me on the Fourth of July, but I didn't get a chance to speak to you. I've heard a lot about you, though."

"Nothin' detrimental to my character, I hope."

The man grinned and winked. "Not at all. In fact it was all to the good. My name's Griffin, Homer P. Griffin, Griff, to my friends. Will you have a drink?"

"Not right now. I just had a few. I'm goin' to get somethin' to eat."

The sourdoughs, who had seated themselves at the card table, eyed the two standing near the bar. "Watch Black John," Swiftwater Bill said, in an undertone. "Remember what John said about it bein' too bad if someone was to shoot Griffin, an' the public administrator got hold of all his cash? I'm bettin' he's got an eye on that cash, himself, an' that he'll make friends with Griffin an' then take him."

"Boy, I hope so!" Bettles exclaimed.

"Griffin, he's pretty smart," Camillo Bill stated. "If anyone can take him, John can, but I'm doubtin' even he could do it."

As Black John started for the door, Griffin said, "I've heard that you're about the cleverest guy in the Yukon."

"Oh? I get along."

The other grinned. "Me too, brother. I guess you and I talk the same language. I claim it's every man for himself. Isn't that right?"

"Yeah."

"Drop in and see me while you're in town. My office is down the street a piece. It has any name on the window. You can't miss it. I've got a hunch that you and I can do business."

Black John eyed the speaker coldly. "I've been hearin' things about you, too, Griffin. An' what I heard wasn't good. If it's true that you're a crook an' a swindler, I wouldn't want a damn thing to do with you."

The other's face flushed a deep red, then turned white with anger.

"Okay, Smith," he growled. "And that goes for you, too." Then he turned abruptly away.

An hour later, as Black John joined the others at the stud table, Swiftwater Bill glanced across at him. "We heard you tell Griffin off," he said. "He sure had it comin'. But we was hopin' you'd sort of play up to him, an' then take him in some kind of a deal. You sure as hell won't never get him in no deal from now on. He hates your guts. Cripes, he was so mad his voice shook!"

The big man nodded slowly as he stacked his chips before him. "That's so, ain't it? Kinda seems like I overlooked a bet. Must be gettin' sort of careless. Well, anyway I had the satisfaction of tellin' him what I think of him."

Bettles grinned. "You sure did. But if only you could of played up to him, an' worked him into some kind of a deal, an' took him for big money… It looks like you paid a hell of a price for your satisfaction."

Again Black John nodded. "Yeah, it does at that, don't it? Come on. Whose deal is it? We can't set here all night cryin' over somethin' that's already done. I'm pullin' out in the mornin'."

ON HIS return from Dawson Black John stepped into the saloon at Cushing's Fort to find Elsie and Bob Baxter about to start for Whiskey Creek with supplies. "How you makin' out, up there?" he asked.

"We're doing all right," Elsie replied. "We shoved an unfinished shaft on down to bedrock, and the test pannings show a lot better than wages. We're down four or five feet with a new shaft, and we're taking out wages practically on the surface. I don't believe we'll make a real strike on that location, but we're on our own. We're not working for somebody else."

"That's right," the big man replied. "An' you can't never tell when you'll strike it lucky. I was talkin' to Bettles, an' Burr MacShane, an' some of the boys down to Dawson, an' they said you two had a location on Ophir."

"We did have," Baxter replied. "But we abandoned it. The test pannings were okay, so we bought it. We worked it all last winter and just about made expenses. The damned crook had salted it. It was my fault. I was a sucker."

"It was more my fault than Bob's," Elsie said. "I should have known better."

"You didn't say nothin' about this swindle when you hit here."

Baxter shrugged. "It certainly wasn't anything to brag about. And there's no use whining about it. Elsie and I are looking ahead, not behind."

"Griffin, this fellow's name is, eh? I ran across a man named Griffin down to Dawson—Homer P. Griffin, he claimed his name is."

"That's the man!" Baxter exclaimed. "The damned scoundrel!"

"Nice talkin' fellow. Wears good clothes. Seemed right friendly."

"Don't have anything to do with him!" Elsie warned. "It was his friendliness, and his nice talk that roped us in."

"They say he's got plenty of ready cash."

"Why wouldn't he have?" Baxter growled. "We heard later that he'd cheated several others out of everything they had in the world."

"Doubtless a contemptible character," Black John agreed. "But, at that, some of them Ophir Crick claims turned out mighty good. Maybe that investment you made wasn't so bad, after all."

"That location will never be any good," Elsie said. "We sank two shafts clear down to bedrock, and the farther we went down the leaner the gravel got. The only money that location will ever make is right now in Homer P. Griffin's pocket. It's the twenty thousand we paid him for it."

"The place to look for something," the big man said, with seeming irrelevance, "is where you lost it."

Bob Baxter grinned. "You mean that maybe Elsie and I could salt a claim somewhere and sell it to Griffin? He'd never fall for a play like that. They say he's mighty shrewd."

"Cripes, no! Claim saltin' is a crude form of skullduggery, besides bein' unethical in the extreme an' downright illegal, if it could be proved."

"Even so," Baxter replied, "I wouldn't have any compunction against paying Griffin back in his own coin. But, after taking us like he did, he'd be doubly wary of any deal we proposed."

"You're prob'ly right," Black John agreed. "But there's nothin' in the book that says you couldn't take him on some deal *he* proposed—providin', of course, that the deal, was advantageous to you, an' he was to lay the cash right on the barrel head."

Elsie laughed. "Any deal he proposed would have to be mighty advantageous. And you bet he'd have to lay the cash right on the barrel head. But, I guess we won't have to worry about his making us any proposition. He took us for all we had, and he knows it.

"We better be hitting out now, or we won't get home before dark. This is the last trip we'll be making till after the clean-up. We shot two moose the other day, and we've got supplies enough now to winter through on. We want to thank you again for letting us relocate that claim of Whiskey Bill's. We're taking out better than wages, and we're wintering in a good cabin instead of a tent. In the spring we can start out from here and make a play for a real strike."

When the two had gone, Cush faced the big man across the bar. "You know, John, when them two first hit here, an' I seen one of 'em was a woman, I started raisin' hell about it. But, by God, she's all right!"

"Sure she is. Cripes, Cush, there's a lot of good women in the world."

"It's a damn wonder a man wouldn't run onto one of 'em, now an' then. Look at the women that's drifted in on us! By God, if they ain't tramps, they're somethin' worse—all but her, an' maybe a couple more. An' look at them four wives of mine! Only one good one out of the bunch—an' she up an' died on me. I'm tellin' you, when it comes to women, the odds ain't right!"

Black John grinned. "Well, hell, Cush, you've got to consider the odds. The reputation of Halfaday bein' what it is, you couldn't expect no hell of an influx of good women. An' about your four wives—one look at you an' a good woman would run like hell the other way."

"Is that so! Well I never seen no hell of a lot of good women clawin' to git at you! You ain't never married even one. An' if you did, she'd have to be ornier'n hell or she wouldn't have done it."

"Set out the box, Cush," the big man chuckled, "an' I'll beat you out of a drink. I need one to help unravel your complicated misuse of syntax," Black John said.

"Sin tax, hell! If there was a sin tax, you wouldn't have a damn ounce of dust left to your name. There. Beat them three fives in one!"

THE SPRING clean-up was well under way on Halfaday when one morning Black John shouldered his rifle and struck off up the creek. Striking into the hills, he paused on the rim of Whiskey Creek and looked down on the two figures who were busy sluicing out the dump on Whiskey Bill's old claim. "Couple of damn fine youngsters," he muttered, aloud.

Descending into the little valley, he stepped out of the scrub and greeted the two who were busy at the sluice. "Hello, folks. How you makin' out?"

The girl was the first to answer, as they turned to face him. "We've done all right," she smiled. "We should finish the clean-up tomorrow. We've already taken out seven hundred and twenty-five ounces. That's more than twice as much as we took out on Ophir, and we've put in ten days less time. We've got a grubstake now that will keep us going till we make a real strike."

"And we've got you to thank for it," Baxter added. "We paid twenty thousand for that Ophir location, and you located us here for nothing. We've wintered in a comfortable cabin and taken out better than three and a half ounces a day."

The girl's smile widened as she glanced at the rifle in the big man's hand. "You must be pretty hungry to be hunting this time of year. Even the yearlings' meat is bitter with the taste of spruce."

Black John nodded. "Yeah, an' it's kinda tough an' stringy, to boot. But it beats no meat. I run out the other day."

"Come to the cabin. We were about to knock off for dinner, anyway. I'll fry you a nice thick steak off a two-year-old dry cow we killed last fall. It's the best meat in the world. How does that sound?"

"It sounds too good to pass up. What are we waitin' for? Let's go," he grinned.

"I don't know how we can ever thank you," Baxter said, as the two lighted their pipes at the conclusion of the meal.

"Like I told you back there at Cush's, Sunset McCarthy has already thanked me for any good turn I could do his daughter. You say you figure to clean up your dump tomorrow. What you goin' to do, then?"

"Why, we're going to hit out and try to make a real strike." He paused and turned to the girl. "Isn't that right, Elsie?"

"Sure, it's right! We'll never quit till we make a strike."

"You're a real sourdough. An' I'm bettin' you'll make good. But it'll be a month yet before you can do any good prospectin' back in the hills. The cricks are all runnin' bankfull, an' the snow is still layin' thick in the narrow valleys."

"I know that," the girl replied. "We could stick around here, but I thought we might run down to Dawson for a few days. There are some things I need that I can't get at Cush's. And there's no telling how long we'll be gone when we hit out into the hills. We could get a canoe at Cush's and slip down to Dawson, couldn't we?"

"Sure you can. I'll loan you my canoe. That'll work out fine for me, too. Fact is, I've got a bunch of dust I'd like to bank, an' it would save me a trip—that is, if it wouldn't be too much trouble."

"There's nothing we can ever do for you that will be too much trouble," the girl replied. "That settles it. We'll hit out for Dawson day after tomorrow. How much dust do you want to send down?"

"Oh, I couldn't say, off hand. Somewheres around fifteen, sixteen hundred ounces, prob'ly."

"Gosh!" Baxter exclaimed. "That's right around a hundred pounds! You must have a mighty good location."

"Oh, it ain't too bad."

"And you want us to deposit it in the bank?"

"That's right. You'll have to stop at the police detachment an' pay the royalty, first. Then take the rest to the bank an' deposit it in your own name."

"In our own name!" the girl exclaimed. "Why, what do you mean?"

The big man smiled. "Don't get excited. I ain't makin' you a present of it. It's a simple business proposition. As you mentioned down to Cush's, the day you hit there, we're supposed to be outlaws up here on Halfaday, an'…"

"Yes, but you're not outlaws! Dad had the greatest respect for you. And Corporal Downey says—"

"Yeah," Black John interrupted, his smile widening. "I'll admit the p'int is debatable. We won't go into details. But, the fact is, there's someone there in Dawson that would fall all over himself to slap some kind of legal attachment on any money he found out I had in the bank. He's a saloon keeper. Runs the Klondike Palace."

"Oh, you mean that horrible Cuter Malone!" the girl exclaimed.

"That's right. He figures I sort of got the best of him, one time on a deal, an' he's layin' for a chance to get even—him an' his crooked lawyer."

"I hope you did get the best on him! Sure, we'll deposit the dust in our name. Then we can make the deposit slip over to you."

"That's it, exactly."

Bob Baxter smiled. "It looks like you're taking an awful chance, trusting around twenty-five thousand dollars worth of dust to a couple of people you've only seen two or three times."

"Listen, son," Black John said, removing the pipe from his mouth and pointing at the girl with the stem. "I'd' trust the daughter of Sunset McCarthy with anything I've got in the world. Sunset McCarthy was a sourdough, an' his daughter is a sourdough. When you've been in the country longer, you'll get to know what that word, 'sourdough' means."

The younger man nodded. "I think I'm beginning to know," he replied, in a voice that choked slightly. "At first I thought it meant just guts and hard work. But I'm beginning, to see that it means something else, too."

"That's right, son—a hell of a lot of somethin' else." He rose from the table and, picking up his rifle, turned to the girl. "That's the best dinner I've had in a long time, sister. It's the kind of a dinner a man don't soon forget. Cush's mouth is shore goin' to water when I tell him about it. I'll be shovin' along, now. By the way, when you get to Dawson, if anyone should offer to buy this location, don't sell it cheap."

"Why, I don't suppose anyone in Dawson has ever heard of it!" the girl exclaimed. "And even if they had, all they'd know is that Whiskey Bill took out better than wages. And even if they found out at the recorder's that Bob and I had relocated it, they wouldn't figure we're doing any better on it than Whiskey Bill did, because we're not."

"That's right," Black John agreed. "That's the way most folks would look at it. But you can't never tell. Someone might get the idea that you'd made a hell of a strike, here... someone like... well someone like this Homer P. Griffin, for instance."

The girl laughed "I'd sure like the chance to sell out to Griffin, after what he did to us down on Ophir. But I'm afraid he'd never invest good money in a proposition he never saw. He's crooked as they make 'em, and smart, along with it."

"He's crooked, all right. But I've noticed that damn few crooked men are really smart. The crookeder they are, the easier it is to take 'em."

"He took us for twenty thousand—every cent we had—and I wouldn't have any compunction about selling him a location we're about to abandon. If we could get our money back, it would serve him right."

"Gettin' your money back wouldn't pay the bill, by a damn sight. Look at the time you wasted. If you hadn't bought that Ophir claim, you might have hit out an' made a real strike. If he shows an interest in this proposition, don't you sell it for a damn cent less than a hundred thousan'. Hold out for a hundred an' fifty thousan'. An' if you deal with him, don't take anything but cold cash or dust. No check, no note, no part payment with more to come later. Make him lay the full amount right on the barrel head—every damn cent of it."

"Okay," the girl said. "We'll do just as you say. That's a promise."

III
PAID IN CASH

THREE DAYS LATER the two outfitted at Cush's for the trip to Dawson. Black John and Cush accompanied them to the landing where the big man placed a small, but heavy, pack in the canoe. "There she is—fifteen hundred an' twenty-five ounces. Pay the royalty at detachment and deposit the balance to your account in the bank, like I told you."

As she took her place in the bow, the girl smiled up into the bearded face. "All right, Uncle John," she cried, as they pushed off. "We'll be seeing you!"

As the canoe disappeared around a bend, Cush eyed the big man with a scowl. "Uncle John," he growled. "Damn near every good lookin' young woman in the Yukon callin' you Uncle John.

An' the way you shove the dust out to 'em, it looks like your unclein' comes damn high!"

"What did you mean—shove out the dust to 'em?"

"What do I mean! Cripes, didn't I stand here an' hear you tell her to deposit the dust in the bank in her own name? It's your dust. Or it was till you up an' give it away. 'I'll be seein' you,' she says. Why the hell wouldn't she be seein' you at fifteen hundred an' twenty-five ounces a see?"

"That dust is still mine. I ain't givin' it to her. She'll deposit it an' make the slip over to me."

"That's what you think. I've warned you a hundred times that someday some good lookin' woman's goin' to take you for plenty. This might be the time. You'd be gittin' off cheap, at that, if it learned you a lesson. One of 'em might take you for a damn sight more. You've been lucky, so far, but luck like yours can't hold."

The big man grinned. "It's an incontrovertible fact, Cush, that your cerebral metabolism is—"

"I ain't goin' to stand here an' listen to no sermon about somethin' which I ain't got neither one of. Come on, I'll shake you for a drink."

As he faced Cush across the bar, Black John smiled. "Just one drink, or maybe two, an' then I'm pullin' out."

"Pullin' out! Out for where?"

"Dawson."

"Dawson! If you're so hell-bent on goin' to Dawson, why didn't you go with them two? Then you could of banked your own dust. Or else, why can't you wait a week or so, till most of the boys finishes their clean-up an' take down a batch of dust an' deposit it? When they begin fetchin' in their dust, the safe won't hold it!"

"Plenty of time to take the dust down later. Fact is, I'm goin' to Dawson to collect a bet. The reason I didn't go down with the Baxters, I didn't want to crowd the canoe."

"Crowd the canoe! Three folks an' a little jag of dust in a two-ton freight canoe! An' you shovin' that young woman better'n fifteen hundred ounces of dust just because she's good lookin'! By God, John, I'd sure as hell think you was crazy, if I didn't know you ain't."

Cutting across by way of the Sixtymile, Black John arrived in Dawson late one afternoon. Registering at the hotel, he seated himself at a window that commanded a view of the door of Griffin's office, and of the Tivoli saloon. "Them young folks ought to be pullin' in tomorrow," he muttered aloud, "an' I'm bettin' it ain't goin' to take 'em no hell of a while to do business with Homer P. Griffin."

He saw Swiftwater Bill and Bettles step into the Tivoli, and a half hour later Griffin left his office in company with two men, and proceeded to the saloon.

Sauntering across the street, Black John burst into the Tivoli, and, without glancing to right or left, hastened toward the little group of sourdoughs who had gathered in their usual place toward the end of the bar. "Any of you boys seen young Bob Baxter?" he demanded, in a loud voice.

Swiftwater Bill was the first to reply. "No, an', what's more we might never see him again. You rec'lect that him an' his wife hit out late last fall way to hell an' gone, an' when we figgered they couldn't winter through an' come out, in the spring with better'n wages, you bet they could. You put up thirty thousan' against our six thousan' apiece for the five of us that they'd make it. What did you come down for—to pay that bet?"

"Not by a damn sight! I'll be collectin' on that bet—not payin' it."

"Have you saw them two this spring?" Moosehide Charlie asked.

"I damn well want to see 'em! I want to buy their location."

"Buy their location!" Bettles cried. "Where's it at?"

"It's on Whiskey Crick. An' accordin' to the Siwash, they busted into gravel that's like some of them rich claims on Bonanza."

"Where in hell is Whiskey Crick?" Burr MacShane asked.

"It's a little crick way back in the hills. They went in by way of the Sixtymile. When this Siwash told me about it, I hit out for there. They'd pulled out, leavin' a note in the shack that they was hittin' for Dawson to bank their dust. I done some pannin' in their shaft, an' in the crick right beside it, an', believe me, I never seen nothin' like it! I want that location. I'll give 'em a hundred thousan'—two hundred thousan', if I have to! The way that gravel is, a man might take out a million."

"I'm damn glad of it!" Burr MacShane said. "Like I told you, last fall, Bobs a damn good kid. He worked for me all summer. You're sure welcome to my six thousan' on that bet, if he's made good."

The other sourdoughs agreed, and Black John nodded. "That thirty thousan' will come in handy, all right. But it ain't a patch on what I'll take out when I buy that location! The Siwash told me they took out better'n fifteen hundred ounces. Think of that—fifteen hundred ounces with just the two of 'em working, an' they didn't hit there till late in the fall!" Out of the corner of his eye, he saw Griffin leave his two companions and slip quietly out the door. "Fill 'em up," he ordered, tossing a well-filled pouch onto the bar. "I'm buyin' one, then I'm goin' to supper. I'll be back this evenin' an' give you boys a crack at that thirty thousan', if you ain't forgot how to play stud."

A MOMENT later he was joined on the sidewalk by Old Bettles, who eyed him gravely. "I don't s'pose you noticed that your friend Homer P. Griffin took in every word you said, an' then slipped out an' left his two pals standin' there half ways down the bar?"

Black John's glance met the shrewd eyes squarely. "Homer P. Griffin? Oh, yeah, seems like I ran across a party by that name last fall. If I remember right, I didn't like him. You say he was listenin'? Cripes, he might locate the Baxters before I do! He might even buy that location! Ain't that hell?"

"I'll bet he's goin' to think it's hell if he does!" Bettles' lips twisted into a grin, and the grin became a bull-throated guffaw, as he dug a none too gentle finger into the big man's ribs. "By God, John, you're a wonder!"

The stud game at the Tivoli lasted all night. After a hearty breakfast, Black John went to bed and slept until supper time. Stepping into the dining room, he seated himself at a table, and a few minutes later Homer P. Griffin stepped into the room, glanced about, and crossing to Black John's table, stood looking down at him. "Hello, Smith," he said, a sneering grin on his face. "Griffin's my name—Homer P. Griffin. You may remember that I introduced myself to you, last fall, in the Tivoli. You told me you didn't like me."

"Yeah, that's right. I ain't got no time for crooks of your breed."

"You call me a crook when everyone knows you're the damnedest outlaw in the country! Smart, they call you—damned smart. Well, let me tell you you're not smart. You're a damned blabbing fool. You barged into the Tivoli last evening and shot off your mouth about wanting to find young Bob Baxter and his wife, about the strike they made on Whiskey Creek, and about wanting to buy their location. And how you'd pay two hundred thousand for it! All right, go find the Baxters! They're right here in town, but they don't own that Whiskey Creek location any more. I didn't relax all day, like you did. I kept my eyes open after hearing what you told the sourdoughs. First I checked the location at the recorder's, then I waited for them to show up. When they hit town, about noon, I was waiting for them. I watched them go to police headquarters, and then checked on the royalty they paid. I followed them to the bank and saw them deposit their dust. Then I steered them into my office and bought their location. And I didn't pay two hundred thousand for it, like you would have done. I got it for a hundred and fifty thousand. It was every cent I could scrape together. But I got it. And now it will be me that takes the million out of that claim—not you!"

Black John grinned up into the sneering face. "Did you pay over the cash? Or are you workin' some kind of shenanigan?"

"Yes, I paid cash—every damned cent of it! I had to. They insisted on it. I wasn't taking any chances. I knew that if I didn't get the claim, you would."

The grin behind the black beard widened. "Prob'ly the only honest deal you ever put across, ain't it, Homer? It wasn't exactly ethical, at that. In fact it was kind of underhanded, knowin' I wanted to—"

His words were interrupted by the voice of Elsie Baxter who, with her husband, had just come into the room. Both made for the table, and paused beside Griffin. "Why, Uncle John! How did you get here?"

"Oh, after you'd pulled out, I remembered a bet I wanted to collect off a bunch of sourdoughs, so I cut across by way of the Sixtymile. Got here yesterday."

Reaching into her purse, the girl produced two slips of paper. "Here's the royalty receipt. And here's the deposit slip for your dust. It weighed in at fifteen hundred and twenty-five ounces. We deposited our own dust, too—the seven hundred and thirty-one ounces we took out of the Whiskey Crick claim. And besides that we sold the claim! Sold it to Mr. Griffin, here, for a hundred and fifty thousand in cash. Isn't that wonderful?" She turned and her glance shifted to the man who stood, his face deathly white, beside Black John's chair. "Didn't we, Mr. Griffin?"

But she received no answer. Homer P. Griffin's knees buckled suddenly, and he crashed face downward onto the floor. Wide-eyed, she stared down at the figure.

The big man smiled. "Looks like Homer fainted."

"But he looked the same as ever when we came in. Why would he faint?"

"Damn if I know. Must of been somethin' you said."

"What I can't figure is how you knew Mr. Griffin would be so anxious to buy our location."

"Who me? I didn't know. It was just a hunch, that's all."

JUSTICE—YUKON STYLE!

I
WELCOME, FUGITIVE!

INSIDE CUSHING'S FORT, the combined trading post and saloon that served the little community of outlawed men that had sprung up on Halfaday Creek near the Yukon-Alaska border, old Cush, the proprietor, set out a bottle, two glasses and the inevitable leather dice box as Black John Smith stepped into the room and crossed to the bar. The big man picked up the box, gave it a perfunctory shake and rolled out the dice.

"I'll leave them three fours in one," he said. "The law of averages says they ort to be good."

Cush gathered up the dice and returned them to the box. "Huh—law of averages! Who made up this here law of averages yer always talkin' about?"

Black John grinned. "The law of averages is not a man-made law. It—"

"Some woman made it, eh?" Cush interrupted. "Er mebbe some kid? Well, any law a woman would make, nor neither a kid, wouldn't be worth a damn, no matter how you'd look at it."

"The law of averages wasn't made by anyone. It is an immutable concept—"

Cush rattled the dice noisily and cast them. "I ain't goin' to stand here and listen to no sermon about somethin' there ain't no sech a thing as. And them three sixes proves it. That's a horse on you, and all the big words you could think up wouldn't change it none. So go ahead and roll out some more laws of averages and I'll show you how to beat 'em."

As Black John gathered up the dice, a figure darkened the doorway. A young man stepped into the room and crossed to the bar, dropping a limp pack sack to the floor beside him. "Is this Cushing's Fort, on Halfaday Crick?" he asked.

Cush nodded and reached onto the back bar for another glass. "Yeah, this is the place."

"Where the hell's my wallet?" he demanded.

Black John returned the box to the bar without shaking the dice. "The unexpected, and I may add, timely advent of this wayfarer precludes the necessity of any further attempt on my part to win. I refer to our time-honored law of hospitality—namely that when a stranger appears in our midst, the house buys a drink for all present."

Cush scowled as he slid the glass across the bar in front of the newcomer. "Law of averages! Law of horspitality! By hell, they ain't no low-down trick that you wouldn't stoop to, Black John, to squinch outa buyin' a drink! Fer a man that's broke every damn law that was ever thought up by God, man, er the devil, from the ten commandments to spittin' on the sidewalk, hollerin' about the law of this and the law of that is plumb redic'lous!"

Black John regarded the bartender gravely. "You are in error, Cush. I have not broken all the commandments. I have never made a graven image." He turned to the stranger, who stood eyeing the two quizzically. "Fill up and pass the bottle before our genial host launches into a career of crime by reclaimin' it and breakin' the law of hospitality. By way of introduction I'll say that my name is Smith—Black John Smith in the vernacular—and the character behind the bar there is Lyme Cushing. I may add that the name of John Smith has become hackneyed hereabouts, and is no longer available to the public."

LITTLE WRINKLES of perplexity showed on the young man's brow, as his glance shifted from one to the other. "I don't quite understand."

"Don't let that bother you none," Cush interrupted. "John don't hardly ever say nothin' that no one kin understand till the next day—and mebbe not then. What he means is—if you aimed to claim yer name's John Smith, you better grab you another one out of the name can there on the end of the bar. They's too damn many John Smith's on the crick already."

"I won't be adding another one," the stranger said.

"My name is Willard Galster. I heard that you men are all outlaws and that the law doesn't dare show up on Halfaday Crick, so I came here."

"You an outlaw?" Black John asked.

The younger man nodded. "Yes, I suppose I'm an outlaw—now. At least, the Mounties think I am. I was arrested for a murder and robbery. With the evidence they had gathered

194

against me, I knew I wouldn't have a chance in the world of being acquitted. So, when he was taking me to Dawson, I watched my chance, knocked him down, jerked his gun from its holster, and made him toss me the handcuff key. I unlocked the cuffs, threw them and the keys in the river, jumped into the canoe and hit out. Later I tossed the gun in the river, too."

"Hmmn, quite an undertakin'. This policeman—it wasn't perchance, Corporal Downey, was it?"

"No. He said his name was Buck."

"Oh, Rollo, eh? I might of known that without askin'. Where was this murder and robbery supposed to have been pulled off?"

"On Moose Crick. I was timekeeper for the Consolidated Dredge Company's operation there."

"Moose Crick, eh? That's in the Fortymile territory. Funny that Sam Steele would send Rollo Buck out on a murder case."

"Constable Buck said that his superior officer had detailed him to count the Indians along the Fortymile. He ran onto this murder accidently, you might say. Mr. Forbes-Allison, the general manager of the Consolidated, was inspecting the work when the crime was committed, and when Constable Buck happened along, Mr. Forbes-Allison demanded that he get on the job immediately."

Black John grinned. "Old Horatio Mutton Chops himself, eh? Well, between the two of 'em they ort to be able to ball up any job."

"Constable Buck jumped at the chance to work on the case. He said it gave him an opportunity to prove that he was capable of handling important crimes."

Black John grinned. "Anyhow, it gave him the chance to keep his record clear. He's been passed along from one detachment to another, clean from Saskatchewan. Sam Steele got stuck with him when Downey passed him on from the Dawson detachment—and poor Sam can't get rid of him without shovin' him clean over into Alaska. So he gives Rollo jobs like office sweepin' an' Siwash countin'. Rollo's tackled several jobs of policin' that he run onto—and bungled every one of 'em. But about this murder an' robbery. You wasn't mixed up in it, I s'pose?"

"I certainly was not! But whoever did do it sure made it look like I'm the guilty one."

"Who was murdered?"

"The messenger who was carrying the monthly payroll from the main office in Dawson. The payroll was stolen. Someone who must have known it was due laid for the messenger a couple of miles down the crick, smashed in his head with an iron bar and made away with the money."

"Couldn't have been no hell of a lot of money involved," Black John opined. "Just the month's payroll for the dredge crew."

"According to Mr. Forbes-Allison it was forty-one thousand dollars. We had a big crew up the creek clearing out the timber ahead of the dredge operation."

"There's been men murdered for a damn sight less than that," the big man said. "How come this evidence that Rollo gathered pointed to you?"

"In the first place, as timekeeper, I knew that the messenger was due with the money. The amount of the payroll was thirty-one thousand, but it seems that Mr. Forbes-Allison had instructed the office to send on an extra ten thousand for his own personal expenses, as he was on a tour of inspection of several Consolidated properties.

"I had sent in the men's time to the main office, and each man's money was in a separate envelope with his name on it. Constable Buck found these empty envelopes in my shack, hidden under a loose floor board. Whoever committed the robbery hid them there to throw suspicion on me. I didn't even know the board was loose."

"And this iron bar the messenger was killed with—was that in your shack, too?"

"No. It was a dredge-frame bolt—made of three-quarters inch iron about three or four feet long, with a square head on one end and threads on the other. There's always some of 'em lying around. Constable Buck found the one the messenger was killed with near his body where the murderer had tossed it. It had some dried blood and a few hairs on it, and he said that if my fingerprints were found on it he'd have an open and shut case against me. I don't know much about this fingerprint business—but I can't see how they could expect to find the murderer's fingerprints on the bolt. Buck and Mr. Forbes-Allison and Bill Emory, the dredge foreman, all handled it—passing it back and forth between 'em, looking at those blood stains."

BLACK JOHN grinned. "If it wasn't for them pay envelopes bein' found in your shack, I'd say Rollo's case was a damn sight more open than shut. If Downey had found that bolt, he'd have picked it up by the threaded end where no finger prints could have showed anyhow, and he would have wrapped the rest of it up so nothin' could have touched it till he'd looked it all over for prints."

The younger man nodded somberly. "Yes, but the empty envelopes were found in my shack. And on top of that I assaulted an officer and took his gun and handcuffs and key and canoe."

Black John nodded. "So, figurin' you're outlawed, anyway, you hit for here aimin' to throw in with us other outlaws, eh?"

"No. I'd never even heard of Halfaday Crick. I didn't know where I was going. I was scared, and all I wanted to do was to get away from there as fast as I could. I had a wild notion of getting out of the country, so when I came out of Moose Crick into the Yukon, I headed upriver. How I ever expected to make it, without any grub or money I don't know. I paddled till evening, and when I saw a little fire on the bank, I pulled in there. I was dead tired, and so hungry I felt faint. There was an old man sitting beside the fire cooking his supper. He invited me to join him, and after we'd eaten he glanced at the empty canoe, and asked me where I was going and howcome I had no outfit along. So I told him just what had happened.

"He was a fine old man. Said his name was Gordon Bettles. He didn't seem to think any more of Constable Buck than you do. He told me I'd never make it outside—that both up and down the river the police would be on the lookout for me. He told me about Halfaday Crick, and about you, and he said to come here and tell you the whole story. You were all outlaws up here, he said, and—"

"Why damn his hide! Wait till I get holt of him! Defamin' our character!"

"Oh, but he didn't. He thinks a lot of you—said you were smarter than all the police in the Yukon put together, and that maybe you could help me some way. Anyway he said you'd let me hide out here where the cops couldn't get me. He shoved the police canoe out into the river and set it adrift, and he took me with him in the morning. When we reached Dawson, he left me on this side of the river, and went across and came back with a pack sack full of grub and some blankets, and then we paddled clear up the mouth of the White River and he told me how to get here, and gave me his canoe. He said he'd flag down a steamboat and go back to Dawson on her. There are mighty few men that would do that for a perfect stranger—and one that was suspected of murder to boot."

The big man nodded. "You was lucky to run onto Gordon Bettles, son. They don't make 'em no finer."

"And you'll let me stay here till—till—"

"till hell freezes over—if the police don't find the murderer first," the big man smiled.

"But what if Constable Buck should come up here?"

"Don't you worry none about Rollo showin' up on Halfaday, son. If he does, I'll take down his didies an' give him a damn good hidin' right where it would do the most good. When Sam Steele's outfit at Fortymile don't pick you up downriver, Sam'll prob'ly notify Corporal Downey. He might show up here, but it won't get him nothin'. I'll take you up and locate you in Whiskey Bill's old shack. It's on a feeder way up the crick, where you'll be safe till this thing blows over."

"But if the police don't catch the murderer, it'll never blow over."

"That's right, son. But I've got a hunch that maybe Downey will have better luck than Rollo did."

"Even so, the Mounties will be after me for assaulting an officer and taking his gun and canoe and those handcuffs."

Black John grinned. "If Downey ever catches up with you for pullin' that trick on Rollo, he's apt to buy you a drink. Rollo's an officer only by the grace of God—not by grace of ability. Cush will fix you out with grub an some extry clothin', and I'll take you up to Whiskey Bill's. You better stay up there till you hear from me. We'll slip you enough grub to keep you."

"But I have no money to pay for—"

"Who the hell said anythin' about money?" Cush demanded. "I'll git out the stuff, and you pack it down to the canoe, and you an' John git a'goin'!"

II
STAMP OF THE OUTLAW BREED

SOME TWO WEEKS later, while hunting moose down the creek, Black John was accosted by a stranger who hailed him from a canoe. "Hey, is this Halfaday Crick? And if it is, where in hell's this here Cushing's Fort I've heered tell about? And where'll I find Black John Smith?"

The big man smiled into the hard green eyes that showed above the stubble of dark beard. "This is Halfaday. Cush's is about three miles up the crick from here, and I'm Black John Smith."

The man beached the canoe and joined Black John, who had seated himself on a fallen tree trunk. "So I got here. But it's a hell of a ways, and I damn near run outa grub. Where does a guy hole up here?"

Black John filled his pipe, his eyes on the lean pack sack that lay in the bottom of the canoe. "You mean you're figurin' on locatin' here on the crick?"

"Shore I'm locatin' here! You boys up here is all outlaws, hain't you? Well, tellin' you about me, I'm an outlaw, too—and a damn good one. I figger on joinin' up with yer gang. You're the boss, hain't you?"

Black John lighted his pipe and blew a cloud of smoke into the air. "W-e-e-l-l, me an' Cush, between the two of us, we sort of look after things around here. You claim you're an outlaw and you'd like to throw in with us. You got any particular specialty? Or are you just a sort of general all-around outlaw?"

"Robbery's my line. I done a stretch in Ohio for armed robbery, and I've pulled off jobs in Ioway and Dakoty and Indiany."

Black John shook his head slowly. "It's easy fer a man to set here and brag about jobs he's pulled back in the States. Up here it's different. We've got the Mounted to deal with—not some hick sheriff. Besides, it looks like you must have botched that Ohio job, or you wouldn't have done time for it."

"I never botched no job!" the man replied. "It was my pardner done it. He got soused and spilt his guts to some woman, and then him and her fell out and she poured it all into the ear of a lawman she was makin' a play fer. I learnt my lesson, and I've played a lone hand ever since I got my parole."

"We don't go much on lone handers, here on Halfaday."

"Up here it's different. You got a regular gang. They hain't none of you boys goin' to git soused and run off at the head, by a damn sight. How about takin' me on?"

"Like I said," Black John replied, "outguessin' the law down in the States don't stack up very high with us. Besides that, how do I know you ever pulled off any jobs. All I've got is your word for it. If there was some job you'd pulled here in the Yukon, it would be different. If a man's runnin' a regular gang of outlaws, he's got to be damn particular who he takes into it. He can't afford to take chances."

The man nodded approval. "That's right, he couldn't. And here's the answer. About a month and a half ago they was a forty-one thousand-dollar payroll knocked off down on Moose Crick. The messenger was cooled with a dredge bolt, and the empty pay envelopes turned up in the timekeeper's shack hid in under a floor board. A constable of the Mounted shows up and pinches the timekeeper, who's a green kid. When he's takin' him in, the kid knocks him down, takes his gun and canoe and makes his git-away. Accordin' to the way you talk about the Mounted, all I got to say is you've got a damn sight more respect fer 'em than I have—when one of 'em can't handle a green kid, an' him handcuffed, without the kid makin' a git-away and takin' the constable's gun and cuffs and canoe along with him! And what's more, all the Mounted Police in the hull damn country has been on the lookout for this kid fer six weeks, and they hain't picked him up yet. They hain't no hick sheriff that couldn't of did better'n that."

Black John nodded as he slowly puffed at his pipe. "W-e-e-l-l, lookin' at it that way, maybe the Mounted ain't so hot."

"I'll say they hain't. Take it from me, John—from now on we kin fergit the damn Mounted, and go ahead and pull off whatever job we want to. The Mounted hain't got me buffaloed, by a damn sight!"

"About you throwin' in with us here on Halfaday," Black John said. "I asked you about some job you'd piffled off here in the Yukon, and you told me about some kid pullin' a forty-one-thousand-dollar payroll job and then makin' a get-away. Where does that tie in with you? If it was the kid that wanted to throw in with us, I might take him on."

The other grinned. "Yeah. And that's why you'll be takin' me on, too. I pulled that robbery. I pulled it so slick that all the evidence pointed to the kid. It's like this: If a guy pulls a job, no matter how careful he thinks he is, some law-dog is apt to stumble onto some little thing that could connect him up with it. But if he leaves some damn good evidence that points to someone else, then the law goes after that guy. Hell, they's three, four guys down in the States doin' time fer jobs I pulled—jest 'cause I was smart enough to plant the evidence agin 'em.

"This here kid he was the timekeeper. He knowed the payroll money was due on Moose Crick. And them empty pay envelopes was found in his shack. On top of that I had gloves on when I handled that dredge bolt so they can't git my fingerprints on it." The man paused and his grin widened. "But they'll git plenty of fingerprints, at that the way this Mounted constable and the dredge foreman and the big boss passed that there bolt back and forth amongst 'em. How about it? Am I good, er hain't I?"

BLACK JOHN wasn't impressed. "Is that the only job you've pulled in the Yukon? One job don't make an outlaw—not one that we'd care to throw in with here on Halfaday. Anyone might pull off one job and get away with it, if his luck held."

"I hain't a guy that depends on luck. I use my head. And here's your answer. I pulled another one two weeks ago on Squaw Crick. I hung around the Moose Crick diggin's fer a week after the robbery, and then I quit and picked up a dredge job on Squaw Crick. The Euriky outfit's workin' there, and I sticks on the job jest long enough to find out when payday comes. I lays fer the messenger and cools him with a dredge bolt, same as the other, and I gits away with a twenty-thousand-dollar payroll. Like the other time, I used gloves when I handled the bar, and I sunk the empty pay envelopes in the crick in the canvas bag the payroll was in. The Mounted is still workin' on that one. How's that fer fast workin'? Sixty-one thousand in about a month's time!"

"If you're tellin' the truth, I'd say you're a competent man in your line. But a more or less intimate association with outlaws of one kind and another has convinced me that most of 'em can lie like hell. And a good share of their lyin' runs to braggin' about how good they are in their line. So you see, before I'd consider lettin' you join up with us, I'd have to have some tangible proof that you actually pulled off these jobs."

Reaching into his pack, the man withdrew three huge rolls of bills and tossed them onto the ground. "There's the dough—sixty-one thousand. Count it."

Black John counted the money and handed it back. He nodded. "The amount checks with what you claimed to have stole. But there's nothin' to prove that you got it like you claimed you did. Hell, lots of folks could show sixty-one thousand in bills—but that don't prove how they got it. Take that Moose Crick job. Prob'ly everyone in Dawson could tell me as much about it as you have. And this other job. Do you claim you killed this messenger?"

"Shore I killed him! By hell, when you wham 'em, wham 'em fer keeps! To hell with jest tappin' em unconscious. They might git a look at you, and when they come to, they would give the law yer description."

"It's undoubtless the safest way," Black John agreed. "But still that don't tie you in with this robbery."

A scowl of annoyance clouded the man's face. "Looks like yer damn particular," he said testily.

"If a man is runnin' a gang of outlaws, he's got to be damn particular about who he takes into it. How long would a gang last if he wasn't."

The man seemed mollified. "Guess yer right, at that," he admitted. "Well, here's how I kin prove I pulled that last job. They wouldn't no one but the man that done it know where he hid the dredge bolt after he'd cooled the messenger, would they?"

"That's right."

"Okay. I'll tell you where I hid it, in under a log, and you kin go there and see fer yerself—and that there canvas bag with the empty pay envelopes what's sunk with a rock in, it, right in the bend of the crick where the bolt's hid. This here bend, you can't miss it. It's about four miles up the creek where the foot-trail swings around a big jam pile. They's a flat rock face right acrost the crick at this bend with a zig-zag white vein like quartz runnin' acrost it. I was layin' fer the messenger behind the jam pile. When you find the bolt, that's proof enough, hain't it?"

Black John nodded. "Yes, if the bolt and the bag are where you claim they are, I'll say that would be proof enough to tie you in with the job. Fact is, I've got to make a trip down to Dawson— I go down about onct in so often to sort of look around. I'll be startin' in the mornin'."

The man grinned knowingly. "Goin' to kinda lay out some job fer the gang to pull, eh?"

"Well, it don't hurt a man to sort of know what's goin' on, here and there. In the meantime you can come on up the crick and throw yer stuff in One Eyed John's cabin till I git back. I'll slip out onto Squaw Crick, and if the bolt and the bag are where you claim they are, I'll know you pulled that job. And I'll take yer word that you pulled the Moose Crick robbery, too."

"Who's One Eyed John? Mebbe he won't want no one movin' in with him."

"He ain't apt to object. We hung him a while back."

"Hung him! What fer?"

"Oh, damn if I remember. Undoubtless it was somethin' he done. One Eye was sort of underhanded. Like I say, you can hang out there till I get back. It ain't far from Cush's saloon, where there's a stud game damn near every night. I ort to be back in two-three weeks. What name do you go by, so I can introduce you to Cush and some of the boys?"

The other winked. "How would Bill Brown do?"

"Suits me. There's no other Browns on the crick, at present. Seems I recollect we hung most of the other ones."

SHORTLY AFTER breakfast the following morning, Black John stepped into the saloon. He was greeted by Cush, who set out the inevitable bottle, glasses and dice box.

Cush was frowning. "This here damn Bill Brown you fetched in last night," he said. "He ain't no one I'm a'goin' to like."

The big man grinned as he picked up the box, shook the dice and rolled them out onto the bar. "Beat them three treys in one," he said.

Cush threw three fives, returned the dice to the box and shook out four deuces. "I'm leavin'"em," he said.

The big man failed to beat the throw, and Cush made an entry in his day book, as Black John filled his glass. "What's the matter with Bill?" he asked.

"Matter with him! Hell, them wicked green eyes of his'n and the way he brags about jobs he's pulled off down in the States. Anyone would know he's a damn liar, and a buzzard to boot."

Black John grinned. "A man shouldn't jump to conclusions, Cush. The fact is, Bill struck me as a rather affable gent, mebbe a trifle boastful, but one who attends to his business in a rather efficient manner. I have reason to believe he has been plenty successful in his previous undertakings."

"You kin cut out all the rest of the big words you know and git down to cases. How much has he got on him? If you've got reasons to believe he's been successful, that means you seen his roll. And by hell, when you come to divide it, I'm in on it, too. If I've got to put up with the damn cuss around here till we hang him, I'm a'goin' to git paid fer it!"

Black John's grin widened. "The man is possessed of sixty-one thousand dollars, which, by his own admission, was feloniously acquired. He claims to have pulled off that Moose Crick robbery that young Galster is wanted for. Inasmuch as the crime, and a subsequent one he mentioned, were committed outside our jurisdiction—"

"Jewishdictions, hell! Moose Crick is a damn sight more contiguous or subterranian to Halfaday than a lot of places is that you claimed was in our jewishdictions! What I mean—if Brown pulled that murder and robbery and put it off on that kid, we'd ort to hang him fer it!"

"In this instance it seems more proper than the Law should deal with Bill. I have a hunch that Corporal Downey will handle the matter more efficiently than Rollo Buck did. Bill claims to be adept at leaving evidence that points to another gent as the perpetrator of his crimes. I deem it fitting that he should, as the saying is, be hoist by his own petard."

"By hell, if anyone would know what yer talkin' about, it wouldn't be me! But go ahead. Only remember I git my cut on that there sixty-one thousand. Ain't you startin' for Dawson today with the gold dust outa the safe? I'll feel better when it's gone, with that damn Bill Brown's green eyes on the safe every time I open it up."

"Get out the dust. I'll throw my stuff in my pack and be back in half an hour. Meanwhile you send somebody up to Whiskey Bill's shack and tell young Galster not to show up here till he hears from me. There'd be hell to pay if Bill Brown was to find him here on Halfaday with official sanction."

Alone in his cabin, Black John tossed a change of clothing and a few personal items in his pack sack. From a secret cache he produced a small flat packet done up in oiled silk, and for some moments stood eyeing the object speculatively as he turned it over in his hand.

When he had found it some time ago among Doc Jones' effects after Doc was murdered, he hadn't turned it over to Downey because a man never could tell when a relic like this would come in handy. Take this Bill Brown. By his own boast, Brown was guilty of two murders here in the Yukon, and justice would be served if Black John should follow Cush's suggestion of calling a miners' meeting and hanging him. But the way Black John looked at it, Bill was entitled to more than just common justice. He was entitled to a sort of poetic justice, as the saying went. A sort of refinement of justice that no one could appreciate better than Bill, himself. In fact, no one except Bill and Black John would be able to appreciate the ironic humor of the situation.

The Law was hell-bent for evidence. Black John deemed it fitting that the Law should handle this case, and, as a right-minded citizen he took it as his duty to see that it was provided with sufficient evidence to meet the ends of justice.

TOSSING THE packet into his pack sack, the big man slung the strap over his shoulder and returned to the saloon, where Cush pushed a heavy package across the bar.

Cush said, "It figgers twenty-five hundred and sixty ounces—forty thousand, nine hundred and sixty dollars at the bank. That's damn close to what the kid says was stole in that Moose Crick robbery. I'm shore glad to git shut of it—with the damn green-eyed Bill Brown hangin' around. I shore as hell don't want him doublin' his money outa my safe!"

Stowing the package of dust into his pack sack, Black John carried it to the landing, nestled it into his canoe, and headed down the creek.

The trip to Dawson was uneventful. After depositing the dust in the bank, he strolled over to the Tivoli Saloon to be vociferously greeted by the small group of sourdoughs at the bar. After a round of drinks, old Gordon Bettles, dean of the sourdoughs, called him aside.

"Did the kid make it to Halfaday all right?" he asked.

Black John nodded. "Yeah, he made it. And I'd thank you to quit shovin' them damn outlaws up onto Halfaday."

Bettles' eyes widened as he stared into the unsmiling face. "Outlaw, hell! That kid was framed. He ain't no more an outlaw than I be!"

"Or me?"

Bettles gulped, then roared with laughter, as Black John's lips broke into a broad grin behind his black beard. "Cripes, John," Bettles said. "First off I thought you was in earnest about the kid bein' an outlaw. He's got to lay low, though, till the police ketches up with the damn cuss that pulled that job off. 'Cause all the evidence shore is agin him."

"The police made any arrests?"

"Nope. And believe me, they're runnin' around in circles, on account there was another payroll robbery pulled off on Squaw Crick. Looks like the same guy done it—both messengers was killed with an iron bar. They got the bar on the Moose Crick job—a dredge-frame bolt—but they ain't found the iron bar that smashed the Squaw Crick messenger's head. Downey figgers it was prob'ly another dredge bolt. How about a game of stud tonight? I rec'lect you got into us boys fer a couple thousand, last time you hit town."

Black John shook his head. "Not tonight. Got a little business out in the hills. Be back in a few days. And I'm givin' you fellas fair warnin' that if you' think anything of your dust, you better keep it in your pocket. I figure my luck's still runnin'."

Purchasing a bottle of whiskey, he sauntered into Al Scugale's store, bought a can of peaches, and with his purchases in his pack sack, headed for the river and stepped into his canoe.

At the mouth of Squaw Creek, he cached the canoe and proceeded up the creek on foot. At a certain bend, he paused, glanced carefully about, and proceeded directly to a fallen tree a few yards back from the bank. Removing the accumulation of leaves and soil, he withdrew an iron dredge-frame bolt from beneath the fallen trunk. Examination showed the trace of a dark brownish-red stain and a few hairs adhering to the rust-covered bolt. Slowly he nodded his head. It was Bill's job, all right.

A half-hour later, after carefully replacing the bolt where he had found it, the big man turned and headed down the creek.

III
BLACK JOHN'S GAME

AT DETACHMENT HEADQUARTERS in Dawson, Corporal Downey looked up from his desk as Black John stepped into the room. "Hello, John! Pull up a chair. How's things on Halfaday?"

"Oh, about the same as usual. Seems like nothin' ever happens up there to break our humdrum existence. How's things along the river?"

The officer frowned. "I'd shore like a little humdrum existence, for a change. Down here it's just one damn headache after another."

"What's the matter? Someone's dog steal a side of bacon?"

"We've got two payroll robberies on our hands—and two murders. Looks like the same kid, pulled both jobs—stove in the messengers heads with a dredge bolt and made off with the payrolls."

"Kid? They don't sound like no jobs a kid could pull off."

Downey nodded. "They shore don't. But I guess he's guilty, all right. He was timekeeper on the Moose Crick dredge job." He repeated the story Black John already knew, including the part about the kid's escape from Rollo Buck.

Black John nodded soberly. "This kid wouldn't have had no outfit along," he commented. "Kind of funny you boys couldn't pick him up."

"It is funny—damn funny. The way I've got it doped is this: The kid got sixty-one thousand out of those two jobs. He's got plenty of money to pay, and pay well, for a hide-out. It's my guess that someone, somewhere, is hidin' him out—for a price."

The big man nodded. "Could be. How about fingerprints? Did you find prints on the bolt the Squaw Crick messenger was killed with?"

The officer shook his head. "We haven't found the weapon yet. Constable Peters looked the ground over, but he couldn't find anything. Then Brock went up there, but he didn't have any better luck than Peters did. They both searched the bottom of the crick for a quarter of a mile each way from where the messenger's body lay. They did find the canvas bag the payroll was in, and the empty pay envelopes weighted down with a rock in the crick, but they didn't find the weapon. It looks like the best way to get rid of the bar would be to throw it in the crick, not only because it would hide it, but because if we did find it we couldn't get any fingerprints off it."

"That's right," Black John agreed. "And maybe the murderer figured that that's jest the way the police would dope it out. So maybe he hid it somewhere else. He might not have stopped to figure about the prints. If I was you, Downey, I'd go down there and take another hunt for that bar. If it ain't in the crick, it's around there somewheres. I ain't got nothin' in particular to do. I'll go 'long with you. Between the two of us, we might turn up somethin'. I shore as hell don't want no head-whammin' son showin' up on Halfaday—kid or no kid."

Downey thumped the desk with his fist. "By gosh, I'll do it! Like you say, that bolt has got to be somewhere around there!"

Leaving the canoe at the mouth of the creek, the two headed up the foot trail with Corporal Downey in the lead. An hour later the officer paused and pointed to a perpendicular rock wall on the opposite side of the creek, and to a huge tangle of drift-wood that had lodged in a sharp bend of the creek.

"This is the place all right," he said. "Accordin' to Peters and Brock there was a rock face acrost the crick with a white band showin' on it, and a big jam pile where the murderer waited for the messenger. Peters fished that canvas bag out of that hole just above the jam pile."

Black John nodded. "I'm bettin' we'll find that bolt some-wheres around here—and not too far neither. The damn cuss would be in a hurry to get away from here as quick as he could. Prob'ly tossed it into the bush, or maybe covered it up with dirt or leaves. We'll keep our eyes open for a footprint, or a broken

210

twig, or a place where the leaves have been disturbed. You work up the crick and I'll work down."

The two separated and began a methodical search of the bush. Some fifteen minutes later, Black John called loudly, "Hey, Downey, come here!"

When the officer reached his side a few moments later, the lips behind the heavy black beard were grinning broadly.

"Better brace yerself, Downey," the big man said. "'Cause if you see what I see, I've got a hunch it ain't goin' to do them headaches you claim you've got any good."

The officer's eyes swept the adjacent terrain and returned to Black John's face. "What do you mean—see what you see?"

"You remember a while back you was up against a couple payroll robberies, same as now—that one on Ophir, and the other right here on Squaw Crick?"

"I'll say I remember! We never did pick up the murderer. And the same as now, both the messengers were knocked cold with an iron bar. I've gone over our reports on both those cases. We got dandy fingerprints, not only on the bars, but on empty peach tins and whiskey bottles. But when we sent 'em in to Ottawa they turned out to be the prints of a dead man—fella name of Jack Brower that died in prison. The prints were Brower's, all right—but our set showed a scar on one finger that wasn't s'posed to be there."

The grin behind the black beard widened. "That's right, Downey. And I've got a hunch that hist'ry's repeatin' itself—that Jack's on the prowl again, and you're in for another round of ghost huntin'."

As he spoke he pointed to a tiny glint of glass that showed through the leaves at the edge of a fallen tree trunk. "When I come around this tree, I caught the flash where the sun hit that glass. It looks to me like the butt end of a whiskey bottle. I didn't touch it, 'cause if it is, I shore as hell don't want my fingerprints showin' up on it. If Jack's runnin' true to form, I'll bet you'll find both an empty peach tin and the dredge bolt under that log."

Dropping to his knees, Downey carefully removed the leaves and dirt along the edge of the trunk, and one by one removed an empty whiskey bottle, an empty peach tin and a dredge bolt.

BLACK JOHN chuckled aloud as, without a word, Corporal Downey wrapped the articles carefully in paper he had brought for the purpose. The officer scowled.

"It might be funny as hell to you, but it shore puts us in a spot. Here we've been goin' all out huntin' that kid that got away from Rollo Buck. We've checked up on him and found out that he didn't come into the country till this spring. He got that Consolidated time-keepin' job a week after he hit Dawson. It's a cinch I'm goin' to find Brower's prints on this stuff, 'cause it's a cinch the same man pulled these jobs as pulled them other two last year. That lets the kid out. And it leaves us right where we were last year—with a lot of good fingerprints and no murderer."

Back at headquarters, it didn't take Corporal Downey long to verify his prediction that he would find Brower's fingerprints on the three articles. "Jest like before. He got his fingers sticky from them peaches, and left prints so plain a blind man could see 'em on the bolt and the bottle and the tin. And old Forbes-Allison and the Eureka outfit squawkin' their heads off about losin' them payrolls, and damnin' the police for not pickin' up the robbers! It's enough to make a man throw up his job an' tell 'em all to go to hell!"

"Oh, I don't know, Downey," the big man grinned. "Policin's about like anything else. Sometimes a man gets the breaks, and sometimes he don't. A man can't expect to win all the time. I jest been kinda wonderin'. Fact is, a newcomer showed up on Halfaday a couple days before I left. Claimed his name's Bill Brown."

"Hold on!" Downey interrupted as he reached for a file and thumbed through a report. "This Bill Brown. Is he six-foot-two, V-shaped scar on his chin, black hair, thirty-two, likes the women but don't touch booze, slight squint in the left eye, hawkbill nose?"

"W-e-e-l-l, I never measured Bill, but off-hand I'd say he's risin' of six foot. His hair's dark, but a kind of ragged beard would cover up any scar on his chin. He could be thirty-two. Can't say about the women—there ain't none on Halfaday for him to like. He takes a drink, but he might of acquired that habit after your report was made out. His eyes are sort of greenish-lookin' and the left one might squint, and his nose might be sort of hawkish lookin'. But if that's Jack Brower's description you've been readin' off, you've sort of overlooked the fact that Jack is dead. This here Bill Brown ain't no ghost. I can swear to that."

"Jest the same I'm goin' to hit for Halfaday and look this bird over—get his fingerprints and compare 'em with Brower's. I'll hustle things up and start day after tomorrow. It'll take me all day tomorrow to get the boys to work on this new angle. When you goin' back?"

"Jest as quick as I can get over to the bank and pick up the cash for that dust I fetched down."

"Why not wait and go up with me?"

The big man shook his head. "Nothin' doin'. I don't care to be seen on the crick in no sech company. Look at it from my angle—yours, too, as far as that goes. If this Bill Brown should happen to be your murderer and you'd arrest him there, the boys would think I steered you onto him if I'd go back with you. My holt on the crick would be gone. The boys wouldn't trust me no more. And you'd lose out on it, too. Because you know there has been times when I've maybe done you a good turn by stretchin' our policy of neither hinderin' nor helpin' the police, when some damn scoundrel foists himself onto us. The way things are, takin' 'em by and large, what with our miners' meetin's and an occasional tip to you, justice seems to work out pretty good on Halfaday."

Downey nodded. "I'll say it does. I don't go so far as to say I always agree with your methods, but in the long run justice seems to work out up there, as you say. I could wish, though, that I'd have more luck recovering the money or dust lost by the big outfits. Lots of times you've turned over large sums lost by some prospector or other individual—but never yet have I ever recovered the losses of big outfits on Halfaday."

The big man grinned. "Undoubtless a mere coincidence, Downey. But keep on tryin'. Like I said a while back, the police can't expect all the breaks. Besides, you've got to remember that them big outfits is ruinin' the country for the poor man."

"If I could pick up the damn cuss that left these prints, I'd have evidence enough on him to hang him a mile high."

"I don't know nothin' about Bill's prints—but it shore wouldn't irk me none if they would turn out to be his. He ain't no one we want sojournin' in our midst, as a poet would say."

"How'm I goin' to spot this Bill Brown when I get to Halfaday? Half the men on the cricks are tall and wear beards, and a lot of 'em have greenish eyes. Will you point him out to me?"

Black John shook his head. "No. Tippin' off a crook to a policeman on Halfaday would be an unpardonable sin. If I was you I'd jest amble into Cush's like it was a routine patrol an' sort of stick around a while. 'Course if you should see anything that might lead you to suspect Bill of some moral irregularity, you could go ahead and arrest him and git his prints, and the boys up there would be for you. We don't stand for no crime on Halfaday—you know that. Well, I got to get goin'. So long, Downey, and good luck to you. Be seein' you."

SOME TEN days later Black John stepped into Cush's saloon and tossed several packages of currency onto the bar. Cush set out bottle and glasses, counted the money, consulted a slip of paper, and nodded. "Forty thousand, nine hundred an' sixty. That's what she figgered. I'm buyin' a drink."

"How's everything along the crick?" the big man asked as he filled his glass. "The kid all right, up at Whiskey Bill's? Bill Brown been cuttin' any unseemly capers?"

"The kid's okay. 'Cordin' to One Armed John he's a damn good kid. He's workin' Whiskey Bill's location and takin' out better'n wages. About that damn Bill Brown—I wouldn't know what a unseemly caper was if I seen one, so I wouldn't know if he's got any cut. He hangs around drinkin' licker and settin' in on the stud game every night, and he's always braggin' about what a hell of a outlaw he was back there in the States. They don't no one like him. The boys would be tickled if we'd go ahead and hang him."

Black John shook his head. "Sech procedure would be unethical in the extreme. Our duty in this matter is clear and unequivocal—merely to set back and let nature take her course. In my opinion the sands in Bill's cosmos are runnin' low."

Cush scowled. "What the hell's anyone's cosmos—and how do you know Bill's has got sand in it? By hell, John, they's somethin' loose in anyone's head when he'll use up all them big words which don't mean nothin' when you git 'em said! When I says the boys would like to go ahead and hang Bill, all you had to say was 'no'—jest one little word you kin spell with two letters. That there nurse you claim dropped you on yer head when you was a baby musta been a damn tall nurse and you musta lit on a damn hard floor, or else she dropped you outa a four-story winder and you lit on some kind of a dictionary!"

The big man grinned. "I disremember the lineal specifications of the nurse, and our lowly cabin in the hills was not a four-story mansion. It was quite a while back. The fact is I've got a hunch that Downey'll show up before long on a routine patrol, and it might be that he'll deem it expedient to take Bill back with him for company. You might slip the Yukon wanteds the tip to lay low till he goes back."

Early in the evening, on the second day after Black John's return to Halfaday, half a dozen men seated themselves around a table in Cushing's saloon and started a game of stud. An hour later, the door opened and Corporal Downey stepped into the room.

Black John greeted him from his seat at the stud table. "Hello, Downey! Pull up a chair and get yourself some easy money!"

The officer declined with a smile: "Nothin' doin'. You boys play 'em too high to suit me." He stepped to the bar.

A few minutes later, Black John shoved his last chip into a pot, and lost. Reaching into his pocket, he withdrew his hand. "Hell, I left my wallet layin' on the table back in my cabin. Wait till I get it and I'll buy another stack of chips."

Rising from the table, he disappeared through the doorway. Ten minutes later he returned, stepped to the table and glared down into the face of a tall, green-eyed man with a ragged beard who had just raked in a pot. "Where the hell's my wallet?" he demanded.

The man looked up, startled. "I don't know nothin' about yer wallet. It's prob'ly where you left it."

"Like hell it is! I laid it on the table just before supper when I changed my pants—and you're the only one that's been in my cabin since!"

"Hell, I only stopped in there fer a minute when I went to cook my supper. I shore as hell didn't lift yer leather."

"Okay, Bill," the big man said. "If you didn't lift the wallet, it's my mistake. It won't take long to find out."

He turned to the officer who stood at the bar. "How about it, Downey? I'm chargin' this here Bill Brown with liftin' my wallet, and I'm demandin' that you search him."

Downey searched the man and failed to find the missing wallet.

Brown turned to Black John. "You satisfied?" he asked, a sneer in his voice.

"I'm satisfied you ain't got it on you," the big man replied. "But I ain't satisfied you didn't lift it, by a damn sight! You went to One Eyed John's cabin when you left mine. I'm demandin' that Downey search that cabin!"

INSIDE ONE Eyed John's cabin, Downey and Black John made a perfunctory search of the bunk, the shelves, and the contents of a pack sack while the other looked on. Finally Downey turned.

"Let's see. This cabin of One Eyed John's—didn't I recover some stolen money from a secret cache in here, a year or so ago? Shore I did!"

He paused as his eyes swept the walls. "There it is, behind where that coat's hangin'. I rec'lect, now." As he started forward, Brown leaped in front of him.

"By hell, there ain't no leather in there! I found that there loose piece of log and stuck my dough in there!"

Downey's gaze met the glare of the green eyes. "It wouldn't be sixty-one-thousand dollars, would it? The forty-one thousand you got on Moose Crick and the Squaw Crick payroll?"

Before the man could answer, the officer brushed him aside, jerked the section of log loose, and thrust his arm into the enclosure. For several moments he groped about the interior, then withdrew his arm, a puzzled expression on his face. In his hand he held Black John's missing wallet, and a flat packet done up in oiled silk.

"This dough you mentioned," Downey said. "It wouldn't be in here, would it?"

The man moistened his lips. "I—I—lied. I never had no dough. I—I never seen them things before—that leather—nor that other thing neither."

Carefully Downey removed the oiled silk wrapping. An exclamation of mingled surprise and horror escaped him as he gingerly fingered the gruesome object—the tanned skin of a human hand!

Black John eyed the object, and pointed to a slight cut near the tip of an index finger. "Looks like you've caught up with Jack Brower's ghost at last, Downey. I'm bettin' a hundred to one that them prints will match up with ones on them crowbars and cans and bottles."

"It won't take but a minute to see," the officer replied, as he drew an inkpad from his pocket. Pressing down the fingers of the gruesome hand on a scrap of paper, he got a set of prints, and a moment later was comparing them with a photograph he withdrew from his pocket.

"They check," he announced. "Believe me, this is one of the most important arrests I've ever made! Not only have I got the guy that pulled these two robberies—but the gent that got away with those two last year."

The prisoner's face went livid with fear and rage. "It's a lie! I don't know nothin' about no robberies!"

"You can tell that to the judge and the jury," Downey said. "And I ain't sayin' it will help yer case any—but that dough you claimed to have shore ain't goin' to do you no good. Why not come clean and tell where you cached it?"

"I lied. I never had no dough. And. I never had them things, neither!"

"Okay," the officer said. "Stick out yer hands while I slip on these cuffs."

At the landing, with Brown seated in the canoe, Black John smiled into the officer's face. "Well, Downey, it looks like you've got enough evidence to satisfy the Law this time."

Corporal Downey nodded, as his eyes met the big man's gaze. "Yeah, I've got the evidence, all right. But I ain't got that sixty-one thousand, and believe me both the Consolidated and the Eureka outfits is goin' to squawk their heads off."

The big man smiled. "Hell, let 'em squawk. Like I told you, Downey, you can't get all the breaks. You got your murderer, and if old Mutton Chops Forbes-Allison and the Eureka boss want their money back—mebbe they can get Bill, there, to tell 'em what he done with it. So long. Be seein' you in Dawson one of these days."

SUPERSTITION

BLACK JOHN SMITH entered the door of the Tivoli Saloon and stepped to the bar to be greeted by a familiar voice that issued from a stud game in progress at a table across the room.

"Aw, I say, Smith, old chap! How are you?"

Crossing to the table, Black John paused and smiled into the face of the man who was regarding him through a monocle.

"Hello, Lordship. I'm able to set up an' take a little nourishment," he said. "But it shore looks like you've fell in with evil companions."

The grin widened as his glance swept the faces of the sourdoughs that smiled up at him from beneath low-drawn hat brims.

"Aw, but these are all good fellows, don't you know!" exclaimed the Englishman. Popping the monocle from eye, he turned to the players. "Gentlemen, allow me to introduce my friend..."

"Never mind namin' him, Dook," laughed Old Bettles. "We've know'd that ol' reprobate ever sense he stock up the American Army over to Fort Gibbon an walked off with their payroll. It's amazin' to us that if you run onto him first, you ever hit Dawson with yer teeth left."

"Aw, but we had a jolly bear hunt together! Didn't we Smith?"

"We had a bear hunt," agreed Black John. "You was the only one that claimed it was jolly. There was too much bear involved to suit me."

"You could buy into this game for a round of drinks," suggested Camillo Bill, with a grin. "Six handed is better than five."

"Shore," seconded Bettles, "buy yerself a couple of stacks of chips, onlest you'd ruther stand around an' delay the game."

"I s'pose I'd ort to—jest to protect my friend, here," acquiesced Black John. So saying, he called for chips and drinks, and drew up a chair.

Moosehide Charlie pointed across the table. "Take a squint at them chips he's got stacked up in front of him, an' you kin see how much protection he needs."

"Yeah," echoed Swiftwater Bill, "the Dook takes to stud like a duck takes to water. We've be'n learnin' him the game fer the past month, er so, an' believe me, it's cost us plenty."

"It's a jolly old game, don't you know! Perfectly rippin'!" exclaimed the Englishman with enthusiasm. "It's the first card that makes it interestin'—the one that the others cawn't see."

"Yeah," agreed Black John, "that's my onderstandin' of it, too."

"The trouble is," said Old Bettles, as he gathered the cards for the deal, "The Dook, here takes it off'n us, an' then lets Cranston come along an' take it off'n him."

"Who's Cranston?" asked Black John, glancing at the corner of his hole card.

"HE'S A dude *chechako* that come driftin' in a couple of months ago. He don't do no prospectin'. Jest buys an' sells claims, an' does a lot of gamblin'."

"So he's be'n takin it off'n you, eh?" asked Black John, glancing toward the Englishman.

"Not at cards. This Cranston is a personable fellow, and I took him for a gentleman. He bilked me in a business transaction in the matter of a claim which he had jolly well salted. I shall endeavor to get it back him at cards."

"Not on his deal, Dook." advised Bettles. "Don't bull no big pot on his deal, no matter what you got. He's a pretty slick article. We'll prob'ly peg his racket one of these times, but until we do, you better lay off the heavy bettin' when he's got the cards."

"Did he take you for your roll?" asked Black John.

Popping the monocle into his eye, the Englishman regarded him with a puzzled expression. "Beg pawdon, did he—er—my roll? I don't quite…"

Black John interrupted with a grin. "That's right, you don't never quite. I fergot. What I was drivin' at, was to ask if this here Cranston separated you from all that syndicate money you was expectin'?"

"O dear, no! It was merely a private investment—a matter of some fifteen hundred pounds."

"An' this here Cranston? You say he buys an' sells claims. Is he a person of means?"

"What's ailing you—callin a pair of kings with nothin' but a pair of sixes. You gone crazy er what?"

Camillo Bill replied, "Accordin' to Curley, he banks anywheres between fifty and a hundred thousan' in the safe here, owin' to whether he's heavy on the buyin' or sellin' end of a deal."

"Hmm, I'd kind of like to meet up with the gent. I'm terrible superstitious, an' I've got a kind of a hunch that mebbe him an' I could do business."

Moosehide Charlie grinned. "You better took out fer him, John. He's slippery. He won't walk right up an' take it off 'n you, like you done the Army."

"'Tain't likely," grinned Black John. "From what I hear, I'd expect him to resort to guile. But fact is, I've got a claim to sell, an' he looks like a likely customer."

"He won't fall fer no salted claim," opined Swiftwater Bill. "There ain't no use tryin' to beat a man at his own game."

"Oh, I don't know," replied Black John. "What's salt fer the goose is salt fer the gander, as the Good Book says. Salt's a funny thing, Swiftwater. Some folks piles it on thick, an' others jest eases it in along with the cookin' till you wouldn't know it was there.

"You boys all know I've got plenty of dust to spend, an' likewise you all know I wouldn't lie to you.

"I'm tellin' you now that I've got a good claim—plenty good enough to sell to a bird of Cranston's stripe. An' also bear in mind that I'm superstitious. I'm tellin' you this in case the gent might kind of inquire around. Some folks is partic'lar about the kind of folks they do business with."

"Speak of the devil, an' up he pops!" exclaimed Moosehide under his breath. "There's Cranston now. He'll be over here d'reckly, wantin' to horn in on this game. But fer my part, six-handed is plenty."

"Let him set in." suggested Camillo Bill. "There's plenty of deals when he ain't got the cards."

"Shore." urged Old Bettles, "If we don't let him in the game, how we goin' to ketch him dealin' crooked. If I get onto his trick, he won't buy no claim off'n Black John, nor no one else!"

The man Cranston bought a stack of chips and seated himself to the left of Black John, who acknowledged Old Bettles' introduction with a hand grip that made the newcomer wince.

The play proceeded for a few deals, when, with a nine in the hole, and a pair of nines showing after the last card had been dealt, Black John raised Camillo Bill's bet of twenty dollars on an exposed pair of jacks.

Cranston, with an eight, a ten, a jack, and a queen showing, raised Black John fifty. Camillo Bill studied the cards and raised fifty. Black John promptly raised a hundred and Cranston raised another two hundred dollars.

The others had dropped out, and Camillo Bill, noticing that Black John had a handful of important chips ready to toss into the pot, turned down his cards with the remark that if either of the two had that case nine in the hole, he was beaten.

Just as he was about to raise Cranston five hundred, Black John's glance strayed to the bar and became fixed on the backs of the drinkers. For what seemed interminable moments, he stared at the row of backs. Then, with a muttered curse, he returned the chips to his stack, and flipped over his hole card, exposing his three nines.

"That's good," he growled, scowling wrathfully toward the bar. "Now wouldn't that have to happen jest when I had the chanct to rake in a good pot!"

"What happened?" asked Swiftwater Bill, eyeing the speaker in surprise.

Black John pointed to the opposite side of the room "Look— thirteen men lined up to the bar! An' me with three nines! It couldn't be no other way than Cranston had made his straight!"

With a grin, Cranston flipped over his hole card. It was the trey of spades.

"Of course," said Camillo Bill sarcastically, "you never noticed that he couldn't possibly have had his straight, bein' as the only nine you didn't have was showin' up in my hand!"

"THAT'S RIGHT," admitted Black John, staring ruefully at the cards. "Mebbe I'd ort to noticed, but when I seen them thirteen backs lined up agin the bar, I know'd I couldn't win."

"But, you couldn't have lost! He couldn't have had you beat! An' what's more, the way you was fingerin' yer chips to raise him made me throw down my two pair!" cried the irate Camillo.

Black John scowled at the speaker. "Sure I could have lost! I did, didn't I? That proves it! Thirteen's an onlucky number. When I seen them thirteen backs I know'd I couldn't win. Them thirteen backs was onlucky fer both of us, Camillo, an' you can't git around it. That jest goes to prove that a man's a fool that tries to go agin luck."

Puzzled glances passed between the sourdoughs as Old Bettles picked up the cards to deal, for Black John was known to them as a past master of the game of stud.

A few deals later, with only a pair of sixes, an ace, and a four showing, he called Old Bettles bet of a hundred dollars and turned over his hole card which was an eight spot. Bettles, who had bet on a pair of exposed kings, stared in astonishment.

"Didn't you see them pair of kings? What's ailin' you—callin' a pair of kings with nothin' but a pair of sixes. You gone crazy, er what?"

"Let's see yer hole card," demanded Black John, gravely.

"What's the hole card got to do with it?" asked Bettles, flipping over the card that made him two pairs. "Them kings that was starin' you right in the face was enough to beat you!"

Reaching over, Black John picked up the other's hole card and examined it meticulously. "It's all right. You win Bettles. I thought you must of had two cards stuck together in the hole, in which case, my pair of sixes would of won, your hand bein' dead."

"Two cards stuck together!" cried Bettles. "What made you think that? Bettin' agin a shore thing on the chanct that a man's got two cards stuck together in the hole! Now I know you've gone crazy!"

"Nope." replied Black John with unruffled calm. "It was jest plain common sense. See that cat over there by the bar? Well, you take notice that he's black, don't you? Jest before you bet, he crossed the room, an' he crossed it from the side from right to left. It's good luck when a black cat crosses from right to left, an' bad luck when one crosses from left to right.

"Accordin' to common sense, I couldn't of lost that pot, an' bein' as the only way I could of won it agin them pair of kings would be to have your hand dead. I figgered, of course, that you must of had two cards stuck together in the hole."

"Well, of all the fool notions I ever heard, that takes the cake!" cried Swiftwater Bill. "Anyhow, you learnt you a lesson. You kin see what believin' in them signs does to a man. How can a cat crossin' a room make a man win a pot, or lose one?"

"Easy enough." retorted Black John. "It lest made me lose one, didn't it?"

"YEAH, AN it proved there ain't nothin' in them signs."

Black John shook his head. "I've got it!" he exclaimed suddenly. "It was my fault an' not the cat's! The sign was right, yes sir, dead right! The sign rightly called fer me losin' that pot, only I read it wrong.

"It's like this—the left side of a room is the side on yer left when you come in the door. I'm settin' facin' the door, so the left side to me is really the right side of the room an' vicey versey.

"What that cat really done was cross from left to right, an' that's bad luck, jest exactly which it proved to be! No sir, boys, you can't beat old man luck. I've proved it a couple of times right here at this table. Come on, Camillo, it's your deal!"

Other glances—glances of real concern—passed between the sourdoughs as the game proceeded, for Black John was a general favorite among them, despite his openly avowed robbery of an Army payroll.

A short time later, after all the others had dropped out of a hand which Cranston had persistently raised, Black John faced the man with only a pair of tens showing in his own hand, against four exposed hearts in Cranston's hand.

Instead of checking, Black John made a substantial bet, which Cranston promptly raised a thousand. Black John studied the cards, arose abruptly, walked around his chair, and then scratched his nose.

"I'm callin' that." he said. "It takes every chip I've got!"

Cranston flipped over the fifth heart and Black John nodded. "That's good." he said. "I figgered you had me beat, an' I was just about to fold up my hand when my nose itched me. When yer nose itches you, it's good luck if you get up an' walk around yer chair before you scratch it.

"That there one ain't no shore thing sign, like the number thirteen, an' black cats. It's just toll'able. I couldn't never of won that pot if I'd of scratched my nose before I walked around my chair. Walkin' around it like I done gave me a chanct at it. Well, I'm quittin' now, I'm broke."

"Here, Smith!" exclaimed the Englishman, "I'll loan you all you want! Glad to do it, don't you know."

Others also offered to stake him, but Black John refused to borrow. "No thanks, boys, it's unlucky to play borrowed money when the moon's on the wane," he said. "Ten days from now the moon will change, an' then it would be different. Borrowed money, in a game, wanes with the moon, an' it waxes with it, too.

"It's just like workin' a claim. I don't never work a claim on the wane of the moon. It would shore peter out on me, an' a man's a fool to go contrary to the signs. That's why there ain't more rich folks. Most of 'em don't know the signs, an' the others don't give a hoot.

"You cleaned me out this trip—but I'll be back. Day after tomorrow I'll hit out for my claim, an' I'll sluice out some dust an' I'll be back. I'd go tomorrow, but it's the thirteenth of the month, an' I wouldn't start nowheres on the thirteenth.

"I'll git to the claim by the turn of the moon, an' I'll work it till the moon turns again, an' come back. I'll have plenty of dust by then, an' I'll be back in the game. An' it won't be with no piddlin' little two thousan' neither."

WHEN THE big man had gone, Cranston turned to Bettles and asked, "Who is this bird, Smith, anyhow? Has he actually got a claim where he can sluice out better than two thousand in a couple of weeks?"

"Must have," Bettles replied. "He's always got plenty of dust on him, an he seems to have plenty of time on his hands. Its prob'ly like he says—he only works on the up of the moon."

"Where is this claim?"

"I don't know. Black John lives up on Halfaday Crick. It's prob'ly up around there somewhere's. I'd shore like to buy that claim off 'n him. It must be a whop dollager, wherever it is."

"Halfaday Creek! Why, isn't that the place where all the outlaws hang out?"

"Well, not all of 'em, There's quite a few up there, so the talk goes. Black John's one hisself. The rumors is that he helt up the Army one time, an' stoled the payroll."

"What—did that dumb egg cop off an Army payroll! They must have left it hanging out on a bush somewhere, if he got away with it! I've seen superstitious men before, but never one like him! He's not only superstitious, but just plain dumb along with it."

"I've known John fer quite a while," said Moosehide, "an' I never noticed he was so…"

"Oh, shore!" exclaimed Bettles loudly. "He's the superstitionest man I ever seen. Ain't he, Camillo?"

"He shore is." agreed Camillo Bill. "His superstition cost me a good pot."

"Yeah, but it cost him more'n that," reminded Swiftwater Bill. "He bought a couple of thousan' dollar stacks when he sat in."

"I wonder if he'd sell that claim?" asked Cranston.

"Well," replied Bettles, "a man will sell anythin' he's got, if the price is right. It must be an awful good claim. He shore spends a sight of dust, an' it don't seem to bother him none."

"I'd hunt him up and make him an offer right now," said Cranston, "but I've got a hunch to wait around till he shows up a couple of weeks from now, and see if he really has cleaned up a big bunch of dust. Do you believe he'll really come back?"

"Shore, he'll come back," replied Bettles. "He said he would, didn't he? Well, when Black John says he'll be back in this stud game, after he's gone an' sluiced him out some more gold, he'll be back, an' don't you fergit it! If you'd care to risk a thousan' er so on him not showing up, I'll take you on."

"You know him better than I do," replied Cranston. "We'll just wait and see. I certainly would like to make a deal with him for that claim. I wish I knew him as well as you men do."

"You will," grinned Bettles. "Black John ain't hard to git acquainted with. In fact, you'll prob'ly know him better'n what we do. We ain't never had no business dealin's with him. Our contacts has be'n what you might say, social."

BLACK JOHN stepped through the doorway of Cushing's Fort and sauntered to the bar, where the proprietor was already setting out a bottle and two glasses.

"Say, Cush, can you howl like a banshee?" he asked, as he poured a drink.

Old Cush, the somber-faced proprietor, poured his own drink, and regarded the other with suspicion. "What," he queried warily, "is a banshee? An' why would it howl?"

"Why would a wolf howl? It howls because it's s'posed to."

"But what is it?"

"Why, its a kind of a ghost, er somethin'."

"How could a ghost howl?"

Black John shrugged. "The fact is, they do. How would I know how they do it? I ain't never be'n one."

"Yeah, well yer liable to be one, if you go pullin' one of yer jokes on me."

Black John grinned broadly. "The joke ain't goin' to be on you, Cush. It's on someone else. Fact is, I'mfiggerin' on pullin' off a drayma."

"Not by a long sight! Not with me in it, you ain't! You can't even pull none off in this saloon! I've had enough of yer draymas! Twict now you've got me mixed up in one, an' onct, if anythin' had went wrong, I'd of got shot. An' the other time, I'd of got married."

"Listen, Cush, it ain't goin' to be in the saloon. This here's an open-air drayma. An' I ain't even castin' you fer a leadin' part. All you've got to do is git out on a ridge an' howl like a banshee."

"Yeah, an' some fool will think it's a wolf an' take a shot at me!"

"No, it'll be at night. The chances is they couldn't see their sights."

"Yeah—the chances is! You're long on chances, John, when its me that's takin' 'em."

"There'll be money in it for you. I'll pay you a hunnert jest to git out on a ridge an' howl like a banshee fer a few minutes. You couldn't make a hunnert dollars no easier."

"What good would that do you?"

"Well, it might help me sell a claim. You know, I'm superstitious, an' I might not like a claim that's in the vicinity of banshees." As he talked, Black John casually poured himself another drink.

Old Cush promptly did likewise, and reaching onto the back bar, entered the two drinks against Black John's account. "I never noticed that you was so superstitious," he said.

"I didn't used to be, but I am now. It's like a disease—it creeps up slow on some folks, whilst others git a big dost of it at once, like I done. Do you want to earn that hundred? You could git down behind a rock when you howl, so no one could hit you, even if it was light."

"But I don't know what one of them things howls like," protested the unwilling Cush.

"Well, howl like you kin, an' I'll tell you if it sounds right."

"When?" asked Cush, in vast disgust.

"RIGHT NOW. We might as well rehearse when there ain't no one else around."

"You'd be makin' a fool of me, an' besides some of the boys might hear it an' think I was gettin' murdered."

"I couldn't make a fool of you, Cush. An' what do you care what the boys think. They'd know different when they got there. I'll tell 'em you was singin'."

"I kin sing as good as what you kin!"

"Shore, but the question is, kin you howl good? Go ahead an' we'll hear what it sounds like."

Throwing back his head, Old Cush let out a tentative howl, and Black John scowled his displeasure. "You don't call that howlin', do you? It wasn't hardly no more than a cross between a growl an' a squeak. Fill yer lungs with wind an' howl!"

Cush complied and Black John thumped the bar in disgust.

"You go ahead an' practice," urged Black John, "an you'll make it, all right. If you git it down right good, I'll double yer pay."

"I won't make no fool nor yet no target of myself fer wages," rebelled Cush. "You aim to sell the claim. Well, I'll howl fer a per cent, er nothin."

"All right, all right!" agreed Black John. "Ten per cent if I make the deal—nothin' if I don't. An' nothin' if you don't put up a good convincin' howl."

"I'll let out the worst noise I kin think of," promised Cush. "An' if it don't sound exactly like one of these here ghosts you was tellin' about, it'll sound like somethin' jest as bad. What ridge have I got to howl off'n? An' what night?"

"There ain't no hurry. We've got a couple of weeks yet. It'll be the ridge that runs along Rat Crick. I've still got the papers fer that claim. An' there's a pole shack on it, with a stove an a few dishes I left there."

Old Cush shook his head in disapproval. "There wasn't one of them claims on Rat Crick that paid even wages. If I was you, John, I'd let someone else cheat folks on worthless claims. That's downright ornery. Where's all these here ethicks yer allus hollerin' about?"

"**THE P'NT** is well taken, an' in the main, I agree with you. But what I claim, it's a pore ethic that won't work both ways. You know that I wouldn't stoop to cheat even a *chechako* on a worthless claim, but the gent I'm layin' fer is a low-down, bottom-dealin', claim-saltin' tin horn, who's so steeped in sin that it's drippin' out of his ears.

"You rec'lect that Lordship saved my life one time. Well this here skunk beat Lordship out of fifteen hunnert pounds on a salted claim, an' I deem it an act of gratitude to bust him flat— not wholly out of revenge, you understand, but to keep him from workin' on other pore *chechakos*. If he ain't got no more capital, he can't deal in no more claims."

"I see," said Cush. "An' was you figgerin' on returnin' Lordship his fifteen hunnert pounds, in case you succeed?"

"W-e-e-l-l, I wouldn't hardly go that far. The way I figger, it would be a distinct onkindness to Lordship to give him back them pounds. A man profits by the mistakes he makes. The lessons that don't cost him nothin' he soon fergits.

"As fer as I kin see, the only profit Lordship got off'n the deal is the lesson he learnt; an' if I was to nullity the lesson by returnin' them pounds, it would wipe out Lordship's entire profit on the transaction. An' besides, it would cut into your percent."

"That's so," agreed Cush. dryly. "You'd ort to be'n a preacher, John, the way you go after the sinful. But what about the rest of this here drayma? All you've told me so far is where I've got to howl some night on a ridge."

"That's enough fer you to know, Cush. There ain't no use in gummin' up what brains you've got with complications. If a man of limited intelligence only knows one thing, the chances is he'll go an' do that thing. But if his brain was to get all cluttered up with a lot of oncorrelated facts, there's no tellin' what he might do."

"Is that so! Well, I don't know as my intelligence is any more limited than yourn! Sometimes a man would think you didn't have none at all!"

"Yeah," grinned Black John, "an' the more of 'em that thinks that, the better I'll get along. I wasn't degradin' yer intelligence none, Cush. What I meant was that yourn more to saloon keepin' than to draymas. An' if you was to buy a drink, that would prove it."

TWO WEEKS later, after a week of torrential rain, Old Cush accompanied Black John to Rat Creek, a small stream that ran parallel to Halfaday, some ten miles to the northward.

Two years before, someone had made a strike on the creek, and the men of Halfaday had stampeded and staked it for miles. But the strike proved to be only a shallow pocket, and the claims were abandoned.

As the two topped the ridge that bounded the little valley, Old Cush gave vent to an exclamation: "Them rains shore raised the devil with this crick! The valley must of run a reg'lar flood. Look at them sluices all washed slaunchways. An' the shafts is all full of water. An' half the shacks is washed away."

*The mirror slipped from Black John's
fingers and shattered against the foot rail*

"It shore don't look like no goin' proposition," admitted Black John, "but mebbe it's better the way it is. We'll go down an' look my claim over."

As Cush said, the creek had risen out of its banks and flooded the valley from rim to rim, and had receded, leaving the abandoned sluices and shacks in sorry disarrangement.

Black John's claim was located close against the rock wall at a sharp bend of the creek. His shack had withstood the flood, though some six inches of sand had been deposited over the floor.

The table and bench were overturned, and dishes and cooking utensils were strewn about, half buried in the sand. Near the water-filled shaft, the rude sluice had been damaged and jammed down against the tailing dump.

Stepping to the lip of the shaft, Black John stood staring down into the water. "This shaft is about ten feet deep," he said. "Bein' full of water, a man couldn't git down in it till it's bailed er pumped out. So if he'd wanted to know what's at the bottom of it, he fasten a bucket on the end of a pole and scrape him up a sample.

"An' he'd stand on this side on account of the dump bein' so clost to the other side that he might slip in. In order that he wouldn't go to all that trouble fer nothin', an' be disapp'inted in the results, I'll jest give him somethin' to look at when he raises his bucket."

Producing a small moosehide pouch from his pocket, Black John untied the thong and allowed the yellow grains to trickle slowly into the shaft. "There's thirty ounces fer him to work on," he said, as he returned the empty pouch to his pocket. "That ort to gladden the heart of anyone—comin' onsight an' onseen right out of the water thataway."

"Yeah," agreed Old Cush, "that ort to be plenty to salt a shaft with. I thought you was goin' liberal on the salt when you draw'd them a hunnert sixty ounces outa the safe. What are you goin' to do with the rest of it?"

"Oh, that's jest property."

"'Course it's property. An' good property. But..."

"**I USED** the term in its more restricted sense," explained Black John, as he tossed a few shovels of gravel into the shaft. "Meanin' its part of the set-up fer this drayma of mine."

"When you ain't usin' big words, yer usin' common ones in a way which they wasn't made fer." said Cush. "Could I ask how packin' seven er eight pounds of dust around in yer pocket is goin' to help yer case any?"

"You could," replied Black John, "but you'd have to git along without an answer. Listen, an' I'll give you a few simple instructions which, if you should forgit any of'em, you don't git no ten percent, no matter how good you howl. I'm hitten' from here to Dawson. In due time I'll be back along with this tin horn, whose name is Cranston. Him an' I will show up at the saloon, an' you'll take yer cue."

"My cue! I ain't no pool player—an' no Chinaman! What do you mean my cue?"

"I was usin' the word in its theatrical sense, meanin' that it's time fer you to begin to do yer stuff."

"You mean you want me to start howlin' at him?"

"No! If you'd shet up an' let me do the talkin', we'd git somewheres. When me an' Cranston shows up at the saloon, you set up the drinks."

"I figgered it would be somethin' like that."

"Also you want to bring in about me bein' lucky to have the only good claim on Rat Crick. An' if I ask you now much I banked in yer safe, you say a hunnert thirty ounces.

"An then you tell me that whilst I was down to Dawson you was over to Red Crick huntin' moose, an' you seen where the high water had flooded all them abandoned shafts, an' mine along with 'em.

"An' I'll let on like it was news to me—like the high water come after I'd went to Dawson—an' I'll growl about my luck, like a man would, on account of havin' to bail out my shaft.

"Then me an' Cranston'll pull out for the claim, an' you foller. I'll time it so we'll git there in time fer him to rig a bucket on a pole an' scrape him up some samples before dark.

"When it gits good an' dark, me an' him will go into the shack an' eat supper, an' then I'll step to the door an' light my pipe. When you see the flare of the match, you howl, an' by God, you make it sound turrible!

"You'll be hidin' there in them rocks on the ridge above the cabin, an' me bein' so superstitious, I'll hit right out fer Dawson an' Cranston'll come, too."

"But, s'pose he don't go with you. Mebbe he ain't superstitious an' would stay on the claim."

"He'll go with me, all right," grinned Black John. "He won't let me out of his sight. I'll tell him I wouldn't spend another night on that claim fer all the gold in the world, an' that I'm hittin' to Dawson to sell the claim to old Bettles."

"An' when you git there you'll sell it to him instaid?"

"You guessed it—the first crack out of the box. An' by the way, there's one more item. You might camp on the claim that night, an' in the mornin' take the bucket an' salvage what you kin of that dust I poured down the shaft. I've heard it's bad luck to waste salt, an' there ain't no use of lyin' in the face of Providence, as a preacher would say."

AT THE mouth of Henderson Creek, Black John camped and hired some Indians to collect a few pounds of the copper nuggets which abound there. Then he placed them in little sacks, with a mixture of sand and gravel, and proceeded on his way.

Arriving at Dawson, he stopped for a few minutes at the detachment in the North West Mounted Police, where Corporal Downey weighed those sacks, accepted royalty on two hunnert sixty ounces of dust, and issued a receipt for it, never suspecting that anyone would tender the fifteen percent royalty payment on anything but gold.

A few minutes later, Black John paused beside some lumber piles and tossed the little sacks of sand and copper into the tall weeds, and passing on, entered the doorway of the Tivoli Saloon and sauntered to the bar to be greeted cordially by Cranston, who had been idly chatting with the bartender.

"Hello Smith. Back already?"

"Yeah, I come back." replied Black John indifferently, as his eyes swept the room. "Where's the boys? I figgered on mebbe gettin' my money back."

"Oh, they'll be along later. It ain't noon yet. Have a drink." When the glasses were filled, Cranston continued. "Well, did you get out some dust?"

"Yeah, I got out a little. It was hot down in that shaft an' I took it easy. Then one day I couldn't work because a eagle that was flyin' over dropped a rabbit that he had, an' that's bad luck. I'd of prob'ly broke my leg, or mebbe my neck even, if I'd of worked that day. A man has got to use common sense, even when he's in a hurry to git out dust. Drink up, an' have one on me."

They drank and refilled the glasses, and Black John drew a well stuffed pouch from his pocket and tossed it onto the bar.

"Weigh it outta there," he said to the bartender, "an' have one yerself."

"Did you dig all that dust since you've been gone?" asked Cranston, eyeing the pouch.

"Yeah. I hired me a helper, though, to crank the windlass. I got out more'n that. Here's another pouch." Producing another pouch, he laid it on the bar beside the first.

"What'll they weigh up to?" asked Cranston, striving to curb his excitement.

Placing the pouches on the scales, the bartender announced the result: "Ninety-one ounces."

"And how many days did you work?"

"We got it in twelve days, the two of us. I paid my helper an ounce a day. It was hot an' we took it easy. We got out 272 ounces, all told."

"Two hundred and seventy-two ounces!"

"YEAH, WE'D of got out more if it was cooler. I give him twelve ounces fer workin', an' I cached a hunnert an' fifty ounces. I always cache half of what I take out, in case I might need it when I git old. It's in Cush's safe up on Halfaday.

"Then here's ninety one ounces I aim to gamble with, an' the thirty ounces I paid fer the royalty on the two hunnert sixty ounces. Here's the receipt. I jest got it off'n Corporal Downey."

The man examined the paper, dated that morning, which acknowledged the receipt of 39 ounces of dust in payment of the fifteen percent royalty on two hunnert sixty ounces of gold.

"But if you left this dust up in the safe on Halfaday, how would the police know that you hadn't misrepresented the amount?"

"Downey knows I wouldn't lie to him. It wouldn't do no good anyhow. He'd weigh up what I had in Cush's safe the first time he come up there, an' if it didn't check with his record of what I'd paid in, he'd make me come acrost. We work hand in glove with the police on Halfaday. They know we wouldn't try to put nothin' over."

"Would you consider selling this claim?" Cranston asked.

"No. Bettles would like to git holt of it, but it's a good claim, an' I mightn't be lucky enough to git another one like it."

"Has Bettles made you an offer?"

"No, not definite. He knows I'd hold it awful high." Black John paused and meditatively twirled his liquor glass between thumb and finger. "I might sell it, though, if..." His voice trailed into silence.

"If what?" asked Cranston eagerly.

Black John paused and downed another drink. "Be you Irish?" he asked abruptly.

"No. What's that got to do with it? Are you?"

"No. I ain't, but my ma an' pa was. I missed bein' Irish by jest the one generation."

"Owing to some sign or superstition, I suppose," laughed Cranston, with a wink at the bartender.

"Well," replied Black John gravely, "it might of be'n some sign. I was so young when I was born, I don't remember. I don't even know if I was lucky er onlucky to of missed it that clost. But anyhow, if that banshee don't quit howlin' nights, I might sell my claim an' git off'n that crick."

"Is there a banshee on the creek?" asked Cranston in evident horror.

"Well, there's somethin' that howls like one."

"Maybe it's a wolf."

"No. I know how wolves howl. This is different. It's a turrible sound. I've heard my ma an' pa tell about banshees. They used to live in Ireland an' I guess they're thicker there. When they howl folks die."

"SURE THEY do." agreed Cranston. "I've heard about 'em all my life."

"It's true, then?" asked Black John, in a voice that quavered slightly. "I was hopin' mebbe ma an' pa might of be'n wrong."

"No, sir! They were dead right. There's no superstition about that. It's a known fact. It's too bad your claim had to be on a creek that has a banshee. That would sure effect the price if you should ever want to sell it."

"I s'pose it would," agreed Black John. "There ain't no one would want to buy onto a crick like that. I don't want to stay on it, neither. I don't want to die."

"Suppose we go up and look this proposition over, just you and I?"

"What's the use? You wouldn't buy into no banshee," said Black John disconsolately. "An' I wouldn't want you should. If you should die, I'd think mebbee it was my fault."

"Well, of course I'd be taking a long shot. I couldn't pay much for the claim, under the circumstances. But if the price was right, I might take a chance."

"It would be flyin' in the face of Providence," said Black John. "Banshees is ghosts or somethin'."

"Let's go look the claim over, and I'll make you an offer," suggested the other.

"But how about that stud game? I'd like to git my money back."

"There'll be plenty of time to play stud after you sell your claim, if I decide to buy it. Come on, let's go."

An hour later, when Old Bettles and Camino Bill sauntered into the Tivoli, the bartender called them aside. "Say," he began abruptly, "Cranston is goin' to beat Black John Smith out of his claim."

"Hmm," replied Old Bettles, "ain't that too bad?"

"It shore is. Him an' Cranston jest pulled out fer the claim. Black John's a good fella. I never know'd he's such a fool. He believes in ghosts, an' such-like, an' he believes that certain things is bad luck. I'll bet that when they git back, Cranston'll have Black John's claim."

"I wouldn't wonder an' he would," grinned Bettles, with a wink at Camillo Bill. "An' I've got a hunch that Cranston'll be believin' that certain things is bad luck, too."

OLD CUSH set out a bottle and three glasses, as Black John entered the saloon on Halfaday, closely followed by a stranger.

"Hello, Cush," greeted Black John, "I'd like fer you to meet up with my friend Cranston. Me an' him's goin' over to the claim."

"Yer claim's be'n under water." informed Cush. "I was huntin' over on Rat Crick a few days back. There was some turrible rains in the hills, an' them Rat Crick shafts is all full of water."

"I know'd I was due fer some bad luck," said Black John. "Rec'lect, Cranston, that noon I upset the salt comin' up! I told you then that it meant bad luck! Did it wash the shack away, Cush?"

"No, but it covered the floor with sand, an' it washed yer sluice around slaunchways."

"I'm glad I only spilt the salt onct," said Black John.

"Yer luck ain't so bad," consoled Cush. "If I had a claim on which I could bank a hunnert thirty ounces right here in the safe, an' take another a hunnert thirty down to Dawson with me, an' pay a helper besides—all in twelve days—I wouldn't figger my luck was runnin' so bad. An' it's the only good claim on Rat Crick, to boot. Would you Cranston?"

"No, but perhaps Smith has other bad luck in mind."

"He's too superstitious. Every little thing means somethin'— either good luck er bad, accordin' to the way he believes," replied Cush.

"A man would be a fool not to believe in them sayin's," replied Black John. "I never know'd one not to come true."

Cranston peered into the mirror and ran his fingers gingerly over his cheek. "I wonder if you'd mind if I'd shave in here?" he asked. "This stubble makes my face itch."

"Go right ahead." said Cush. "I'll have someone fetch you some hot water, an' you kin shave right there at the end of the bar."

The water was brought, as the man secured his shaving outfit from his duffel bag.

Black John was an interested spectator. "It's bad luck to shave," he opined. "I know a fella onct, whose beard had grow'd fer ten years, an' the day after he shaved the police got him."

"The police!"

"Yeah, before that they didn't know he was him."

Cranston laughed. "I'll take a chance. The police aren't hunting for me."

"Nice lookin'-glass you've got," opined black John, picking up the small silver framed mirror that the man had set up on the bar.

The next instant it slipped from his fingers and shivered into a hundred pieces against the brass foot rail, while Black John stared at the splintered glass in wide-eyed horror.

"Now I've done it!" he cried. "Now I've done it!"

Cranston smiled. "Never mind, Smith. Accidents will happen. The thing was of no particular value. I can easily get another."

"**NEVER MIND** the value!" cried Black John. "I'll pay you whatever it's worth! But I broke a lookin' glass! Seven years of bad luck on top of what I've had! Seven years! An' no gettin' out of it! I'll bet my banshee charm won't never work now!"

"Did you have a charm?" asked Cranston.

"Yeah, I sent a hundred dollars down to Madam Griseldy in Seattle, an it was a little kind of a box, which she said I dastn't open it er it wouldn't work. It come to Dawson, an' I fetched it up last trip. I buried it like she said, an' all them twelve days me an' the man was on the claim, the banshee never let out so much as a yip.

"I figured mebbe I had it beat, but now… seven years of bad luck! If that thing howls tonight, I'll know it ain't no use. I'll hit straight fer Dawson an' sell the claim to Old Bettles. He'll give me a good price, an' he don't know about the banshee. Come on, let's git it over with. I ain't got the heart to drink no more licker."

Hours later, as the sun was topping the western hills, Black John and Cranston entered the little valley of Rat Crick.

"Old Cush was right," said Black John, as he peered somberly down at his water-filled shaft. "Bad luck follers me whither ever I goest, as a poet would say. Let's git out of this valley. I don't want to be here no more nights."

"Would you mind if I—er—just sampled a pan or two of gravel from the shaft?" asked Cranston.

"No," replied Black John, wearily. "I wouldn't mind nothin.' But there's more bad luck! How kin you sample a shaft that's full of water?"

"Here's a bucket," replied Cranston. "How deep is the shaft?"

"Only ten er twelve foot. But it'll be a sight of work bailin' out all that water."

"I wasn't thinking of bailing it out," said Cranston. "It won't take long to cut a sapling and make the bucket fast to one end, and scoop out a few samples from the bottom. I can find out all I want to know very quickly. You've got a pan here, haven't you?"

"I don't know," replied Black John lugubriously, "I'd ort to have one in the shack. But with the luck I've got, the high water prob'ly worshed it away. You're smart to think up that bucket stunt."

"You go look for the pan while I cut a sapling and fasten the bucket to it," said Cranston, drawing his belt ax.

Black John returned a few minutes later with the pan. "I found it," he said somberly, "but my luck is shore runnin' porely. The shack's all messed up, an' everythin' strung all around. It'll take an hour to pan the gravel an' git supper, an' then it'll be dark.

"An' that banshee'll prob'ly howl. But it won't git me! I won't stay here an' die fer no banshee! One squawk out of it tonight an' I'm gittin' outa here as fast as my legs'll carry me!"

HE STOOD by and watched indifferently as Cranston collected gravel from the bottom of the shaft with his improvised dredge and panned it, his eyes fairly popping from his head at sight of the rich butter-yellow layer that remained in the bottom of each of the four test pans.

Later in the cabin by the light of a candle, he weighed up the dust while Black John prepared supper. "Seven ounces," he announced. "Near two ounces to the pan!"

"Uh-huh," replied Black John indifferently. "She's gittin' richer as she goes down. I never got a color out of the top strippin'. But what good is it if that charm don't work? I won't stay here an' die even if it was two pounds to the pan! Why did I have to break that lookin' glass?"

The two ate in silence—Black John in a somber, brooding mood, and Cranston in deep thought.

As the meal was finished, Black John paused in the filling of his pipe and assumed a tense listening attitude.

Then, pipe in hand, he stepped cautiously to the door and threw it open. Silence greeted him as he stood framed in the doorway.

He struck a match on the jamb and held it to the bowl of his pipe, and the next instant the silence of the night was shattered by a horrible prolonged shriek that rose and fell in a sort of weird cadence, and trailed off into an eerie, moaning wail.

Without so much as a glance at Cranston, Black John reached for his hat, swung his pack to his shoulders, and bolting from the room, struck off down the valley as fast as his legs would carry him in the dim starlight.

Behind him he could hear Cranston's feet thumping the ground as he followed.

From time to time the man called, but Black John, alternately running and walking, gave no heed.

Three miles farther on, the fleeing man turned up a shallow draw, and ten minutes later paused all out of breath, on the rim of a broad plateau where Cranston overtook him.

"We're out of the valley!" panted Black John. "We're safe! What did I tell you? Breakin' that lookin'-glass shot Madam Griseldy's charm all to pieces! I'm hittin' fer Dawson to hunt up Old Bettles! No more Rat Crick fer me! I'm through!"

"What will you take for your claim?" asked Cranston.

"Bettles'll give me a hunnert thousan'. But what do you care? Didn't you hear it yell?"

"Yes, but I've got a hunch. It's like this—I'll give you a hundred thousand dollars, if you'll throw in Madam Griselda's address."

"But her charm ain't no good. It didn't work!"

"You forget," reminded Cranston," that I didn't break a mirror."

"That's so," said Black John. "It worked fer me till I broke that lookin'-glass."

"Exactly. How about it? Wouldn't you just as soon sell to me as to Bettles?"

"Have you got the cash?"

"I'VE GOT seventy five or eighty thousand in the Tivoli safe. I'll turn that over to you as soon as we hit Dawson, and you give me 24 hours to raise the rest. I'll have to sell a few claims I'm holding."

Black John nodded. "Yeah, I'd ruther sell to you than him." he said. "You know all about the banshee, an' yer takin' yer own chances. Bettles don't know about it, an' if I was to tell him, he might back out. Bettles ain't no fool—he might not want to die no more'n I do."

"That's right," agreed the other. "I'm satisfied."

"It's a deal then," said Black John. "Come on, let's git goin'. The moon'll be up d'reckly, an' I don't like this crick, nor even to be near it."

In Dawson, Cranston promptly transferred the money deposited to his credit in the Tivoli safe to Black John, and at the end of the 24 hours, he called him out of a poker game.

"I couldn't raise but fifteen thousand more in cash," he said. "It's every cent I can rustle, beg, borrow or steal. How about it? Will you take my I.O.U. for ten thousand? I'll promise to pay you with the first ten thousand I take out of the claim. You've got ninety thousand in cash."

"Well," considered Black John, "I don't like to be hard on a man. Go ahead, write her out. It's a deal,"

With the I.O.U. in his hand, Black John turned to Cranston and said, "Come on over to the table an' I'll buy a drink. The boys'll be glad to hear of our little deal. Corporal Downey's settin' in with us tonight. He don't play very often."

"Sure thing," agreed Cranston. "But I'm afraid I can't play. I'm broke, and will be till I get back up to Rat Creek and take some dust out of that claim."

"Boys," announced Black John, as the two paused beside the table, "I jest sold out my Rat Crick claim to Cranston. I wanted you all should know about it, so if anythin' should come up that maybe didn't look jest right—like I'd took advantage of him, er somethin'—you wouldn't blame me. There's—er—somethin' a little peculiar about the deal."

"It's all right," grinned Cranston, reassuringly. "I entered it with my eyes open, knowing all the facts. If there's anything wrong with it, that's my business. It's nothing I can come back on Smith for, I assure you. All I've got to add is—I'd hate to have Smith's luck. I've just bought a claim from him that I wouldn't sell for a million!"

"I'll say you won't," echoed Black John solemnly.

And as he resumed his seat, he thoughtfully folded Cranston's I.O.U. and placed it in his pocket.

"I'll turn this paper over to Cush. It'll pay his ten percent," he muttered to himself, as he picked up his hand and scanned the pips of his cards.

WHITE HELL

"THERE'S FOUR SIXES to beat them four fours you shook. Shove the bottle, Cush, the drinks are on you," Black John said, gathering the dice from the bar.

"Not by a damn sight they ain't! By god, that there last six was a trey till you turned it over with your sleeve! I seen you do it!"

The big man grinned. "Why, my good man, I assure you that if any such incident occurred it was entirely accidental, and unpremeditated, and—"

"Yeah," Cush interrupted, as he took the day book from the back bar and made an entry. "And my four fours beat them three sixes, and you're charged with the drinks, and all the big words you kin think up or make up ain't goin' to change it!"

The door opened, and a man and a raven-haired woman stepped into the room, pushed back their parka hoods, and stamped the snow from their mukluks.

Black John smiled. "Why, damned if it ain't Louis Harpe! An' Angela, too! How's everything on Ladue Crick? By Cripes, girl—seems like you get prettier every time I see you."

The big man laughed, and turned to Cush. "Shove out a couple more glasses—and by the way, the unexpected advent of these estimable folks obviates the necessity of my payin' for this drink, it bein' the immemorial custom that upon the advent of strangers the house sets 'em up. So if you'll rub out that last entry in your book an' shove out the glasses, we'll—"

"We'll have a drink, all right—on the house. But that there book entry stays right where it's at. We've got another one comin' that you're payin' fer, that's all."

Harpe laughed. "Always you two fightin' over the drink. By gar, sometime I'm come in here and find you both dead on the floor, the bottle and glasses on the bar."

Cush scowled, as he set out the two glasses. "I'd trust John with every damn cent I've got and never lose a nickel—but, when it comes to shakin' dice for the drinks, they ain't no ornery trick he won't try to squinch out of buyin' one. That's two times he's tried to git outa payin' for that drink—both of which didn't git him nothin'."

Black John grinned and winked at Harpe as he shoved the bottle. "Fine language, English, ain't it, Louis? You ought to learn it some time."

The girl poured a little liquor into her glass and glanced at Cush. "I'll fill it up with water," she said. "I don't like whisky straight."

Black John turned to Harpe. "How you doin' over there, Louis?"

"Doin' good. Got good location. My test pan she get better all the time."

"There was a Siwash come through here the other day from Sebastian's Village, an' he says a couple of young fellas filed in below you on that feeder."

"*Oui.* Me, I'm locate Discovery claim. Angela, she got Number One Below. Last winter we take about three time better

"Get these damn dogs off!" he bellowed.

as wages. And like I'm tell you, this winter she get better every day. This spring comes two young feller—Bill Mason and Joe Preston. Mason locate Number Two Below, and Preston got Number Three."

"Ain't they pardners?" Cush asked.

The girl smiled. "No. They came in together, staked their claims and went out and recorded them. Then they came back and built a cabin on the boundary between the two locations. They worked all summer together getting out wood to burn in with. Joe Preston wanted to work the two claims in partnership, but Bill don't want it that way. And I don't blame him because Preston's kind of lazy. And besides, Bill's got the better claim, I'd guess. It lies next to mine, which we know is good. So they divided up the wood and are going it alone."

"Hum, get along all right, do they?" Black John asked.

Louis Harpe glanced at his daughter and grinned. "*Oui*, seem like they get along pretty good."

THE GIRL blushed, the smile faded from her lips, her brow puckered slightly, and she groped for words. "You see, both of them have asked me to marry them."

"An' you can't make up your mind which one it is, eh?"

"My mind's made up, all right," the girl replied. "But papa needs me there on the job, this winter—and I won't leave him till after the clean-up. But I haven't given my promise. You see, with both of them there in the cabin all winter, I figure the other one might—well, something terrible might happen. So I told them both that I wouldn't marry either one of them till spring, that after the clean-up I'd marry the one that could show the most dust. You see, I know which one will win. But if both of them think they've got a chance, they'll work hard clear up till the clean-up. And by that time the danger will be past."

Harpe drew a paper from his pocket and tossed it onto the bar. "Got to get supply," he said.

Black John glanced at the long list. "Cripes, looks like you've got enough stuff listed there to last you all winter! It would take a six-dog team to haul it."

The Frenchman grinned. "Got the seven dog team. Angela, she work hard on the windlass, she eat like hell. By gar, the man she marry better take out plenty dust to keep her goin'!"

Cush glanced through the list. "Some of this here stuff, like raisins, an' chocolate, an' powdered sugar I ain't got none of. Looks like you'll have to wait till Chris'mas an' fetch that stuff up from Dawson."

"Oh, we're not going down to Dawson, this Christmas!"

"What—not goin' to take in the Chri'tmas jamboree!" Black John cried. "Cripes sake—an' here I figured I'd have a dozen or more dances with you! An' how about Louis, there? If he don't go down, who's goin' to sing all them French songs for us there in the Tivoli?"

Again the girl laughed, and glanced affectionately at her father. "Papa sang too many French chansons last Christmas—and not only in the Tivoli, but in the Monte Carlo, and the Blue Elephant, and the Dominion, and the Borialis—and even in Cuter Malone's Klondike Palace! And every time he sang the crowd would buy him drinks. It took me two whole days to get him in shape to hit for home. So this year I decided we'd pass up the jamboree."

The big man glanced at Harpe with a grin. "How about it, Louis? What did you decide?"

"By gar—that Angela! She just like her mama. Me, I'm take few drink—that all right. Take lot of drink—hell to pay! Angela say we no go Dawson—we no go Dawson. That damn good thing you ain't got no woman tell you when you can take the drink."

Black John grinned, "Well, takin' it by an' large, as the Good Book says, bein' an abstemious man, I never felt the need of one."

"Huh," Cush grunted. "Whatever that there big word means it's prob'ly a damn lie. John, he, don't git loaded very often, but when he does, all the women in hell couldn't stop him."

"Maybe that so," Harpe grinned. "But, Angela, she ain't in hell—she right there on the crick. Me, I'm buy a drink, and then we pull out when you get the stuff ready."

"You hittin' right back?" Black John asked. "It's a good three days on the trail to your place with a loaded sled. If you'd wait till mornin', you'd only have to camp two nights instead of three."

Harpe shrugged. "Don't make no differ'—two night, four night, six night. Got the good tent. Got the good little stove. Got the good snow, now. Got the good back trail. Get more snow, take more longer, more hard work on the trail. When we get home I'm lend the dog outfit to them two young fellers. They come over here for get supply. And if they ain't got the money or the dust to pay, you give 'em what they need an' charge to me. They can pay me back after clean-up in the spring."

Later when the Harpes had gone, Cush eyed Black John across the bar. "Now we'll have that there drink I've got you charged up with," he said, shoving the bottle. "That there Angela Harpe's a damn good looker, ain't she? By god, I wouldn't mind marryin' her myself—if I was twenty year younger—er her that much older. She's smart, too. Figgerin' not to promise neither one of them fellers till spring so's they'd both work like hell all winter to git out the most dust. It looks a damn sight safer over there on that feeder than it might of been."

Black John nodded. "Yeah," he replied, dryly. "About as safe as a cocked gun, an' an idiot foolin' with the trigger."

LATE ONE afternoon, some ten days after the departure of the Harpes, a dog team drew up before the door of Cushing's Fort, and a young man entered the saloon to interrupt a cribbage game between Cush and Black John. "I'm Bill Mason," he said. "Joe Preston and I came over from Ladue Crick for a load of supplies. I expect we'll have to spend the night here. What can we do with the dogs?"

"Pull the harness off an' toggle 'em," Black John answered. "You'll find stakes an' chains out back."

As the two stepped into the room a few minutes later, Cush set a bottle and four glasses on the bar. "Fill up," he invited. "This un's on the house."

When the liquor was poured, Black John glanced at the two. "I'm Black John Smith, an' the character behind the bar there is Lyme Cushing. Old Louis an' his daughter were over here a few days ago. They said you boys would be along later."

Preston nodded. "We got an early start yesterday morning and made it through in two days. Louis said it's about forty miles. There hadn't been any snowfall lately, and we could follow Harpe's trail."

The glasses were emptied, and Black John ordered another round as Mason tossed a paper onto the bar. "Here's the list of supplies we need. We're new at this game—*chechakos*, I guess you'd call us. Angela made out the list for us."

Cush glanced at the list and laid it on the back bar. "I'll git the stuff out after supper," he said. "We can eat there at the table. I'll have the *klooch* fetch the grub in. You boys'll be wantin' to hit back whilst the weather holds. Better git an early start in the mornin'. You'll be three, four days on the back trail with a load if you have good luck. If you don't, it could be a damn sight longer."

The two newcomers each bought a round, and Black John noted that Mason cut his drink to a mere token. "There's the last damn cent I'll have till after the clean-up," Preston said, as he tossed a bill onto the bar. "And, by the way, Harpe said he'd fixed it up with you to charge these supplies."

"Only charge half of it to Louis," Mason said. "I'll pay for my share. It sure is handy to get the stuff here instead of having to haul it clear up from Dawson."

"Yeah," Black John agreed. "And, speakin' of Dawson, I s'pose you boys'll be hittin' down to take in the Chris'mas jamboree."

"The what?" Preston asked.

"The Chris'mas jamboree. There's always hell a-poppin' in Dawson around Chris'mas time—roulette, faro, stud, dancin'— and from what I hear, the churches all have big doin's— Chris'mas trees all lit up for the kids—everyone kicks in some dust for presents, and everyone has a big time. You boys ought to go down. It'll do you good. Most of the boys from the cricks show up. Kinda breaks up the winter. It's a hell of a while till spring."

Bill Mason nodded thoughtfully. "That's not a bad idea," he said. "It'll be the last chance to get any mail till spring, and I'd sure like to hear from my mother. I'll bet she's written several letters by this time, and I can write her and tell her not to worry if she don't hear from me the rest of the winter."

"We could make it in five or six days, traveling light," Preston said. "We know the trail across to the Sixtymile and on down to Dawson. Came in by way of Ladue Crick, but when we went back to record our claims Louis Harpe told us about the short-cut across the Sixtymile." He paused and grinned. "There's a grouchy old cuss living in a cabin at the mouth of a little crick that runs into the Sixtymile at a big bend. We stopped on the way down to ask if we could do any errand for him in Dawson, and he reached for his gun and told us to get to hell out of there and mind our own business!"

Black John grinned. "Old man Quinn. He located a pocket two, three years ago on that short steep gulch and struck it lucky. He's taken out plenty of dust, all right. But what good does it do him? He ain't got a friend in the world. Never spends a cent. Never goes off his claim. One of the Siwashes over in Sebastian's village hauls his supplies out to him twice a year."

Preston shrugged. "Hell of a way to live. It might be all right for a while, but I like to hit the high spots now and then, get a few drinks under my belt, swing the gals high wide and handsome, and I wouldn't mind sitting in on a little stud—that is," he added, "if I can borrow enough dust off of old Louis for a stake. I guess we'll take in that Christmas jamboree."

After the two had departed with the sled load of supplies the following morning, Cush turned to Black John. "How come you was so damn anxious them boys took in the Christmas jamboree down to Dawson?" he asked.

"Like I told 'em," the big man replied. "It's a hell of a while till spring. You know even a couple of sourdoughs winterin' together on a crick get crusty as hell before spring. An' *chechakos* are a damn sight worse. Especially with Angela Harpe danglin' between 'em. Men have been murdered over women a damn sight harder to look at than she is. The Chris'mas jamboree busts up the long winter—gives 'em a chance to blow off steam. I'd hate like hell to have anything happen to Mason. He's a damn good kid."

II
JAMBOREE!

EARLY IN THE morning of the second day after Christmas, Black John stepped, into the lobby of the Northern Hotel just as young Mason turned away from the desk and reached for his pack sack on the floor beside him. "Stirrin' around kind of early, ain't you? Pullin' out, or just gettin' in?"

"I'm pullin' out. We hit town the day before Christmas. I picked up my mail and a few things I wanted, wrote a few letters, mixed around with the crowd, here and there. But I'm not much of a drinker, those dance hall floozies don't interest me, and I don't care much for cards, so I'm hitting back to the crick."

"How about your pardner? He goin' back, too?"

"Joe? No. He's having too good a time where he is. Hangs around there at the Klondike Palace. He keeps pretty well liquored up. Dances and plays cards all night. He's up in his room—just rolled in a few minutes ago. I stopped in there and wanted him to come with me, but he says he's doing all right playing stud, and hit a couple of lucky numbers on the wheel. He wanted me to stay a few days longer, but I told him nothing doing. I came up here to dig gold—not to hang around saloons."

"Pal, of yours, was he—back where you come from?"

"No. I met him on the boat—the *Islander*. We landed on Dyea beach and came on in together. We're not partners. We share the same cabin, but each works his own claim. You're up kind of early, too. Are you pulling out for Halfaday Crick?"

The big man grinned. "No, just pullin' in from the Tivoli. Got to catch me some sleep. Set in a stud game all night with a bunch of sourdoughs an' got into 'em for about eleven thousan'. Told 'em I'd give 'em two nights to try an' get it back. Whether they do, or don't, I'm hittin' back day after tomorrow."

The going was good on the big river, and when the short day waned Mason had no trouble following the hard-packed trail by starlight. Late in the evening, with thirty miles behind him, he spent the night with Art Harper, who had camped in a tent on a point, on his way down from Selkirk. The following night be spent with the trader at Ogilvie opposite the mouth of the Sixtymile. Near noon the following day, some ten miles up the Sixtymile, he met an Indian with a six-dog team traveling light down the river.

The good weather held, and in the evening of the second day thereafter, he paused and gazed for a full minute at the light that showed in old man Quinn's window. He was dog tired, and hungry after a long day on the trail, and the cabin looked inviting. Spending the night in the shelter of a cabin, even if he had to sleep on the floor, would be much more comfortable than building a fire in some spruce thicket, squatting in the cold to eat his supper, and rolling up in his robes in the snow. He was about to turn from the river when the thought of the crabbed old man deterred him. "Nothing doing," he said aloud. "The old cuss would probably tell me to get to hell out of there, like he did before. I'll camp in the bush rather than have anything to do with the old devil."

He camped in a thicket a couple of bends farther on, and got an early start in the morning. Toward noon the light, easterly breeze freshened, and filmy clouds scudded across the sky. As darkness fell the clouds thickened, and Mason increased his pace. The wind-packed snow made good footing, and he shoved on, following the white lane of the ice-covered river that wound between the black walls of spruce. The wind increased to a gale, its steady roar in the spruce tops broken now and then by the crash of a falling tree. Flinty snow stung his face—fine as flour, it bit into his skin like the points of hot needles. "That abandoned cabin!" he exclaimed as he skirted a stretch of open rapids. "It can't be far from here. If I can only reach it while I can still see. I've got to make it. I couldn't even build a fire the way this storm is building up." Lowering his head to the icy blast, he shoved on, and an hour later, with a shout of relief, he stumbled up the bank and shoved open the door of the substantial log cabin he and Preston had spent the night in on the way to Dawson. Taking a candle from his pack, he lighted it and thrust it into the neck of an empty bottle. "I'm sure glad we left this wood and kindling here," he muttered, as he knelt and kindled a fire in the stone fireplace. "And, I'm glad that whoever built this cabin thought of a fireplace. It's the only one I've seen in the country. I'd have had the devil of a time cooking my supper outside tonight."

Mason slept soundly through the night and breakfasted by candle light. The steady gale of the previous evening had broken into fitful gusts that sucked the flames from the fireplace furiously up the chimney one moment, and the next a fitful downdraft filled the cabin with smoke. Shouldering his pack, he opened the door to be greeted by a swirl of fine snow that all but blinded him. The next instant the air was clear, and he watched the funnel-shaped snow eddy disappear down the river, bouncing against the walls of spruce as it was whipped from side to side by the ever changing gusts of wind. Other flurries appeared above and below whirling furiously for a few moments and disappearing, while high above the spruce tops the sky was obscured by a swirling chaos of white.

Closing the door, Mason tossed his pack onto the bunk. "Guess I'll lay over for a day," he muttered. "I've been shoving right along the past six days. The rest will do me good."

Picking up his light ax, he crossed the tiny clearing that surrounded the cabin and attacked a dead spruce tree, chopping trunk and limbs into firewood lengths which he carried into the cabin. Then he worked on another and another. It was well toward noon when he stepped from the timber into the clearing with an armful of wood and the storm struck with a force that all but knocked him off his feet. Out of the northeast it came—a solid wall of fog-like snow that bit into his lungs as he gasped for breath, and completely obliterated the cabin, scarcely ten yards distant. A few moments later he slammed the door against the icy blast, and as his eyes accustomed themselves to the gloom of the interior, he regarded the two piles of wood, one on each side of the fireplace that reached from the floor to the rough split log mantelpiece. "Boy, I'm glad I didn't hit out this morning!" he said aloud. "This storm might last two or three days—and I'm sure glad I put in the time cutting wood."

AT EXACTLY six o'clock in the morning Black John Smith, shoved his chair back from the card table in the Tivoli Saloon in Dawson, and eyed the other players. "Game's over," he announced, as he stacked the chips before him. "I got into you boys for eleven thousand, and told you I'd give you two nights to get it back." He paused and grinned into the faces of the sourdoughs, old Bettles, Swiftwater Bill, Moosehide Charlie, Burr MacShane, and a character known as Buzz Hornet. "I'll admit you tried like hell, and only lost about four thousand more in the attempt. Let that be a lesson to you. If you're bound to play stud, pick out someone you can beat."

The sourdoughs grinned sheepishly. "Yeah," Bettles chuckled, "I s'pose you've forgot about last summer, when we took you for eight thousan' between Dominion Day an' the Fourth of July."

"An' how about that game up to Ogilvie last September. If I remember right you didn't do so damn good then, either."

"Mere come-on amounts. Cripes, if I won all the time I couldn't get anyone to play with me, and it would be lonesome as hell in Dawson without a card game, now and then." Pausing, he raked the chips and slips of paper into his cap. "I'm cashin' in this stuff at the bar. You boys can settle with Curley for these markers. I'm goin' to get breakfast and be on my way."

"You mean you're hittin' the trail without no sleep?" asked Moosehide Charley.

"Sure I am. A man's got to get straightened around sometime. Here in town it's all right to play stud all night and sleep all day—but on the trail it's a damn sight handier to travel daytimes, and sleep nights."

As Black John stepped across the room and dumped the contents of his cap onto the bar he was joined by Buzz Hornet. "Say, John—that there marker of mine—how much is it?"

Selecting one of the slips of paper, the big man glanced at it. "It calls for five hundred and fifty dollars. You want to take it up, or shall I get it from Curley?"

The man cleared his throat nervously. "Well, you see—it's like this here. I ain't got no credit with Curley. He won't cash my markers no more."

"Why not?"

"It's on account of because—here a while back I got a load of liquor off him on credit. I aimed to pay for it when I'd sold the liquor. But fact is, I got in a game over in Louse Town, an' lost the hull works, so I couldn't pay him."

"I thought you got your liquor from Cuter Malone down to the Palace."

"Yeah, I allus did, till he shut down on me a while back, on account I'm owin' him fer a couple of batches."

"So, seein' as Curley won't cash your marker, you want to take it up yourself, eh?"

The man shifted uneasily on his feet. "I would. But, facts is, I ain't got that much on me."

"How much have you got?"

"Nothin' to speak of—mebbe eight, ten dollars."

"How come you set in the game—with only eight, ten dollars on you, an' no credit to back you up?"

"Well—I—er—I figgered I'd win, an' mebbe git enough to stake me to a couple bar'ls of liquor."

"This liquor—where do you sell it, mostly?"

"Oh, here and there—on the cricks—wherever the Siwashes has got enough fur to buy it."

"How do you get it to 'em?"

"Dog sled."

"You got a good dog team an' sled?"

"Sure I have. Six damn good dogs and a good sled."

"What do you hold 'em at?"

"I wouldn't sell 'em. Cripes, if I sold my outfit, how in hell could I git out on the cricks with my liquor?"

"I'm tellin' you, Hornet, you ain't goin' to get out on the cricks with no liquor for a while. I'm takin' your outfit in payment for this marker. I can pick up good dogs here for fifty dollars apiece. But I'm givin' you seventy-five—that makes four hundred an' fifty, an' I'm allowin' fifty for the sled, an' fifty more for the harness. That just takes care of your marker. Here it is—where's your outfit?"

"By god, I won't let that outfit go!"

"The hell you won't! Listen, old Sebastian from up on Ladue crick and ten of his Siwashes are in town right now. And every damn one of 'em are willin' to swear that you sold two barrels of cut liquor to the Siwashes up there on Ladue Crick, last month, and cheated hell out of 'em, at that. And Corporal Downey's just itchin' to get the goods on you. I'm tellin' you that I get that outfit—an' get it right now—or you go to jail with an iron-clad case against you—an' believe me, Judge Stowe will throw the book at you. And by god, he ought to! You're nothin' but a low-down, hooch-peddlin', Siwash-swindlin' son of a gun! And my takin' over your outfit might save some poor Siwashes their winter's catch. You're well named, Hornet. You've stung plenty of folks—but you ain't stingin' me by a damn sight. Come on now and turn over that outfit—and then you better hit out down-river, and don't stop till you hit the Alaska line. Because I'm goin' to slip Downey the word that you're in town—and Sebastian's Siwashes, too. So you better begin pickin' 'em up an' layin' 'em down damn quick."

WITH THE excellent dog outfit he had won from Hornet, Black John made good time on the trail, reaching Quinn's cabin at noon of the third day to find the oldster drawing a pail of water from a hole chopped through the ice of the river. The man scowled as he drew up beside him. "Huh, it's you, eh?"

"Yup," the big man grinned. "Me—in person."

"What you doin' with Buzz Hornet's dogs?"

"Drivin' 'em. Only they ain't Buzz Hornet's dogs. They're mine. I won 'em off him in a stud game."

"If you win his dogs, how the hell's he goin' to peddle his liquor? I'm needin' a jug right now. Mine's damn nigh empty."

"He ain't. That's why I took his dogs—to keep him off the cricks. He's a damn, low-lived skunk, the way he's be'n cheatin' the Siwashes out of the fur they need for clothin' an' grub."

The scowl deepened on old man Quinn's face. "What's it any of your business if he cheats the damn Siwashes? Accordin' to the tell, you're the damndest outlaw they is in the country, yerself."

Black John chuckled. "I've heard the rumor. But you've got to remember Quinn—there's a damn sight of difference in outlaws."

"When I seen them dogs roundin' the bends I figgered it was Hornet, an' I could git a jug off'n him. Now I gotta wait till that damn Kumtak gits here with my supplies, an' the damn lazy buzzard'll prob'ly lay around Dawson three, four days 'fore he even starts back. He mightn't git here for a week."

A vicious gust of the rising wind picked up a cloud of loose snow, and Black John glanced upward at the scudding clouds. "He damn well mightn't. It looks from here like a storm's kickin' up, and, comin' from the northeast, she might be a humdinger. I might even be persuaded to put up here for the night—if I was asked."

Again the old man growled. "You ain't asked. I ain't got only the one bunk, an' I don't keep no boarders, no how. Las' spring, couple young fellers come down the river an' stopped to ask could they do nothin' fer me in Dawson. But, hell, I know'd what they was up to. They figgered on hangin' around and locatin' my cache. So I grabs up my rifle and tells 'em to git to hell outa here. They come on back, but you bet they didn't stop that time, nor when they come sloggin' down agin a few days 'fore Chris'mas. I mind my business, an' by god, other folks better mind theirn! No one kin play me fer a damn fool!"

"They'd be wrong as hell if they didn't, Quinn," the big man grinned. "Thanks for the hospitality. I'll be pullin' on. Got to locate a good campin' place before this storm really hits."

PUSHING ON in the face of the rising gale, Black John camped early a few miles above Quinn's, and morning found him again on the river. The gale had broken into fitful gusts picking up swirling eddies of snow that seemed to strike from every direction at once. "I don't like it," he muttered, as he cracked his long-lashed whip over the heads of the dogs. "Mush, damn you, mush! The way this storm's ribbin' up, I'll be damn lucky to reach the

Baron's cabin before it hits—and if I don't make it I'll prob'ly put in the next three, four days holed up in a snow bank chawin' frozen fish with the dogs."

Toward noon an ominous calm succeeded the swirling eddies. Overhead the opaque gray of the low-hung clouds blotted out the mountain peaks. The sled runners rasped harshly on the windpacked snow as, with his hand on the tailrope, he urged the dogs to their utmost. A solitary raven rose from a thicket, circled high, and slanted earthward emitting a raucous jumble of hoarse squawks and croaking. "You're damn right," the big man grinned, "when she hits, she's goin' to be a hell-winder—an' by god—here she comes!" As the words left his lips, a dull, all-encompassing roar sounded from behind, and glancing over his shoulder he saw the approaching white wall bearing rapidly down from the northeast, blotting out mountains and timber—an opaque smother of whirling white.

"Mush! Mush!" he cried, cracking his whip about the ears of the straining dogs. "We've got to bore through it—but we ain't got to face it! An' we can't get off the river!"

The storm hit with a fury that seemed to tear the words from his lips. The air was filled with snow, fine as fog, that blotted out sight of the dogs, filled his eyes, and plugged his nostrils with flinty particles. Tightening his hold on the tail rope he pushed on. The pace had slowed to a walk. In vain he shouted at the dogs, but the words, torn from his lips by the wind and smothered by the snow, scarcely reached his own ears.

For an hour the outfit pushed on, the dogs blundering, now against one of the steep banks of the river and then another as they managed to negotiate the numerous bends. Then the outfit stopped with a suddenness that sent Black John sprawling over the sled. Regaining his feet, he shouted and plied his whip, but the dogs did not respond. Making his way forward, he found the dogs crouched flat on their bellies, whimpering and whining. Then, as he inched his way on, he heard it—the muffled roar of the rapid! And he heard it in the nick of time—another step, and he would have been in the water. Crouched beside a dog he saw that the animal was squatting braced back, saw that he was the next dog behind the leader, saw also that there was no leader, only a pair of traces, stretched taut, disappearing over the edge of the ice. Baring his hand, the big man succeeded in drawing the belt knife from beneath his parka and severing the traces. Grasping the front dog by the collar, he managed to turn the team and, step by step, work the outfit to the bank and onto the portage trail that skirted the rapid. Here he paused, and words rumbled from beneath the black beard that now was a mat of frozen snow. "It ain't so far to the Baron's cabin from here," he muttered. "An' hour, maybe—two hours, if I can keep goin'. But without a lead dog, I don't know." Cutting the long whip-lash from the handle, he made one end of it fast to the collar of the front dog, threw the lash over his shoulder, and shoved on, groping his way step by step along the narrow trail through the ever-deepening snow that might at any moment give way and plunge him into the icy white water.

It took an hour to reach the head of the half-mile rapid, and it was with a mighty sigh of relief that he found himself again on the comparatively smooth ice of the river. On and on he slogged, half leading, half dragging the leaderless team.

THE EARLY darkness had fallen, slowing his pace to a crawl as he felt his way with his feet. Suddenly he tripped and fell forward over a dead spruce that had fallen onto the ice, and the next moment the dogs were upon him, growling, snapping at each other in a frenzy of rage and fear. Smashing out right and left with his mittened fists, he tried to fight his way out from under the fighting dogs, only to find himself hopelessly entangled in the harness. In vain he yelled and cursed and guarded his face with one hand from the vicious fangs as the terrified dogs snapped and tore at each other. Then, suddenly, a voice reached his ears. Strangely muffled and far-away it sounded, yet the big man knew that it must be close to be heard at all above the medley of growls and yelps and the all pervading roar of the storm. "What's the matter, there? Who is it?" came the words.

Filling his lungs Black John bellowed. "Get these damn dogs off me! Club hell out of 'em! Cut the traces! Kill 'em if you have to!" A few moments of silence followed, then the sound of a thumping club, and sharp yelps as the dogs ceased fighting and cringed on their bellies. It was but the work of a few moments to disentangle the twisted harness and release the entangled man, who regained his feet, and thrust his face close to the other's in the darkness. "Who the hell are you? An' where'd you come from?"

"I'm Bill Mason!" the other shouted, "and I came from a cabin there in a little clearing at the top of the bank! I've got a good fire going in the fireplace. Come on in."

"I'll turn these dogs loose first, and be right with you," the big man shouted, and jerking off his mittens busied himself with the harness. Ten minutes later he stepped into the cabin, and dumped a huge pack onto the floor. "Bed roll, dog feed, an' a little grub of my own," he explained as he glanced at young Mason who was eyeing him with a grin.

The grin widened. "Oh, I thought you were Santa Claus, white beard, pack, and all. A little late—but why—say—aren't you Black John Smith, of Halfaday Crick?"

"The same, and in person," the big man replied, as he stepped close to the roaring fire. "And when a couple of pounds of ice melts off my beard, you'll see that it's black—not white."

"But how did you manage to get here in a storm like this? I'll say you're lucky."

"Lucky's the word—damn lucky! So lucky that if you hadn't showed up just when you did, folks would have been wonderin' what become of me from now on."

"I was mighty lucky myself to reach this cabin. Then this morning it looked so stormy, I decided to lay over for a day and put in the forenoon chopping wood and carrying it in."

The big man nodded. "We're both damned lucky. If you hadn't made that decision, we'd neither one of us lived out this blizzard."

"I'm glad whoever built this cabin put in a fireplace. A man would have the devil of a time doing his cooking outside—and it would be mighty uncomfortable inside without any heat."

"Yeah, the Baron used to live here. Worked a claim for a year or so, but it wasn't nothin' to brag of. He was a peculiar sort of cuss. A German—Baron von Hutton, his name was. Had a lot of books. Used to set around readin' most of the time. Prob'ly done better if he'd throw'd the books in the fire an' leaned a little heavier on his shovel. Pulled out a year or so ago." As he talked, Black John opened the pack and extracted five frozen fish. "Got to feed the dogs," he said. "And I'm damn glad it's fish they're eatin' tonight—an' not me."

III
MURDER!

TOWARD NOON ON the tenth day after the big blizzard, Corporal Downey looked up from his desk at detachment headquarters in Dawson as an Indian stepped into the room and sidled to the desk, clawing the cap from his head. "Me Kumtak," he said. "Take the dog, git load supply for ol' man Quinn on Sixtymile. I'm stay in Dawson till the big storm quit. Then I'm go to Quinn with supply. Get to Quinn cabin. Ol' man Quinn he dead on the floor. Got the hands tie. The feet tie. Got the shoe off. Got the feets burn. Got the nose smash. Got the eye black. I'm think mebbeso something happen to ol' man Quinn. I'm throw the supply in the Cabin and come back like hell to tell police about that."

"Yeah," Downey agreed, "it does look like somethin' might of happened to him, at that. You say old man Quinn hired you to haul him a load of supplies with your dog team? Where do you live?"

"Live Ladue Crick—Sebastian town. Ol' man Quinn aint got no dog. In the fall I'm haul him load supply in canoe. He say you come back Chris'mas time haul me another load supply with dog. So I'm do that."

"Did you start out from Quinn's cabin?"

"Yes—ol' man Quinn give me the paper with the supply wrote on for give Al Skougale at the store."

"How long did it take you to get to Dawson from Quinn's?"

"Fi' day."

"And you got to Dawson the day the storm hit?"

"Yes."

"And you hit out the day after the storm quit?"

"That right."

"How long did it take you to get back to Quinn's?"

"Six day with load supply."

"Then you got back here in four days—is that right?"

"That right. I'm come jus' so fas' the dog can run."

"On your way down after the supplies, did you meet anyone— on the Sixtymile, or the Yukon?—See anyone goin' up when you were comin' down?"

"On Sixtymile, about half day up from Yukon is one white mans comin' up the riv'. Got no dog. Got the light pack. On Yukon is Mr. Dickson, and Gene Laporte."

"This man you met on the' Sixtymile—did you ever see him before?"

"Yes. Las' spring cum' him and another mans up Ladue Crick. Go on up the crick and locate the claim on little crick by Louis Harpe claim."

For several minutes Corporal Downey sat drumming on his desk top with his fingers. "Okay, Kumtak. You done right in comin' to the police. It looks like a murder from here. Stick around till mornin', an' I'll hit out with you to Quinn's place. I s'pose you'll be goin' on to Sebastian's Village?"

"Yes—me, I'm go home."

Five days later, as the two reached Quinn's cabin late in the afternoon, Corporal Downey stepped into the cabin and emitted a low whistle as he eyed the interior in the fast-fading daylight. Stepping over the corpse, he lighted the tin bracket-lamp and turned to the Indian who stood in the doorway. "Come on in and shut the door while I get a fire goin'," he invited.

Kumtak shook his head vigorously. "No! Not come in there! Not stay in there in the night with dead mans! Me, I'm go' home!"

Downey grinned. "Okay. Go on home, then. But stick around there in case I need you."

The Indian hesitated for a moment and pointed to the clock shelf. "Me, I'm want my dust."

"Your dust? What, do you mean—your dust?"

"Ol' man Quinn he weigh out my dust for pay for haul supply. Twelve ounce dust. He put in the poke and lay by the clock. Say I'm get that when I'm git back with supply."

Downey picked up the poke, hefted it and set it aside. "I'll give you a receipt for this. You'll get it later. I might need it for evidence."

Pocketing the receipt, Kumtak turned away, and the next moment headed upriver.

As the Indian had said, Quinn lay on the floor with his hands and feet tied. The stub of a candle lay on the floor beside the feet which had been blistered with its flame. That the man had received a terrific beating was attested to by the broken nose, bruised lips, and blackened eyes. He had finally been dispatched by a knife thrust through the heart, but not before he had been repeatedly prodded about the hands and chest with a knife. Downey recovered a sheath knife from beneath the table, where it had evidently been tossed, and also a letter that lay partially concealed beneath the dead man's body—a letter that had evidently dropped from the murderer's pocket as he leaned over his victim. Tossing his blankets onto the bunk, he cooked and ate his supper, and, shoving aside the dirty dishes that littered the table, he used his own. He lighted his pipe and stared at the corpse on the floor. "It's a murder, all right, and a damn dirty one. I wonder if the old man told where he had his dust cached? He must have got it just before, or durin' the blizzard. There wasn't a track in the snow when we got here." His glance strayed to the sheath knife that he had placed on the table together with the bloody envelope. "It ain't a common make of knife, all right, but even so, I might have had a hell of a time locatin' the owner, but findin' this letter was a break for me. I sure wish every damn crook was that careless. In the mornin' I'll hit for Louis Harpe's crick, and, if the hombre Kumtak met on the river is this William Mason, he's going to have to do some pretty fast talkin'."

Carefully wrapping the knife in an old newspaper, he placed it, together with the letter and the poke of dust in the pack sack. Covering the corpse with a blanket from the bunk, Downey spread his own blankets, blew out the light and turned in.

TOWARD EVENING of the third day after leaving old man Quinn's, the officer tapped on the door of Louis Harpe's cabin to be greeted by Angela. "Why, it's Corporal Downey! Come on in! You're just in time for supper."

"By gar, Downey, throw your pack in the corner and take off you things! We got good supper. Two, three days ago I shoot yearling moose. Angela, she throw another big steak in the pan."

"I'll say it's a good supper," the officer grinned as he slipped off his pack and removed his parka. "I've been livin' on trail rations for the last eight days. It'll shore feel good to be able to shove my feet under a table."

"You got somethin' on you mind? Or just take the little walk for you health?"

"I'm takin' a walk, all right—but not for my health. Know anyone by the name of William Mason?"

Fork in hand, Angela turned swiftly from the stove where the steak sizzled in the pan. "Bill Mason!" she cried, her eyes on the officer's face. "Oh, where is he? Is he all right? The blizzard caught him somewhere on the trail—probably on the Sixtymile. He was coming back from Dawson, and it's eighteen days since the blizzard let up—and—Bill never got here."

"Friend of yours?" Downey asked.

The girl brushed a tear from her eye with the back of her hand. "He was more than a friend—he—I—we were going to be married after the clean-up in the spring. Oh, why did you ask about him? Has—has something terrible happened?"

Corporal Downey nodded slowly. "Yes, Miss Angela," he replied gravely. "From your angle I'm afraid it's somethin' pretty terrible." Downey told them about what had happened, and insisted, saying, "And it looks from here like Mason murdered him."

"No!" The word exploded from the girl's lips. "Oh, how can you say that? If you knew him you'd know that he never murdered anyone! He's the nicest, kindest man in the world!"

Facing about the girl turned the steak in the pan, as old Louis eyed the officer with furrowed brow. "Me, I'm know you long time, Downey. I'm know you smart mans. But this time I'm think you wrong. What make you think Bill Mason kill old man Quinn?"

Stooping, Downey reached into his pack sack and, removing the covering, drew out a sheath knife. "Do you recognize this?" he asked. "It ain't one common to the country. Prob'ly fetched in from the outside."

Harpe eyed the knife and nodded. "*Oui*, that Bill's knife, a'right."

Angela's face showed paper-white in the lamplight as she stared at the knife in the officer's hand. "Yes—it's Bill's knife. I—I'd know it anywhere. Where—where did you find it?"

"I picked it up off Quinn's floor where the murderer tossed it after killin' Quinn." Again he reached into the pack sack and withdrew a letter. "I picked this up off the floor, too. It's addressed to William Mason, Dawson, Y.T. It laid partly under Quinn's body. It's got blood on it—Quinn's blood."

Angela broke the awkward silence. "That's Bill's knife and Bill's letter," she said in a voice that sounded flinty hard. "But Bill Mason never murdered old man Quinn. If he was murdered, someone murdered him and tried to put it off on Bill. The murderer might have murdered Bill first and taken his knife and that letter—that may be Bill's blood on the envelope, and not old man's Quinn's. Is that all the evidence you have?"

"Not quite all. A Siwash met a man headin' up the Sixtymile alone half a day up from the Yukon, travelin' light, and the Siwash recognized him as one of two men who shoved up Ladue Crick last spring and located on this feeder."

"It could have been Joe Preston, then!" the girl cried, "Joe got back here about noon on the fourth day after the blizzard."

Corporal Downey's brow furrowed. "It's possible that this Preston's our man. This Siwash, Kumtak, his name is—lives in Sebastian's village. He'll know when he takes a look at Preston, whether he's the man he met on the run. It's Preston's cabin I passed a little ways down the crick, I s'pose. A light showed in the window, but I passed it up, wantin' to talk to you folks first."

Tears streamed from the girl's eyes. "That's Bill's cabin, too," she said in a low trembling voice. "Only Bill isn't there now. Bill Mason may be dead—but he's no murderer."

"For your sake I hope you're right, Miss Angela," Downey said in a low kindly voice. "All I can say is that I'll personally keep on the case till it's closed."

"And I'll keep on it till it's closed, too—if it takes me all the rest of my life," the girl replied, as she slipped the steak from the pan onto a platter which she placed on the table. "Let's eat. No use letting the supper get cold."

The meal was eaten in silence. The girl cleared the table, and, as the two men lighted their pipes, Downey turned to Harpe. "Tell me about Mason and Preston."

"Ain't so much we know. Black John tell them about the jamboree in Dawson. Bill have some money left—but Joe is broke and he borrow twenty ounces dust from me, say he pay back after clean-up in spring. Bill, he don't come home. When Joe git here, he handed me back my poke of dust. Say he don't have to use it. Say he lucky on the card—on the wheel. That all we know."

"That's all," Angela added, "except that I love Bill Mason. I don't like Preston. I put them both off because if I accepted Bill I was afraid of Joe Preston—and—and with the two living together there in the cabin all winter…" The words trailed into silence, and Downey nodded.

"I know what you mean. Lots of things have happened when two men winter together. But I want to talk to Preston. We'll get him up here. But first let's see if we can get any clear finger-prints on this knife handle. I've been careful to touch nothin' but the blade—had the handle protected as you saw with a paper wrappin'. If I can get some good prints—when Preston gets here I can compare them with his, and if they check, maybe we can close this case, here an' now—right in this room." As he talked, Downey produced some light powder from a container and dusted it onto the hilt of the knife while Angela and her father watched in breathless suspense as for several minutes he scrutinized the hilt from all angles through a pocket magnifying glass. Finally he looked up and shook his head in disappointment. "No good," he said. "Not a clear print anywheres. All smudged up—like his hand slipped. Let's get Preston up here. I want to ask him some questions."

HARPE DONNED cap and parka and stepped from the room, and Downey, noting the tears of disappointment in the girl's eyes, sought to comfort her. "Don't give up hope, Miss Angela.

It looks bad from here. But you never can tell. I promised I'd stay on this case till it's closed—an' I'll keep that promise."

The girl nodded. "I know you will. And I know you'll find that Bill Mason didn't murder old man Quinn. But where is he? I'm afraid you'll find that he's—that he's dead—that—the one who killed Quinn killed Bill first—or how else could he have gotten Bill's knife—and that letter?"

The door opened and Harpe stepped into the room followed by a younger man. "This Joe Preston," he announced. "And, Joe, this Corporal Downey. He say ol' man Quinn git murder—try to fin' out who keel heem."

Preston smiled. "So that grouchy old cuss got murdered, did he?"

"You knew him?"

"Met him once—and believe me, once was enough. He told us to git to hell out of there and mind our own business. Black John Smith told us he was a cantankerous old cuss who was taking out plenty of dust but didn't have a friend in the world—and I can well believe it. And you bet I passed him up when I came back here from Dawson after the Jamboree alone."

"You say you and Mason went to Dawson together for Christmas. Why didn't you come back together?"

"Well, I like to have a good time. Bill don't care for such things, so he hit out. He wanted me to come, too—but my luck was running at cards, so I stayed on for a couple of days."

"You hit out alone, then?"

"That's right."

"Meet anyone on the trail—on the Yukon, or the Sixtymile?"

"Why, yes. On the Yukon, just a little way below the mouth of the Sixtymile, three fellows had pulled off the trail to fix a sled runner. I stopped and offered to help, and they pulled out a bottle, and we had a drink or two—no one I knew. While we were there, Black John Smith passed us on the trail. He had a dog team and was going like the devil—didn't stop."

"Meet anyone on the Sixtymile?"

"No."

"Didn't overtake Mason?"

"Of course not! Bill's pretty good on the trail, and as I told you he left Dawson two days before I did."

"Where did you hole up durin' the blizzard?"

"It was above Quinn's cabin—about halfway between there and that open rapid, I guess. An Indian had swung off the river just before the storm hit and was trying to pitch his tent. It was a crude affair—not much more than a tarp, and I helped him with it. It was the devil of a job—with the wind and the fine snow—but we finally made it, and crawled in and laid there under our blankets till the storm let up."

"Didn't build a fire? Didn't do no cookin'?"

"Hell, no! Why you couldn't see your hand before your face. The whole air was filled with snow as fine as dust. We just laid there for three days. I had some chocolate, and the Indian had some smoked meat, and we chewed that."

"Who was he, this Siwash? Where was he from? Was he one of Sebastian's?"

"I don't know. I didn't ask him his name or where he came from. I'll tell you this, though. I hit out early the morning the morning the storm quit, and spent the night in a cabin above the rapid. There was a lot of freshly cut wood in the cabin that wasn't there when Bill and I went down to Dawson, and evidence of a recent fire in the fireplace. I figured that Bill had holed up there during the storm. But, if you say old man Quinn was murdered, it might have been his murderer, and not Bill."

"Didn't see any tracks?"

"No. The wind still held pretty stiff, and loose snow was drifting along the ground. There were no tracks visible. Poor Bill—it sure was a shock to me when I got here and found out he hadn't showed up. I hate to think of him lying out there somewhere under the snow."

Downey nodded. "Yes, we've had reports of several others that haven't showed up since the storm." He reached for his cap and parka. "Harpe says you and Mason lived there togther, in the cabin. Guess I'll go down and look it over. Might find out somethin'—I s'pose he's got some private papers, letters and whatnot."

Preston nodded. "Yes, our bunks are at opposite ends of the cabin, and each has a box for our personal effects. I'll go back with you."

When he returned to the Harpe cabin, half an hour later, the girl eyed him expectantly. "Did you find out anything—anything of importance?" Downey shook his head. "No, nothin' to speak of. His location papers and a few letters from his mother, down in Michigan. Guess I've found out all I can around here. Fact is, I looked into the Baron's cabin on my way up, an' found that, as Preston said, someone evidently holed up there durin' the storm. I'll slip on over to Halfaday Crick. It might be that Black John holed up there—or maybe it was the man who murdered Quinn. Anyway Halfaday Crick is a good bet. Most every crook in the country hits for there, sometime or other."

"They say that Black John is the worst outlaw in the country," the girl said. "But I don't believe a word of it. I like him."

A slow grin overspread Downey's lips. "I like him, too, Miss Angela. He's what might be called an outlaw's outlaw. Meanin' that plenty of crooks an' outlaws have hit for Halfaday with their loot. Some of them are allowed to go on their way. Some of them are hung. And some of them, in a roundabout sort of way, are turned over to me to be dealt with accordin' to law. But, their loot never goes with them. If it was taken from some worthy person, it always somehow finds its way back to him. If it was taken from some crook or from a big outfit, it simply disappears. While Black John's ethics might be open to question, he's done a lot more good in the Yukon than most of us has—and that's what I call a man."

Harpe nodded. "That right. By gosh, that Black John good frien' to have!"

"Oh, I hope he can help you find the man that murdered old man Quinn!" the girl cried, as tears welled in her eyes and trickled down her cheeks. "Even if—if poor Bill is lying out there somewhere under the snow, I want his name cleared."

"If anyone can help, he can," Downey replied. "Like I told you, Miss Angela, so far the evidence points strongly to Mason as the guilty man—but the case ain't closed. When it is, you can rest assured that justice will have been done. Guess I'll roll in, now. Harpe's bunk, there, looks big enough for two, and I want to get an early start in the mornin'."

IV
THE MURDERER!

TOWARD EVENING OF the second day after leaving the Harpe cabin, Downey stepped into the barroom at Cushing's Fort to find Black John and Cush at the bar, the inevitable dice box between them. The big man greeted the officer as Cush slid another glass across the bar. "What the hell brings you up here? Did someone steal a sock of candy off the Chris'mas tree? Or, are you jest takin' the census?"

Slipping off his pack, Downey removed his parka and stepped to the bar. "If anyone stole some candy the crime ain't been reported. And the way the damn *chechakos* are pourin' into the country, the census ain't the same no two days runnin'. Any strangers showed up on the crick since Chris'mas?"

"Nary a stranger."

"Know a fellow named William Mason?"

"Bill Mason? Yeah, I know Bill."

"How long since you've seen Mason?"

"Oh, mebbe half, three quarters of an hour. I come over here to shake Cush for the drinks, and with a horse apiece the damn cuss claimed he shook four treys, an' there was only three…"

"Like hell they was only three!" Cush cried "By god, they was four treys layin' right there on the bar, an' you grab 'em up almost before they quit rollin' and claimed they was only three! And you can argue your head off and it don't do you no good, 'cause the drinks is charged against you!"

Black John grinned and winked at the officer. "No wonder Halfaday's got a bad name, the way Cush carries on. But, as I was sayin', while we were discussin' the merits of the case, half an hour or so might have slipped by."

"Where's Mason, now?"

"Over in my cabin. Want to see him? Or just makin' a casual inquiry?"

"Yes, I want to see him. Old man Quinn was murdered in his cabin on the Sixtymile, and all the evidence points to Mason as the murderer."

The grin widened on the big man's lips. "You mean all the evidence, Downey? Or just all the evidence you've got?"

"It looks like I've got enough to convict him, all right. It looks like him for sure."

"Old man Quinn couldn't be considered a loss to the community, but I s'pose he had a right not to get murdered. Howcome you figure Mason done it?"

Downey told him, and Black John said, "Anything else?" refilling his glass and shoving the bottle.

"Anything else! Good lord, man, plenty of men have been convicted on a damn sight less evidence than that!"

"Yeah. An' plenty more will be, too. That's the trouble with the law, Downey—it goes too much on evidence. Take a miner's meetin', and we…"

"The Harpes, both Louis an' Angela, identified that knife as belongin' to Mason," Downey interrupted.

"Do they think Mason murdered Quinn?"

"No. Neither of them do. Angela's afraid Mason got bushed in the blizzard and is layin' dead somewheres under the snow."

"When do you figure Mason killed Quinn?"

"I figure it was either just before, or durin' the blizzard. If Mason's alive, it's a cinch that he holed up durin' the storm either at Quinn's or the Baron's. No *chechako* could have weathered it without some sort of protection. He either killed Quinn just before the storm and shoved on to the Baron's cabin—or he stayed in Quinn's till the storm let up. When did he hit Halfaday?"

"It was a couple of days after the blizzard."

"Then he must have been the one who holed up in the Baron's cabin. He couldn't have made it here from Quinn's in two days. He murdered Quinn just before the storm, and shoved on to the Baron's."

Black John chuckled. "That's a true sayin', Downey—'you can never tell by the looks of a frog how far he can jump'."

The officer frowned. "What's jumpin' frogs got to do with it?"

"Nothin', except you shore made a hell of a long jump to reach that conclusion."

"Did Mason have considerable dust in his pack when he got here—Quinn's dust, for instance?"

"He didn't mention havin' it."

Downey's frown deepened. "You don't believe Mason's guilty, eh?"

"Nope, I know damn well he ain't."

"Then, tell me this—why did he hit for Halfaday after the storm, instead of shovin' on to Harpe's Crick where he belonged?"

"It was me done the shovin'. I hauled him here with a dog outfit. Mason come down with pneumonia there in the Baron's cabin. I brought him here where I could dose him up with whisky."

"You mean that you an' he both holed up in the Baron's cabin durin' the storm?"

"That's right."

"But," persisted Downey, "Mason could have murdered Quinn a couple of days before the storm, or even the day before, and made it to the Baron's."

"He could have—but he didn't. I stopped and talked with Quinn late in the afternoon of the day before the storm hit. I shoved on, an' the storm caught me well below the rapids. An', by god, I'm tellin' you she was some storm! If it wasn't for Mason, I'd be dead now. Guess he'd got sweated up choppin' the wood the morning before she hit. He complained of feelin' rotten the second day, an' the third he had a hell of a pain in his chest an' was delirious an' runnin' a fever. I had a quart along, an' I fed him doses of liquor all that day and the followin' night. In the mornin' I hooked up the team and sure burnt the snow till I got here. It didn't look like he'd pull through the first few days, then he got over the hump, and he's comin' along fine."

CORPORAL DOWNEY nodded, slowly. "You're sure lucky—both of you. You for bein' alive, and Mason for havin' a perfect alibi. I'm mighty glad of it. Angela Harpe's a fine girl, and it would have broken her heart if Mason had been found guilty. Guess I'll talk with Mason. There's some things I want to ask him."

"Better wait till mornin', Downey," Black John said. "He's kind of weak, yet. Another night's sleep will do him a lot of good. Cush can put you up, an' I won't tell Mason about the murder tonight."

In the morning as Mason swung his feet to the floor, Black John greeted him with a smile. "How you feelin'?"

"I feel fine. Just about normal again, thanks to you. Gosh it gives me the shivers to think that I'd be lying there dead in that cabin if you hadn't happened along. I don't know how I'll ever repay you."

The smile widened on the big man's lips. "You paid in advance, this time. Where the hell would I have been if you hadn't happened along? S'pose you keep an eye on them steaks in the pan while I slip over to Cush's an' fetch a friend over to break-fast. He's Corporal Downey of the Mounted. He wants to ask, you a few questions."

"Yeah—there's a little matter he wants to clear up, an' he figures you might be able to help."

Downey told Mason about the murder over breakfast, and, after; he glanced across at Mason and extended a knife toward Mason. "Ever see this before?"

Mason glanced at the knife, and his eyes widened. "Why—that's my knife! I missed it in Dawson, and bought another just before I started back."

Downey nodded, and produced a letter.

"This is yours, too, ain't it?"

"It sure is—it's from my mother. I got it in Dawson, along with several others. I didn't know it was missing. Thought I put all the letters in my pack."

"I found both it and the knife on the floor under old man Quinn's body. I stopped in to Harpe's on my way here. Louis and Angela both identified the knife. And Joe Preston said you and him went down to Dawson together, and you pulled out a couple of days ahead of him."

Mason nodded. "That's right. He wanted to stay a few more days, but I was anxious to get back."

"Now," Downey said, "is there any way you can think of that anyone—Preston, for instance—could have got hold of that knife and the letter?"

"Why—yes. I suppose Joe could have gotten them. We had adjoining rooms at the Riverside Hotel. And neither of us kept our door locked. I suppose plenty of other people could have gotten them, too."

Downey nodded. "How did you two get along, you an' Pres-ton?"

Mason's brow furrowed slightly. "Why, we got along all right. But lately Joe has seemed kind of moody. We filed adjoining claims. We built our cabin on the line between the two claims, and when we were building it I noticed that he rather shirked—that I was doing most of the work, so I insisted that we each work our own claim. The test panning has showed that the gravel is richer on my claim than on his. Then there's Angela. She's a wonder girl, and we both fell in love with her. But I have reason to believe that I'm the one she will marry—and I rather think that Joe feels that he has lost out. But even so, I can't believe he would commit a deliberate murder and try to put the blame on me."

Corporal Downey eyed the younger man. "I think you'll believe it, all right after I've done a little more investigatin'. Preston says that Black John passed him on the Yukon with a dog team, and John reached Quinn's cabin the evening before the storm, which hit about noon the next day. Preston could have reached Quinn's just about the time the storm hit. He claims to have weathered the storm, holed up with a Siwash above Quinn's place, but I don't believe he could have got above Quinn's. He got back to Harpe's Crick on the fourth day after the blizzard. It would take him just about that long to get there from Quinn's. It took me three days to make that same trip—an' I shoved right along. I doubt if any *chechako* could have made it in that time. I believe that Preston spent the three days the storm lasted in Quinn's cabin, and I believe I can prove it. I spent the night in Quinn's cabin and used my own dishes. I shoved the dirty dishes that were on the table to one side. If Preston did stay there durin' the storm, it's a cinch that his fingerprints will be on some of those dishes."

"You say Quinn was tortured," Black John said. "I wonder whether he told where his cache was?"

"I've got a hunch that he did," Downey replied, "an' that he'll show us where he recached it. That'll come later." He turned to Mason. "You stay here, and John and I'll slip down to Quinn's an' get those fingerprints. Couple more day's rest won't hurt you any. When we get back we'll all go over to Harpe's Crick for the—"

THE WORDS were interrupted by a sudden thumping on the door, and at Black John's invitation to enter, the door burst open and Angela Harpe burst into the room. At sight of Mason her eyes suddenly widened, and she turned to Corporal Downey. "Oh, you've arrested Bill! And he's innocent! I told you he didn't kill old man Quinn—and he didn't! It was Joe Preston who killed him—and I can prove it!"

The officer smiled as his eyes met the girl's. "Did he confess?"

"No, he didn't confess! In fact he told me that beyond a doubt Bill is guilty. He said that with Bill's knife and that letter you found on Quinn's floor you had an ironclad case against him. But—"

Downey's smile widened. "Did you tell him about me findin' the knife an' the letter?"

"Why, no. He knew about it—I thought you must have told him."

"That'll about cinch the case—even if I can't find any fingerprints down to Quinn's. The reason he knew I found that knife an' letter was because he put 'em there, and knew I couldn't help but find 'em."

"And I've got some other evidence!" the girl cried. "That's what I came here for—to show you this dust. Joe Preston borrowed twenty ounces from papa just before he left for Dawson, and when he returned he handed papa back his poke—said he hadn't had to use the dust as he'd been lucky gambling. Papa put the poke on the scale and the weight was right, so he put it on the shelf. Yesterday I opened the poke to put the dust in the cache, and I saw at a glance that it was different from any dust we ever had—there were flakes in it—thin flakes. I showed the dust to papa, and he said that they had been pried from rock fragments. And he said he knew that old man Quinn did some hardrock mining—that besides his placer work he did a lot of blasting on a quartz vein that showed on the side of his gulch. So I put the poke in my pack and hit for here. I had a moon most of the night. I just got here and Mr. Cushing told me you were here."

The girl paused and reaching into her pack tossed the poke onto the table. "There's the dust—you can see for yourself! I told you Bill Mason was no murderer! And now you'll turn him loose, won't you?"

Corporal Downey picked up the poke, opened it, and poured some of its contents into the palm of his hand as all stared at the flaky particles of gold.

Black John nodded. "That's hard-rock gold, all right. And I know that Quinn done considerable blastin' up there in his gulch."

Downey poured the dust into a saucer and reaching into his own pack drew out a small poke. "Here's some dust I know was Quinn's," he said. "He had it all weighed out to pay Kumtak for makin' that trip to Dawson. The Siwash pointed it out to me on the shelf in Quinn's cabin. He wanted me to give it to him, but I told him I might need it, so I give him a receipt for it, and took the dust along."

It was evident to all at a glance that the two samples were identical, and again the girl appealed to Downey. "So now you'll turn Bill, loose, won't you?"

Gravely the officer shook his head. "I can't do it, Miss Angela."

"But why can't you?" the girl cried. "You just said that—"

"I can't turn him loose because he's loose already. He's never been anything but loose, as far as I'm concerned."

The girl's eyes flew to Mason's face: "Oh, Bill I—I thought you were dead, that you'd been bushed in the storm! If you're all right why in the world did you come here instead of returning to your claim after the storm?"

White teeth flashed beneath the black beard as Black John answered the question.

Downey glanced at the girl. "Well, I guess Cush can put you up, Angela, and Bill can stay here in John's cabin while he and I slip down to Quinn's for those fingerprints. We'll be back in three, four days, and then we'll all go over to Harpe Crick for the show-down. I've got a hunch that Joe Preston is goin' to do some mighty fast talkin'—especially when he shows us where Quinn' dust is cached."

Black John eyed the officer quizzically: "What makes you think he'll show you where he cached Quinn's dust? Why would he? Cripes, he's got nothin' to lose by clammin' up. And, what with all the loopholes there is in the law, if he shouldn't be convicted, he'll have that dust to fall back on."

"Just the same—I'm bettin' the drinks he'll show us the cache."

The big man grinned. "You wouldn't care to lay about ten ounces on top of them drinks would you?"

Downey returned the grin. "Ten ounces? Why yes, John—anything to accommodate a friend—that is, if you're sure you can afford the loss."

"I hate to take your money, Downey. But it's the only way I know to teach the Law not to gamble."

TOWARD THE middle of the afternoon on the sixth day thereafter, the four descended from the rim into the little valley of Harpe's Creek to be greeted by Joe Preston who had just lighted a fresh fire to thaw the gravel in a shallow shaft on his claim. The man's glance rested for a moment on Mason's face, then switched to Downey's. "So, you caught up with him, officer? To tell the truth, I didn't believe you would. I figured he'd either doubled back to the Yukon, or else had got lost and died in the blizzard. But it seems that your hunch that he'd hit for Halfaday was right."

Preston turned to the girl. "I suppose you're convinced now, Angela, as to who murdered old man Quinn?"

The girl nodded. "Yes. Perfectly convinced."

"Kind of cold standin' around out here," Downey said. "How about goin' in the cabin?"

Inside, Downey's eyes roved about the interior for several moments before they centered upon the floor at the opposite end of the room. "When I stopped in here on my way to Halfaday, Preston told me that's your end of the cabin. Is that right, Mason?" The man nodded. "I noticed the cracks between the puncheons were pretty well filled up with sand and dust—all but that crack there. Have you pulled out that puncheon lately for any reason?"

Mason shook his head. Downey said, "I'll just pry that puncheon out and see what's under it."

Without a word Preston stepped from the room and returned a moment later to hand Downey an ax. It was but the work of a moment to pry up the puncheon, and all stared wide-eyed at the collection of moosehide sacks.

Preston was the first to speak. "A-ha! I've got it! Instead of doubling back to the Yukon, or becoming lost in the blizzard, Mason murdered Quinn and then came directly here, watched his chance, and slipped into the cabin without either Angela or her father seeing, him, cached Quinn's dust there under the floor, and then hit for Halfaday Creek, to lie low until the search for Quinn's murderer died down! He may have holed up in Quinn's cabin during the storm, might even have been in there when I passed the place the day before the storm hit." He paused and glanced at Downey. "So, Corporal, I guess that cinches your case."

Downey nodded. "I figure somebody besides Quinn holed up in that cabin durin' the storm. If I could prove it was Mason, it would look kind of bad for him."

"But surely you must have found—that is you—you—visited the cabin since the murder—a man could hardly stay in a place like that for three or four days without leaving some—some evidence of some kind."

"Like Bill's knife and the letter you told me Corporal Downey said he found on the floor?" Angela asked.

Preston's face flushed. "I never mentioned any knife or letter!" he cried.

Downey eyed the man coldly. "You knew about them because you put 'em there, Preston. You cached Quinn's dust there under the floor, too. The man that murdered Quinn holed up there durin' the storm, and he left plenty of plain fingerprints on Quinn's dishes. What's more, that dust you returned to Louis Harpe, tellin' him you didn't have to use it, was dust from Quinn's cache. It was flake gold—not dust from Harpe's claim. I'll have an iron-clad case against Quinn's murderer, Preston, when I compare your fingerprints with the ones I got down to Quinn's."

Preston whirled sharply, and the next instant a loud report rang out, and Joe Preston crashed to the floor, his hand still gripping a revolver, as red blood flowed from a small hole in his right temple.

Black John was the first to speak. "Guess you win the drinks an' ten ounces on top of 'em," he cried. "Preston sure showed you where he cached Quinn's dust when he forgot to resand that crack."